The Last Fairy Tale

By

LAURA DAWN

Nightflame Books

For Kevin, who watches over me,
and Gavin, who believed in fairies.

"These siths or Fairies… are said to be of a middle nature betwixt man and Angel, as were daemons thought to be of old; of intelligent Studious Spirits, and light, changeable bodies."

Robert Kirk, "The Secret Commonwealth of Elves, Fauns and Fairies"

1

CHAPTER ONE

Many, many years ago, long before fairy-tales, were fairies. Not fairies as you and I would know them; these were real fairies.

Fairies are of quite a normal height. Many of them would be rather offended to see the pocket-sized figures they are shown as today. Some of the boy fairies, especially, pride themselves on being at least a head taller than the boys of humans, for fairies are the children of angels who, as everyone knows, are very, very tall.

As for the girl fairies, if they were ever seen by a human lady they would be instantaneously hated. The human ladies all look much older and less pretty than a fairy. A fairy does grow up – their lives would be frightfully dull if they did not – but no matter how many years pass, a fairy will never look a day above thirty. Thirty, for a fairy, is quite old enough. Thirty is the limit; thirty is nearly ancient. Fairies stop at thirty, because they are magical. Some of this magic has clearly seeped into our world; I am sure you know several people who have stuck at thirty, or thereabouts, for what seems like several years. Well, if you do, you are very lucky, for you have probably met the descendant of a fairy.

For those of you with less fortune, do not feel left out. We are going now, altogether, to see a fairy, and a very beautiful one too. But we must all keep deadly quiet as we creep along the dappled wood in the brightening dawn of this new day. It is a hushed and calm wood, like a green tent filled with cool air. Little mice, or rabbits, or they could be squirrels – you cannot catch a glimpse of them, they move so fast – scratch in the bristling hedgerows which line either side of the cart-track we are stealing down. Every now and then, a bird readjusts itself in the arms of a tree, to get comfortable on its branch. Sometimes the flap of its wings sends a shower of fresh green leaves dancing downwards. Other birds whistle out sweet snatches of songs, then stop, for birds cannot often remember all the words. One bird makes a whizzing sound like a firework, but he does not seem to explode. Even if he did, you would not see it through the thicket of trees.

The trees are old and worthy. Gnarly and rugged barks twist into every imaginable shape. The bark is a deep, greyish brown, which gives off a heavenly woody smell. In places, the trees are stained with green dribbles of moss. Small saplings with delicate branches start up near the floor, wishing they could be tall already.

The cart track gives way to softer dirt and the crunch of fallen leaves. A stick cracks, although no-one has trodden on it. The trees seem to double before our eyes. It is very green now, in all different shades, and very, very quiet. You feel as if you could sleep in the gentle beauty all around. The colours look just perfect to the eye – neither too bright nor too dark – it is pretty, but not so pretty you need to stare at it, or pay attention.

Your eyes begin to close. They are suddenly so heavy! There is a still, warm and easy feeling deep inside your chest. The scurrying of animals and soft birdsong begin to tickle in your ears like a lullaby. Green shapes, silhouettes of branches merge in your eyes so that all you see is a hazy, woody mesh. It is the perfect way of seeing. You are very nearly in a doze by now, almost asleep. Your eyelids begin to close – and then there is a flicker.

There! Did you see it? It is the only way to find a fairy. Look again! Yes, there she is! There is our fairy, deep within the grove!

She sits in cavernous hollow; a leafy cave spotted with falling sunlight. Ivy snakes around her tree and drapes like curtains behind. All the bushes, flowers and baby trees around her are so dense, that it looks like there is no gap at all in the green and brown expanse. Thin fingers of twigs and branches make a fragile net in front of her. But through all that, we can still see she is extremely fair.

One leg, as pure white as fresh snow, hangs down from the deep dip in the oak tree upon which she is seated. How unbelievably white it looks next to the dark, rugged brown! It is a wonder we did not see her standing out from it like a bright star long before now. But then again, we were not looking properly.

She wears a pearly, shimmering robe. It looks as if it were made of liquid, so closely does it ripple over her skin. Her clothes do not hang at normal angles. This robe is falling off one shoulder, and looks much longer at the back than it is at the front. How odd it is! So odd that it is amazingly beautiful. It is almost a toga, yet it is almost a spider's web.

Leaves begin to rustle. Her dark head snaps up in attention to a distant pounding. The hair which falls away from her pale face is a rich, deep brown, glossy beyond compare.

It is as if a miniature earthquake were taking place inside our little glen, and inside the fairy too. Something is brushing past the reaching branches of trees at a fast rate, snapping twigs, trampling flowers. Fairies can feel these things. They can feel the alarm of the field-mice starting out of the way, and the despair of the family of ants who watch their tall powdery tower of a home perish beneath a charge of hooves. Horses are coming. Our fairy can tell this.

She breathes quickly. Little jolts of excitement, mixed with a creeping fear, are tingling through her cheeks and stomach to the time of the hoof-beats. She arranges the careless folds of her shining dress. She climbs a little higher in the tree for a better view. All her movements flow fluid and graceful, with the poise of a ballerina. Her blue, blue, ridiculously blue eyes sweep back and forth. They are so blue! As vivid, strong a blue as two new jewels twinkling in a ring. She licks her lips. To move any more, she feels, is impossible. Her body feels stuck, although inside she is writhing. We can see all her whizzing feelings in her skin. It is so smooth, so transparent, that it almost seems to glitter.

Here comes the conquering hero! The rattle of metal clicking in the distance suggests it. Yet the clouds are darkening to warn of imminent rain. Small blobs bounce off the tree tops, swaying the leaves and sounding a threatening whisper. Whinnies of a horse reach the fairy's ears. They startle her. In her tension, she starts again, as two ravens flutter out from a bush, diving right in front of her in a never ending game of chase.

Looking through the cover of branches, she can see the black outlines of a team of riders now. She flinches. The movement casts aside the last delicate blossom of the tree, which spirals and spirals as it falls to land softly on her dark head. The riders are nearly upon her now. She begins to shake her head. They are too many.

Powerfully built horses thunder through the peaceful glen. Their muscles gleam beneath their shining bay and black coats. They wear a kind of mask over their faces of bronze and dark red. It must be uncomfortable, for they

4

toss their heads about with great snorts as they stalk through the undergrowth, searching. Our fairy makes herself very small. But the problem with animals is, they can sense fairies without even looking properly.

The horses' rumps are clothed with chequered cloths in the same colours as their masks. The fairy can see the patterns weaving about the edge of her wood. Terror mounts in her throat. The men on horseback call to each other. They are not dainty like the fairy. Huge suits of armour with sharp points make them look like great beasts of men: monsters of metal. One sits in the saddle with a little more grace than the others. His legs are splashed with dried mud and he carries a long lance, which has clearly seen a few battles. He edges so perilously close to the fairy that she can smell the warm smoke coming from his horse's nostrils and count the beads on the great ornamented sleeves which cover the reins. If only she does not move...

The song of a blue-tit slices the silent tension from directly above the fairy. She had not even noticed him alight on her tree. She gives a gasp – that is all – and the graceful man's horse dances on his forefeet. He has seen her. All the horses have seen her.

With great speed the horses break through the last barrier of the thicket, their knights slashing away the branches like a hot knife through butter. Now that they know where to look, they can see the fairy too.

She looks upon the carnage of her trees, and responds in fury. An injured tiger driven into a corner, she rears up, snarling a terrible cry. Foxes give a similar scream in the dead of night, at springtime. The fairy rises, proud and terrible, on great wings of the Red Admiral butterfly. These were quite invisible as she sat, and shock all the more for being previously concealed. Nothing could prepare the knights for the dazzling sight of this giant canvass, fragile and yet intense with its stripes of warning red and metallic blue spots. The great wings vibrate savagely as blinding sparkles pulse through the fairy's skin.

The sheer wingspan of fairy, the striking colour and that awful, awful noise would frighten some of the young knights away. They rein their horses back and cry out in gruff, angry tones. But not the graceful knight. Beneath the bars of his visor, his glinting eyes are not thrown by the parade. The gleaming circles of colour do not distract his gaze from the most vulnerable part of the wing, as they are designed to do. He pulls back his arm, aims his lance, and throws.

The weapon soars through the air with the speed of a bullet. It is badly aimed. Nevertheless, it hits the fairy in the side. She gives a yelp, and sinks slightly. The knights are encouraged. Suddenly, they all discover themselves to be brave men. Arrows, lances and daggers fill the sky thick and fast. The fairy is flying dizzily, trying to escape without the strength to manage it. Giving out horrible laughs, the knights throw nets of thick, scratching rope about her. She is fluttering franticly now, screaming again. Her screams no longer seem to bother them. She is caught in this twine cage, gnashing her teeth. All her beauty looks crumpled. She is so strong that she manages to break several of the cords, but it is not enough. The graceful knight has already spoken.

"The wings, you fools!" he cries. His voice is detached and hoarse.

A lithe young knight in shining, new looking armour leaps off of his horse with a swing of the leg. He runs at the fairy pulling from his scabbard a jewelled knife. He jumps, high and nimble, making a slashing motion. From the heart-wrenching sound which flows out of the net, it is clear he has cut her wing. A great sigh, or groan, more tragic than terrible reverberates around the glen. A rush of wind seems to radiate from the fairy, and now she is bleeding.

Her blood flows like a fountain, but it is not human blood. It is a runny, sticky liquid like honey – it even smells a little like it – but it is purple in colour and laced with glitter. The blood alone is almost more beautiful than the fairy herself. It looks like liquid amethyst stone, and it smells like heaven. It is her life force.

Once that has seeped from her, she will evaporate and be gone forever; not just her spirit, but her beautiful body too. It is the way fairies go.

She has just time as her body folds down amongst the debris of leaf skeletons on the forest floor to glance up and see a face beneath the chain-mail hood. It takes her dying breath away. It is *him*.

2

CHAPTER TWO

Aurora gazes out, bored, from the circular window flooding the cave with light. Her wings, cranberry blues, droop even more. They are already held back by tight strings which, although they appear made of the thinnest cord, are stronger than iron chain links. Cynthia is incredibly late.

Aurora looks around the white cave. Stalactites and stalagmites wink at her in diamonds. They remind her of something, and she glances down at her fingers. On the trim middle finger of her left hand is a moonstone ring, encased in an intricate framework of delicate silver. The ring on her right hand is of a cruder setting, gold and housing a pearly rose quartz.

Letting out the minutest sigh, Aurora shakes her hands. She can see by the way the sun beams are rippling off the glassy pool inside the cave that the hour for expecting Cynthia is long past. Only a small crease in between her eyebrows suggests she is slightly worried. It would not be unlike Cynthia to arrive late, having forgotten an appointment in daydreaming. Not quite *this* late, however…

Deciding to go and look for her wayward friend, Aurora takes a piece of material which resembles a sari and wraps inside it berries and some dried flowers. Being now completely ready, she emerges from her cave into the land of Laseri, where the fairies live.

It is a large, cool, round kingdom, forming almost a perfect circle of white Romanesque palaces inside the tangle of the forests beyond. The air appears to be tinged with a golden colour, illuminating the carpets upon carpets of multicoloured flowers which poke out from fresh green grass. Towards the centre of Laseri's circumference the landscape grows rockier, mounting up in dark hills and springing out tinkling waterfalls. At the utmost peek presides a grand Colosseum, waving grand banners, where handsome Deucalion, King of the Faries lives. Naturally Laseri's commerce and bustle centre round this great oracle. At the base of the hill the rocks give way to marble colonnades and shimmering tents, spreading out in a vast market place where the soft clang of wind-chimes can always be heard. Aurora must skirt the edge of this busy bazaar. As she does, her dainty chin stuck out resolutely, the eyes of a female fairy – a fay – follow her from behind a stall selling tall phials of golden, sticky nectar, with hardly a benign expression.

"I wouldn't believe it!" the customer she is serving hisses in a shocked whisper. "The assurance, the heedlessness she walks with! As if she didn't know every eye was upon her! It *must* be Aurora Optilete. Never, until now, could I credit that the stories about her were entirely true."

The stall-keeper casts a jealous look over her produce, checking it has not suffered any contamination from its near brush with peril. "Not true?" she repeats, apparently without the ability to modulate her voice to the civil, sniping whisper of her customer. "You saw for yourself the appalling hair, lopped off in scrags. Tell me, would great Deucalion submit to that ultimate shame any fairy who could possibly be innocent? Say," she adds, nodding towards the majestic palace guards in burnished armour, "very loudly you think just Deucalion could be wrong."

The appearance of the guards somehow lessens the customer's prepossession in Aurora's favour. With a look like a frightened rabbit, she comments: "No, I would never *consider* that. Only it is so strange she has not lost her flight! You *know* she would have done, if she had borne a pixie, or even…"

"But the freckles! Actual freckles! Did your mother never tell you that we fairies are so pure that if we ever have reason to blush we will be marked forever with freckles? Or could you not credit that to be entirely true, either?"

"Well, she does have freckles," concedes the customer, running her hands meditatively over her phial of honey-coloured nectar. "But you know it is our job always to hope for the best…"

"Take my word, she's a traitor alright, in some way or other," is the kindest allowance the stall-holder can grant Aurora. "And I will take three coins for the phial, before those guards come any closer. I'm sure they heard you doubt Deucalion."

One of the guards, slim and youthful, hears their conversation and breaks off from his regiment. Discreetly he slips away and follows Aurora's path. Once free of the market stalls he spots her, gazes around to make sure that no-one sees, and breaks into a run, the plume from his helmet flying in the wind, his white Apollo wings, after which he is named, shivering.

Soon he is by her side and, as he is somewhat vertically challenged for a male fairy, only just manages to keep trotting along at her pace. Aurora acknowledges him with a slight nod of the head. In her childish days, Aurora was foolish enough to practise her spells upon poor unsuspecting Apollo – to wit, a love potion, which she thought at the time would be particularly amusing. After so many years the results have failed to stay amusing. Apollo is certainly not in love with Aurora – her magic was not good enough to produce that result – but he has developed a tendency of following her about, and acquired the need to always stand at only an inch's distance from her body. Aurora is terribly fond of Apollo, yet she does not think this is the kind of behaviour which ought to be encouraged, so she says nothing.

"Where are you going?" pants the black-haired Apollo.

"To find Cynthia," she replies with purpose.

"Oh. Is she missing?"

"No... not missing. It does not qualify as missing. I do miss her – I lack a Cynthia – but you guards would not call that missing. You would say she is merely late. Embarrassingly late." Aurora shakes her head again. "It is not like her," she says to herself.

"It is very like her," corrects Apollo, taking off his helmet and walking a little easier now she has slowed down. He does not have a great regard for Cynthia. She is more a necessary appendage to Aurora than a thing to be acknowledged. After all, Aurora is nobility – however shamed in recent days – and Cynthia is unremarkable in everything; everything except her lateness.

They reach the edge of the wood as Aurora grinds to a halt and looks at him. "No. It is different this time. I feel it is somehow different." Silence reigns until Aurora glances over Apollo's shoulder. "Shouldn't you be back guarding the gates?"

Apollo puffs out his chest. "No. I am coming with you."

The information does not cheer Aurora as much as it might. "Won't you get in trouble?"

"A guard following you will not be looked upon as a strange thing," Apollo points out sadly.

Aurora gives a grim smile. He will be someone to talk to, at least. "Very well," she says, swinging her arms together, and walks with a jaunty step towards the trees.

Apollo is scampering after her in a flash, haphazardly jamming his helmet back on. "Wait! You're going in there? You're going into the woods?!"

"Certainly," Aurora shrugs. "You know she sometimes sits in a tree, close to the kingdom boundaries."

Apollo recalls with perfect clarity that regrettable habit of Cynthia's. It makes him, a fully fledged guard of the gate, shudder. "Yes, and the more fool her for it! It is not *safe*!" He tries to make himself a barrier between Aurora and the shade of the heavy forest. They are within touching distance of the rough barks now; one more dainty step and they will leave Laseri.

Aurora steams with impatience. She knows that the most important fairy of all lives in this forest, and it irks her to be reminded she is not thought as wise and brave as this great fairy.

"My dear Apollo," Aurora begins her lecture, "What is the purpose of every fairy?"

"To find the one they were made to protect," he delivers immediately.

"And if they can, bring them into the grace and sanctuary of Laseri, so they may be like the fairies," finishes Aurora. "It pleases our ancestors, the angels."

Apollo nods. "But you were not made to be Cynthia's guardian."

"No, a human's. So next tell me this – how do you propose to meet that human, much less bring them into Laseri, if you never leave?"

He blinks blankly at the gesture she makes around the kingdom and her provoking tone. "No fairy has stepped far past the boundaries since the last war when the kingdom shrank. It is not safe," he repeats.

Aurora puts on an air of gravity. "No. It is certainly not safe. But luckily I will have a brave guard of the palace looking out for me."

Apollo is left stuttering as she raises her eyebrows and stubbornly walks on. With all the bravado of mortification and reluctance, he intrepidly follows.

3

CHAPTER THREE

It had been under very different circumstances that Aurora first set foot in this wood, Green Glow Forest. She recalled the same sick feeling of a distant danger – not immediately upon them, but creeping slowly like a damp night mist.

Her beautiful dapple grey horse, Blanchard, was below the thick swag of her crimson velvet cape, restlessly pawing the ground as it stood in the white cobbled courtyard of the Noble Village. Beyond the pointed towers Aurora saw a ghost-like trickle of smoke winding upwards, and wondered where it could come from. It must be one of those many strange things from the human realm – but then, Laseri was so very large in those days, it was rare that any signs of life from the outside could be seen.

The courtyard was strangely deserted. Fairies that did pass were in a great hurry; dirty stable fairies diving to and fro, only nodding their heads to her if they happened to catch her eye.

At last the movement Aurora had been waiting for erupted from the Palace. A noble looking female was drifting across the mess of straw and dirt on the floor, great folds of deep blue and purple material flowing behind her in a train. This great fairy looked more dishevelled than Aurora had ever seen her. The jewels in her hair were lop-sided, and lines of worry sat in her thirty-year-old face. She had only two soldiers in attendance; the number had been dwindling gradually.

"It is time. Your father says you are to leave immediately." The fine fairy leant upward and kissed both of Aurora's cheeks.

"This is ridiculous," declared Aurora, sitting firm. "What kind of fairy runs in the time they are needed most?"

Her mother drew herself up proudly. She inspired awe despite her loosely arranged hair and small guard. "A fairy of noble family. A dutiful fairy." Leaning forwards, she soothed with a softened tone: "Not *running*, Aurora. Never running. But you are the last female with a direct line to the royal blood. A thousand males with the claim might stay here and fight, and one will probably live. But *you* – ! What are a hundred of them to you? You were born to bear kings, Aurora Optilete, and do not forget it. The very future of the royal fairies could depend upon your survival."

Aurora could not defy the impassioned speech from her strong, stately parent. Looking towards her with great respect, Aurora sighed: "Why only me? Amongst all the fairies! When *you*, my revered mother -"

"Shall stay where I belong," interrupted the elder fairy, stepping back, tightly controlled but with an expression of great loss in her face. "Go, go, my child. May speed be in your wings and a blessing on your head."

Reluctantly Aurora loosened the grip on her reins and tucked in her feet. She was half resolving inside herself to ride to the outskirts of the kingdom and join up with a brigade. Casting a last look at her mother, she spurred grey Blanchard on, and set off at a swinging canter.

She was leaving, maybe for the last time, the marble enclosures. The rapid hooves of her steed were nearly touching the verdant grass and leaving the Palace far behind, when a blonde youth threw himself into her path.

Struck with panic to the core, Aurora gasped and recklessly wheeled her horse to the left. Her hands were pulling back so hard that it hurt; she shut her eyes tightly, and it was with difficulty that both she and her mount kept their balance. Finally all was still, and she gingerly looked up. There, in the exact spot he had leapt, stood the Prince. She gazed at him in mute astonishment and wonder.

"You should be gone by now," he said reproachfully. "But praises be that you are not." He strode assuredly over to her steed, took hold of it under the chin-strap and led the pair back to the courtyard.

Aurora did not know whether to be affronted or honoured. "It is largely owing to your honoured father's intervention, I believe, that I am made to leave at all."

"Certainly," replied the elegant figure below without looking up. "He intends you for my bride." With a grim chuckle he added, "If I have the fortune to live."

"Nonsense," said Aurora evenly, again hardly decided upon what she felt. "No royals will die. Barely any fairies have died. We have never known war before this, and it is not so bad *physically*." She looked about the undamaged beautiful land and said with confidence, "We will triumph, and blessed peace will be restored."

There was a pause. "They have taken Majeseerum," Prince Deucalion threw in, almost off hand.

The information electrified Aurora. She gaped at the startling white-blonde head of her Prince, convinced that all could not be right inside it. "Impossible!" she practically spat out, with vehemence.

The Prince raised a jet-black eyebrow, and said no more until they reached the Noble Village.

Now both her parents were standing together, with far more soldiers. Beside them was gracious King Iubdan himself, the amazing Spotted Fritillary wings common to

16

all of his royal family rising out of a pine-green robe. Aurora nearly tumbled off of Blanchard as she rushed over, quickly nodding her head as her only mark of respect, for no fairy ever kneels to another.

"My son has told you the fate of the great city," boomed his sonorous voice.

"Your Majesty, it is impossible. Those walls can never be breached."

"And yet they have been," said the wise King sadly. "Without it..." He trailed off. It wounded his kingly pride greatly to admit, in an undertone so that the soldiers could not hear, "I am no longer certain we can win this war."

"The staff," Aurora demanded desperately. "They do not have the blue staff?"

King Iubdan shook his head. It was one of the most beautiful sights Aurora had ever seen. It filled her every vein with sweet relief.

"No, no. We can only be thankful it has not gone that far. The frozen fay that bears it escaped to her lodge in Green Glow Forest. But how safely she may remain there..." he trailed off again and coughed, ever conscious of the soliders.

Young Prince Deucalion let go of Blanchard and came towards them, dauntless. His clothes were tighter and more practical than his father's. Though they were richly adorned, they made his figure look lithe and ready for action, like a tightly coiled spring. "Caves in flames, whole fields burnt out, fairies slaughtered by the dozens, the little ones too," he listed, heedless of his effect upon the soldiers and their ever-delicate moral. "Oh, they have some kind of seer. They must. One of ours, perhaps. But they have some link to the Greater Powers, when -"

"When we should be their link," finished Aurora. She wrung her hands and stamped her foot in uncontrollable despair at the ignorance of people. "Who would use such a

17

gift for this evil?"

There was silence. Deucalion looked pointedly at King Iubdan.

The King took Aurora's very white hand into his own and made her turn away from the guards. He was very close to her, and his face looked earnest. He appeared so fatherly at that moment, though he was a formidable fairy, with great high cheek-bones and severe brows. Aurora could not describe the closeness she felt to her King just then, completely surrounded by him and his grief for his fairies. All she could see, beyond the green velvet rise of his shoulder as he put his arm around her, was the distant face of Prince Deucalion, who was so tall that she could make him out. "Who indeed, my dear. That is the question. If we stand any chance, we must find this out."

"My liege, how can this be done? You must send a fairy inside the Castles of the humans... and they have never taken kindly to our entering their domains," Aurora smiled wryly. "Even when we are not at war."

"Ah, just so. You are a quick fay. A fairy must go in, and earn the trust of these people. A fairy must have a way of getting information out... without being sure of getting out themselves. Is there such a heart in the whole of Laseri?"

Aurora grimaced. "I doubt it," she muttered. "So many have become cowards and turned from our calling." Her pearly teeth flashed in a wave of anger. "I do not think there is a soldier left alive who remembers what it is to be a fairy."

"That is why," smiled the King, "we have chosen you."

Aurora was dumbfounded. Her large eyes looked up, demanding clarification. "You - you would let a young fay take this task alone?" To be doing something at last! This was what she had been waiting for. She would still be leaving Laseri, but she would be *useful*.

King Iubdan chuckled. "My son insisted none but you would do for this job. I trust his judgement, in this case, implicitly. But you will not be alone. There is a young girl from the Limenitis family chosen to play your handmaiden. You will intercept her near Rainbow Glen."

He stood back, satisfied, and began to move. Everyone looked about to be resuming business as usual. Aurora looked confusedly about her.

"Where am I to ride – my wings – how will I know this girl? I have just been told I must save myself because of my royal blood, and now I am being cast upon the most dangerous mission! It does not make sense. Please will someone explain?"

But her mother, with a gaze locked constantly upon her, was being ushered into the Palace by her father, through the glistening ranks of the guard. Only Prince Deucalion remained, owning the Noble Village with his presence, pointing his index finger at her. He was deep in concentration as he spoke.

"You were selected for your ability to improvise and solve these little problems. It will be rather a wonderful test for me to see if you would make me a good wife. And as for your blood, the way things are going, I daresay it will be safer out of Laseri than inside it." Small sparks were beginning to fizz from his finger now. They were growing gradually, and occasionally ran right through his hand, illuminating the moonstone ring which all fairies bore. "I have concocted a spell to shrink your wings. They can be tucked safely away from human view in those huge capes they wear. Only sudden immersion in water will make them grow again – just in case you need your flight." Aurora eyed with distrust the mini-streaks of blue and purple lightning that were rippling out of his hand. "It is quite safe," he laughed, "I have already used it upon

19

Cynthia Limenitis." He shrugged. "But if it goes wrong, at least you might not have to marry me after all."

The blinding wave of mauve had hit her with less force than the sight of the gnarly oak tree hits her now in the peaceful glen.

Aurora freezes. Although she is at a distance, the sparkles which reach her in the sunlight, reflecting on the pool of blood, tell her all that she needs to know. Her tears hang suspended, as if they too cannot credit the vision enough to actually spill out. Apollo dashes forward with a great cry, kneeling beside the grim puddle, and contemplating in horror for an instant the moonstone ring floating in the middle of it. Then a glimpse of something not foliage catches the corner of his eye. It is tall and dark grey, like a dirty pillar. The fallen leaves swirl around its base.

Apollo walks toward it. When he sees what it is, his brow contracts violently. He pulls the sword out of the ground and holds it up to Aurora. She follows his dark gaze to the hilt, where there is emblazoned a coat of arms with a prominent letter: J.

CHAPTER FOUR

"I tell you," insists Aurora, exasperated, as she throws herself down on the rose-petal floor of the Colosseum, "this is not the act of King Joel. Trust me, as the only resident expert in the matter!"

"Surely she is the one fairy who has ever been among them," says one of the astral fairies. They are tall creatures, advisors to the King, with coloured rays of light streaming from them. "She must know their ways."

"Perhaps she does, and perhaps she is trying to buy them time," throws in another bright astral. "How can we ever know for sure with her?"

Aurora sighs pitilessly as she hears the same arguments again and again. She takes another apple from the little serving maid, Dirne-Weibl and looks at the amazing palace instead of listening. If these fairies weren't so distracted by their ears and rumours, she thinks, they would see more clearly. The walls in the room are painted with exotic scenes of palm trees, climbing plants, fruits, fountains, vases and terraces. Parts of it are real, like the boughs of shiny ripe apples that hang down under the weight of their fruit. Live birds are soaring above, round the moulded ceiling decorated with great frescos of blue skies, powerful clouds, and magnificent depictions of their great ancestors the angels. One colourful parrot swoops and lands upon the fine helmet of Apollo.

"I told you," Aurora hisses to Apollo from across the room, "you should have let me deal with this. Why did you bring it in here, to start all this madness again?" she can feel another war approaching like pins scuttling down her flesh.

"It was my duty," replies Apollo without flinching. "I could not jeopardise the safety of Laseri, or have a secret from my King on my conscience.

"Indeed," agrees Deucalion, biting into an apple, "you can rest assured you would not keep your place if you did." He looks impressed with the flavour of the apple, and drops it into the lap of one of his advisors. "Aurora, Aurora!" he coaxes. "Do you expect me to stand idly by while one of my fays is slaughtered? My council will not allow it!"

"No," admits Aurora, toying with the fruit in her lap. "But what example are we setting if we retaliate with violence? If we hurt humans, we are only hurting ourselves – and I am convinced this is a matter to be resolved by them, in their own realm. King Joel has made peace with the fairies. This cannot be his doing. There is a rebellion against him..."

"But this is King Joel's sword!" cries Deucalion, bounding over to Apollo and snatching it from him. He wields it impressively and points it at Aurora. "I warned him! And he was not very cordial to *you* the whole time you were his guest. Why should you object to my teaching him a lesson? I think, my little Cranberry Blue, you do not want action taken against the King lest it impacts on the *Knights*." He smiles saucily as Aurora bites her lip and two more freckles appear on her face. "But remember I do not know which one you favour," Deucalion shrugs, leaning on the sword, "so there is a chance he might survive."

Everything blurs and sounds muffled for an instant. Aurora recovers herself and looks up defiantly from the carpet of petals. "Fairies launching a war against humans is wrong! All the dark fairies will reappear in the forest, countless numbers of us will be bereft of the ones we are meant to guide – "

"The fairies are not *starting* the war! Is not the murder of a fay – who was your dear friend, may I remind you – provocation enough? But I am being benevolent. I am not going to carry out what I threatened Joel with last time. That would involve traipsing through the Green Glow Forest to find Cailleach Bheur and her frozen blue staff, and I haven't the energy. Listen to what I mean to do." Deucalion rests the sword of Joel behind his neck, across the tops of his shoulders. "We go into Auchriachan. The dark fairies you mention are on our side, for the main part."

Aurora scoffs. He knows nothing, but she allows him to continue.

"We have ways of making them do what we wish. We are smaller in number, but Tethys assures me we could tempt the pixies to join us. I do not say pixies will be reliable, but we will do what we can with them. I do not deny many humans will die. It does not signify; they have forfeited their claims to our protection," looking at an astral, "have they not, Gaia? Yet the few good ones remaining – those pure of heart, and noble – shall be taken prisoners of war. Thus they shall be bought into Laseri. If the pixies do not betray us, I will acknowledge them. Green and monstrous as they are, we will let them in," he says simply. Deucalion begins to list the virtues of his plan on his fingers. "Peace will be forever established, the darker fairies will vanish, and the three kingdoms be united."

A great stir arises the second the King closes his fair mouth. The astral fairies begin to flicker and flash.

"*Acknowledge* the pixies?!"

"The noblest plan ever concocted! How he has heeded our advice! What greatness of mind!"

"Three kingdoms united! Why, this is the bravest, most brilliant King ever to grace Laseri!"

"Humans into Laseri! Genius, sheer genius! I am sure I gave him the idea. "

"Can it be so simple? This is a thing often talked about, but -"

"Your Majesty," exclaims Apollo ardently. "This is the sole purpose of all fairies. Your Majesty is the only King in history brave enough to attempt it. We must all dedicate our lives to this chivalrous cause, and I pledge mine now."

"Good!" says Deucalion brightly, slapping the soldier on the back. "But I cannot afford to promote you."

Aurora has dropped her apple and stands now, trembling. "With all respect, the plan has the right intentions, but you will be killing thousands of humans! Your Majesty has never met a human – except in battle – and still sees them as things which can be disposed of if they have not yet come round to the right way of thinking. Let me go to Auchriachan and talk with – "

There is a general scoffing and Apollo says jealously: "Oh yes, you would like that!"

"- talk with King Joel," carries on Aurora bravely. "There is a chance this proposal will be acceptable to him without violence."

The astrals laugh. Deucalion, however, hears her out with interest.

"Is not every human's secret desire, somewhere within their heart, even if it is blackened over, to enter Laseri and live here forever?" shouts Aurora in response, now desperate.

"Small little cherub," says Deucalion in his most patronising tone (and he has several), "you are very idealistic. Joel is proud. He will never abandon the stronghold of Iblees. He has been brought round – or so I thought until today – to realise he cannot just butcher us, but I fear giving up his self-importance and control of his own life is a pitch beyond his puerile brain."

"At least let me go and try!"

"Absolutely not. As your King, I forbid it." Deucalion's violet eyes twinkle. "Don't make me tie up another part of your body."

Aurora marches steadfastly up to the great wooden throne, wound with creepers and flowers of white. She stands for a second, and drops upon her knees. The astral fairies gasp. Apollo nearly falls over. Dirne-Weibl drops her basket of apples. "Shave my head, clip my wings, only let me know I did all I could to prevent this horrible war!" The disgraced fairy begs.

Deucalion looks at her with respect and tries to raise her to her feet. "No. I cannot risk it."

Aurora spills tears of frustration. "Oh, I wish I had married you!" she howls, to the deep scandal of the astrals. "As Fairy Queen you would have to acknowledge my wishes! You would have to let me go, or else it would appear you did not trust me!"

"I do not trust you," confesses Deucalion, taking her hand. She has revealed a feeling that he has longed for her to acknowledge for years: her regret. "You are too smart and cunning for me. You know I would have made you my Queen when you returned, but for this." He taps her rose-quartz ring. An old thorn twists in his side and is reflected in the annoyance of his tone. "What promise does this bind you to? Your stubbornness over it gave rise to the rumours, and forced us to thus humble you."

"No promise," Aurora says, closing her eyes. Behind their dark cover she sees the moment again. "It is only a symbol, but I must insist on keeping it with me."

Deucalion thinks about this. The sight of this rose

quartz ring does not give rise to the same suspicious and bitter feelings in him that it used to. "A symbol of something that prevents you from being a monarch of Laseri?"

Aurora looks impassioned. Her face turns red and white by turns. "No, no indeed! I have told you this before!"

"Then why are you not my Queen?" Deucalion asks. It is not the first time he has posed the question, and before he was obliged to disgrace her, it had been uttered far more eloquently. But then she had refused, and then by necessity she was naturally disgraced. "I could use you on my side in this war," he adds. She is already proving more troublesome to him than he expects the humans will be.

"I could not consider it at that time. There was too much..." Aurora feels he is playing with her, and will not look at him. She feels the same frustration she felt years ago, when she was trying to save the humans and everyone else was concerned with trivial fairy matters.

The astrals and soldiers are silent to hear their conversation. They still do not trust Aurora, but the King seems almost like he does. After all, the crimes they disgraced her for never came to fruition. Perhaps she was innocent after all. Could the long awaited marriage really take place now, after all that has passed? It would certainly be a comfort to have the succession secured, especially with a war on the horizon. And none of them can forget this partnership was the last wish of King Iubdan.

Deucalion hesitates and chews his thumb nail. Lines of concentration appear in his forehead. At last he takes Aurora's chin in his hand and turns her face to him.

"And now? Could you consider such a thing now, if I offer it again?"

Much time has passed since Aurora last found herself in this position, and she looks very thoughtful. She is older and appreciates more fully what she can do with a position like Queen of Laseri. There is a long pause. "If I were your Queen, would you let me do as I now wish?" she asks, tonelessly.

Deucalion hesitates. He looks to Aurora, to his advisers and back to Aurora. "Yes. But I would not stop my preparations for war until you returned. I would go on just the same." He shrugs. "But you would be free to go, as you please."

Aurora stands up before him. "Then, your Majesty, I will marry you."

5

CHAPTER FIVE

Let us look back now to the time before Aurora first entered the human realm of Auchriachan; a time after the estrangement, but before a war between humans and fairies.

Spring had just touched the landscape of Auchriachan. Small pink blossoms embellished choice branches, and the grass began to poke out from the ground in denser crops. It was a good thing for the flocks of Asher and Joel. Keeping sheep was hard enough in that land, where the trees were sparse and scattered, and the earth was dry and patchy.

Asher cast a troubled eye onto the skinny sheep. Their wool was growing coarse and rugged. "The foliage spreads thicker around the Castles," he told Joel, who was sitting cross legged on the floor, drawing in the dirt. "We should head near one."

Joel scoffed. "And they would let us graze on their land, do you think? Don't be ridiculous."

"They want to wear our wool, don't they? How can they expect it to be fine and soft without putting in a thing?" snapped back Asher. He was tired and hungry as well as the sheep.

"The King is dying, the succession is in crisis. Fine people who live in Castles have better things to worry about than quality wool."

"I wish we did." Asher replied glumly.

Very few inhabitants of Auchriachan lived below the poverty line. The extremely large majority were all Knights and ladies. They were split in to five main tribes, and the spin-offs of those tribes. Each was determined to compete for the title of the strongest, wealthiest, most respected and most powerful tribe.

The tribes were named the Emberlights, the Riverons, the Moordales, the Amorettes and the Boanerges. They had been named in the days of old; the Emberlights for the combustibility in the summer months of the thick wood and gorse-land on which they lived; the Riverons, quite simply, because they lived on the river; the Moordales, unsurprisingly because of their habitation on the moors. The Amorettes had some debates over whether their name stemmed from their prowess at making and maintaining the finest armour, or if it was a corruption of the word *amour*, and they were very desirable lovers. The Boanerges knew their name meant "Sons of Thunder" – they said it was because they were mighty in battle. The Amorettes, who were their closest neighbours, maintained it was because they made a lot of noise.

In all these tribes, women were rare commodities – all those that did exist were ladies, although some of the less fortunate ones were obliged to take on duties like the care of fowl and needlework, in order to keep the Auchriachans living in fine style. Very poor women were ladies in waiting on the finer ladies. But they were all ladies.

Men who were not lords became Knights. Most men in Auchriachan, therefore, put a Sir before their name. Unless they happened to be the really unlucky ones: the workers, or the shepherds, for example. Because everybody was so very fine, no one was quite unrefined enough to do the work to keep everybody fine. So those in the hapless minority born as workers were obliged to work twice, if not three times as hard as any worker you will ever know.

Scraping his foot across the unyielding ground, Asher suggested warily: "We could take the flock into the forest."

Green Glow Forest was not half so large in those days. But beneath the shade of the trees, and so close to the fruitful soil of Laseri, fattening grass might grow.

Joel nearly choked on laughter. "The forest?!" he repeated.

"Yes," maintained the undaunted Asher. "There will be grazing enough there. Who knows, the grass could have magical properties, being so near the fairy land."

"I've heard stories," muttered Joel distrustfully, shaking his head.

"Fairy stories?" Asher asked saucily.

Joel did not appear to find it funny. His face looked dark and ominous. "Yes, stories about fairies. Dragging people out of that forest to Laseri, from where they never come back."

Looking around the clumpy earth of Auchriachan, the idea did not seem too terrible to Asher just now.

"And then there's that seer," continued Joel.

"The one who foretold the King's death?" Asher raised his eyebrows. He wasn't sure he believed this seer existed. It was probably a story made up to keep children from wandering off into the forest. A group of somewhat unstable Knights had come back from the forest once, repeating a prophecy of his – a prophecy which was now running uncomfortably parallel to reality – but that was the closest to proof anyone in Auchriachan had come. "Isn't he meant to reveal the future King?"

"Yes," said Joel, who knew much more about these things – or everything, it seemed to Asher sometimes. "That's why this succession is taking so long. There are so many tribes in the nobility! There are no direct heirs. The

Boanerges think they have a claim, but the Riverons were closer related in the blood line. There are those waiting for the seer to appoint a leader, and others who say they will not accept his King, even if he does choose one."

"Well then," said Asher consolingly, "if we go to the forest, we might find this seer. He can tell us who the new King is, and everyone will be so pleased with us they'll let our sheep graze on their land. Even better, they'll reward us, and we'll never need sheep again."

His tone was half-joking, but Joel stopped and meditated on Asher's words. Joel bit his finger nail. At length, he stood up.

"Another of your hair-brained schemes I've been talked into." Joel readjusted his sheepskin vest. "If any fairies steal our ram, you'll be for it."

Asher moved forward in pleasant surprise. He could not think what had caused this sudden acquiescence in Joel – unless it was hunger. His heart began to beat fast with the promise of adventure. He could imagine fairy land, with its plump lambs, shining in unapproachable light. These dreams amused him all the way to the forest edge. But as the trees neared, and the dream became a reality, the joy was swallowed up in the clutches of uncertainty.

All was painfully still near the forest. The trees on the side of Auchriachan were twisted and gnarled. Peeking through the interwoven twigs and branches, the young men saw that it looked threatening and dark inside. Branches gave mournful creaks in the wind. Asher thought, or rather sensed, the promise of something sweeter in the centre. Over the scent of wood, he caught the hint of a flower; the lack of light within suggested rich leaves. He rallied his courage, and took the plunge inside. Deeper and deeper he walked in, using his crook almost as another leg. Joel trailed reluctantly behind.

The tinkling of a small bell tied around the neck of

one of their sheep was all the young men could hear as they trod the beaten animal paths. Gradually, the intricate trees opened into a little glade, and an expanse of gorgeous green lay glimmering before their eyes. Precious, precious grass!

The scrawny sheep found a burst of energy to gallop forward. A pretty sylvan scene they made, frolicking like new born lambs. They bleated merrily to taste this luscious meal after so many months of thistle, bramble, nettle and twig.

Joel and Asher laughed and hugged one another for joy. The sun bounced off the grass in a bright light which made them squint; they could almost taste it themselves.

"Oh it is too wonderful! I knew it, I knew!" cried Asher. Peace and happiness flowed like a river through him. A thousand futures full of fat sheep and comfort pulsed through his glad mind. He laid down on his back, crossed his arms behind his head, and looked up to the sunny sky.

Joel, who was slightly more practical, shielded his eyes from the rays to observe the flock. It looked larger, spread about the small rustic space; but it was smaller. One sheep was missing. This was enough to shatter their entire world.

"Blackberry!" Joel exclaimed in a leaden voice, immediately registering the absence of his favourite. Blackberry was their only male lamb. He held the future of the flock in his woolly coat.

Asher gave a start, and sprang up. He started counting the sheep as fast as he could. His head was muzzy with panic but he reached the same conclusion: one short. There was no joy in his thoughts now; only terror on every side.

Almost the second Asher finished counting, they heard a pitiful bleat. Joel did not hesitate; his alarmed eyes met Asher's, and he ran towards the sound.

Leaping over shrubs, winding through trees, he followed the increasingly frantic little pleas of Blackberry. The sound grew so loud that Joel knew the lamb must be very close by. His eyes were dazzled by the nets of twigs and moving foliage. He looked down, and in doing so, came across a ditch, pilled with dead leaves. He skidded to a shuddering halt. His feet stopped just in time, tottering over the edge.

Joel peered warily into the ditch. The little lamb Blackberry was inside, a spot of grubby white, stuck where his tiny foot had become trapped underneath a tree root. Joel relaxed and took a step back. His heart cried with immense pity for the poor thing. He must speed to its rescue.

By this time Asher had caught up. He had been very reluctant to leave the flock alone. Looking over at the ditch, which was a dried out pond, he stood stock still and called to his friend in a low, urgent voice.

"Joel, hang back."

Joel saw too, at that moment, the sinuous movements of an adder weaving closer and closer to the frightened Blackberry. Starting up, Joel only moved faster to the lamb's aid.

"Stop!" yelled Asher. "Joel, leave him be!"

"I won't have him killed," Joel stated firmly.

"Neither would I, only – better the sheep than the shepherd! Look, look, it will pass him by, only be patient."

Patience had the misfortune to form only a very small part of Joel's character. He saw a fallen alder tree, leaning like a bridge across the ditch, and began to crawl across it. Asher could only look on in suspense and despair.

"There now," Joel spoke gently to the lamb. "Stay very still." He shifted slowly across the trunk. It gave an ominous creak.

The snake cocked its head and seemed to inspect the lamb from both eyes. It glided around Blackberry. Joel held his breath, but the serpent passed and remained stationary at about half a metre's distance.

Joel took his opportunity and gingerly put out one hand. "Come on then, little one." Blackberry gave a pitiful cry. Joel's fingers touched the rough wood of the tree root entrapping his sheep. He groped to reach the lamb's foot. The snake hissed.

The foot was caught fast. Joel gave it a small push on the hoof. No movement. He grasped the base of Blackberry's leg and pulled. The lamb whimpered in pain. At the noise the snake drifted forwards.

"You'll break his leg," murmured Asher.

It did indeed seem impossible to free Blackberry without laming him for life; and then what use would he be to them anyway? But Joel could not abandon him.

Thinking quickly, he reached for his back pocket. The branch wobbled. Joel regained his balance and drew out a small knife of dull metal.

Putting one arm under the soft fleece of Blackberry, Joel held on to the branch with only the strength of his legs. With the other hand he began sawing the tree root. The scraping noise attracted the snake. Through the shards of wood flying near his eyes, Joel could see the sinister shape hovering towards him. He sawed faster. The snake moved faster.

Sweat beaded on Joel's brow and his limbs ached with the effort required from them. He closed his eyes. Abruptly, he felt his knife fall down as the root gave way. He lifted his arms up as the snake reared up. He turned on the log, throwing Blackberry to safety. In hurling the lamb he lost all grip with his legs. Asher, dashing to scoop up Blackberry, saw him fall to the adder's sting.

Asher waited in mute horror. The adder had

achieved its aim and slid triumphantly around its prey. All was now still in the wood. The birds continued to chatter tranquilly, like nothing had happened. The adder became bored and, giving another hiss, it sloped off into a dense bush. Only then did Asher move toward his friend.

He half galloped, half fell down the steep banks of the ditch, and skidded on his knees by the side of Joel. From the pain, or the shock, or perhaps the fall, Joel had passed out. Blackberry nuzzled his unresponsive hand.

"It is only an adder," Asher realised, finding himself talking aloud. An adder could not kill a human, he remembered, but it was poisonous. He felt for a pulse on the dirty neck. Joel was alive. But Asher knew he was going to be very, very ill. And then there was the awkward way in which he had fallen. There was a nasty graze on his temple beneath the matted locks of his hair, and a small spot of blood on the left corner of his mouth. Asher could not take these to be good omens.

It took all of Asher's wasted strength to hoist his friend's inanimate body over his shoulder. He stumbled and fell in clawing his way up the bank, but eventually he reached the top, Blackberry trotting docilely behind like any dog.

Where to get help? Certainly Joel needed aid, but how could Asher leave the flock? He was not even sure he remembered where the flock was anymore. Towing the increasingly heavy weight of his friend, Asher walked, deeply involved and lost in the woods, for what seemed like hours. The trees began to swim and blur into one. He could not find the flock.

Asher laid Joel gently down and sat on the floor, his head on his knees in exhaustion and defeat. It hurt to catch his breath. Blackberry, equally exhausted curled up in a little croissant shape. But the lamb could not get comfortable. He bleated repeatedly and coughed a sweet little lamb cough.

Poor Asher thought his luck was really in. An unconscious friend, a lost flock, and the only sheep he had was expiring. Only a few hours ago it had seemed as if he would be rich and happy for life. He had not taken very good care of his opportunities. He began to mentally abuse himself for all he could have done. He should have controlled Joel's mad rescue attempt – he should have kept an eye on a sheep as important as Blackberry in the first place...

Asher was able to take in large breaths as he panted. He too began to give a few chokes, like the lamb. There was something in the air: a delicious, warm smell of burning.

His head snapped up, almost convinced he would see a forest blaze. It would be in keeping with the rest of his day.

But no. He saw a dark tendril of smoke – just one – drifting upwards in uniform style. That could only come from a chimney! There was a house!

Finding a new lease of strength in this wonderful spring of hope, he hoisted Joel up once more and nearly ran in the direction of the smoke. He was not thinking clearly enough to beware of strange houses in the woods, which of course was a very silly thing for him to do.

The sun was beginning to sink as he reached an open plot of turf, strewn with mossy grey boulders. A small fountain pumped out twinkling water beside a lopsided house. It was made of clay and wooden logs, and had a dirty straw roof. Just outside, on the floor, was the black stain of a coal pit, with a trivet and a few pans.

Asher made straight for the fountain. Sitting on a tree stump and nursing Joel's head in his lap, he washed the wound and splashed water over his face. Blackberry gratefully lapped up a drink with his tiny pink tongue.

Once he had finished cleaning Joel, Asher slumped back. It was all for nothing. There was no-one about to help, and Joel had still not woken up. Asher's eyelids were terribly heavy now all was gentle and quiet again. He did not know how, but he fell asleep.

Only when he was aware of feeling very, very cold did he wake up. He gasped in fright. Everything was pitch black. Joel had gone.

Panicked, Asher stood up, the blood rushing to his head. He ran toward the house, and nearly collided with a sudden vision that sprang, as if out of the ground, to confront him. A figure of a man in spotless white struck his eyes against the darkness of the night. The figure had a very pale face and was covered like a bride in an eerie floating white veil. In between his hands the figure held a burning candle.

"Do not be alarmed," said the apparition in a fluid voice. "I am Roddag."

This intelligence did nothing to slow Asher's crazed heart beat. "I know who you are!" he answered, shuddering. "The seer!" As he said the words, Asher's faculties and all his native courage began to return to him. Roddag was only standing quiescently and nodding. "Well," cried Asher, ""See" where my friend has gone. He is sick and I must find him!"

With a benign smile, Roddag stretched out one hand mantled in gold and silver jewellery. "Come."

Asher eyed him warily. At last, though his face still spoke deep distrust, he clamped his rough, brown hand into the seers.

They entered the narrow door into the cabin-like house. It smelt of wood-chips and hay. It was very plain inside, with heavy wooden furniture and leaves for a carpet. Looking up, Asher became aware of exotic birds perching on the rafters of the ceiling. In fact, there were creatures everywhere. A fawn was nuzzling his hand as he moved along, and Blackberry was galloping after squirrels, which shot up the walls and looked unimpressed with the duo. Roddag tapped him on the shoulder, and gestured toward the homely blaze of a fire.

On the most comfortable article of furniture in the room – a sort of truckle bed covered in rags – sat Joel, beaming up at him.

Asher catapulted to his side, laughing and embracing him with relief. Something, however, was strange. Not right.

Asher held Joel's face in his hands. There was no graze. No scar, even. His eyes ran rapidly over the now clear, unharmed skin of Joel. No bite, no wound! Baffled beyond words, Asher looked mutely from Joel to Roddag, Roddag to Joel.

"You have been extremely lucky," said Roddag, pretending not to see Asher's astonished reaction by instead fixing his gaze on a minute white mouse running over his hands. "It does not do to go playing with snakes."

Joel scoffed indignantly. "*Playing*!"

Roddag busied himself about the fire. "Not playing? I suppose you trod on it. Well, something hot to drink and then you will be on your way."

"He's not very good for a seer. So much for being the link between *them*," meaning the fairies, "and us; he does not know what has happened, let alone what will."

But Asher saw a twinkle in Roddag's eye which checked him from joining in with Joel's mockery.

"I know," said Roddag, "That you went seeking that snake. It did not come to you."

Joel sat up proudly. "Yes I went seeking it, and had the branch held out, I would have sliced its head clean off too for daring to come near Blackberry."

Roddag turned with sudden interest. The fire flared

mystically in his face as he studied Joel.

"Could it be..." he breathed to himself. "But you are only a worker, a shepherd boy. This, I take it, is Blackberry?" he looked towards the soft white creature bleating at his heel.

"Yes," said Joel, scooping up the lamb. It nestled into his neck and closed its eyes.

Roddag looked at the pair, thunderstruck. "This – this is your *only* sheep?"

"No," sighed Asher leadenly. "The rest are still out there... somewhere. I do not know if we will ever find them again."

Roddag's bright gaze widened. His now extremely large eyes looked like they had galaxies swirling around inside them. The magical look unnerved the young men. Suddenly, Roddag started laughing. "Of course! Of course! The water, the sheep, the snake – why did I not know?" He threw off his white veil and began to bustle about the fireplace.

He poured some of the pure water from the fountain outside into a huge silver dish. "Ah, but I would have thought, since you were holding the lamb, it would have been *you*," chattered away the seer, wagging his head at Asher. He sprinkled something into the flames, and they suddenly flared up silver, underneath the dish of water. "But I see it in your face, young Joel – that defiant brow of yours! *You* left all you had in the world, to save this one skinny little creature – and then you fell prey to that you would snatch it from! Quite fearlessly!"

Joel hadn't been entirely fearless, but he did not see the necessity of telling Roddag this, if he couldn't see it himself. Moreover, he and Asher were entirely confounded by the seer's cryptic words and strange behaviour. Roddag had suddenly become less dignified than became a seer – his pale face was sparkling, and he looked hungry, and excited.

The water began to make bubbling sounds. Roddag took the dish from the fire, and shoved it onto Joel's lap. Joel winced, in expectation of it burning his legs, but it did not. It was actually very, very cold. The water inside looked like liquid crystal.

Roddag calmed, and opened with great reverence a glass case hanging on the wall. From it he took a tall golden candle, like a church candle. He gave a gentle blow upon the wick, and it burst into flame.

Walking over to Joel, Roddag took one of his hands and clasped it firmly around the base of the candle. "Let the wax drip into the water," he said in an urgent, hushed voice.

The warm, shiny wax trickled quickly into the water as Joel tilted the candle. It set almost immediately as it touched the surface. Solid and white, the wax had formed a shape unmistakeably resembling a sword. Even Joel and Asher, simple as they were, knew what this meant.

Joel nearly upset the bowl of water on his lap, but with true heroism, steadied the dish to save Roddag's leaf carpet. When he looked up, both Roddag and Asher were staring at him in unaffected awe.

Roddag began to laugh, in a kind of triumph or relief. "You are! You *are!*" he crowed, pressing Joel's hand. "My purpose is fulfilled; I shall not live long now."

Joel wanted to laugh too, but could not make a noise. There was an odd fizzing in his chest, and a proud glow on his cheeks. Still more urgent, there was a tight knot of apprehension in his stomach. He did not feel at all worthy of Asher's suddenly adoring looks. Asher was kneeling to him, suddenly, mouth ajar. "You are the chosen King," Asher whispered in wide-eyed wonder. "The King whose reign is to change the future of Auchriachan forever."

It was an awful lot of responsibility for an obscure

shepherd boy. Joel did not feel in control of any of it. "How can I be?" he asked Roddag. "What am I to do now? I have no power to make myself King! Who will believe a dirty, poor shepherd – who probably only has one sheep left to his name by now – when he tells them he was lost in the wilderness, and appointed King by Roddag the seer? They'll hang me for treason."

"You seem to have one pretty staunch follower already," commented Roddag, looking at the awe-struck Asher. Roddag did not seem able to concentrate on anything but Asher. "It is strange," he murmured to himself, "you are certainly a very fine young man. Do you not feel wronged boy, to leave with nothing, when I have given your friend a kingdom?"

"Oh no," Asher stood up and shook his head. "Joel is far braver and smarter than I. He will be a wonderful King."

Joel said very earnestly, and a bit touchily: "Asher will never want for a place of respect while I am sovereign. But we are talking madness! I cannot believe it! What do you expect me to do now, Roddag?" Joel put the bowl from him shakily.

"Exactly what I tell you. You will recover your flock – they are still all safe and well – and you will travel with them to Iblees. Do not be afraid. You will hear your own fanfare playing there, and will enter triumphantly. Then you will know that I am near."

Joel looked pained, and nodded thoughtfully. He thought that perhaps if he nodded enough it would look like he believed Roddag.

"And you, young man," continued Roddag to Asher, "must make sure he gets there safely."

"I will do my utmost – "

"I will guarantee that you do more. When I am gone, you will know the signs. Here is my gift to you." He laid

41

his hand on the messy head of Asher. There was a spark from the fire, and the boy passed out.

CHAPTER SIX

As Joel, Asher and their herd approached Iblees, they heard a great commotion. It was truly the only element needed to complete the absolute panic of their journey. Joel drew back and hid himself behind a cart piled full with hay and manure.

He could see the domineering turrets of the castle rising up in intimidating majesty. All the walls were heavy, wearing a mantle of creeping ivy. It was all far more vegetatious than the landscape Joel was used to, being littered with rough gorse and gnarly trees which seemed to rise up with each branch as a twirling helter-skelter.

"This is a crazy idea," he whispered to Asher. "What were we thinking? Roddag is playing a game with us; he wants to kindly lead us to a painful death without the mere grief of doing it himself. Can't you hear the fighting?"

Asher listened carefully. His sense of hearing was strangely altered since Roddag had touched him; he heard things no one else noticed were there, and was only learning gradually himself what these odd new sounds really were. Today he did hear a clash of metal, but it sounded more tuneful than armour would. Suddenly he made out a tambourine, and as he did, a picture flew into his head, fully formed.

"It is not a fight," Asher told him. "It is the Amorette

43

tribe. They are dancing in the town square. It was an impromptu thing, and no one knows why they are doing it. Come and see."

Joel took a few begrudging steps. "*You've* been acting strange the whole journey too," he grumbled. "Saying these queer, fairy things."

Asher did not reply as he walked alongside Joel over the flat table-land of Iblees. The truth was, he had *felt* different the whole journey. Little daydreams that flitted over his brain suddenly became true about an hour later. He seemed to know instinctively now what paths to take and if routes were safe. Most of all, he began to observe omens. He saw an omen in nearly everything; he saw a good one now, as they walked over the vast purplish moorland, in two magpies hopping together amidst the dried heather.

As they neared the stone cottages and smoking huts on the outskirts of the great Glass Mountain Castle, the sound of music became clearer. Evidently Joel believed enough in Roddag's good opinion of him to feel he needn't admit he had been wrong.

The stronghold gates flung open suddenly with a huge crash. Joel and Asher did not look very kingly anymore; they leapt about a foot in the air and clung on to one another. But it was only a gay procession of brightly coloured dancers, girls with plaid belts and men with bells leaping to the sounds of the tambourines, flutes, harps and lyres. Ribbons fluttered in the air and short dresses swirled as the happy company pranced. Only a few of them appeared to notice the shepherds; one was a naughty maiden who made a joke of their bewildered faces by kissing Joel on the cheek and skipping off. A Moordale tutted, and Joel blushed furiously, but Asher chose to interpret it as another omen.

The swirling parade looked about to pass them by

without further incident, towards the Moordales and Boanerges who were having a serious discussion over the succession and were distinctly unimpressed by this show.

But at that instant a sonorous boom broke the spell of the music. The King's heralds on top of the battlements had made the sound, but were looking at their trumpets as if unsure the instruments had not started playing by themselves. Asher knew then what he should be looking for, and he saw it: Roddag stood authoritatively on top of a barrow, like he had that moment pushed himself up from underneath it as a flower does.

The crowd collectively took in a sharp breath, and stood still. A shiver of wind passed over the undulating moors.

"People of Auchriachan," called Roddag. "Long have you interrupted my solitary life with requests for a King to unite the tribes and factions of your race. Today I bring him to you. Mourn no more for the ruler of Iblees, cold in his grave, for there stands one whose reputation shall be immortal."

Roddag raised his arm, as a shaft of light cut through the low grey sky to highlight Joel. The shepherd boy blinked, but stood defiant and tall. A King would never show misgiving or doubt, he knew. The very circumstance of the ray of sunlight, and Roddag's words, gave him a confidence and a rush of power beyond what he had ever felt before. Perhaps Joel felt a little too strongly his distinction, but he was new to being a King, and had not yet learned that a good King mingles humility with sovereignty.

Some good Emberlights, overawed by Joel's spotlight, did not help to teach him this lesson; they fell immediately upon their knees. The majority of the crowd, however, buzzed in an excited whisper.

"The King, the King! At last! Is he really here?"

"Can you see him? I dare not look! It is him, it is really him!"

Still others, who also struggled with the lesson of humility, took on a sceptical tone.

"That," pointed out the dead King's widow in no very pleasant way, "is a shepherd boy."

Those upon their knees seemed to feel the full justice of this accusation, and looked a little chagrined.

"Do they expect us to bow to a worker?!" exploded many Riverons. Some of the Emberlights upon their knees got up.

The kinder Moordales accepted Joel for what he was. They found his origins a thing to be proud of.

"A worker, of course!" they laughed. "So unexpected, so like the way of the prophecies!"

"He has had all the disadvantages and hardships which lead to certain success!"

Joel did not know what to say. He did not even know if he wanted to persuade them in his favour yet. However, the queer way in which he stood, merely staring, inspired the crowd to take to him. He looked strong and manly, touched with some great power of thoughtfulness. An ambition to prove himself burned slowly in his gaze. He was not sure he *wanted* the responsibility of King, but he knew he did not want to be laughed at as incapable of taking it.

"Say as you will, I give you a leader," proclaimed Roddag. "And I give to this appointed one all authority over you. Whether you chose to accept it or not is your own concern. Each of you must decide himself where his allegiance lies. But surely as the sun rises in the sky, here is Joel, King of Auchriachan, in accordance with what was foretold."

Just then a very strange thing happened. The overcharged sky dropped its heavy burden of rain, just in one place. A fast shower of fat drops descended immediately over Joel's head. All of Iblees stared in disbelief as the sprinkles formulated, very gradually, into a shimmering crown upon the young man's brow. At that moment, Joel was aware of something surging within him. It was as if he was waking in the morning after a long, long sleep in an unknown place. He felt he had finally become what he was meant to be, and secretly knew he was meant to be since the day of his birth. Joel felt secure of fulfilling his destiny, and the consciousness of that took away every last scrap of fear.

Only one in the crowd failed to be amazed by the magic. He was a large, square built man with a thick beard and a very little neck.

"Aye, pretty tricks, very pretty tricks," he called in a gruff voice. He clapped his hand in mock applause. "An' we're all meant to bow down to this scrap of a lad because you say so, am I right?"

Everyone felt suddenly terribly uncomfortable. The joyous spirit had been ship-wrecked, and the crowd were now a little ashamed of themselves for getting carried away. When it was put like that, the coronation of King Joel seemed a silly idea indeed. Inside, in a secret place, many people knew they *should* accept King Joel, but could not say why, and could certainly not explain it to one with such a stubborn mind as Dybuk.

Dybuk, you see, was a Boanerge, and one of the dead King's personal bodyguards. He was very powerful and influential, although rather vulgar, but vulgarity was something that could carry you a long way in Auchriachan.

"Sir," Joel ventured to say calmly, "you seem to be one who served the crown well, I think, and will not go unrewarded. I will immediately Knight one of your sons, and appoint him to my select staff."

Dybuk chewed on a fat lip as he mulled this over. "Which son?"

"Kish," threw in Asher helpfully. He was not altogether sure how, or if he knew Dybuk had a son called Kish. But it soon became clear that there was a Kish, for a tanned and sturdy young man with quick eyes perked up and looked very eager as this was said.

"What gives you authority to do that?" Dybuk came back with. "Come on," he said to those around him, "we're not to be told what to do by one man in a white frock. We have the power, not him, and we choose our King."

"He's right," piped up someone else. It was probably another Boanerge. "We can't trust someone who was fairy led as a child."

"Roddag's spent too much time being tricked by the winged creatures," decided another of Dybuk's sons. "They're impish, deceitful creatures. Always trying to lead us off from our homes."

"Didn't he once live among them? He must be on their side!"

So it was that a disgruntled group of burly men separated from the masses and turned their backs on the new King.

"He's not our King, that measly worker," said Dybuk for all of them. "And the Boanerges tribe will agree with me," he threatened. No doubt he was going to rally that tribe, from whence came the deceased King's mother, into revolt.

The astute Kish did not follow his father and brothers as they went off. He had been promised a knighthood after all, beside which the ties of family rather pale into insignificance.

In fact, many did not follow Dybuk. They stood, chastised, less certain, but still loyal. One in particular, an elder and advisor to the previous King, whose name was

Alfred, came forward and drew from his cape a shining leather volume.

"This is the book of instructions to the King," he told Joel respectfully. "All the seers, even your patron Roddag have contributed to it. It has been passed down for generations. If there is anything I can explain, do not hesitate to call upon me, my liege." Joel thanked him.

Alfred clapped his hands. "Well!" he ordered the lower Knights and ladies-in-waiting who made up the castle staff. "What are you doing? Take His Majesty inside and show him his apartments."

Joel found his way back to Asher, whose hand he seized, before he was led into the huge grey castle. It would be less daunting, somehow, if Asher were just there, with his soulful looks and newly acquired snippets of useful information. They both turned to look for Roddag. It did not seem right, or even possible, to go ahead without his lead.

Where the seer had stood upon the hill, a healthy pink hyacinth bloomed. A hyacinth, on this barren moorland where only heather and gorse could take root! Its beautiful bells nodded defiantly in the breeze. The flower was puzzling beyond words. But weirder still, Roddag was not there; neither at the top nor bottom of the hill. He was not in the crowd, he was not among the advisors. He had vanished. When later that evening, the recently instated King Joel sent a rider to the site of the hut, it too had vanished. And Roddag was never seen again from that day.

CHAPTER SEVEN

King Joel was soon firmly rooted as the monarch of Iblees. He saw wonders beyond his imagination in the shining halls of Glass Mountain Castle. He sat at the head of huge tables filled with magnificent feasts; he walked down corridors of chequered black and white which clicked with his footsteps. He saw the statues of past kings and seers which lined so many walls, and his heart swelled inside him to think he was now was one of them.

Yet in all this, he was painfully insecure. The cold, hard faces of the statues were so wise, so noble! Joel looked at his own frightened expression and young brow, and could not be sure that Roddag had chosen the right person for the job.

Joel knew he was not intelligent, or particularly strong. The learned advisors surrounding him only served to brand it more clearly on his notice. If it were not for Alfred's incessant council and clear determination to instate him, Joel suspected the elders would not even consider accepting him as a ruler. He had a deep conviction they did not like him. He did not trust even one of them.

Nonetheless, Joel was doing well. Asher's new talents for farming forecasts meant the people could enjoy a fuller harvest than they had ever yet known. Sir Kish proved a handy accomplice. He had a shrewd, fast mind and was not at all loathe to lend it to the King who had chosen to favour him. Kish seemed very keen indeed to remain friendly with one who could give so much. So Joel trusted Asher and Kish, most of the time. But a creeping little shadow in his heart worried that he would be branded a fraud, merely gaining applause by exploiting the genius of others.

"A King must not always expect victory for himself," Asher read to him from the Book of kings. "He must submit when powers beyond him have chosen for him to be humble. For all is planned; it is good and wise for a King to listen to the council of those whose souls are woven to the soil, and those who see the signs of the angels." See, it is normal to be guided and helped," Asher encouraged. "A King should never be stubborn and act alone." He put the book down in his lap and bit his lip.

It worried Asher that with so many references to the signs from the angels and from the fairies, the humans remained estranged from them. Why try to follow their prompting, if they were creatures to be feared? It did not make any sense to him. Asher resolved to research the matter further and talk it over with Joel – when he was calmer.

"I should know this myself!" groaned Joel furiously, twisting his sceptre round and round in his hands. "I should have read the entire book by now, not you! I feel so stupid!"

He felt especially stupid since he had caught a glimpse of Alfred's granddaughter, the Lady Ganieda. She was always around in Glass Mountain Castle, watching in silence with eyes that sparkled like diamonds. The dark hair that fell in ringlets to her waist was the most beautiful sight Joel had ever seen. He was always very bright red, very uncoordinated, and very unable to do any task properly when she was around. And she was around far too often.

Over the period of the next few weeks, Joel reacted as frightened, insecure souls often do. He assumed an air of great pride and assurance. He spoke harshly, so that he did not appear vulnerable, and he acted with insolence to persuade himself he did not shake within. He became, in fact, like the bleak, foreboding expanse of moorland he presided over; unyielding, tough and undulating, with the ability to sing in the sun or scream amongst the clouds. And as they regarded the land, the people began to regard the King; they marvelled at the rugged beauty and ferocious majesty, yet feared the rolling winds that came sweeping down the hills.

One day Joel, Kish and Asher were out making their royal progress along this boggy terrain. The sky was laden with darkness, banked to the hilt with long stored up rain.

"Perhaps we should go inside," suggested Asher sensibly.

But Kish broke off from the group, without the King's permission, which was an incredibly bad thing to do. Yet he had already acquired that assurance around Joel, and impressed upon the young King his own superior worth, that Joel would not think of chastising him.

Kish jumped down into a long trough between the wild hills. He walked along for a moment, intensely studious. Then he began to pull away the undergrowth in the moist spots. Amid the rustle and flying leaves, a woven fence of hawthorn was slowly revealed. It was a fence that looked a bit sorry for itself; where it did not have holes, it was wonky, but it dug in its heels and kept standing like a good fence should.

Kish stood back beaming, like he had uncovered a great wonder. "Look, sire," he pointed to the fence. "Generations ago my tribe erected this. It goes all along the border of the wood."

"That is ... admirable," said Joel, sharing a bemused look with Asher. "What use is it to me?"

"Your Majesty!" exclaimed Kish indignantly. "Surely I need not tell *you*. If you are as keen as I thought you were to keep the fairies at bay... you did say something of the sort to me, but perhaps you have changed your great mind. I hear kings do that."

Joel's bottom lip stuck out in a proud pout. Kish was practicing his particular talent of making Joel feel like an imbecile again. The King shook his great red velvet cloak and replied haughtily: "Sir Kish knows we are ever anxious to prevent our subjects from being enticed away to – to –"

"Laseri," supplied Asher. His eyes were roaming the fringes of reed and straggling tufts of bushes.

"Yes, Laseri," Joel began again, somewhat severely. "I was *going* to say, before I was rudely interrupted, the Land of the Dead. For that is what my Knights have been telling me it is. No one has ever been, of course, but it is certain once they enter they can never return."

"That doesn't quite make sense-" started Asher, but Kish spoke over him. Asher sighed. It was useless, he knew, to argue against these distorted stories conceived in fear. He had spoken to all the elders regarding the fairies, and learned they considered fairies as a thing to be respected, though not meddled with. That was why they had the seers to teach them, and would not dare break through the forest.

"Well, if that is so, all the more reason to repair and maintain these fine fences," exclaimed Kish, putting his hands on his hips and throwing out his chest so the coat of arms on his tabard expanded. "For everyone knows fairies respect the boundaries of the hawthorn. And a firm framework of iron would be as good as putting a gaping sea between us and them."

Joel offered his hand to help Kish out of the ditch.

"Then we shall do it," he declared. "What do you say, Sir Asher?"

Asher might have been a very good Knight were his head not always in the clouds. He did not hear the King, for he had taken off his chain-mail hood so that he could see better, and was wringing it in his hands. The movements of nature beneath the frowning sky today fascinated him. Upon a half-starved tree he saw two grey squirrels running helter-skelter down the trunk, winding round and round each other. Then there was a loud flap of wings, and a pair of pigeons, he saw, were playing chase. They flew about with such fury and pace it made him want to laugh.

It piqued Joel to be ignored. "Well, we do not need *his* opinion," he said to Kish. "It shall be done. You may superintend it yourself, if you like. The brutal kidnapping of our dear people must stop."

"This will stop the horrors of changeling babies, curses, stolen milk and hag-ridden horses," mused Kish, calling up every superstition about fairies he had ever heard. "It is how to prevent the people from going *out* that I struggle with. They will always be enticed by the glamour and preternatural beauty of these creatures." He gave a laugh, "A pretty face makes people do some very foolish things."

Joel coloured. He was beginning to understand that himself.

"Laseri is reputedly the loveliest place in the world," recommended Kish. "There are scores upon scores of female fairies, jewels and flowers beyond imaginations. Of course it all turns to dust sooner or later. Be that as it may, the people – particularly those Riverons – would risk everything just to see it. They are so heedless they would give their lives to despair and captivation rather than go without having one moment of boundless beauty." He gave a snort of contempt. "And what has dear old Iblees to offer in the way of that fresh, graceful allure? With all respect, your Majesty, you do not measure up besides a lithe young fay!"

"You must take a wife," said Asher before they had even begun to laugh properly. He still said it half in a dream. It was becoming slowly clear to him through a haze of thoughts. "You *must* take a Queen. The signs say it would be a good thing."

Kish and Joel looked at one another.

"Well, if that is your solution to combat the beauty of the deceitful fairies!" laughed Kish. "What do you think, your Majesty?"

Joel looked rather strange as he said, "Well – if it is for the good of the kingdom."

CHAPTER EIGHT

Queen Aurora strains her shoulder blades. They feel locked, and her face is screwed up with the effort. Finally, she gives a huge shrug and deflates, exhausted.

"I see what you mean," says her husband in contemplation. "Do not worry." He fingers her blue wings gently, like a petal. "They are weak from lack of use. They will work again. Eventually."

He sits on a decaying log and resumes picking at the luscious grass.

Aurora pulls round her almost violet fore-wing and looks at it. She can see the creases and small breaks where the cord bound them for so long.

She had been so happy, when first seated on her rightful throne with the whole glittering host of Laseri before her, ready to respect her once more, and Deucalion had loosed with his golden knife her heinous chains. That dear, bright joy had been a wasted emotion. She cannot feel them at all. Somehow, she thinks the ever wily Deucalion knew this would happen.

She looks across the flowering meadows, divided by hedgerows of bright primrose. Small tents are erected on the grass next to the wheat-sheaves. The reigning sun catches glints of metal in its course across the lustrous sky.

"Delay the march of the army," Aurora says in a small but steady voice. "Wait until I can fly again. It is only fair.

Give me some chance."

Deucalion laughs. "My dear, my dear! There is much I have to teach you about being a monarch. You did not stipulate your being able to fly as one of our terms. It is regrettable, but you see how far affairs have moved along. I am utterly, utterly powerless." He folds his arms behind his head and lays down upon the log, gazing at the sky, a picture of contented idleness.

Aurora blows out a deep breath. Her eyes close then open. She sits down upon the log and strokes the golden threads of the King's glorious hair. "I thought that perhaps you might make an exception. It is not safe, you know, for me to travel so far on foot. The dark fairies..."

"I am not afraid of the dark fairies. I keep telling you this. They are *fairies*; ergo, I am not afraid of them."

"But I am," Aurora admits, as if she hates herself for it.

Deucalion slaps her heartily on the shoulder. "Ah, well. You're a brave girl; you'll take care of yourself."

He stands up and leaves Aurora gaping on the log in indignation. "What sort of husband are you anyway?" she cries angrily.

"A very good sort," Deucalion acknowledges, as far as his modesty will allow him. "I took your suggestions; I am already establishing the equality fairies were designed to practice. Do not imagine you know more than me about the obligations and great purpose of fairies. I may not get in a pet about it, but I feel it in my soul all the same." He gives a yawn. "Anyhow, what would it signify my ranting and raving now? I can do nothing, you know, without my newly elected council."

Aurora feels a little ashamed as she realises the truth of this. "Can you not persuade them..."

"I *did* persuade them. The council wants a war. I persuaded them too much. They will not let me delay it now. One law for all, you recall."

Aurora hides her face in her hands. She does not doubt that an enigmatic fairy like Deucalion can talk anyone into doing whatever he likes, even those pig-headed astrals. But he does have a point. How would it be ethical to sway his council one way, and then the other? How would it be any different, in fact, to the old system she had previously complained of?

"You are a very great King," she proclaims, and she really means it. He flashes a lightning bolt smile towards the log. "But you are mistaken in this war."

He does not look perturbed even for an instant. He is so used to believing absolutely in himself that he cannot even let in a chink of conflicting advice. "Perhaps; perhaps not," he says graciously. "The fates will favour your feet or my armies with speed. As the angels will it." He kisses her on the forehead and leaves her alone on the log, watching the white phantoms of dandelion seeds drifting in the air.

This is the moment Aurora swore she would see through, but she finds it very hard to do it. The courage that swells her heart in moments of passion has subsided to a dull thudding that she feels mainly in her neck. She looks from the peaceful pastoral scene to the dank-smelling forest. Something odd is already taking place there. Shadows move imperceptibly beneath the trees.

She remembers during the last war the young fees standing, just about where she is sitting now, trying to prove their bravery for dares and prizes, if they made a certain length of time.

"*Le Barboue* is going to get you," she can still hear them singing. She tries to recollect what it was this threatening creature of their imaginations was supposed to do to fairies – then decided that she would rather not remember.

The coolness, the stillness within the trees begins to

enthral her. Magnetised, she walks closer and closer to the gap in the trees. The promise of something deeper, something more fascinating within the forest pulls her irresistibly forward.

It is so different now to when she stormed in, heedless, to find Cynthia. The dark fairies, the Deevs, could have risen up even now. Leaves flap on the outside, near her hair. Her breath comes heavily now. She does not move her gaze. If she dares…

Litterfall and dust are swooping in the filtered spots of sunlight, softly, gently, calling her name. Can it be so dangerous? If she takes one more step, as she yearns to, will *Barboue* really get her?

She steps forward, helpless, drawn recklessly on. Something touches her.

Aurora gasps and pants, turning wildly around to bat at the heavy weight on her shoulder. Her whole skin has turned to ice and pure fear is pounding relentlessly in her head; she cannot open her eyes. She begins to shriek uselessly as she senses whatever it is winding itself around her, capturing her, squeezing her. She is held tight and she cannot move.

"Aurora! Aurora!"

The voice brings her vaguely to her senses. Every limb is trembling, but her mind is calmer, resigned.

Whatever binds her is not holding her as tightly, anyhow. Its arms are slipping from her entirely, in fact. She feels the cool breeze on her arms, and knows herself to be at liberty. Gingerly, she opens her eyes.

It is Apollo; only Apollo all along! The brightness of his fine shining fairy armour makes her squint. Apollo.

"You didn't think I'd let you go alone, did you?"

CHAPTER NINE

Circumstances improved for King Joel after his wedding to the Lady Ganieda. Life has a habit of looking better when you are married to a beautiful woman. There were two of them now, in the spotlight; two to stand as a team against slander, insurrection or criticism. Two was a far less scary number than one. King Joel did not often feel stupid as part of a pair.

Of course, he had felt utterly ridiculous when he first attempted to follow Asher's advice. He blamed Asher greatly. Joel could not, he found, just go up to Ganieda and propose to her. It seemed something of an insult to obtrude his presence on her, let alone ask her to allow him to stay beside her for any length of time.

Moreover, Joel did not exactly know Ganieda very well. He knew she looked like one of a heavenly race, that she occupied his head all day long, that she was what he prized more than anything else in the world, but that was all. And all he could offer her was a share in the entire kingdom and the lifelong devotion of himself. It appeared to Joel a rather insufficient bargain for the poor girl.

So Joel spoke to Alfred. The King had decided to marry. He had chosen to honour Alfred's family and thank that humble servant for loyal service to the crown by selecting a bride from amongst his family. The Lady Ganieda was of noble blood and well suited to embellish the role of Queen of Auchriachan. The King would leave the family to discuss it amongst themselves and consult the fair lady's inclinations.

Unsurprisingly the fair lady was very inclined to become a Queen, and more than a little impressed with the rugged, brooding looks of the King. Therefore they were married in a triumphant festival witnessed by all in Auchriachan, with showers of confetti, rich satins and furs and great sprawling bouquets of the wild flowers which grew on the moors, before they had really held many conversations together. Again Joel felt very stupid he had not possessed courage to ask her himself; he thought his wife must regard him as a great, mute coward.

Luckily, the Lady Ganieda was precisely the species of girl fitted for King Joel. She was graceful, soft and indulgent. Lady Ganieda owned enough confidence to talk first to King Joel, in a way that he was obliged to respond to. It was her talent to make great decisions, without seeming to give an order at all; she relished the role of helpmate and advisor to the King, although in appearance she never guided him. Ganieda could start an idea rolling in someone's head, and by the time it had reached fruition, they were convinced it was purely their own invention. Ganieda never corrected them; she always smiled.

The Riveron tribe from which she sprang were delighted with this turn of events. Those that had begrudged Joel his place now ceased to do so, since one of their tribe was in a manner on the throne. It was the next best thing to a Riveron heir becoming King. The Riverons were now the only tribe connected to the Royal Family, and that must count.

"You and I have never known much family," said Joel to Asher. They sat in the long throne room; a vast, rectangular hall terminating in grand stone steps up to the plush red chairs of state. They were alone, sitting close together, looking for all the finery of the thrones they occupied just like two shepherd boys huddled over a fire. Their voices echoed just like they had done when they had been stuck in valleys together, protecting the sheep from wild weather.

"Well, the sheep – and each other," Asher corrected with a wry smile.

Joel gave a half-laugh. "Yes, but it is a marvellous thing, this family. I wonder it escaped me before." Joel looked like his mind was many miles away, and he began to beam at something Asher could not see. "She is perfect, is she not? A wife! That is all you need! Why it is mother, sister, daughter, aunt and friend. The kingdom loves her; I love her – it was a mighty good idea of ours, Ash. One of the better ones." Since it had proved successful, the idea had become joint property of the two.

Asher flushed proudly, but disclaimed with almost believable modesty: "Well, we have been blessed with the signs."

Joel leaned back a bit more dignified in his throne. He looked out of the large arched windows at the purple-stained hills in healthy blossom. "All is well. We are strong, and nothing will defeat us. I begin to feel, for the first time, this *will* be the great reign to change our future. I will be remembered. Food supplies are flourishing, wool is richer and softer by the month, and look at our Queen! The charms of fairies will always fall impotent beside her. They have no chance at all, against our rare, ethereal Ganieda!"

"I wish you would tell Sir Kish that," replied Asher glumly.

Ganieda, too, had not failed to notice, with her large, lustrous eyes and her not so large but nonetheless pretty ears, how Sir Kish had leaned upon her husband regarding the subject of fairies. He had leaned so hard, in fact, that he was nearly falling over. And Joel... let him.

"It is his unquenchable sweetness of temper," thought the partial Queen to herself. "He is so keen to oblige others, and so wary to refute their logic, that he does not see how all this fairy paranoia is twisting his mind."

She decided to raise the subject one muggy summer evening, lying on their stately white bed with the gauzy curtains fluttering around it. The room was tall and grand, with black and white mosaics embellishing the heavy pillars holding up the ceiling; a proper room for a serious conversation.

"Sir Kish," Ganieda said languidly, in response to one of Joel's comments, "is a frightened little boy. Undoubtedly the fairies are powerful, but is that reason for these absurd rituals?"

"Less absurd, I think you would find, if our kingdom came under threat," retorted Joel hotly. "There is no such thing as being too careful. You cannot comprehend what it is like, my love. I lived in the open for years on end; we heard things. Noises, stories." His voice dropped, low and solemn. "Fairies can do well nigh anything. They are an irrepressible evil. What with their glamour, and their magic... Some say they are fallen angels. What can they not do, if they choose it? They are all-powerful." His face twisted for a very small moment out of its loving expression into something Ganieda did not like at all. "I know *your* tribe, the Riverons, are convinced they are our spiritual guides. That blasted Book of Kings Alfred keeps throwing at me! Kish told me the Riverons wrote it. Nearly all these "seers" were Riverons, and only the Riverons listen to them!"

Ganieda stared at him, undaunted. "It does not matter what I believe. I only wish that you would discredit the seers, for it was a seer who brought you to your throne."

The suspicion faded from Joel. It was replaced by a

slow burning blush of regret and shame that went all the way to his eyes. He looked like he would say a lot, but could only say: "Ganieda..."

She rolled over on the bed and nestled her head into the soft white pillow, so he could only see her long loose hair cascading down her back.

"I love you Joel, and I believe you are the true King. I would never ask you to build your Kingdom on my principals. But if you refuse, as every King before you has, to admit fairies into that role of protector, you must provide something to replace it. Your subjects should be able unleash that side of their nature, safely within Iblees. You must find something that will appease the spirituality of the Riverons and not upset the Boanerges. The fairies would hold less allure for people to wander after them, if we had some greater goal to work towards together here. If there was settled peace, I do not see why Iblees could not be as beautiful as Laseri."

Joel jumped up on the bed. This softer, simpler way felt like a cool cream being smoothed over his whirring brain. "Of course! Of course!" he cried. How great he would appear! No scared King running from winged elves! "I will build a Temple," he decided, his voice running fast with excitement. "The most gorgeous feat of architecture ever realised. A Temple of peace! It will immortalise my reign – it will keep Asher happy, he can use it to sit in and listen to his signs! Kish cannot complain – we will be safe. There will be peace in my Temple, and no one will be allowed to sit in tribes." He lifted up his wife laughing and danced her about the room. "We will beat those fairies! Our Temple will be so beautiful, the most beautiful building – as beautiful as the Queen herself!"

"You can take the ripest grain, and the prettiest flowers to present in the Temple," smiled Ganieda. "Then when the people think of those wonderful things, they will think of you, like I do."

"I will do whatever my lady commands! Yes, yes it will be ideal! It will look just like I am providing the people with bountiful gifts! That I am better, stronger, more munificent than the fairies!"

"As you are, my dear. As you are."

That was how the great Amber Temple came into being; that huge Temple with carved wooden eagles, woven tapestries of the finest thread, a giant bronze altar, deep bronze bowls full of fragrant water, windows stained in amber so that the sunlight came through golden, amber jewels in every door. Great wooden Doric columns stood by the door, as did all the moorland flowers that could be gathered.

Four of the tribes brought their individual expertise into the making of it. Some of it they actually made themselves; most of it they directed the workers to make. But they had made an effort, for the good of peace.

Such an immense structure was extremely challenging and stressful to build. It was rather lucky perhaps that the exiled tribe of the Boanerges did not hear about it until after it was completed, for they would have caused far more stress. They were not happy.

They were not happy with a King picked by a man who was probably a spy for the fairies, and they were doubly unhappy that by these fine ceremonies he seemed to honour the fairies. He *said* the ceremonies were to honour peace, but they were unclear as to the meaning of that word, and did not trust one who used it.

So they picked that convenient time, after the Temple was all done and dusted, to do a very inconvenient thing. They picked that time to launch their rebellion.

10

CHAPTER TEN

The strong clean air soaring over the moorland became thick and musty with smoke. Wherever he wandered around the straw huts of Iblees, Asher could hear a regular rhythm of clang, clang. Blacksmith's hammers fell with a metallic beat upon red hot iron. Copious amounts of swords were being produced for the army of the King's Knights; piles upon piles of glinting silver weapons lay shimmering in the clouded daylight, ominous and inappropriately showy.

Asher circled round the forges, eyeing the produce with distaste. Swords looked to him so lumberous, heavy and dull. He did not hold out much hope of wielding one himself. Could he defend himself with such an object? These swords were baubles; incapable of performing a noble action. And he could not reconcile himself with carrying around all day an object drenched in other men's blood.

A flame flared from within the forge; sparks flew up: a pause, and then the clanging, like an unstoppable headache, marched again.

Asher shivered and sat upon a rock. He watched the blacksmiths in their greasy aprons shoeing the tall, muscular horses. In the opposite field, targets were erected, and young men were being taught to combat with freshly forged swords. The ladies in waiting had donned humbler apparel and stood at tall tables preparing rations, or sat weaving banners and painting designs upon the shields.

Ironically, for all the choking air, heat and toil, now was the time to be a worker. Only a few of them would be made to risk life and limb against the Boanerges. Hard as they laboured, they were not dignified enough for that glory.

Although Asher knew he must fight, he did not doubt for an instant that his place was among the workers right now. Call it habit, or empathy. He simply gravitated there, plonked himself down and played idly with his pocket knife and a long twig he had picked up from the blackened ground.

The squalor did not bother him greatly. He had dreamt dreams the night before of a wide, open meadow and a pale sky in the morning. This image lived vividly enough in his memory to satisfy him for the present. He could not tell yet what the dream meant. He sensed it was only partly revealed; there was more to come, but who could guess what or when? It was hard to see the signs amidst stressed conferences, talk of blood and battle, and a head full of strategies, pounded by the clash of metal upon metal as swords were made and trained with. Why, all he had of nature near to him was this paltry twig in his hand!

Asher stopped. He looked at the twig. He had unconsciously whittled it into a point at the end. Streamlined, beautiful. Then his attention was drawn to the hens pecking for scraps about his feet. That was it: arrows!

Queen Ganieda moved uneasily about her sitting room in one of the towers of Glass Mountain Castle. It did not feel like her home recently. A strong scent, and almost a taste, of the damp stones became noticeable to her, though she had never remarked upon it before.

"Oh Rubezahl," she said to her lady in waiting, "I have great misgivings." Ganieda wearily removed her tall, pointed veiled hat, put it upon her lap and stared at it, as if the answers were buried somewhere deep within the beaded designs upon it.

Rubezahl looked up from the great swath of rich material she was sewing industriously with a whole circle of ladies in waiting. "Why, dear me, your Majesty, there is no need to worry! You would not have the King give up his preparations for battle?"

"Of course not," Ganieda replied dutifully. She fingered the large, segmented gold necklace about her neck in thought. "Insurrection cannot be endured. This war was bought upon us by necessity; if we do nothing, our lives stand in peril." Which was a longer, more Queenly way of saying she was scared, but knew she must put up with it, or else something even more scary would happen.

"Yes, my lady," returned Rubezahl, sewing without looking, as if by second nature. "Those wicked creatures are already closing in around Eodain, I heard some of the Knights say in the stable yard. Was that not where her Majesty's kinsman, the great counsellor Alfred was born?"

"Yes, yes, I know what you are saying. Obviously I wish to see it protected. It is only – only a foolish thing; the woman, not the Queen in me talking." Coming over to where the ladies in waiting were sewing, Ganieda ran her hands over the beautiful tapestry and asked them, ingenuously: "If my husband goes into battle, will I ever see him again?"

Ganieda could not add, as a Queen, that she feared Joel's ability to lead a military campaign, having only ever been a worker. Greater still was her inability to express that even if Joel did return, it would not be Joel as she knew him; how could the horrors and hardships of a war fail to leave an impression upon the mind that would dent it for the rest of its life?

Yet what she did say was enough to win the ladies' sympathy; indeed, she had their unswerving devotion already from her unassuming ways, good influence upon the temper of the King and kind treatment of them. They gathered round and caressed her with pitying sounds.

"What nonsense! King Joel, appointed leader by Roddag: how can he fail to return victorious?"

"Absolutely. He will come home, and your Majesty will be safely delivered of a boy."

"An end to that rebellious tribe of Boanerges. I never cared for them anyhow. You remember Rubezah, even when Sir Dybuk was here, how there was something I disliked, something underhand in his family's faces. Only Sir Kish is worth a fig."

"Yes, your Majesty, the King will be with the fearless Sir Kish. Only conceive how comfortable he will be!"

"Bless me, you do look pale, your Majesty! Let us get you to a window."

"Yes, yes, give her some air."

Ganieda was conducted to sit on the cold stone floor besides a long, narrow window. There was not much air to be had, only smoke and the sight of artillery: a combination which was likely to do her more harm than good.

But then the sound of a small twang reached her ear. The Queen's eyes followed the sound, and she blinked for a moment.

Round targets of blue, red and yellow stood in a line by the forest. Asher was there. He raised his arm, dropped it, and a volley of arrows shot from the young workers he had placed opposite his targets. Nearly every one hit the bull's-eye.

The Queen laughed. "Asher!" she said, as if that in

itself was an announcement. "Asher the archer!"

How had she forgotten? Asher would look after him. She had more faith in that slim, untidy figure with his motley crew of bow-shooting archers than Sir Kish in his chain-mail, wielding a broad sword.

Choirs of angelic voices raised songs to the rafters of the Amber Temple. They were crying, or screaming perhaps, in desperation for their soldiers to come safely home; yet it sounded beautiful. If nothing else, the impending threat of the Boanerges attacking had brought the tribes to work together, and to feel together. Whatever mauled the hearts of the singers came out haunting, mystical, and just like the voice of guardian angels themselves – or so Ganieda thought.

The whole ceremony felt somewhat ominous to Ganieda, and the clouds of white cedar incense were making her queasy. Everything did since the child had started to grow inside her.

Sir Kish sat down heavily beside her, trying to get as far away as possible from these highly reprehensible proceedings. His fine face looked black. The strange, clever glint in his eye had reappeared, but mutated somehow. Not in a good way. He looked just like he was ignoring the rituals, and thinking of something else. But he wasn't.

A bit of sick came into Ganieda's mouth. "Yes my little Prince," she thought, "you do not like him any better than I do."

They both watched, in prickly silence, as a strange little goat decorated with bells was lead up to the burnished altar before the King. We do not like to go into details about what happened to the goat. Suffice to say, it was not exactly pleasant, least of all for the goat. Admirably, the Queen did not throw up, which is all the comfort we can take from the situation.

"I wonder, my Lady," she heard Sir Kish's firm voice saying in her ear, "that you do not discourage your husband from this – this hocus-pocus." If he had not been talking to a Queen, he might have used a stronger word than hocus-pocus.

"For an extra chance of his safety, and that of our brave Knights, I would not discourage anything the King wishes to do," murmured Ganieda. "Besides which," she added pointedly, "King Joel is my King too, and it is not my place to question his actions."

Sir Kish was very clever, and knew when to stop his trap; meaning that he shut his mouth, but said his angry words all the same, only inside. Which is a far more dangerous thing to do...

Balmy evening had fallen, and the air felt as hot as it had at the height of midday. The dried heather bells on the moors nodded contentedly, letting out a soft whoosh of perfume as King Joel and Sir Asher brushed past them with their long cloaks.

"I am only saying," explained Asher patiently to the shadowy profile of Joel, "that I do not think it was the wisest thing you ever did." He could not say what the wisest thing Joel ever did was. Joel was not given to doing wise things of his own accord; without others shoving and persuading him into it. Unwise things, he was very given to doing of his own accord; despite others pulling and persuading him out of it.

"For an extra guarantee of the safety of my Queen and unborn child, there is nothing I would not do," declared Joel. "Besides which, though we were shepherds together once upon a time, I am your King too, and it is not your place to question my actions."

Of course it was true, but Asher did not feel easy with it. And he knew how dangerous it was to let uneasy feelings fester inside him.

Night time blurred and dimmed the features of Joel's face, so Asher could make believe he was not talking to a King. "Just suppose," he thought, "instead of arguing with this grand King foretold by prophecy, I was just talking to Joel. Only *suppose* we were still shepherds, cold and hungry, and I was trying to talk him out of one of his hair-brained schemes."

Imagination gave Asher courage, and he finally said aloud: "The goat you sacrificed looked to me like a Ki-lin. Do you know what a Ki-lin is?"

"I am the King, of course I know what a Ki-lin is. It looks like the goat I just sacrificed."

Asher sighed, closed his eyes and then opened them. "A Ki-lin," he recited off by heart from the Book of Kings, which apparently the King himself was too grand to read, "is a very holy creature. It is like a unicorn. You saw the tiny horn it had – only one, mind you – tipped with flesh, to show it was not for violent purposes. It often heralds the birth of a great person, or the reign of a brilliant ruler."

They began to climb up hill over one of the tors. "So it does," panted, Joel. "My son."

"Yes, but you have killed it. Killed a creature so gentle it will not step on a blade of grass too hard for fear of hurting it. Every time you hurt something helpless, something dark is born to avenge it. This cannot be a good omen."

Joel rolled his eyes, but Asher could not see in the dark. "Nothing ever is a good omen with you. You always see the bad ones. Can't you start looking out for good stuff?"

"I saw something very good: a Ki-lin. But then you..."

"A kind of unicorn," interrupted Joel thoughtfully as they reached the peak of the tor. "Sounds like fairy business to me."

"Exactly, that is why-"

"Better to get rid of it then," Joel interrupted again, for although he was King he had very bad manners. "Stop it bothering us. And what can offend them about our sacrificing one of our finest animals, nominally in their honour, in the Amber Temple?"

There was a fine prospect of the Temple from where they stood; they could see nearly all the kingdom, and in particular the huge wooden building with the glowing yellow lights inside.

Asher looked towards the Temple, agreed it was very beautiful; but something being very beautiful does not excuse doing something very wicked. "Fairies love goats. They are their favourite animal," Asher tried to tell Joel. "Why, the only thing worse would be hurting a tree. I have read that a tree chopped down for no good reason -"

"My dear fellow," said the King, putting his arm around Asher's shoulders. "Enough of this nonsense. You are not King; you cannot understand. The incense and the songs were enough to get the women behind the war; they like a nice bit of incense and some songs. But what will you do for the men? There are more of them, and they must be pleased. Nothing pleases a man more than a goat slaughter. You can play your tunes and burn your white cedar all you like, but for the men it has to be goat slaughter. Nothing else will do."

Seeing that Asher was not as amused or impressed as he might have hoped, Joel cut his losses; or rather, he let go of Asher and sprang up the hill. He was enough satisfied with himself and his own kingly judgement to be able to care less and less what Asher thought of him.

"Only look what I am doing," he called jovially over his shoulder as he reached the top of the hill and the three stately cedars that had managed to thrive there in spite of everything. "Fairies love the trees, don't they? Kish tells me he has heard a strange whispering around these three trees in particular. They were the first to grow, just before Green Glow Forest was born. If this doesn't keep the winged ghoulies quiet, nothing will."

The King produced from the folds of his great cloak a poesy of primroses, tied with a green ribbon. Sweeping a low, theatrical flourish, he said: "Hail green ladies!" and presented the bouquet at their roots.

Asher could not help experiencing the funny feeling that the trees, although they were made of motionless wood, could tell Joel was not being quite serious.

11

CHAPTER ELEVEN

A black day for Auchriachan. All her brave sons, young and old, gathered tightly together in units and brigades, glittering like a silver ocean in heavy armour. There was too much going on inside their hearts for them to rejoice that four of the tribes at least were now united in a common cause. Excitement and fear ran through them like a nervous twitch. Though they were so many, they were deadly silent, awaiting their leader, their King.

Some of the Ladies had taken to weeping softly, and clinging in a highly embarrassing way about the Knights.

Less emotional ladies in waiting plaited together stems of gorse and heather to strew the path of the warriors with. Horses were pawing at the ground; everyone felt on the edge of a high cliff, waiting for the fall, waiting, waiting…

The drawbridge of Glass Mountain Castle began to wind down, clicking and creaking. Immediately the Knights let out a cheer, sonorous and deep. Joel came galloping out to the sound of their applause, sword raised to sky. His brave steed, covered in tassels and embroidery, snorted as it moved like a whirlwind across the bridge with its mane flying in the wind and its cropped tail swishing. Behind him came streams of cavalry, Sir Kish and Sir Nehemiah – a young Moordale of great skill with all weapons – leading the charge.

After came the Queen and the Ladies of High Descent, trailing banners of burgundy and bronze, riding in a more dignified, Queenly manner. Guarding their flanks, on foot, were Asher and his archers, more agile and swift in surcoats and leather breeches.

Weapons flew up in salute to the King. All were eager to be off and prove their worth. To the Ladies' amazement, the Knights were more thrilled than appalled by the woeful scenes they were about to be thrown into.

The mood changed to become gentler, like the whispering breeze stirring the trees, as Queen Ganieda, now heavily pregnant, took off the wispy scarf about her neck and tied it to the right arm of her King. In the hush of the ceremony, Asher listened carefully to the wind. His eyes flickered back and forth to the trees, and the cedars on the hill with an eerie unrest.

Ganieda, courageous to the last, finished off her knot and kissed her hand to Joel. As Auchriachan erupted into raucous applause, Sir Kish surprised her with an unexpected act of kindness – which here means, he cruelly took away for a minute all the pleasure she had in disliking him.

"Your Majesty," Sir Kish whispered, jostling close beside the King on horseback. "Should not someone stay with the Queen?"

Truly, Ganieda had looked rather ill of late – or, as ill as someone of her beauty could. She could feel the arrival of her child marching upon her like a volcano inside. And must we confess, even the valiant Ganieda felt a twinge of fear? She had to admit, even though it was Kish who had suggested it, to have someone remain with her was her secret wish. Therefore she said nothing as Joel looked at her in surprise.

"She has her ladies in waiting, does she not?" said Joel. "If the time comes, they are the best qualified to care for her. And if it is men you want, the workers, the medics-"

"- are largely marching under Sir Asher," finished Sir Nehemiah, casting a glance over his shoulder. "But there are some left - as many as would be necessary, I think."

No one spoke for a moment. Sir Kish shuffled awkwardly in his saddle. "I will stay with the Queen," he decided. "If the fairies take advantage of our absence to attack, you will need me to-"

"Oh, no, no. There can be no call for that," Ganieda found herself saying. It was probably not the wisest thing to say, but the horror of spending so long alone with Kish propelled it out of her. So suspicious had her mind become towards that Knight, that she could not even credit his goodness in this concern for her; she was convinced it was a secret plot against her husband.

"Don't talk nonsense," joined in Joel, readjusting his reins. "Who would lead the army?"

Kish bit his lip. "Asher, then. Let Asher stay with her – he can read the signs and warn of impending danger..."

Joel scoffed. "Asher? *Asher*?! What are you thinking, man? We need him with us in battle for that very reason! Do you want us to win this war or not? Kindly cease treating Queen Ganieda like a child, Sir Kish. Auchriachan knows of her strength and ability. She will reign well in my stead. My Queen does not need anyone, do you?"

Putting up her chin, Ganieda did a silly thing. She lied. "Of course not," she said levelly, not wishing to look weak, or contradict her husband. "If you feel I do not need a Knight to remain, then it is true," she finished, but she was looking at Kish, rather longing for him to insist.

Their eyes met, dark against light blue. Sir Kish raised an eyebrow. "The King has spoken," he said, bowing his head, "and it is not my place to contradict his actions."

Collectively the Knights spurred the horses and

galloped off in a cloud of dust, to the cheers and weeping of the Ladies. As the archers ran behind, Asher took a last look at the Queen, pale and frozen on horseback. He continued to look over his shoulder until she was but a spot on a very large horizon.

Horrible, horrible sights replaced the Queen in Asher's eyes, left, right and centre. All the untamed grandeur of the moorland became but a tangle of sedge, spotted with bilberries. The spongy banks were striped with large puddles – perhaps puddles of water, or perhaps something more sinister. Asher found it hard to tell, for a shadow was casting itself over the landscape of the warring Auchriachan; tendrils of fog and smoke from the cannons of the Boanerges wound like the legs of a giant squid around every Knight, masking their view.

Each foggy day and hazy night they marched blurred into one. So far there had been only skirmishes. Runners were sent out from captured Eodain to slow the progress of the King's army. These unfortunate Boanerge soldiers had met a speedy death at the hands of Kish and Nehemiah, who charged together with such fury that their lances could have flung the runners all the way back to Eodain as a warning to Dybuk.

Kish reined his horse back to the ranks of the archers after one such thunderous stampede. Mud clung to his armour and the sweat poured from his forehead. "Chin up, Asher!" he called, noticing Asher looking soulful. "You'll get your chance at the gates of Eodain!"

Strangely, the reminder did not cheer Asher up. Kish shrugged – such a creature was beyond comprehension – and cantered his foaming horse back to the place of honour.

The archers passed the bodies Kish had created, eventually, as the long crocodile of an army wound itself over the windy hills. Men crumpled in every position, looking ludicrous, tragic, unreal. But one in particular caught Asher's sad gaze: a Knight lying with his helmet off, so close by the feet of the archer's that their surcoats nearly swept his face. White as wax he lay, an unspeakable shock in his broad eyes.

"He looks so like he could be a relative of Alfred," Asher mused to himself. "A younger Alfred. So young, so brave, but no advisor in Glass Mountain Castle; he is only sprawled in a moat of his own blood without a drawbridge to lead him back again." Curious, how the blood only looked like berry juice. Asher found himself, rather morbidly, studying it. He followed the swirls and patterns, his mind glided through and through it, mesmerized, until he suddenly stopped, electrified.

"A clot! A clot!" he exclaimed in a terrible whisper, and collapsed into the ranks of archers behind him.

When Asher awoke, he found himself being hauled through the very triumphal arches of Eodain, confronted with the solemn statues peering down from them. Asher gasped and drew back, supposing himself in a hideous nightmare.

There was no time; there was no opportunity to speak to the King of what he had seen. He could not reach the King, far away at the front of the file, powering along on a fresh horse, not stumbling on two pumped-out, shaking legs. No sooner had Asher come fully to his senses than he was called upon to use them. All thoughts of blood clots were catapulted from his mind by the immediate danger of suffering one himself.

Already the Boanerges were prepared. A hissing sound reached the archers, and pitiful screams rent the air; molten lead was being poured in a thick black stream down the cobbled streets from the fort on the hill.

Men and horses alike were swept away by the flow. Asher ran, leading his archers uphill to the right. Shrill whistles rang out, and murderous bullets flew among them. Asher would not turn back to watch some of his archers fall as he jumped and climbed with all his might up the huge medieval fountain into the Entrance Square.

Clambering with hands slippery with sweat and blood, he reached the huge fish spouting water at the very top. He had not really given thought to what he would do next. Once he was not in the face of molten lead, everything became rather less clear.

He looked down, for the briefest of moments and went giddy. His archers were following him; soon there would be no more room on the fountain and those at the base would be carried off by the terrible tide of hot lead. Asher judged the distance to jump to the neighbouring cliff. It was not far; but when he thought about what he must do, it suddenly seemed a lot further away.

There was no choice; he closed his eyes and took a leap.

He did not so much see as feel his flight. There was a moment of weightlessness; he reached out. The skin on his hands was scraped away as they caught at something rough. Straining his arms, Asher scaled the rocky wall and drew himself up panting to the top of the cliff.

Now that part was done, the next course of action seemed almost easy. "We must cover the Knights!" he shouted as the bedraggled archers found their way after him. He pointed towards a distant grey structure at the entrance of a kind of cave, covered in statues of horses and eagles. "Let them get through the Main Gate. Archers ready! Fire!"

A shower of arrows, oddly beautiful, littered the sky. The spectacle gave hope to the Knights of Auchriachan on the ground. Boanerges on the battlements of the fort dropped their carbines, or fell, headfirst, into the stream of lead they had been pouring.

From the lower level, Sir Kish threaded his troops through the piles of dying men and the rider-less horses running spooked and caught up in their reins. These Boanerges who shot at him so fiercely had once been his relatives. He did not let the remembrance bother him as he hacked through the infantry. It was not a special occasion, after all.

Kish knew Eodain; he knew the back passages, and he knew the tactics of his kinsmen. Creeping off from the ancient climbing streets to a hollow track, Kish steered his cavalcade under a waterfall, and through the slick, dark corridors there.

"Have you the cannon?" he hissed to the Knights closely trailing him.

"It has come through," they confirmed. "Only just. Those carrying it on the left-"

"Good," cut in Kish, feeling it would do no good to dwell on what happened to those Knights on the left "Bring it forward."

The long muzzle of the cannon passed through the ranks of Knights.

"Hold it stead and keep as quiet as death," commanded Kish, "or you will soon meet your own. When you hear a commotion and a volley of shot, we charge forward and to the right. It will bring us straight to the gate. By then we should find it undefended, and ready to batter down." He gave a grim smile. "Or, if we don't, we shall have to make it undefended, even if we are the ones to be battered down in the process."

The Knight behind him gulped and nodded.

12

CHAPTER TWELVE

Bang. Bang.

Queen Ganieda felt every thrust of the battering ram, prolonged and urgent, but from the inside. It welled up in strong waves, interspersed with moments of glorious pause, when it seemed the troops were mustering their strength for another try.

Soon she was laid up upon the bed. It beat furiously now, without intermission. Ganieda, head swimming, felt she would faint from the pain. All the defences of her body were being slowly worn away.

Bang, bang, bang.

"Is it normal for her to be in so much pain?" whispered Lady Rabezahl to the gaggle of ladies in waiting clustered around the door. Straining over the sea of shoulders and jostling heads, she could see the Queen doubled up as if hugging herself, pale as snow.

"It must be a boy," chirped up Lady Morgan. "A strong Prince puts up a fight to come out."

"Or a wicked child," Lady Kenna suggested brightly. "Did you ever hear the story of Princess Genevive and her horrific pregnancy?"

The group of ladies in waiting soon heard all the horror stories of terrible births. Luckily, Queen Ganieda was too far away and occupied in her straining to hear them too, for they hardly would have leant her the assistance her ladies in waiting were meant to.

"My stomach feels full of poison!" Queen Ganieda panted to her kinswoman, Lady Urvasi.

Her body convulsed, and the sheets became soaked with her blood.

"All will be well," the doctors, fighting their way through the crowds about the door, told Lady Urvasi. "Knot a sheet across the bedposts and her Majesty can hold on to it when the pains come."

Lady Urvasi did so quickly.

The doctors felt Queen Ganieda's forehead, and frowned as she sweated and tossed her head on the pillow.

"She would be easier if the King were here," explained Lady Urvasi, biting her lip.

One doctor nodded. He waved a hand before Queen Ganieda's fixed gaze. It did look like she was staring far away, trying to see her husband. "It is only odd she does not cry out," he observed.

The moment the words had left his mouth, Queen Ganieda lurched forward, and vomited. Lady Urvasi rushed forward to hold back her wringing hair. Suddenly the Queen let out a groan of renewed pain, and the baby's head broke from her body.

All in an instant out came the baby in a slithering rush, a red mess on the white sheets. Queen Ganieda slumped backwards and was silent.

The ladies in waiting, now there was an actual baby, sprang into life, Rabezahl reaching the child first. She scooped it up in a clean sheet and wiped the blood from the tight little face.

"A boy!" she cried in triumph. "It is a Prince!"

Instant pandemonium. The infant was sent squalling as it was passed from lady to lady in a lap of honour. Even the worker doctors became so caught up in enthusiasm for their future monarch that they rather forgot about their current one.

Only Lady Urvasi, who was slightly more sensible, as became her noble birth, ventured inside the wispy hangings of the bed and saw her Queen's teeth chattering.

"The placenta," she said tonelessly to the head doctor. "Where is the placenta?"

The head doctor turned his red smiling face towards her. "Hmm?" he asked dreamily. "Did it not come out with the Prince? It does that sometimes, you know," he explained in a painstaking voice.

Lady Urvasi merely tossed back her head and gestured to the sheets.

"Oh," said the doctor dully, his ruddy smile disintegrating. "Oh."

"Look at the Queen!" panicked a more observant doctor. "She is shivering. Stoke up the fire, for goodness sake!"

"The placenta is not out," his college murmured to him.

"Heaven help us," the more observant doctor, turning pale, replied. "We shall have to go in and get it."

A huge crash made the earth move beneath their feet, then nothing; only the steady rush of the waterfall pounding in their ears.

"We shall have to go in and help them," declared Sir Kish. "Are you ready?" He did not wait for an answer, which was as well considering it was not forthcoming.

Throwing forward his sword, Kish let out an unearthly cry. His Knights were propelled forward as it echoed around the cavern and infected them. They ran and emerged, a great wave of fury bursting through the curtain of the waterfall.

A scene of devastation lay before them. Sharp javelins filled the heavens and the ground bubbled up in piles of slain men. Across the ranks Kish could see the able Sir Nehemiah on horseback as he smote the last few guards of the gate on the helm of his sword. Finding with a cry of exaltation that they had enough space to prime the cannon, the Knights fell to their artillery.

One heavy blast was enough to tear the gate to pieces like a lion, and send a Boanerge leader behind it sprawling on the very same ball.

Men streamed forward, clambering uneasily through the splintering wound of the gate. They could see the tall towers King Joel's unit had managed to erect alongside the fort, each with a drawbridge from which more Knights were spilling out.

Great roars of panic and fury erupted as the Boanerges tried in vain to cut the ropes attaching these towers to their fort. Rhesus, a brother of Kish, came within a hair's-breadth of succeeding. He hacked with an axe at the fraying rope – but Asher sailed out of that very tower he was attempting to topple, his arrow flying straight and true. He had not missed today, even by a hair's-breadth.

On the confused battlements, where the floor was slippery with blood, Asher bumped into his King. Spinning like a wild animal with claws (or in this case, a bow) poised, Asher recoiled in momentary horror at what he saw.

The King stood before him, but in soiled rags. The Royal emblem upon his chest and the crown worn over his helmet teethed with writhing maggots. Little white tails licked Joel's forehead as he laughed at his friend.

"Asher! It is only me." A cloud moved, throwing a small amount of light – a strange, white light, as one sees when it is summer but overcast – over Joel. The maggots disappeared.

Asher blinked. He understood. "I must speak with you," he urged.

"A time and a place!" exclaimed Joel, looking around him. The scene leant him a strange energy; his dark eyes glistened and looked to be relishing the bloody scenes they fell upon. "This is a great victory for us," he carried on, which seemed to Asher, looking at the piles of vanquished men, one of the stupidest remarks he had ever heard. "Still, we are not safe until Dybuk is captured."

Asher regained use of his reason and senses. Dybuk, the instigator of all this, must be brought to justice: it was the only way to secure peace.

If Dybuk remained at large (and he was a very large man), he would store up his forces and keep launching rebellions. Joel's life would be continually at risk, and, what Asher was beginning to fear more, his very spirit would be constantly clouded in this terrible smoke of war. Asher could not be sure, judging by his friend's now eager and almost ravenous face, that the dark fumes around them would not take him this very instant.

At that moment a single raven crossed the dimmed sky, a blacker spot on a nearly black canvass. Asher, standing straighter as if suddenly called by name raised his eyes. He heard no more of what the King said; he merely patted Joel's shoulder, and ran full pelt after the raven.

Letting out a coarse caw, the raven alighted on the stone ledge of a belfry. Asher's feet did not stop. They were running away with him, even when his brain felt it wanted to pause and assess the situation. Dodging catapults, arrows and bullets, he became vaguely aware of Sir Nehemiah and a file of Knights tailing him. With a strength he never knew he had, Asher ran crashing into a sturdy wooden door and burst straight through it into a small, crowded room.

Treasures, food supplies, used cutlery and material cluttered every available surface. Every precious thing had clearly been snatched in a hurry and stored in this room for protection.

The Boanerges leaders, counting themselves as precious things, stood in the centre, huddled, but nonetheless ready for combat with sharp weapons raised. They let out a war cry and started forward the moment they were disturbed, ready and quite able in number to flatten the troops of Nehemiah still outside.

Asher let loose an arrow from his bow which flew, faster than a swallow, to nest in the chest of mighty Dybuk.

The great Boanerge stumbled; his followers baulked. Asher's nimble bow poured forth another and another charge, until Dybuk fell under the relentless stream, and night came upon him.

There was no time for the Boanerges to react, or unleash half their wild fury. Fleet-footed Nehemiah and his followers descended on the strong-hold, and the rebellion came crashing down.

13

CHAPTER THIRTEEN

The wounded, the dirty, the valiant and the strong sat cowering on the muddy turf, huddled like sheep in a field on a cold winter's eve. Crumbled stone and parts of buildings jutted from the earth, as did the smaller debris of spent arrows and broken swords.

Sir Kish had to steer his horse around these obstacles as he paced forwards and backwards before the hostages.

Sir Nehemiah was seeing to the rounding up of all animals that were not injured; dividing the livestock and treasures of the tribe among his troops.

"Well, what do you expect, as prisoners of war?" he reasoned with the sullen faces of the Boanerges. "Don't worry though – you'll still be able to care for them: as our workers."

Apparently this consideration was not a pillow of comfort for the surrendered Boanerges.

"Workers?" repeated Sir Kish from his lofty height. "They should be lucky. It is an honour too great for them. I wouldn't be surprised if they were sent into exile."

"To muster their forces again?" cried an Amorette Knight. "Too dangerous."

"Exiled without food, livestock or money and with no way of getting it, they would die soon enough," his comrade pointed out with happy inspiration, and everyone was easy again.

A trumpet blared. Every head turned to see the King and his train picking their way through the rubble, their steeds now cloaked in a quaint animal version of a victory dress.

"Hail King Joel!" spoke up Kish as the Royal Progress neared. "We await your Royal commands as to the fate of our wretched prisoners."

The King inclined his head as if to wisely ponder the situation.

When Nehemiah saw Joel's pondering glance had alighted upon some well-fleeced sheep, he felt it necessary to explain: "We took the liberty, reverent Majesty, of separating the enemy from their livestock. If it pleases your Majesty, I have presumed to hope you might see fit to reward the courageous Knights with a goat or two."

Before King Joel could respond to the flattering speech, Sir Kish gave a whistle.

"Of course," Kish added, as he motioned to some ready Knights, "we were bold enough to reserve the choicest, most beautiful ox as our own poor mite of an offering to so worthy a ruler."

A meaty, shining beige ox was bought forward, bedecked with ribbons and tossing its proud horned head.

"The foolish custom of tribes died out so long ago that I doubt it has been worth your Majesty's while to remember them all," continued Sir Kish. A very clever, a very subtle way of avoiding the fact that Joel, as a worker, had never really belonged to a tribe.

Sir Kish could easily gloss over anything to make it fairer to the eye. The truth did not matter, since it was never mentioned, and there was glorious pretence to take its place. And if the Knights pretended long enough, they began to forget, like King Joel, that the truth ever really existed; Kish's flattery became real, and the truth like a horrible dream that rampaged through the mind and died quietly long ago.

"But it may please your Majesty to hear that our tribe – I mean, the tribe to which I used, most erroneously to belong," Kish recovered himself swiftly, "puts particular significance upon this beast of burden. In each generation one ox always thrives, and it is seen to be a symbol of the tribe's glory and strength. Therefore it is fitting," Kish folded into a very smart bow, "that this ox should pass to you, the victor of the tribe."

Kish's ex-tribe gave him no very cordial looks. The daggers had been taken out of their hands, but they had grown in their eyes instead.

"Good, good," replied King Joel. "Bring all the oxen forward."

Some Amorette Knights mumbled, but gave up their brief prizes nonetheless. There was a scuffle of movement, a little patter of hooves and a low background mooing, then all the oxen stood next to Sir Kish, swishing the flies with their long tails.

"Good." King Joel looked to the henchmen by his side. "Hew them to pieces."

The deed was done; done before the Boanerges had begun their wail of enraged protest; done before the taken aback Kish and Nehemiah had time to blink. The earth turned slushy as it ran with a wine-dark stream. The Boanerge women sobbed softly.

King Joel, his face and tone unchanged, said levelly: "This is what will happen to anyone who does not follow me." And with that omen, he turned and rode away.

Asher rooted about through the caverns of the cool stony room where Dybuk had fallen. Like a shadowy treasure trove, each grimy corner threw up new discoveries: horns of prize oxen, medals, old coins, family transcripts and crinkled parchment dating back to the very start of the Boanerge tribe. He began to sift through them eagerly. Early exclusion from tribes and their ways had left him fascinated with the minutiae of the customs and the stories.

As Asher turned over leaf after leaf, the edge of his manuscript caught. There was a loud crashing sound as a bowl and its contents went spinning off the heavy wooden table.

Cursing, Asher fell to his hands and knees, collecting whatever he could of the spill. Whilst he was gathering rings and small glass beads, something else under the table caught his eye. There was a vague shape in the dusty darkness.

Asher reached out, picked up the object, and turned it over in his hand. It was a small, dull flint arrow head. As it sat, a dark blot on his dirty palm, Asher noticed a thin lightning bolt engraved into it. For some reason best known to himself, Asher gave the arrow head a squeeze and put it in his pocket.

This strange souvenir looked like it had fallen from a small package of white cloth tightly bound with red string.

On it were inscribed the words: "Fairies beware" and "Death to the ice staff" in the old Boanergian language.

Carefully Asher untied the strings. The package unfolded in a rush onto his lap.

It contained a small white mountain of salt, round iron discs, a glove, a sprig of mulberry and a pocket mirror. Fearsome weapons indeed.

"I begin to discover why you lost the war, Boanerges," Asher muttered wryly to himself.

"Surely because they dared rise against the True Chosen King," answered a voice from the doorway. Asher started so suddenly that he nearly hit his head on the table.

Crawling out, he saw his visitor was Joel, and walked into his arms.

"Glad to see you still alive," said the King, releasing his friend from his embrace. "Do you find great treasure from the ever-so-mighty Boanerges?" he added sarcastically.

"Not at all, though I am sure it means something to them. Will we return it? It can be of little use to you. But what shall become of the fallen tribe?"

Joel shrugged and started to poke through the useless paraphernalia covering the table. "The youngest, strongest ones will be kept as our workers. It pays to keep them in our sight. And most of the women, of course, we shall take home to Glass Mountain."

Asher did not look happy, but managed to say: "Queen Ganieda will be very grateful for some companions."

"Will she indeed? *They* should be grateful to be allowed near the hem of her robe!"

"Certainly. What of the others? Did you give them terms?"

"Oh, they wanted to make a pact, brazen fools. *They* would have dictated terms to *me*. I refused, of course. I must show my power. The main leaders were hung there and then for their impudence; the rest are exiled to the Far Lands, without their supplies. I must keep a constant guard around the Far Lands to make sure none cross the border. If some of them do not die of want, how will they ever learn the lesson? I have some idea of building a wall to keep them out. You must help me."

Joel did not notice Asher staring at him, mouth agape. He continued looking through his spoils, and gave an appreciative chuckle at some bizarre drawing of a blue sceptre.

It was very difficult for Asher to pick his words. At first disbelief took away his entire vocabulary. But then he had to consider how best to influence, how to respectfully advise the King. He must suffocate his own anger for the good of Iblees.

For how could Asher address Joel? He fluxed so rapidly between the imperial King and the old friend that Asher could seldom predict his response.

"I – *am* going to try and help you," Asher replied quietly. "But first – what has been done to the bodies of those you hung?"

"A good question! I am glad you asked that. I was going to bury them – a mass grave would be easier to achieve, I thought. But the soldiers have conceived such a confounded love of my Amber Temple, that they want to burn the bodies on the altar to honour my victory. I am a condescending King, so I have allowed it."

Asher burst out with words before he could stop them. They leapt straight from his brain to his mouth like an undamable tide of raging water. "You cannot – cannot! That temple was not made to honour you! That Book of Kings, which you will not trouble yourself to read *also* states it is wrong to refuse pacts with those who surrender; it is wrong to make slaves of prisoners, it is wrong!"

Asher was forced to stop while he panted for breath.

"Wrong? Do you dare call me wrong?" Joel asked with a genuinely astonished look. "I have been merciful!" He drew himself up. "Well. You do find out who your friends are. I know – I think – I *hope*," he continued, stalking round Asher, who stood breathing heavily with a rebellious face, "you are only trying to help me. But if you remember, you always did have strange notions which I was obliged to talk you out of. Now, regarding this book: I realise you are anxious because you believe in these ghoulish little spirits and happy skipping fairies. But don't you see that these old superstitions are not *needed* any longer: I am the promised King appointed by Roddag. Roddag himself! Roddag appointed ME; I do not require a spiritual guide."

Asher regarded the King with a soulful expression. "Joel, Joel," he repeated despairingly. Then, sidling closer to him, Asher wrestled within himself for a moment and thus began: "Words have been brought to me in secret. You know before we met Roddag I hardly believed any more in these things than you – but he has done something to me. These things I see – I think I am supposed to *replace* Roddag. On a warm summer night, as I lay sweating in bed, the wind from the moors blew over the hills and in through my window. It glided like a whisper, like a spirit passing over my face. It tells me you will not be King for long. It tells me this was your purpose: to defeat rebellion and unite the tribes. You have done it, and done it well; you have built your temple. But my friend, the time is coming fast on our heels, like a panther chasing us through the forest, when I will call you my King no more."

A face of stone met Asher's speech. Joel was silent for a long time, his jaw working convulsively. Finally, he patted Asher on the shoulder. "Thank you, thank you my friend for telling me these things. You are a loyal subject. Now, now," he began to pace about the room, "we must stop them from happening."

"Stop them?" repeated Asher blankly. "Is it even possible? Your time has passed: this is the way it has been decreed. My research convinces me more every day that the fairies, the descendants of the angels who -"

"Ah, the fairies!" spat out Joel, his expression almost ravenous. "I knew it would be the fairies. They are stirring panic amongst us with their tricksy signs they show you: we must stop the fairies."

"No, no; you do not understand. Lately I have dreamt of a wide field in the apple-tinted morning – I flew above this field on golden wings. Besides me was a fairy. We were the same, Joel, just the same! It must mean the time has come for fairies to rule us. I cannot say which fairy, or when, or how, but the fairies are to come and take your well-conducted place!" Asher realised how unconvincing he sounded the moment he spoke; how talk of his dreams and strange interpretations of everyday events would not be sufficient evidence to make Joel want to abdicate.

Joel's face contorted in such a strange way that his eyebrows, lips and pupils seemed to stand out like a raised surface. "Then every fairy," he declared, with dreadful finality, "will die."

14

CHAPTER FOURTEEN

Smoke again. Wherever Asher turned he saw billows of obscuring smoke. This smoke, though, was the strangest of them all; it was the vapour of a personality, a human life. With all the complexity of the human character, he would expect the smoke to be a rainbow: shards of mixtures, vivid rays and subtle shades. In reality, it had no colour at all; only a smell: a sickly sweet compound of sticks of incense trying to cover the stench of burning flesh.

Some Emberlight Knights had ridden on ahead with the carts heaped up with fallen Boanerges. They had begun the ceremony so that it would serve as a greeting to the King as he came over the hills.

Iblees had never looked so beautiful. The moors still stood, eternal and immovable, but minute parts of them were changing, fluctuating. Heather burst out in purple riot and the crickets exploded in their crazy chorus of summer.

"Look at all this: nature itself blooms to salute my homecoming. This is a sign indeed, eh?" Joel smiled to Asher as they rode along.

If Asher did see any signs, he silently vowed to keep them to himself from now on.

He was beginning to think they might be hints that his mind was not quite sane.

They halted briefly to watch a procession pass to the

The Last Fairy Tale

Amber Temple. Ladies, their hair all netted up with beads, walked solemnly along in heavy dresses. Knights all shining in full plate armour carried woven banners, many others sprigs of heather or of gorse. They all bowed low or curtseyed deeply as they walked before the King.

"I will go and watch," announced the King. "But first - " he looked over to the distant shape of Glass Mountain Castle. "I want my wife to be with me." He spurred his horse and galloped off, plume flying.

The sullen Asher trotted half-heartedly behind.

A delicate female figure pelted out of the keep almost as soon as the hooves of Joel's horse touched the drawbridge. She was holding a small bundle in her arms. Joel leapt, rather than dismounted from his horse and ran as fast as his armour would allow him to embrace her.

But as he reached the lady, Joel saw she was only his kinswoman by marriage: Urvasi. He kissed her cheek.

"How now, Lady Urvasi, what is it you have there?"

Joel looked with wonder as Lady Urvasi silently and gently revealed the red and wrinkled face of his child.

"Good Heavens," said Joel, speaking as quietly as if he were afraid a louder voice would hurt the baby.

"It – it... I mean he – is a Prince," Lady Urvasi told him, swallowing repeatedly.

Suddenly moved to life, Joel snatched the child from her arms and laughed. "A Prince, Asher!" he called, holding the babe up to the sky. "Do you see, Iblees? A Prince! Oh! But where is the Queen?"

Lady Urvasi was wearing a horse-shoe shaped hat, falling low over her forehead. It made her brow look especially lined and furrowed as she said with a shaking voice: "The – the Queen cannot come down, your Majesty."

"Too tired, eh? Well, who can blame her – she has done a fine job. Producing such a handsome Prince must take it out of you – show me to her. I must speak to her of my plans regarding the fairy folk."

A single tear rolled down Lady Urvasi's cheek. "She – she is sleeping, sire."

Joel ceased to croon over the child. He comprehended everything from those few words, yet they were too dreadful, too awful to take on board. Surely it was only his over-active imagination. "What," he said with a half-laugh, though it did not reach to his eyes, "can she not wake up to see her lord and master?"

"No, your Majesty. She cannot wake up."

Joel felt some great reaction was expected of him, but he hardly knew what to do. He could only stand, blankly, and feel it was impossible. "Go, go to your Uncle Asher, there's a good boy." Joel passed the child, now staring at it detachedly and with a hint of venom. "Take me – take me to the Queen nonetheless," he commanded Lady Urvasi.

The Lady swept a curtsey and led him off. Never had the hallways of Glass Mountain Castle felt more dark, gloomy and airless as when she lead her King through them. Feeling the presence of its mistress leave, the Castle seemed to be closing in, preparing itself for the dreary hermitage it was to become.

The Lady Urvasi faltered by the door. "I – I would advise against looking at the body, sire. It is not a pleasant thing; she is not as we knew her. You must prepare yourself for an alteration. It was necessary to perform certain operations – you must not become angry."

Joel's heart was too full for speech. He shook his head, unable to take on board Lady Urvasi's words as well as his own rampaging thoughts, and burst into the room.

The doctors stopped speaking and looked around. Joel did not see them. With a trembling step, he reached the bed and fell upon the posts, having to hold onto them for support.

The body itself was not horrific. The blood had been

cleaned and her shining eyes closed. Yet Queen Ganieda's hands glistened with something. They were like miniature pincushions, with silver needles poking out from every available space on her delicate skin. Her rosebud mouth being slightly ajar, it was possible to see it filled with tiny glass beads, like a hoard of fish eggs. Actual eggs lay resting under her armpits. Joel looked on in horror and confusion. "What – how?" flew from his mouth, and the two monosyllables seemed to convey everything.

"Your Majesty must excuse the liberty we took with the fair body of our late beloved Queen," said a Moordale doctor reassuringly. "We had some fear of the Langsuir."

"*Langsuir*?" repeated the lost Joel, his eyes unmoving.

"Yes, your Majesty recollects: sharp nails, green robes, floor length long black hair..."

"What?" barked Joel.

"An evil vampire fairy," whimpered the doctor in return. "Surely your Majesty knows a woman killed in childbirth is very liable to become a fairy herself. I read it! These rituals will prevent her rising as a Langsuir, at least."

Joel stood frozen. "Fairies," he breathed, the same ice in his voice. "Fairies again. They steal my very wife now, do they?" He ground his teeth and pushed his way from the room.

Asher, waiting at the drawbridge, saw the King walk by with resolute steps and ran after him, baby in tow.

"Joel! Joel, where are you going?" Asher called ahead, for he could not walk as fast as the King for fear of dropping the child.

"Honour the fairies, Joel. Give offerings to the trees, Joel," the King yelled back in bitter mimicry. He did not look back over his shoulder. "Well, your damned signs didn't stop this from happening, did they? I should have listened to Kish. What do you use your crazy visions for but your own glory? You had to kill Dybuk yourself and take the honour from me! You and your hateful advice!"

Asher did not like where this was going. He had a horrible feeling that Joel's sudden wrath would bring more wrath upon them in return, though he could not say from where.

Joel broke into a run, gaining the top of the hill which over looked the Temple. Hymns and burnt offerings were still drifting upwards on the air. Joel gave a dry sob as he saw them. He unsheathed his sword.

"No! Joel, don't do it!" Asher clutched the baby closer to him and struggled with all his might up hill. "If you only take note of one decree in your life, let it be this: do not act in anger. The bad energy will – " Joel was heading towards the three trees. Asher gasped. It was worse than he thought. "No! No! Even Kish said those trees were special. Do not mess with something you know so little about. Dire consequences may – "

But Joel, with an almost inhuman strength, planted his sword into the thick trunk of the closest of the three trees. Sap flew as he hacked at them by turn in blind rage.

"I don't care! I don't care what the Book of Kings says! I suppose it warns against hurting dumb, unfeeling plant life does it?"

Asher was flinching with every slice. "Actually – you may remember I told you that when you hurt something helpless, especially in malice, a force of revenge -"

"My wife was helpless! She believed in that stupid book! My son is helpless there, in your arms!" Joel took another almighty swing at the tree trunk. "And this is nothing but a tree, Asher! You superstitious, crazy traitor! A tree!"

Suddenly, there was a flare from one of the funeral pyres. The smallest of the three trees, swayed, and came groaning down with snaps and an almighty crash. The smoke of the dead Boanerges washed over it.

Asher did not know if the smoke was thicker on this hill, but all about him had become dark, like an eclipse of the sun. Thunder rumbled low in the sky. A few streaks of lightning darted across the darkness like a web. He pulled his cape around the Prince.

Next to where Joel knelt, now exhausted and sobbing, a little gust of wind was twirling, catching the leaves up in it. Like a tornado, this dark mist began to swell in size. Stronger and stronger, round and round it span; now not only making the sound of a gusty wind but a hideous cackling.

Darker than darkest night the wind spread out in tendrils, waving up and down in its own gusts. Asher shuddered as he thought one of the smoky wisps resembled an arm with pointed fingers.

Boom. There was a deep rumble through the earth; the growing tornado pulsated, and Joel was blown backwards. Noticing for the first time the strange phenomenon, he scrambled backwards, looking up at it with frightened awe.

Another crack of lightning and Asher's worst fears were instantly confirmed: Deevs. Misty figures were flying up and separating from the body of dark wind, laughing horribly. Asher could see their cavernous mouths and wild hair. Looking death pale and half starved they floated and gaped awhile with pleasure at the horrified population of Iblees. The grass beneath them was withering and dying.

Suddenly, there was a crash and they separated; zoomed would be a more appropriate word. The Deevs burst outwards like frenzied birds of prey, dashing off from the centre at all angles, blowing behind them a hot smoke. The entire landscape was sizzling and scorching. In their wake there was no longer green grass but pale, dirty sand.

The two remaining trees exploded from the roots, and Asher saw no more.

15

CHAPTER FIFTEEN

Though it is night, darkness has not yet fallen properly. There seems to be a light behind the blackness, like a lamp shining behind a veil. Apollo finds it very strange, and moreover, thinks the stillness of the wood is eerie. It should not be so still. Where are the animals scuttling, where are the noises of trees settling?

He is tired, hungry and fed up, but cannot propose that they stop for three reasons: one, it would look like weakness before Queen Aurora, whom, for some reason, he is determined must always have the highest opinion of him; two, it is still light enough to see their way; and three, he does not really fancy standing still in this creepy atmosphere.

Instead, he takes out his frustration by grumbling. "Far be it from me to criticise you, Aurora – Queen Aurora, I might add – but if you had been a soldier, it might have occurred to you to bring provisions for such a long journey."

"I *did* bring provisions," she reminds him, not turning round.

Apollo colours. "Well," Apollo mumbles, "*More* provisions."

Aurora leaps lightly over a log; Apollo can flutter over it with tired wings. "My food allowance was perfectly adequate for one fay. I did not count on a second.

Especially," she adds, "one who eats enough for at least two fairies!"

Apollo blushes. "I am a guard of the palace. I need my strength; I am a growing young fairy!"

Aurora looks up and down his short stature. "I have yet to see any evidence of *that*."

They walk on for some minutes in what Apollo evidently considers to be an offended silence.

Being silent around Aurora is not one of Apollo's many talents. Mysteriously, he feels compelled to engage her in conversation and make her smile at him.

The ink blot of real black darkness begins to seep through the sky. "Speaking of provisions," Apollo throws forward in what he hopes is a casual voice, "what have you brought as a guard against Deevs?"

Aurora gives a secretive smile and taps her moonstone ring. "All safe in here."

"Like what?"

"I cannot tell you. They will know our weapons if I do. What if they are listening now? The trees have ears, Apollo!" Aurora is half-serious, half trying to frighten him.

Her laughter dies suddenly and her smile falls to a startled expression. They can hear something in the undergrowth.

Close by, nearly in their ears, an owl hoots. Apollo and Aurora exchange wide-eyed looks and take off into the night at a stunningly rapid pace. Apollo can fly, his wings moving faster than a humming bird, and he grabs Aurora's arms to pull her with him.

They dash through the air in a mad panic. The wind hits Aurora's face with a cold shock. At first she is afraid it is something attacking her, but then she remembers. She has not felt this sensation for a very long time. Not since the day Deucalion disappeared her wings, in fact.

At last, as their breath slows and the blood ceases to

pound in their throats, they decline gradually. Apollo steers expertly and lands on the crunchy carpet of leaves.

"I was afraid you were going to fly too high," pants Aurora. "Who knows what Deevs could swoop out the top of the trees and grab us?"

As she speaks, Aurora looks to the heavens. It is darker, and in the velvet sky, shining bright through all the foliage is one very large star.

She frowns, and thumps Apollo on the shoulder so that he looks.

"It is nothing," he says.

He does not look entirely convinced by his own opinion, but he is being soldierly and brave. He looks at the faint white pool the star has spread over the darkened forest. It is much less spooky with that light, and he is thankful for, rather than frightened of the star.

"Do not worry, Aurora. I said I would look after you, and I will." Apollo sits down on the ground with a noise of relief and leans back on his arms. "Besides, like you said, we have our moonstone rings. Can a Deev really hurt us when we have them?" A sudden inspiration comes to him. "Of course, my ring! Why didn't I think of it? Sit down and rest; I will conjure us some nice food."

He extends his finger.

"NO!" Aurora moves with freakish speed and clamps his hand into a tight ball. She holds it with such force Apollo thinks she will break his fingers.

"Ow! What are you doing?"

The Fairy Queen makes a hushing sound with her lips. Her eyes are drifting forwards and backwards with a heightened alertness. Green Glow Forest is very, very still and dark once more. Apollo feels goose-pimples run up his arms.

"We cannot use our magic for food," she impresses upon him in an urgent whisper. "It will attract attention to us."

Apollo nearly laughs. "There is no one here to pay attention! How do you think *she* lives – Cailleach Bheur – out in this forest all alone with her blue staff?"

Aurora looks down and brushes her dress. It ripples in flowing waves. "I may be the Fairy Queen, but I do not pretend to be on a level with the one who bears the most precious fairy relic of all time. I must protect *us* as best I know how. And that means that while we are in this forest, we will have to live without magic for a while."

Had she hit Apollo in the chest with a bolt from her ring he could not be more dumbfounded. "But – but – we will have to live like *humans*?!"

Aurora twists her face into a wry grin. "How ironic. Perhaps it will bring us closer to them."

"I do not *want* to be close to them! I want to live. I came to look after you; not partake in some human and fairy relations experiment. I thought it was a mad enough scheme for two fairies to venture into Green Glow – but two *humans*..."

"We will use our magic if necessary; if attacked. But otherwise- "

Apollo is pouting in such a thoroughly insubordinate way that Aurora loses all patience with him. She does not bother to finish her sentence. She did not *ask* him to come; she does not need him to be disheartening her the whole journey. Blowing out a long vexed breath, she turns and walks off, as if she knows precisely where she is going, into the dark mesh of foliage.

"Go home if you want. Go home and be like the rest of them. Your heart is not in this," she tosses back at him as she walks.

Apollo never likes Aurora to be angry at him. He likes it even less when it means he is left on his own in a potentially lethal forest. It is looking even darker than ever now, if that is possible.

A leaf moves against his shoulder. His blood drops to freezing temperature. Through his fear, Apollo's pride forces him to stay seated and silent until the count of ten.

"Aurora," he begins in a tone that is an apology in itself.

She does not turn around. For some reason Apollo is mentally calculating that if he was attacked now, Aurora would not be able to run back and help him in time.

"Aurora, please. I'm sorry."

She turns her pretty blond head. Her angry violet eyes just begin to relent towards him. She takes a step, and disappears with a frightful scream.

"Aurora!"

All tiredness forgotten, Apollo is on his feet and at the tree in a breath. He looks around frantically; left, right, behind and upward...

There she is, above his head! Her dainty ankle is cruelly snared in a vine. It is wrapped around her leg tight enough to stop the purple blood. It pulls upwards like a rocket; Apollo's eyes can still make out her figure shooting further and further away, her white hands reaching out towards him in ardent distress.

Apollo knows what he must do. Great white wings unfold behind him with a rustle like silk. His feet lift gently off the ground, and he rides the wind once more.

Twigs snap against his head as he rises. It is a painfully, prickly ascent, like hacking through a blackberry bush. He strains his hand up. He can almost reach her hand...

"Apollo be careful!" he hears her groan over the sound of wind and breaking branches.

He listens more carefully; yes, he can hear it too now – the sound of laughter. Wicked, inhuman laughter.

Every morsel of his flesh recoils from that sound.

"Aurora, I'm sorry. But this living like a human; it's not going to work."

Before she can exclaim, he is ready to fire; a white bolt splits the air and shatters the tranquility of the forest.

His aim is that of a true soldier; the vine breaks, and the Fairy Queen tumbles instantly into his arms.

"Go! Go quickly!" she shouts the instant he catches her. He rather wishes she had said thank you first.

The gravity of the situation is clear; they are Deevs, real Deevs! And they are coming for them.

Apollo turns and flies like shooting star. A fork of deep red lightning narrowly misses his shoulder.

"Can they do that? Can they fire at us?!" Apollo had never truly considered a Deev might be an equal match for him. He was so used to being a mighty warrior of Prince Deucalion – or guard of the gate, at least – second to no other fighting force. But whatever was in this tree seemed not only intent on, but actually able to kill him!

Another fork of red. He swerves to miss it and nearly hits a tree.

"Sorry!" he shouts to Aurora.

He swerves away but still he is close to the canopy. There are hazards all around; heavy branches, flowers, twigs, leaves – and *that*. Apollo dives downwards as a black misty arm with fingernails like razors reaches out to grab him. But there are more of them here; there are grabbing fingers sliding out of every tree. Apollo makes a turn; it is ill-timed, and one of the talon-like fingernails cuts his cheek.

It is enough to throw him off balance. The fairy duo plummet for an emergency crash landing. Aurora rolls out of Apollo's arms and pulls him to his feet.

"Run, run, there is no time!"

Apollo follows her blindly. He looks over his shoulder to see if they are escaping. The whole forest appears to be moving and alive. And there – snakes! No, not snakes, but those awful vines again, slithering across the turf and intent on grabbing them...

Aurora pulls up short. Apollo does not notice – he is too horrifically engrossed by the vines – and fails to stop. He smacks into her with an incredible force, and they fall over.

He can see – or rather feel, now – why Aurora stopped. They were at the edge of a precipice. And now they are tumbling, falling and bouncing painfully over logs, rocks, dead leaves and other large objects. They fall and fall and he thinks they will never stop.

Crack. He hears before he feels his head smack against the rock. Then he feels and hears nothing at all.

Apollo wakes up reluctantly. His head is throbbing with more pain than he thought physically possible. In the first daze of consciousness he wonders where he is. The recollection comes flooding back, and he sits up with a jolt, gasping.

Aurora is there. She is already standing up. This takes the edge off the panic slightly.

Apollo stumbles to his feet, his hand pressed against his temple.

"What are you looking at?"

She is staring fixedly up at the sky, her blond hair spilling down her shoulders. Apollo is more interested in the surroundings; there are strange piles of leaves, and wood that looks as if it has been cut with an axe. It looks very nearly like civilisation.

"Look," Aurora says at last. "That star. It is still there. Look at it."

By the time he does, another has appeared – and then another pops out, and another next to that. The sky is soon full of stars and each star is making the sound of a tinkling bell.

Then, one falls. Just falls clean out of the sky. "I am too late," thinks Aurora. "It is happening already: the world is ending!"

The stars extinguish one by one. As Apollo strives in vain to remember the part of his soldier training which dealt with such occurrences, the tinkling stops. In the dark silence, Apollo and Aurora drop their eyes to look at one another – and recoil in horror.

Behind the other – surrounding them in a tight circle – stand squat, pointy eared creatures with globular grey eyes. In the dark Aurora can just make out the slightly green tinged skin that cloaks them. They wear a fine film of gossamer covered by dead leaves.

"Who are you?" demands Aurora in a commanding voice. "And what do you want with us?"

One of the creatures nearest her hisses at her with a singularly hungry look. "Fairies," it sneers to a companion with utter hatred. "Fairies do not pass here," it informs Aurora, not very cordially.

She is not afraid of it; all the creatures look skinny and childlike.

With a contemptuous toss of the head Apollo takes Aurora's hand and begins to flutter upwards on his white wings. Yet no matter how he rises, the circle of creatures is rising around them. The air is full of the sound of wings: the short, grey and brown mottled wings of these creatures. The wings look almost furry: moth wings.

"So this is what pixies look like," says Aurora with sudden recognition. Her eyes are full of pity.

Apollo switches the hand in which he dangles Aurora and holds out his moonstone ring. It sparks, like the beginning of a fire when you blow it. Yet before the ring has time to ignite, a web of light materialises around them. It collapses, entraps them, and they fall to the ground, entwined in a thick net.

"You had forgotten some of us can perform magic," says a pixie tauntingly. "We got that from *you*."

Aurora shoots a warning glace at Apollo.

"Do not use magic against such creatures, how will it ever teach them?" Aurora whispers.

"I wish to *kill* them, not *educate* them," Apollo barks back. "I wish to put a termination to their existence; the welfare of their intellect means nothing to me."

Aurora sighs. "We were not given magic for that purpose. Besides, they are half fairy. It would be a disgrace to harm one."

A pixie, though not hearing in entirety their hushed conference, seems to gather some of its import. "Yes, you see what we are now. The height of ignorance in fairies increases! To disregard us to the length you have no idea what a pixie looks like! We are your children, we are from your bodies, and look what you reduce us to! Can you imagine we would let such a depraved being as a fairy pass in peace?"

There is a general titter of evil, disgruntled noises.

"Look," says Apollo in a key a little higher than his usual voice. "You must let us pass. We are very sorry for your misfortunes and all that... But we are on a mission to stop the humans, who you also hate. So it is in your interest to let us go. We will give you something in return."

The pixies look vaguely inquisitive. "We will give you fairy gold," announces Apollo, devoutly hoping they have not heard of fairy gold's worrying tendency to disappear.

"To stop the humans from war?" asks a girl pixie, revolving her huge eyes. "What do we care if there is another war? The hateful races will kill each other, and pixies inherit the earth. In fact," she adds in a bitter tone, "a war would probably add to our numbers."

Other pixies agree with the statements and close inwards.

Like a parent that has too long humoured a child, Aurora blows out a gust of air, and easily as shaking a fist evaporates the net.

The pixies know fairy magic is much stronger than theirs. Yet they have a dark kind of magic which produces nasty results. It is not as important for a nasty spell to be very accurate; for even if the gist of it is right, the sufferer will not experience a pleasant time.

"Kill them!" shrieks a voice, and the pixies close in again.

Aurora and Apollo move their rings together...

"Wait!" It is an inquisitive looking, perceptibly darker green pixie who has halted the proceedings.

"This had better be good Demetrius," snarls one pixie or the other.

Demetrius picks up a long branch from the floor and waves it in the direction of Aurora. Clearly he thinks closer contact will contaminate him.

"Look at her," he goes on, as if examining a specimen. The end of the branch pokes Aurora's short, bright, hair. "Her wings. Her *freckles*. She is a disgraced fairy." A shocked murmur ripples through the green people and Aurora seems to develop another freckle. "She must be the mother of one of us."

The murderous look in the pixies pine-coloured faces increases in a truly filial fashion. Apollo hardly looks less disgruntled.

"We should not kill her. We should demand of her why her kind gave us up!" roars Demetrius.

"You have no idea who you ask!" replies the indignant Apollo. "She is no mother of yours. And if she were, why should she keep a strange, unwanted creature forced upon her by those vile humans? You are unfortunate reminders of a hateful war, that is all..."

The pixies look offended but only Demetrius speaks. "It would be becoming of a fairy to keep and care for a poor, unwanted creature rather than participate in the moonlight revels and saucy tricks on humans they have more recently found a taste for, under King Deucalion. Unless my studies of fairies have been in error," he adds, though with an expression that makes it abundantly clear he sees no chance of it.

"Demetrius is quite an expert on the subject," says a pixie begrudgingly. "If he thinks we should not kill you, we ought to follow his advice."

The pixies are all regarding Aurora with tilted heads, trying to trace in her regal face some resemblance of their own features. "We will take them to the fort and speak to the others before deciding what to do with them."

Apollo and Aurora find themselves wrenched to a standing position and their hands hastily bound behind their backs, rendering their moonstone rings next to impotent. They are frogmarched over rocky, potholed ground.

Nobody speaks, but the bells around the pixies' necks shrill out with every step. Aurora feels it must be at least near to dawn by the time the trees give way and they reach the scraggy ruins of a stone fortress. But still the only light is the glint of the huge pixie eyes, peaking out from crumbling window shapes and behind mossy rocks.

"The sun does not shine here," Demetrius tells her, noticing her furtive glances at the sky. "We do not belong in any place; even the light chooses to ignore us."

The prehistoric structures look uncomfortable, but they are surrounded by sturdy clumps of elm trees, and afford an unlimited view of the sky thick with stars. Aurora considers, depending on what eyes you look at the place with, the kingdom of the pixies could either be extremely depressing or mysterious and glamorous, in a dark sort of way.

Demetrius flutters ahead on his moth-wings to the top of the decrepit fort and rings a large rusty bell. Pixies run out of every crevice and begin to gather in what looks like the remains of a keep.

Two identical girl pixies appear and trot alongside the guard leading the fairies. They are roughly shoved aside; one falls down and rolls over on the rocky ground.

"We do not call a meeting for *you*," sneers one of the guards. The pixie on the ground begins to weep. Her twin hisses and shoots out a jet of fire which narrowly misses the offending pixie's pointed ear.

Aurora tries to reach out to the injured pixie but cannot. "Who are those... girls?" She asks a pixie to her left, whose name she gathers is Doamna.

"Scum," replies Doamna in no uncertain terms. "All of us are the produce of human fathers and fairy mothers. There are very few women in Auchriachan. One can almost understand the temptation of the human men when they have so many fays as prisoners of war... But *them*," Doamna points her head contemptuously at the retreating figures of the twins. "They have a human mother. Only think of that. It is disgraceful for a fairy to act in such a way."

Aurora is shocked for the whole of fairy kind. And yet her words suggest she suspected it as she says: "Yes. They did have a human mother."

Aurora and Apollo are pushed again into the centre of a circle of pixies. This time, all the pixies are seated, and there is a warm fire next to the fairies. All the pixies are pacified and basking in its glow.

"We bring before you two fairies," a pixie called Kenna stands up and proclaims, "found wandering in our part of the forest."

There is a low boo.

"They *claim* to be on a mission to thwart the humans. They *claim* to mean us no harm. Yet the short one has openly avowed some very ungenerous sentiments towards us already."

Apollo bristles but Aurora shoots him a warning look.

Kenna continues: "Demetrius has stopped us from killing them outright. There is some sense in it. They have survived the Deevs so far and must be powerful. We can at least take their knowledge before disposing of them."

This meets approval. Apollo is unsure whether to plume himself on being thought powerful and knowledgeable or resent the implication he can be easily disposed of.

"This much is clear," contributes Demetrius: "That fay is disgraced, and the mother of a pixie. I propose we make them explain their voyage into a place they do not belong. That fay must tell us which pixie is her child. She must give us an account of her unnatural behaviour in abandoning it. Then, if her cause is worthy, she may pass."

Some pixies look mutinous. It is apparent they are struggling between their noble, fairy tendencies and their baser, human instincts.

Before being asked Aurora stands. "You are creatures of the dark. Your eyes are unaccustomed to the light, and you cannot see clearly. But though you cannot see, hear now that this is but a disguise, and I am mother of no pixie. My name is Aurora Optilete: Queen of the Fairies."

She closes her eyes and a small, colourful stone with a hole through the middle floats out of her pocket and levitates in the air before her.

"A holed stone," whispers Demetrius, agog. "Symbol of marriage between fairies! Look how at sparkles! The colours! It must be the King's stone."

"I say we kill her now!" It is the ostracised girl pixie that shot a jet of fire who screams this out.

"We do not ask *you*, Daireann," says Doamna in a bored voice. "No doubt if you had spent less time in a filthy mortal womb you would be wise enough to realise this is a valuable hostage."

"If you will listen to me," Aurora speaks authoritatively over her, "you will perhaps decide there is no reason to kill me or hold me hostage at all. Or," she adds at a look from Apollo, "my good friend here."

With their rapt but suspicious green faces gazing up at her in the firelight, she explains to the pixies all that has happened: the death of her dear friend Cynthia, the clues pointing towards a murder by Knights despite her strong reasons for doubting this, her marriage to the King of the Fairies and his permission for her to go as a peace ambassador.

"And so you can see the need for haste," she stresses, her whole face begging the point. "An age of peace like the old golden days can and will be established. I am certain. And you, pixies: will you establish it? Will you play your part? I, a Fairy Queen, ask for your help. A return to these halcyon days cannot happen if I do not reach my destination."

"How will the Fairy Soldiers possibly reach Auchriachan before you?" Demetrius has a sceptical expression around his mouth. "You have said you cannot fly because of your bound wings and if the soldier here carried you the Deevs would attack you. How does the Fairy King mean to overtake you on foot, if he sets out afterwards?"

"They *will* fly," Apollo says with an impatient roll of the eyes. He cannot comprehend how pixies know so very little about military manoeuvres. "There is more protection in a large squadron. One or two fairies will fall, that is normal – but all in all a large number of them will reach Auchriachan a long while before we do." There is a faint note of regret in his voice that he is not with them.

The pixies whisper hurriedly among themselves in their low, mysterious voices.

"It will be good for us to make a friend of the Fairy Queen, whatever happens," decides one pixie.

"We should be on the fairy side, no doubt about it," chips in another. "They are bound to win with their superior strength. Let them pass."

"But how can we be sure these fairies before us will keep their word? Even if we let them go on terms favourable to us, they will betray us. They have no feelings. They need to be watched at every turn. What kind of unnatural mother gives up her child, after all?"

Aurora stands silent and proud awaiting their decision. Apollo fidgets on the spot, watching the air and Aurora alternatively.

"We will allow you to continue with your quest for peace," announces Kenna at last. "As children of war we know how desirable that state is. But you will not go unprotected – we will give you a pixie guard."

Apollo guffaws and Aurora gives a wry smile – she does not believe for an instant they are over anxious for her safe passage.

"You may smile, but pixie magic is of a different sort to yours. We are better accustomed to dealing with Deevs and know these woods far more intimately than you can. You will take Demetrius with you – he is wise in fairy law."

"I shall be extremely glad of his company," replies Aurora politely. Apollo bristles slightly.

"And two others…" begins Kenna.

Aurora can see Kenna's plan to outnumber her with pixies. She admires the attempt, but in the stately way of a

Fairy Queen interrupts the pixie. "Yes, the twin girls," she declares, and there is no room for contradiction in her tone. "You," she says, turning backwards and pointing out the astounded Daireann in the distance, "and your sister."

"Do you know what you are talking about?" cries a tall, skinny pixie in rage. "A fine guard! That dirty, scowling thing and her sister indeed! The little whimpering one cannot even *do* magic!"

"Then she is to be pitied," says Aurora sympathetically. Her eyes have not left the dark figure of Daireann. "And that gives me all the more cause to take her. You will not miss her, I think?"

"Of course we won't!" roars Domna. "Their mother wasn't even a fairy!"

"Oh no, she wasn't'," agrees Aurora, picking her way towards Daireann and staring her full in the face. "Certainly she wasn't. But sometimes her eyes, like yours, had something other-wordly in them."

"What do – do you mean?" stumbles Daireann.

"Oh yes," smiles Aurora. "I knew your mother."

16

CHAPTER SIXTEEN

Everything that could change in Iblees had changed. The moment the Deevs had streaked across the sky, they had burnt the fertile land to a crisp waste of dirt and sand.

They had burnt Asher's fortitude with them. The worst thing he had ever read of had happened. He did not know how to live with the reality of that.

Joel changed too, in every aspect except his mind. He was still bent on going to war with the fairies. Kish thought it was a splendid idea. So they went to war with the fairies.

That was the final blow to Asher. All bridges between him and Joel seemed burnt forever – burnt as thoroughly as the land he had once loved. Asher drew within himself, shell-shocked.

The walls of Glass Mountain Castle had crumbled in the wave of Deevs. There was a great deal of dust and extensive repair work going on; but still Asher sat in his chamber, regardless of the mess and the noise. He had been born amongst mess and noise, and it soothed him in some strange way to be amongst it now that he felt as if he had died.

There was only one way to distract his mind from painful wanderings: he must concentrate on something. There was only one book in his possession: The Book of Kings.

Ironically this was his escape. He read it from the moment he woke to the moment he fell asleep, his eyes blurring from the constant strain. Often he wept over a passage, as he realised how far his people had fallen short of the ideal. But this weeping in itself was a great relief; it gave Asher a sense of morbid satisfaction to dwell upon his misery and let it possess him.

One day, Asher awoke to find less light flooding his bleary eyes than usual. Confused, he looked around the entire room from his bed. Something *was* different. The walls had been patched up. Every wall had been patched up, and he had not even noticed the workers begin the task.

So it was for more days and nights than Asher could count, for they all merged into one another. He read his Book, and read his Book again, seeing nothing, hearing nothing, feeling everything. So it was until the day he reached his favourite passage once more.

As always, the instant he read the words tears filled his eyes against his wishes, and his chest became an intolerable weight. Asher was obliged to put the book down and hold his head in his hands. And it was then, in the acutest agony, that he heard a noise.

Perhaps the only reason he noticed it was because it reflected his own grief. It was the most pathetic, harrowing cry he could imagine. And then he realised it was the baby.

Asher raised his head from his hands. It was swimming with a rush of logical, non depressing thoughts trying to break through the mist of woe he had created there. He had forgotten about the baby.

Instantly Asher felt less sorry for himself. He was overcome with a tingling wave of pity for the child. There it was, all alone, motherless and with *such* a father! Though it was a Prince, it had been born into a wasted Kingdom and a crumbling Castle. It did not have much going for it at all.

Asher went to return to his reading. It felt scary and unsafe to come out of his blanket of gloom. The real world had hurt him beyond words; he had no desire to start living in it again.

The words ran around the page and would not make any sense. Asher read three sentences six times and still had no idea what they were about. The baby filled in his mind.

The baby. The baby who would grow to be a King. Reluctant as he was to let himself hope, Asher had to admit there *was* hope in that. That small, wailing Prince may grow to be a good King – a King who not only *read* the Book of Kings, but followed it. A King who righted all this wrong that had crushed them.

Asher stood up. Pushing aside his wooden seat he took some tentative steps towards the door. His hand trembled on the handle.

It had been so very long since Asher had stepped foot outside this room. He did not know what he feared on the other side of the door, but he was petrified at the idea of opening it.

The baby cried again. Asher pulled his door open, just a crack, and let a slither of light into the room. He put one brown eye to the opening and looked down the corridor.

There was no one about. The torches burned on the uneven walls, but there were no people basking in their light. It gave Asher the courage he needed. Very slowly, he slipped through the door and followed the sound.

He had decided: he was going to visit the Prince of all Auchriachan.

His whole body was trembling as he wound his way through the passages. He was worried he may turn into the wrong room – or perhaps Joel would be with his son?

The mere thought of that nearly turned Asher back. But every time he nearly lost his nerve, the baby cried again, and Asher knew he must see it.

At last the wailing became so loud Asher knew he could not have the wrong room. Now he could not only hear the crying of the baby, but the gurgling of its mouth and the movement of its small limbs.

The room was at the end of a small corridor, a turn off from the main passage. The door was ajar, and sunlight was glowing within. Asher braced himself and entered.

The door creaked open to reveal a large room hardly fit for a Prince. On the badly repaired walls hung the remnants of the decorations Queen Ganieda had so lovingly prepared. For the most part they had been blasted and ruined by the Deevs.

There was no furniture at all except the great monstrosity of a carved wooden cradle in the centre of the floor; at least eight babies of great girth could fit inside it – one infant on its own must have felt very lost indeed. In fact the cradle was so large that Asher was entirely in the room before he noticed the lady in golden embroidered lemon robes standing over it.

Her head, covered with a small pointed hat, snapped upwards. She looked surprised to see him, but not unfriendly. "Can I help you, Sir?"

Asher struggled to find his voice. He had almost entirely forgotten the art of speaking. "Oh. Oh I am sorry. I did not realise anyone would be here."

The lady smiled and came towards him. Asher had an absurd urge to run away. She held out her hand.

"I am Urvasi. The Queen was my cousin."

Asher took her hand and worried about how long it had been since he had washed his. "Asher."

Lady Urvasi smiled. "I know who *you* are. Who does not know the slayer of Dybuk? Ganieda was very fond of you."

Asher looked down and did not reply.

"Well, Sir Asher, would you care to see your Prince? You are one of the few people who has tried."

Asher looked up and saw Lady Urvasi regarding him with great approval. He trusted her instantly.

"Yes. Yes, I really would."

Lady Urvasi walked over to the side of the gigantic crib and beckoned him to join her. Asher came to her side. He nearly had to stand on tip-toes to peer inside.

In the centre of a nest of white linen, there was curled a very small, thoroughly helpless baby. Asher's heart ached to look at his tiny fingers, his pretty bow shaped mouth and the downy hair upon his head. The Prince was just like a little angel, surrounded by a cluster of clouds. He seemed to glow with a divine radiance, and from that moment Asher knew he would do anything – everything – to protect this precious child.

"What is his name?" Asher breathed in an awed whisper.

"He does not have one."

Asher was so surprised that he prised his eyes from the baby. "Joel has not decided yet?"

Lady Urvasi looked ashamed and angry. "Joel has not come to see him yet. I have tried my best. Joel does not want anything to do with him."

"But surely he is a comfort to him? He is half Ganieda! That must be balm to his grief?"

Lady Urvasi shrugged. "I am this baby's family now. Perhaps I will name him one day. You may help me, if you like. If you'd like to keep visiting, that is," she added uncertainly.

Asher smiled very warmly. His mouth felt very odd to be in that position once more. "I would like that beyond all things."

From that day on Asher stopped reading the Book of Kings. He went to see the Prince and Lady Urvasi constantly. In fact, Asher visited this baby so frequently, that it was him, and not the King, who gave him his name. He named him Elihu, because he wanted someone to explain his troubles.

When they had decided upon this name, Asher and Lady Urvasi went down to the Throne Room to run the idea past Joel. They knew he would not like to be reminded of the baby's existence, but it did not feel right to name him without his father's input.

It was the first time Asher had seen Joel since the Deev episode. His heart beat thick within him and every nerve vibrated at the idea. But Joel did not seem to recollect they had spent anytime apart at all.

He was pouring over charts and maps with Sir Kish and Sir Nehemiah when they entered.

Lady Urvasi was the brave one who broached the subject. Joel did not even look up from what he was doing.

"Well, I suppose you must call it something," he said. "I'm sure that will do as well as the rest. Now, Asher, I would be obliged if you would stop playing around with infants and coach the archers. There is a war going on, you know."

And then he started talking to Sir Nehemiah.

The sun was setting over the sand dunes, staining the sky with broad red streaks. Already the temperature had dropped dramatically. Sir Kish and Sir Nehemiah huddled inside their armour.

"I wish I knew a way to break their strength," continued Sir Nehemiah. "They are unlike anything I have ever thought before. Such strange weapons! Like miniature cannons on their fingers."

Kish looked out across the horizon. "I have tried to

inspect them closely. From what I can see they are almost like rings. If we could gain possession of one – we could take it from a dead fairy – we might examine it and see how it works."

Nehemiah kicked the sand. "There *are* no bodies; that's the problem. You've seen the way they vanish in mid-air! Purple glitter: that is all we ever find. I am not sure if that means they are dead, or have transported themselves; I just do not know. That is what bothers me." He looked at Sir Kish earnestly. "Does it not bother you?" Kish thought for a moment. The sunset was warming his face with an orange hue. "Certainly it is not as simple as fighting the Boanerges. I knew what I faced there. But if there is one thing I will always be proud of about my exiled tribe, it is the hatred of fairies. Since the foundation of Auchriachan, it was always the Boanerges who suffered the greatest outrages from their kind. I believe in this war, and if many of our men have to die to annihilate these detestable creatures, I shall not count it a loss."

He looked intently at Nehemiah, his eyes on fire. Nehemiah sighed. "Perhaps you are right. I am a simple Moordale, and my family never minded fairies one way or the other. I don't think we even spared a moment to consider them. I hope I will always be a good Knight and follow my King. But..." Nehemiah glanced to Glass Mountain Castle, its wreckage illuminated by the dying sun. "I worry about King Joel's decision. He is still grieving for his wife. He is taking risks with the future of Iblees by meddling with a force we know so little about." He gestured to Green Glow Forest. It was far away now, over many long and tall dunes. "Is it just me, or has that forest gotten bigger? What's happening *there*?"

Kish followed his arm to the dark mass of trees. It *was* significantly larger, even though it was further away.

"There is so much we do not know!" recommenced

Nehemiah in an impassioned voice. "Of course I want to kill the hideous black creatures that ruined our moor lands – but the fairies we kill do not look like them!" Nehemiah wrapped his arms around himself and tried to stop the cold seeping in.

Sir Kish laughed. Nehemiah appeared very small and afraid positioned so. "Come man, what kind of cowardice is this? You are tired; you are not sure what you are saying."

Nehemiah sighed and blushed. "Perhaps you are right. I *am* tired. And it is so very cold. Should we not turn back before night falls?"

Kish shrugged. His eyes took in the waning sunset, and flicked back to the forest. "You go. I want to take the air for a little longer. The cold helps me think."

Nehemiah regarded him a little oddly. "Very well. Be careful. It would not do to lose one of our best Knights to the desert!"

Kish nodded. Nehemiah said goodnight and turned around. Kish watched him trundle towards the Castle with all the zeal of a comrade and friend. When he was quite out of sight, Kish turned, and began to wander towards Green Glow Forest.

It was a long walk, and Kish knew it was dangerous to be out in the desert in the dark. But a small flame within compelled him. Curiosity spread through his limbs and drove them onwards. He must see if the fence his ancestors had built was still there. He was not sure why this was so important, but he must see it.

As he walked, black night gradually covered over the streaks of red in the sky. The yellow sand transformed to grey. Everything looked unreal, like a misty dream.

Nehemiah's words floated through his head. They took his mind off the cold. Kish was overwhelmed with a terrible homesickness. He thought of his tribe, and his large family of brothers. He could use their help now. They would know what to do; they would understand why it was so important to kill the fairies. The Boanerges would know that it did not matter if the fairies who destroyed Auchriachian did not *look* like the ones they were fighting; the Boanerges had learnt the tricks fairies could practise from the cradle. He wished more ardently than ever he had not turned his sword against them. This was the greatest fight of his life, and they were not there to see it.

Kish thought of Joel and the baby Prince. It began to trouble him again that Joel was, after all, only a worker. And if he meant to ignore the Prince as studiously as he had done thus far, that Prince would grow up to be an ill-qualified leader too. Kish did not know what to do for the best.

An upsurge of frustration and ambition swelled in his breast. He could guide the King, but he was a stubborn person. And it all took so *long*. It might take too long. But even if he was able to convince Joel down the right paths in time, why should Joel get the credit for his ideas?

He wandered on through the unchanging desert, consumed by worry and resentment. His stride slowed, but he kept his eyes on the forest. It was nothing now but a darker black mass on a dark black mass.

At last he arrived. The trees smelt sweet in the night air. Somewhere in the distance he thought he heard a cricket chirp.

"I am sure I am not afraid of Green Glow Forest," Kish thought to himself. "It charms the senses and is very fair. I do not need to worry about being alone in the dark. If a fairy comes, I will kill it."

He bent down and began to dig among the brambles with great self satisfaction. It proved to be hard work. The thickets hurt his hands and Kish wished he had brought a lantern to throw some light over the shadows. He was working all by feel.

The darkness would have distorted his bearings anyway, but Kish was at a loss as to where he actually was in relation to his ancestors' fence. The forest was so altered he was convinced it had been chopped down and a new one rebuilt. But still he scrambled through the tangle of foliage and thorns, undismayed.

It soon felt like a dream, rummaging through the leaves. Kish was so tired from the walk that his body began to act automatically. The concentration made his eyes heavy, but that was a good thing, for while he concentrated he did not give way to superstitious fears.

But it was so cold, and so late, and he was so tired...

Kish felt his eyelids giving way, and woke up with a start. Onwards with the dig. The moon was high now, and its light began to flutter on to his hands. It would help his search. But his eyes were aching even more than his scratched hands. They did not listen to his rigid self-command; they shut again.

"Kish."

Kish sprang awake violently, his heart thumping. He rose to his feet and spun around. The grey dunes, stretching far as his eyes could see, were deserted and did not bare the marks of any footprints. He looked past the hedges into the trees, but it was as dark as being blind inside that forest.

He could swear a voice had just spoken to him in a warm breath against his ear.

"A dream," he said to himself, and the sound of his own voice reassured him.

He bent down to his knees once more.

"Kish."

Kish sprang upwards like a tightly coiled spring with a cry of fear.

"Who's there?!" he demanded, with a much stronger

and more commanding voice than he had dared hope would come out of his lips.

No one replied. Nothing moved. Kish had an impulse to turn back to Glass Mountain Castle, but he knew he would run forever on the sand and still be in sight of whatever was there.

Shaking, he looked at the forest. It was dark and serene. And then out of nowhere a hazy light blared into his eyes. They were so used to the dark now it blinded Kish momentarily.

He shielded his face with his hand and drew out his sword. "Fairies," he muttered.

"Kish!" the voice called.

Kish gritted his teeth and followed the light.

The trees looked like an enormous cavern. Kish had the feeling of being sealed inside a pit as he stepped inside the forest. But the same heady smells filled the air, and the same gentle noises of a light breeze and the odd insect were all that troubled his ears.

Soon Kish could lower his hand and look with open eyes. He kept his sword held in a guarding position. The light was a dull yellow white, oozing through the black pillars of trees.

Kish came as near as he dared. He found a little spot peppered with budding bluebells and crocuses, where he could stand and observe the light, still out of its immediate glow.

"What do you want?" he asked.

A light mystical voice floated towards him. Many echoes followed it. "Want? Why, we want the same things you want, Sir Kish of Iblees."

Kish grinned wryly. "I doubt that."

"We do not want the Boanerges roaming around here picking berries. We do not want the fairies to pass through here. So far, I think, we want the same."

Kish swallowed. "Are my kinsman reduced that far? Are they starving? Are -"a sudden backlash of pride and suspicion stopped Kish's mouth. "No! I know your tricks. You want to play upon my sensibilities. I will not listen to this."

He turned and went to walk away, but the ground before him spontaneously ignited. Kish jumped backwards, gasping.

"Stay," the voice beckoned him, still honey sweet. "Stay, and perhaps you will learn how to do that."

"I do not want to learn your fairy tricks!" spat Kish.

"Fairies?" the voice sounded suddenly dark and menacing. Kish regretted his harsh response. "We are not fairies! You insult us. We hate the fairies!"

"Then – then what *are* you?" Kish looked up at the light, and found it increasingly mesmerising.

"We are everything a fairy is not. We are the anti-fairies. We are here so that they will not be."

Kish digested this. He frowned. "You are what Sir Asher calls Deevs. I know nothing of Deevs. The Boanerges only know about fairies."

The voice gave an airy chuckle. "Your King; does he know about fairies?"

"My King," announced Kish without hesitation, "knows nothing."

"And this Sir Asher of whom you speak? His praise has travelled past this forest. He must be a wise and learned warrior?"

"No!" Kish heard his voice ring through the forest and startle a small bird. "No. He has done nothing but sit and dream all day. All he has done worthy of note is – is kill my father. And I am supposed to worship him for it." A half-suppressed sob erupted from Kish's lips. This was the first time he had really let himself consider who he had lost in ending the Boanerges rebellion. A twinge of guilt pricked him.

"You did the right thing," the voice interrupted his meditation, almost as if it had read his mind. "You always did the right thing, Sir Kish; it was those around you who failed."

Kish had to agree with this.

"You, who know so much about fairies – surely you should be in charge of this war. Only you would be able to destroy them."

"I think I could," said Kish eagerly, coming forwards. "I just need the support and to be listened to. It takes so *long* to persuade the King…"

The voice turned incredulous. "*Persuade* the King?! He knows nothing; you know everything. Why does he not listen to you straight away?"

Kish took a moment to consider this. "I suppose, because he is the King. And a bad one at that."

"He is a bad King," agreed the voice mournfully. "Oh, your poor people! Would it not be better, Sir Kish, if *you* were King?"

Kish burst into whoops of laughter. "Yes, it would be better. Of course it would be better. But you do not just make yourself King."

"Did you never wonder, Sir Kish, why we appeared? At that very moment too, when your King was doing the most foolish of all things?"

Kish looked confused. He hung his head, and said: "You are a – you are a punishment to the King?"

There was a low hum. "Perhaps. Perhaps you may see it like that. But remember, our purpose is to destroy the fairies. They will not be destroyed with a fool like Joel for a King."

Kish wiped his forehead. His nagging doubts were now hurtling through his breast with the full sorrow of conviction. He felt very bitter.

"No. I guess not. But we must try our best." Kish thought he would try for his father and his brothers.

"Oh," sighed the voice. "Noble and noble again. So you will try that way, will you? You do not want to be our King?"

Kish did not know whether to take them seriously. "I am not one of you. I cannot be your King."

"No, but with our help, you could be King of Auchriachan. You could help us kill the fairies, and be King of Laseri too."

The latent ambition in Kish's veins thrilled through him to the quick. "I would be a better King than Joel," he said. It was not the first time he had considered this fact. "But why would you be willing to make me King of both these places? You could do it yourself."

"We have no purpose to stay and rule," came the sickly sweet voice, cooing. "Just to destroy the fairies, and settle the world as it should be."

Kish was about to say he did not believe in that sort of thing, but then he remembered how deeply he believed the fairies were evil spirits, and did not see why he could not believe in good spirits too.

"I will not be pixie-led," he said at last. He was going to turn on his heel again but then he remembered the fire that had appeared before. He looked at it, still flaming viciously beside him and decided to ask to be released.

But before he could open his mouth, the flames were filled with an orange image.

Kish saw himself within the fire, receiving a double-tiered crown. He saw a scepter in his hands and crowds of people cheering around him.

"The people do not want a shepherd boy for a King," whispered the voice.

Kish shook his head fiercely and shut his eyes. "I have heard too much of the deception of fairies to listen to this. Kindly release me. I will say nothing of you to my King."

"Very well." The flames of the fire went out. Kish head a fluttering sound above him, and something brushed against his head. Opening his eyes, he looked at the ground in front of him. A scrap of parchment lay at his feet. Warily, he picked it up and turned it over. It resembled a map.

"You are the type of person, Kish of Iblees, who desires proof. Here is what we offer you. We will not reject you with the same scorn you reject us. Follow this or do not. But if it turns out to be useful, you will come back and see us."

As quickly as it appeared, the light had vanished. Kish began to shiver once more, and stared, dumbfounded at the map in his hand.

17

CHAPTER SEVENTEEN

Years of war passed. It was hard to even dream of a time without the war. The days when Iblees had looked over moors and the scant grass Asher and Joel used to feed their flocks upon were irreconcilable with the present.

Like all wars, this one had begun with the promise of early victory. Joel, the prophesised King, could not doubt he would succeed; the fairies felt confident of defeating the human onslaught in a week. But neither side was quite as good as they considered themselves to be, and a draining stalemate ensued.

Perhaps the only reason the humans stood a chance was the strange effects of their attacks. The fairies took them very much to heart. Iblees was not a happy land of bliss any longer. Fairies wept, became ill and inexplicably disappeared. Their confusion and distress at being suddenly set upon was evident. During the first few battles, indeed, they were reluctant to harm, let alone thoroughly murder, any human at all. But being shot at soon cured this malady, and the fairy soldiers began to acquire an enthusiastic taste where before had been hesitation and peacefulness.

Despite their paltry weapons, in the way of wooden spears and other such frivolous apparatus, the fairies looked in a fair way to winning through their magical powers. That was, until last week.

Last week, Kish had found the route to the fine fairy city of Majeseerum. He had captured it with incredible style. No one knew exactly how he had found or captured it, but the Knights he had taken with him were now his devoted followers.

King Joel rewarded his victory as if the victory itself were no reward at all. He built, or rather, ordered that someone else build, Kish's very own castle. Nonetheless, Kish was not satisfied. A fairy had escaped, he said, with a very important object.

However, Kish's dissatisfaction did not stop him ascending rapidly over every inch of ground he had left to gain in the King's trust. Kish was the honoured Knight now; Kish was the King's personal friend.

Poor Asher was left with nothing but training the young page boys who wanted to be Knights and fight in the war. They probably wanted to fight under Sir Kish. Asher submitted to his lot without complaint.

Though he was a bowed and weary spirit, there were times when Asher came to himself and ached for an escape from his teacher role. Long after the exercises had passed, he could still hear the dull thud as young soldiers rode past the quintain and hit the shield on its spinning wooden arm.

Today was one of those days. He woke up, dressed, and looked out the window at the altered view. Still the thumping in this head.

A heat haze hung over the now dry and dusty landscape and Asher could not believe this was all there was in life. He felt as restricted in his inner being as if metal hoops were wound around him. He was not the same optimistic Asher as years ago, who believed in his visions and his purpose in life.

He decided to do something drastic. He saddled his horse alone, hours before anyone else awoke, and rode.

As his horse tripped and stumbled in the sand, Asher thought back over the past years. Ardently did he wish to hear the birds singing and the insects humming. He longed for the scent of a flower; he longed most to be a simple wandering shepherd again, who had not done the things that he had done. He wanted the land before the Deevs, before Joel had launched the war with the fairies, before the humans had captured the finest fairy city, before the moors had been gobbled up and scorched into an arid desert.

On and on he travelled under the rising sun. The landscape awoke in a pale yellow wash. The sun was soon too bright, but Asher rode on, squinting, seeing nothing of the way he took.

Just when Asher knew he must turn back to avoid being late, he felt the cool lick of shade on his sweating face.

"Only a dried up acanthi tree or a budding palm," he thought, and drew up his reins. In order to turn, Asher opened his eyes properly. He saw green.

Thinking the sun must have played so long on his eyelids that it was causing him to see colours, he continued to wheel round. And then he heard the low whistle of a bird.

The horse stopped. The sun was no longer glaring in his face. Asher turned back to look over his shoulder.

A forest. A huge forest stretching out like a border, as long as the eye could see. Asher blinked at the varying colours, unable to believe they were there.

"That is the forest that used to be! The way to fairy-land!" he exclaimed to himself. "Kish mentioned it when he spoke of his route to Majeseerum. I thought he was lying!"

Thoughts of returning on time to supervise the pages in battle skills flew from his mind. How cool and inviting the leafy recesses looked to him! Entranced, he kicked the horse on and entered the forest.

Ducking under branches as he went, Asher rode with a bewitched look on his face. The very sight of all this foliage made him want to leap for joy. It was too much to cope with, and too much to take in.

Gradually he became aware of sound. There was a delightful bubbling in his ears. Asher looked in the direction of the sound and saw he had found a cool stream. He dismounted instantly and rushed to bathe his face in it.

The clean water on his face made him feel like a new creation. Smoothing back the wet hair from his forehead, Asher raised his head: and met another pair of eyes.

The most exquisite creature he had ever seen was gazing back calmly at him as its tongue gently lapped the sparkling water. It had the delicate bone structure of a lean and agile deer. Small fluted horns curved gracefully up from the top of its head, and its coat was the snowiest, smoothest white imaginable.

Unaware of what he did, Asher murmured "Beautiful" and stretched out a trembling hand towards it. He forgot his proximity to the water. The motion unbalanced him and he fell forwards with a sudden splash.

The liquid brown eyes of the beauteous animal widened in fright, and before the water had settled again, it had fled with the speed of a bullet.

"Wait, wait!"

Asher vaulted on to his horse and set chase after the fleeing white rump. He rode wildly, keeping the bounding animal always just within sight. He did not even know why, exactly, he had to chase it. Asher only knew that, having seen it once, everything else would seem dull and commonplace. Somehow, he was sure, that white hart carried with it the secret of life, and the essence of the world before he and Joel had chased the wayward

Blackberry.

On and on he rode, branches snapping against his face, hearing nothing but the snort of his horse and the delicate hooves of the hart. And then: a scream.

An appalling, blood-curdling scream sliced through the air and pounded into Asher's concentration like a slap in the face. He sat back heavily in his saddle, just for one beat, and his horse tripped forward a few steps due to the unexpected shift of weight. Asher's eyes momentarily left the white hart. By the time he re-adjusted his horse and raised them again, it had completely disappeared.

Frustrated and panting, Asher slowed to a trot. Gradually his horse stopped, and Asher regained his breath, listening to the sound of his own heart beat in his ears. As his pulse slowed, Asher could hear the scream again. He furrowed his brow, unsure whether to trust his senses. It came again; long, high pitched and murderous. It sounded like a young girl.

Immediately alert, Asher was recalled to a sense of his situation and blamed himself for being so foolish. He was alone, in the middle of a war, on enemy territory. He had no idea what kind of creatures lived in this forest, and even less idea which route he must take to get home.

The horse's ears flicked back and forth as the scream grew louder. In a sudden resolution, Asher kicked the horse on and followed the noise.

"If it is a human Lady being harmed, I, as a Knight, must rescue her," he told the reluctant horse. "If it is a fairy... well, it will be my comrades doing the harming, and I can ride back safely with them."

But strangely, when Asher was sure he had reached the source of the cry for help, there was no one there at all. His eyes searched the vacant branches of the trees above, and the dark, still bushes. Only the sound of the stream reached him. Asher's horse pawed the ground.

The scream came again, incredibly loud and extremely close. Asher dismounted and span about in confusion.

"Where are you?" he called, gazing upwards.

When the scream was repeated, Asher realised he had been gazing in the wrong direction. The noise was coming from below him.

Running alongside the stream, he found it soon swelled into more of a river. Across the river, he found a large wooden bridge, nicely built in a neat arch, complete with a hand rail. Quickly Asher knelt down upon the wood and stuck his head under the rail.

"Hello? Do you need help?" he cried.

"Help me, help me!" called a strange voice. "I'm drowning!"

"I cannot see you. Tell me where you are."

"Lean lower!"

Asher laid down flat on the bridge and dangled more of his body over the edge. Blood filled his head.

All that met his eyes was the darkness under the bridge. He peered closely. He could see something, almost… something white.

Suddenly the white exploded on his vision. Around his face there was something scratchy and sticky. He fell from the bridge, but instead of meeting the water, he bounced back up as if on a bungee cord.

Asher became aware that he was spinning, and could move neither his arms nor his legs a fraction of an inch.

"Do not fight the spider's web," cackled the same voice that had called to him in such desperation. "That would make your muscles all taut… and that wouldn't taste very nice at all, would it?"

Asher heard an evil little laugh, and with it the dreadful wailing of several other voices. Each tortured cry sounded even more forlorn than the scream which the wicked little creature that had now captured him had made. They made the hair stand up on the back of his neck.

"Do you mean to eat me?" asked Asher, spitting out cobwebs. He had never believed fairies so truly monstrous before. In his nightmarish frame of mind, he began to struggle with, amongst other things, the painful idea that Kish was actually right.

"Oh, do not worry yourself," soothed the voice in a mocking tone. "I mean to drown you first."

With a jolt Asher felt the web give way. There was a rush of air past his face, and suddenly his head was in the water.

He had not had time to take a gasp before he was plunged under. Asher's lungs burned in his chest as he strained for a breath but met only choking water.

His vision clouded. He tried to swim, but still could not move; the web held him tight, with just his face submerged in the river. Soon he had no energy left to struggle any more. He felt the life beginning to ebb out of him, and it seemed as if he was about to drift into an inviting sleep...

A flash of colour crossed the dark inside of Asher's eyelids. There was a muffled crash, and the water appeared to pulsate around him. All was silent for an instant. Suddenly Asher felt himself travelling upwards, and cold, cruel air rushed past his face.

Gasping, he felt himself hauled up upon the bridge, weighed down like a block of lead in his sodden clothing and rusting pieces of armour.

Opening his eyes, which were still bleary with water, he dimly descried a figure dressed in spotless cream. The figure was holding a small, squirming, ugly thing with a bright red nose.

"That is the last time, Boag!" said a stern female

voice. "Back you go, to the mercy of those you had no mercy upon!"

The unknown lady dropped the ugly red-nosed creature from the bridge. As it fell, Asher saw it was tied in a thick cord, almost like rope, but he could not call it such. He expected the wicked little thing – Boag, this strange lady had called it – to hit the water and drown, but it did not. As it neared the surface of the tumbling river, a fog rose up and entwined it. That ghastly mournful scream, like a wolves howl, sounded again. Asher saw shapes like ghosts appear from the fog, their eyes mad with delight. They blessed the lady on the bridge and with long fingers dragged down the shrieking Boag. He and the drowned souls disappeared with a great gurgling bubble. Then all the wood, and the surface of the water, was just like nothing had ever disturbed it before.

Asher dashed the remaining drops of water from his eyes and stumbled to his feet. "I – thank you. What – what *was* that... that *thing*? Who are you? I thank you, I thank you indeed."

It was only then Asher saw there were actually two female figures before him. The one that had dropped Boag from the bridge turned and smiled at him. She was decorated in crystal jewellery and had long white blonde hair flowing down in a shining sheet over her shoulders. There was a sparkling, v-shaped belt around her waist and a long train to her robe, embroidered round the edges with golden thread. A neat chain of gold was clasped around her forehead.

"My name is Lady Aurora," she said in a very regal way. "And this is my lady-in-waiting – the Lady Cynthia."

Lady Aurora gestured to a girl standing beside a fine dappled grey horse. The Lady Cynthia looked more like Asher was used to seeing girls look – her hair coiled up in plaited wheels over each ear, and a net with gems in it crowning her head. She held a curious small white dog with red ears.

"I do not recall…" began Asher.

"We are from the tribe of the Boanerges," Lady Aurora cut in. She gave him a provocative look, which seemed to say "banish us again if you dare".

Asher's hand moved to the hilt of his sword. "Is that so? What brings you out this way?" he demanded.

The Lady Cynthia looked from Asher to his sword, to Asher again, and began to cry. Asher was confounded.

Aurora very calmly and precisely told him: "Other than your peril, an attack on our encampment brings us this way. We are unsure as to where my family has ended up, and we did not care to remain in the company of the brutish soldiers who are left. We come to beg the assistance of the King, or if he will not give it, a few weeks sojourn in Auchriachan until we have news it is safe to return."

Asher looked dubiously at them. Cynthia's wailing was starting to embarrass him. "Very well," he muttered, "you have saved my life."

"Oh yes. We Boanerges take great pride in our ability to deal with fairies," smirked Aurora so dryly, that Asher was led to believe she was out of humour with her tribe. The supposition could only recommend her to him.

He let go of his sword. "The King will not admit you into his presence as a guest," he told them decidedly. "If you come, you must come as my prisoners."

Aurora shrugged. "So we are."

Asher stood for a moment without seeming to know what to do. Too much had happened to him in the past hour for his brain to function as it usually did.

"Good," he said at last. "Mount your horse, my lady, and I will lead you back."

He watched the graceful figure silently and obediently spring into the saddle. Giving the sniffling

Cynthia something like a reassuring pat on the shoulder, he took the reins of the white horse and began to retrace his erratic steps out of the forest.

18

CHAPTER EIGHTEEN

Asher knew nothing about where the Boanerges had moved to following their exile. He was led to believe they must now live in a very strange place, judging by the reaction of the two ladies as he bought them out of the forest.

He could not know that they were comparing the yellow, scorched expanses of sand which Auchriachan was now reduced to, to Laseri. Even if he had known it, he could never comprehend, having never seen the wonder of Laseri himself, how the alteration startled them.

Every direction they faced, the sand dunes looked identical. There was no juicy grass, no musical lagoons, and the air was not filled with a thousand opal shimmers; it was dusty, muggy and oppressive.

"You have not seen Iblees for many years," deduced Asher.

"We have never seen it," replied Aurora calmly. "We were far too young when our tribe left to be able to remember it."

"Oh madam," squeaked Cynthia, her eyes appalled. "Have you ever beheld anything like it? Beige, beige; cruel bleak beige as far as the eye can see!"

Asher asked no further questions. It would not do for him to seem too friendly towards two Boanerges, even if they had saved his life. Besides, the ladies were holding a

144

whispered consultation for a large duration of the journey. This whispering was not only extremely rude, in purposefully excluding Asher from the conversation, but it made him feel awkward, unwanted, and moreover, increasingly paranoid that they were whispering about him.

He did not point out to them, therefore, that there were different tones of sand; he rode straight past the cliffs, and the patterns, and the oases. He did notice, from time to time, the Lady Aurora's eyes flick to observe such sights, but said nothing. Nor did he tell them the story of how all of this had been rolling moor land until the Deevs were released, bringing with them a blight to the land, hot winds and a scorching sun. He did not tell them that he held the memory of green foliage and the smell of heather bells as precious in his mind. He simply led them past the worker's hovels, which now looked like stone chameleons on the desert, up to a much altered Glass Mountain Castle.

The Castle was now contracted into a piled up square keep which towered over the kingdom. Not that it truly deserved the name "Castle" any longer; it was an ungainly mishmash of the old stones and the dusty, neutral coloured dirt walls which had been glued in to support the structure. Here and there were winding climbers of ivy from days gone by, now choked and crisped by the heat. Asher noticed the ladies eye these suffocated plants with distinct distaste.

The bailey was already awake and alive with the sound of fletchers and blacksmiths at work. Asher and his companions left their horses and walked in on foot.

Newly fledged squires were chasing around with their first real swords, whilst their younger counterparts, the pages, were loading up the Knights with the weapons and shields they would need for battle. This sight made Asher anxious that he was now so late as to fall under the

King's displeasure. A few of the preparing Knights viewed Asher with curiosity. Nearly all of them nudged each other and nodded towards the strange ladies with raised eyebrows.

Asher was very eager to reach the Castle before King Joel descended, but apparently this was not the plan of his two prisoners. There was a sudden squeal of pleasure behind him and someone, he thought it was the Lady Cynthia, breathed a strange word he did not recognise.

Asher turned in amazement to see the ladies fawning over a herd of goats, caressing and twittering to the beasts, their faces shining whiter than the sun with sheer pleasure.

Knowing that he was in trouble and being extremely fatigued made Asher angry with this pointless delay, despite the fact that the ladies were very pretty, which must be their excuse.

"What is this?" he roared, stalking over to them. "Do ladies often roll around on the ground in your tribe? Do not tell me they don't have goats in the Boanerges?!"

The ladies looked up with impish faces. Cynthia repeated the word "goats" and they both giggled.

As Asher began to drag them to their feet, the trumpet sounded. The door of the Castle went up, and out flew the excitable and yapping dogs of King Joel.

The dogs bounded at them, panting wildly. Asher was surprised to feel his prisoners writhe and struggle in his grasp. He saw the Lady Aurora's jaw set, and her face go pale, while her lady in waiting was giving out small shrieks and twirling about like a captured bird.

If they disliked dogs so greatly, Asher wondered why Lady Cynthia was clutching that odd little canine so tightly to her bosom and muttering "Farvann, Farvann! Oh Farvann, protect me!" But the antipathy was clearly mutual. After springing merrily all over Asher, the dogs approached the new comers with hackles raised. They sniffed the train of Lady Aurora's gown as she stood, immovable as a waxwork.

"There is something not right about these ladies," thought Asher to himself. "The Boanerges are certainly a very strange tribe." It began to explain a lot about Kish.

One dog growled suspiciously. Another let out a short, sharp bark. Lady Cynthia screamed. The dog ran towards the noise; the Lady Cynthia ran away, and soon the whole pack of dogs was chasing her around the bailey.

Being a valiant and good-natured Knight, Asher would have helped her, had he not been pounced on from behind by another eager and happy creature.

"Well, hello there Elihu!" he smiled warmly, sweeping the young Prince up. He was grown now into quite the miniature monarch; a pretty, charming little child. "What do you think I have brought for you today? Two ladies, look, and their odd little dog."

"For me? Thank you. I will have the dog," beamed the child. He thought a moment, wrinkled his nose and added very seriously: "But you can keep the ladies, if you don't mind."

The heavy thud of feet marching and metal clanging beat through the ground. Asher did not hear it in his delight to see little Elihu.

"Elihu, Elihu!" Asher laughed, gazing adoringly at him. He was such a lovely boy with bright eyes and thick light hair. "Where is your father?"

"Your King is here, Sir Asher," said Joel irritably as the guard of sergeants parted for him. "And you are late."

Asher put down Elihu and ruffled the boy's hair as the signal he should run along, which he was more than ready to do.

"On the contrary; I am early. I have been up since the bright dawn and caught two Boanerges for you already." Asher indicated Aurora. Cynthia was clinging about her, dishevelled and frightened. One dog continued to worry at her stocking.

A hush fell. King Joel looked displeased, but moved to a position where he could see both ladies very clearly.

Aurora calmly returned Joel's gaze as his deeply ringed eyes swept up and down her and his strained forehead furrowed.

"What madness of yours is it to bring such people into the capital?" Joel asked Asher broodingly. "They are dangerous traitors – even if they are only ladies; you put the lives of my subjects and your Prince in jeopardy. If you wanted to please me you should have brought me their heads. What good are they to me?"

Asher did not remonstrate about the lack of ladies in Auchriachan, or explain that it was better to keep Boanerge ladies prisoner than fairy ones, which they certainly had done in the past few years. He could not honestly defend his actions – he had spared them out of gratitude, pity, humanity: in short, nothing that King Joel would understand.

"If you please, your Majesty," began Aurora staunchly with a deep curtsey. "We do but look for shelter. Our tribe is scattered without your powerful Majesty to protect us; our homes…"

"We owe you no shelter!" interrupted Joel, flicking out his cape. "Rebels cannot come whining back to the monarch when they are in trouble. It does not work like that! Do you think me a fool?"

"No indeed," answered Aurora. Asher admired the way she pointed out her little chin with dignity. "We only trusted in your grace and mercy, having been so fortunate as to receive it once before, when you spared our father's lives."

It seemed to disturb King Joel to look into her bright face. "I thought I had placed guards on the boundaries of the Far Lands. How did you get out? Were my guards killed by the fairies, or did you kill them? How can I know? You allude to your father's desertion. Why should we trust such people again?" he returned in a shaking voice.

The onlookers drew up in surprise as Aurora disentangled herself from Cynthia and actually approached him, holding out her hand.

"Look," she beckoned, flexing the finger bearing her moonstone ring. "My lady in waiting has one too. You know what they are, of course: fairy rings. We have defended ourselves against fairies to get them. In our journey we have killed many a fairy in loyalty to you. This knight here," nodding at Asher, "saw me kill another." Asher gave a look of confirmation. "We are valuable fighters. Fairies will see what we wear on our hands and quake. If you have... seers is it? Interpreters of those strange signs which are supposed to come from the fairies – but I am sure they do not. It is the angels that -" She stopped and recollected herself. "If you *do* have such people, perhaps they can help us learn to use the powerful magic inside the stones. All this considered, can you really afford not to have us on your side?"

A great heaviness sat on Joel's brow, which was working furiously. He pushed Aurora's hand away and looked fleetingly at her face. Then his eyes fell again and pondered the ends of her rippling blond hair.

"You wear your hair down," he said very cautiously.

She saw no other lady did. Her cheeks went hot as she devoutly hoped this was not a fatal mistake. "I do, your Majesty. It is unusual, perhaps."

There was a silence before Joel said: "Our Queen wore it so. I trusted her implicitly, and I will trust you. For now."

He snapped out of his nearly tender mode and

waved a royal hand. The ladies were surprised to find themselves seized by the arms and frogmarched out of the keep.

"There is no time to establish you in our hospitality now," laughed Joel grimly, mounting his horse. "You signed up for this – if you want to stay with us, you must come along with us." He was evidently enjoying their discomfort.

Asher had a brief consultation with another Knight and came back to them.

"Reports have reached us that a village is in distress," explained Asher. "We go to bring aid and defence."

He watched the two ladies roughly hauled forwards until they were out of sight. The King rode up beside him and they moved along together.

Joel leaned over and grinned nastily. "For all those fine speeches, let us see what their stomachs are really made of."

19

CHAPTER NINETEEN

No one truly expected Niebelheim to still be on fire. The diminutive houses made of whattle and daub blazed like torches lighting the way along a corridor. There were screams and moans, and the air was permeated with rancid smells. Thatched roofs, food supplies and hay stacks were either scattered or roaring in flames. Asher had never seen eyes grow wider than those of Lady Aurora and Lady Cynthia as they were bustled into the tumult and confusion of the scene.

Sir Nehemiah was already there, sweaty and covered in sand. He rode up on his foaming, snorting horse to meet them.

"Livestock all taken," he told them without waiting for a word of greeting. "Most of the women gone too."

"Casualties?" asked the King in a business like manner.

"Many of the children. Some of the workers tried to defend themselves, but every one who did has perished."

King Joel nodded and began to give orders for the distribution of the supplies they had brought with them. Water in huge earthen-ware jugs was thrown upon the burning huts, as other Knights tried to herd together the injured and frantic.

However, the fire in the granary looked to have taken the strongest hold. It seemed entirely impossible to put out without risking the combustion of many Knights. Asher saw Lady Aurora watching them attempt it, and withdraw scalded.

"Children?" Asher asked, taking his eyes away from the pretty lady. Many of these children were looking curiously at Asher. They seemed to know who he was – the Seer, the one who killed the leader of the Boanerges – and were whispering excitedly amongst themselves. "What cause have fairies to injure children?"

"One hundred and one," a voice said, surprisingly affably, from behind.

Kish, just as dirty and worn out as Nehemiah, had walked over to join them. King Joel nodded to him in welcome.

"Mainly to sabotage our race. If they take a hair, a bit of skin, they can swap them for changelings at any time. If, that is, the fairy glamour hasn't already infiltrated their blood... they could be transforming even now. It would be safer to dispatch them all..." He was prevented from carrying on with his iniquitous speech by the eruption of one of Lady Cynthia's suppressed sniffs.

Sir Kish's attention was suddenly drawn to the face wet with tears below the elaborate hair style and beads. Its pretty distress reproached him.

"Well, who is – how did?" he began, confused, to Asher. "I was not aware any ladies lived in Nibelheim. I thought them all workers and whelps of workers... unless -" he turned pale and whispered: "Tell me they are not the mothers of these children?!"

Despite the attendant tragedy, Asher could not help feeling that it would have given him the greatest imaginable delight if Kish's fear were true.

"They are not," he reluctantly relieved Kish's discomfort with. "They are a little lower. Do you not recognise them at all? You should: they are Boanerges, your old kinswomen. This one here has saved my life today," he tacked on gratefully, fearing his rivalry with Kish had made his speech too harsh.

He turned towards Aurora and saw her still gazing at the granary. But the fire had completely gone. All around the structure were looking up at it in wonder. He was then too astonished to continue.

Kish's face broke in relief, and all his natural assurance returned. "Indeed? Actually I did think, my Lady," to Cynthia, "I knew you from somewhere. I am glad, for you will both understand better than anyone the twisted fairy magic lingering in this place, and join with me in urging King Joel to…"

Lady Aurora's head suddenly snapped up to face them. Her cheek bones were suffused with red and her eyes glistened violently. "Fairies… *fairies* did this?" she questioned, her voice shaking with either indignation or grief.

There was a silence. "Undoubtedly," ventured Sir Nehemiah gently. "On my honour as a Knight, I saw them leaving with my own eyes."

More silence as they all watched Aurora in curious fascination. Some emotion – none of them could tell what it was – stopped her mouth.

Asher spoke at last, warily. "Perhaps the Lady Aurora would be so good as to take Prince Elihu and assemble the remaining livestock. She has already proved herself a fan of goats – it should pose few problems for her."

"Yes, yes, why not?" shrugged King Joel. "Once we can see what is left us, we will know what action to take." He looked round at the tail of his horse. "Where is the child, anyway?"

Prince Elihu had somehow materialised at the Lady Aurora's side. Clearly glad to have someone to be strong for, she took his hand, spread a smile over her face and said: "Now, will you help me find a cow?"

The boy's face lit up so that Asher feared his fondness for the child would show too strongly if he looked at him. Asher was obliged to look down at his hands on the reins and smile; by the time he looked up, they had gone.

Sir Kish took this opportunity to seclude Lady Cynthia. Was she not, after all, as much a lady as the Lady Aurora, with the same feelings, although she bore the infamous tag "in waiting"? He took her arm, in a very knightly way, and escorted her to the village entrance, where the air was less thick, and workers were washing the soot and ash from their faces in a long trough of water.

"So, you and I are from the same tribe," he said conversationally. "You look a very young lady. I do not remember you at all, though I suppose everything changed after the exile; people grafted in and out. Tell me, who was your father?"

The change of subject did not have the desired balming effect upon the Lady Cynthia. Her wide, frightened eyes declared her even more reluctant to speak of her family than about the slaughter of workers by fairies.

"Oh sir!" she wailed, "Do not make me speak of him. He is – he is dead!"

This topic was therefore fruitless. "I am sorry for your loss. I can understand – not to the same degree – separation from a family member. From a whole family, in fact. Tell me, where *are* our tribe now?"

Asher was gravely unhappy. Every day he was experiencing fresh proof that they were all doomed, body and soul. He had not been seen outside the Castle walls for a very long time now, and each horrible circumstance of war was pressed upon his vision anew. He had forgotten how bad it was.

"When will it stop? Can we ever really win against this magic? Look at the lightness, the fragility of this life – how easily it is taken away! I think the time is coming, Joel, when we will have to surrender, or lose every spark of life in Auchriachan." Asher looked in vain to the clouds as they walked along. They told him the same things he was telling Joel.

The King's tightly grouped features relaxed in sudden exhaustion. He looked suddenly as sad and tired as the workers. "Lightness? Lightness? You are wrong, Sir Asher; you are only a Knight and cannot understand the incredible heaviness of being. The sheer effort just to carry on existing – no, life is a weighty, weighty burden."

Asher gave a sympathetic half nod. If he could keep Joel in this dependant, open mood, if Kish stayed over near the village entrance with that girl, he might just be able to guide the King, ever so slightly, down the right path...

"But not all the Knights feel it is so. How can we ask them to fight an unknown..."

The end of Asher's sentence was lost as he nearly tripped over a tiny gaggle of dirty children, laughing and singing to the rhythm of a skipping rope. He pulled up, smiled at them and walked around. He was about to start speaking again when the words of their song suddenly became intelligible to him.

"Joel is our King, our given King,
He drives the tribes asunder.
Asher is a Knight, a much better Knight,
He slays the fearful Dybuk.
Joel kills thousands,
But Asher kills hundreds of thousands.
How many thousands did he kill?
One, two..."

Asher felt himself turning a peculiar colour and just dared meet Joel's eye. The hardened brow and tense demeanour had returned. Asher suspected from this his opportunity of persuading the King had probably passed for today.

Before either could speak a word, an extremely over-exited worker came scampering up to them.

"Sire, sire!" he panted in wide-eyed ecstasy. "One cow – we had only one cow left – but it is the only one we will ever need!"

After being upbraided for speaking nonsense, the worker was finally coerced into taking them over to where they had left the Lady Aurora and young Prince Elihu. Practically the whole village of Niebelheim were now assembled at this point, looking as wild with wonder and thankfulness as they had been with despair but moments before.

Sir Kish, markedly less pleased than the workers, beckoned for them to join him at his place right at the middle of the circle.

"It was her – the fine Lady – who first discovered it," babbled the excitable worker as they pushed their way through the crowds. "It just keeps coming!"

Over many shoulders, Asher could see the one remaining cow, standing placidly as fair white fingers moved nimbly over its udders. The Lady Aurora, sitting so that her golden hair swept the ground was milking very easily and merrily, although a great circular wall of shining, brimful buckets around her suggested she had been at this occupation for some time.

Elihu, enthralled by this new trick, danced around the animal, passing buckets to the malnourished children who gobbled and squeaked with glee at the thick white liquid.

"I think that will do for today," said the Lady Aurora, wiping her brow. "But there is more in her, I am sure of it." She pressed the velvety muzzle of the animal and murmured the words: "Good Cro-sith".

Asher was sure there must be some sign in this – he felt that people were looking for him to reveal a sign, at any rate. He himself could only be full of thanks and awe that there were supplies for these unfortunate people. Moistening his mouth to speak, he parted his lips and – was beat to it by Kish's ready tongue.

"Monstrous! Monstrous!" he called out. "I cannot comprehend, King Joel, how you came to allow your subjects to touch such a substance!"

Bemusement filled the faces of the crowd, gradually vacuuming out every scrap of wild happiness from the edges to the very centre. Children who had trembled with joy now began to quake with fear, and their little shaking hands slopped the precious milk onto the floor. It was, after all, a very strange thing; and when something was strange, it was possibly a wonderful thing – but far more likely, from the experience of the workers, to be a frightening thing.

"I allowed nothing," declared King Joel, which scared the workers even more, for fear of being proved disobedient. "Do you not see I have just arrived? Many of my Knights were on the scene – they are to tell me what has happened here, and advise me of the facts, in order that I might make my judgement."

The Knights, on the lead of Sir Kish, bowed. "But of course. It was very relapse in us not to speak at first, Your Majesty – allow me now to do it on behalf of us all."

King Joel inclined his head in token of being prepared to listen. Asher saw the workers, quivering, watching Kish with ravenous interest. The Lady Cynthia, too, observed him with expectation, apparently astounded he had the bravery to speak like this.

Asher, however, and the Lady Aurora, kept their eyes firmly on Joel.

"Why," began Kish, striding up to the cow in evident enjoyment of the attention he commanded, "would one cow alone escape? Sheer luck? Or the mercy of fairies? I think we can see," waving his hands significantly at the burnt homes, "that alternative is highly unlikely."

The Lady Aurora slumped a little.

"Well, let us call it fortune. But if we do, you must tell me – who here remembers this cow ever shedding such bountiful produce before? If someone knew of this cow's special properties, it was an offence not to report it to the King, so that he may help feed the other starving workers ruined by fairy attacks. Clearly that is the case. I must presume someone knew this cow was special, and took the trouble to save it amongst the other livestock. I would be extremely interested, and so would, I daresay, King Joel, to know who this was."

Silence fell completely, as if even the wind was afraid to blow.

"I agree," boomed King Joel, looking affronted. "Occurrences like this do not go unnoticed. I charge each and every one of you to explain yourselves. Reveal to me this moment who knew."

Prince Elihu looked very serious all of a sudden, understanding vaguely it would one day be him having to make the firm expression on his father's face. The children around him began to cry.

"No one – no one knew!" wailed a worker.

"Ah. I see. Ah, then." Kish shook his head knowingly. "It is as I thought. More sinister powers are at work here. The fairies left this cow, but not out of mercy – oh, no! They have left us a hexed cow, as a mark of appreciation. That is fairy milk we are suckling children of Auchriachan on! Fairy milk! Look at these ignorant workers! Everyone knows that once a child has drunk fairy milk, it is easier for the winged blighters to turn them into changelings. They mean to infiltrate our race from the inside!"

The workers screamed and clutched at their children. Some even tried to make them vomit.

In the pandemonium, the Lady Aurora stood up. "Really," she tried to say to King Joel, "this cow is but – "

"Kill it," ordered King Joel, and a spray of blood mixed with the spilt milk.

20

CHAPTER TWENTY

Majerseerum had once been the jewel of the fairy crown, glimmering with canals and twisting wooded walks. The architecture had risen to the sky: great domed, pillared buildings, pure white with swags of the most exotic materials forming curtains and doorways. Coloured mosaics filled the floors and doors. Round stain glass windows illuminated all in the tints of a smiling rainbow. Aurora could remember all of this in a misty corner of her mind, as she gazed into the iridescent ring on her hand and saw what it had become.

Trees were cut off in mid growth, blackened and blasted. Splinters of their wood lay scattered in huge chunks all over the churned up ground. There was no lingering trace of green, only mud. The ground of this once gorgeous landscape now looked like the mutilated surface of the moon, dotted with huge craters full of muddy water.

"Oh, if only I knew what to do!" sighed Aurora, tearing her eyes from the painful sight by stuffing her hand into a glove.

"Hmm?" Cynthia looked away, dazed, from the window she was staring out of.

They were in the room assigned to them by the King. Each wall was washed roughly in beige, and contained a pointed arched alcove. Clay pots stood almost decoratively in the corner. Here and there roughly circular patches of

160

the wall had peeled back to reveal the original small grey stones. Small shuttered windows, very far up on the walls, were the only source of light available.

Aurora watched Cynthia dismount from her standing position on the bed. She had been peeping out of one of these windows. Aurora tried to give a half-smile.

"You are supposed to be helping me change into something suitable for a feast," she reminded her pretend lady-in-waiting.

"Well I do not know what to do either!" pouted Cynthia, wrinkling her face. "Who can understand these odd human dresses, with all their fastenings and clips?!"

Aurora put her golden head into her hands. "I am meant to be sending information to King Iubdan. I have written down the names of the main Knights, how many they command; who he trusts with certain tasks – the relative fighting merits of Sir Asher, Sir Nehemiah-"

"Sir Kish."

"Yes, Sir Kish too..." Aurora drifted off thoughtfully. After a short reverie, she restarted with great intensity, "But tell me, Cynthia, can you still perform this task with a clear conscience?"

Images were flashing and overlapping in Aurora's mind: the children of Niebelheim; the injuries and devastation; Majeseerum as it was; the blood of the cow; Majeseerum as a wasteland.

Seeing Cynthia's mute bewilderment, she further explained: "I did not – though there was a war, and I heard stories of battle – I did not think fairies could, or would do such things. Those things that we saw this morning." Aurora shuddered.

Cynthia wished to reply very wisely, but did not have time to construct a sentence at all, let alone a wise one. The sound of a huge gong shivered through the sand and stone walls; within a few moments there was an insistent banging on the wooden panels of the door.

The surly constable of the castle, with jangling keys at his waist and wearing important looking chain-mail, met their tentative peep.

"Your presence is demanded by the King in the Banqueting Hall," he told them, in no very condescending manner.

Aurora visibly swallowed something – it may have been her hackling pride – and said with perfect calm: "We are prisoners at the King's pleasure, and will be honoured to do whatever he requests of us."

The Constable sniffed, and stood back from the door with a smirk on his face. Aurora issued from the room with dignity, Cynthia trotting edgily after her.

They were led to a spacious hall, covered in huge wall hangings that were mainly obscured by dust and washed out by sand. Rushes were scattered the length of the grubby stone floor.

An open fire roared on the ground in the bottom left corner, warming the rows upon rows of benches that filed down vertically from the Head table.

They were purposefully seated as far from this Board of Consequence as humanly (or fairily) possible. The constable, after jilting them along with the smellier, dirtier members of the banquet with a visible sag of relief, made his way up to the raised platform.

The fairies could only turn about with confusion and alarm as the feasting began. A jangling chord of music started up painfully close to their sensitive ears. Lutes and little trumpets tooted along as entertainers burst into the hall, blowing fire, tumbling about and waggling their fingers with their thumb against their nose.

"I think Prince Deucalion would like it here," was all Aurora could think to whisper to Cynthia.

But this was where the similarity to fairy practice

ended. Neither was very able to conceal her horror as a whole stuffed peacock with its tail fanned out was paraded through the tables, closely followed by a line of chickens on a spit.

"What – what have they done to those animals?" demanded Cynthia in the desperate tones of a child wishing to be reassured that her over active imagination had been deceiving her again. Aurora saw her friend's eyes welling with tears and looked down at her trencher on the table.

"Am I supposed to eat this? What *is* this?!"

Amid the raucous noises of the feast, they were suddenly interrupted by a deliberate cough behind them. Cynthia clattered her cutlery loudly as she jumped round to see Sir Asher and a tall, elegant lady beside him.

"Sorry – sorry," stumbled the Knight, half amused. "This is Lady Urvasi, kinswoman to our beloved Queen…" he trailed off awkwardly. No less awkwardly, he met Lady Urvasi's gaze and indicated the fairies. "These are our – well – the – they come from the tribe of Boanerges, as I told you," he finished, as if that would explain everything.

Aurora let out a snort, which perhaps sounded more contemptuous than she intended. "Alas, Knights are always in battle and ill qualified for such graces as introductions. Your friend means we are prisoners seeking asylum. My name is Lady Aurora – this is my girl in waiting, Cynthia."

Lady Urvasi nodded politely and looked almost like she wanted to smile, but could not quite let herself.

"We thought it a very rude action to seat you so far away," she explained calmly. "Though you are *prisoners*, as you consider yourselves, you are still human beings – and moreover, ladies. If you were Boanerge Knights, I could understand the possible danger – but a lady deserves to be treated like a lady."

She showed her clean teeth very quickly and sat herself next to Aurora with perfect ease.

"That is very noble of you. I can see you were related to the Queen," Aurora invented with the barest hint of a blush – though Urvasi did not see it, for it appeared as a freckle.

A few dishes were now petering down to their distant table. They looked much plainer than the delicacies at the top table, much to the relief of the fairies.

"I am afraid it will be cold and tasteless by the time it reaches us," Lady Urvasi commented touchily, adding under her breath a sentence from which Aurora only caught the words "abominable rudeness".

As fairies never eat cooked food, and are very unused to anything but nuts and berries, this remark caused Cynthia to cast the most bemused glance at Aurora which said "Why on earth would they – they wouldn't – they couldn't have *warm* food? Surely?!"

But if Lady Urvasi did see this guileless look and think it odd, her musing on it was interrupted by Sir Asher, who had until now sat gazing with glazed eyes and his chin propped up on his hands.

"Besides, it would benefit the King to befriend you," he came out with irrelevantly. "As Boanerges, you are well versed in fairy law. Is that not right? I found some documents once, in a Boanerge stronghold, which lead me to believe if anyone knows how to beat the fairies, it is your people."

The irony almost prompted the fairies to laugh, but Aurora managed to catch herself in time to reply: "Certainly, we know much about the ways of the winged people."

Food reached them. The humans began heaping spoonfuls onto their trenchers, and the fairies, after viewing it dubiously for a while, were forced to follow the example.

"Sir Asher is right, of course," nodded Lady Urvasi after swallowing her first mouthful. "You only have to see what Sir Kish did to Majeseerum to realise what the Boanerges can do with all their learning and superstitions."

Cynthia, who was bravely raising a morsel to her mouth, paused mid way and put it down again. "Sir – Sir Kish was the one who managed to break the defences?"

"Practically all by himself," Asher answered sullenly.

"Gracious!" breathed Cynthia, and gaped at the bronze and dark red Knight sitting at the head table with frank admiration. Aurora also turned towards Sir Kish, but her look was of a different nature.

"How did he do it?"

"A fairy ring, I believe. He managed somehow to use their magic against them, which proved disastrous to their armies." Asher shook his head as if he disapproved deeply of Kish's risky tactics. "Why, the fairy armour from all accounts was little other than gossamer and leaves; their weapons but spears and wooden frivolities. They obviously became complacent, little thinking they would need something other than their magic."

"Of course," gasped Aurora. "Fairies should never, ever fight against one another... I cannot imagine what would happen if magic was used against like magic." Then, feeling she had said too much, added: "Even our tribe's extensive knowledge has not discovered *that*."

"Well, Kish discovered it. He discovered many things, from the tales he tells. Of course, they could just be tales – with Kish I would not be surprised. But the stories he has of fairy land! Laseri, I think they call it. You would not believe it: colours no human has ever seen, every gust of wind sounding like a symphony."

Simultaneously, Aurora and Cynthia closed their

eyes and sighed, desperately trying to recall that place and those feelings it inspired. It all seemed so very, very far away now.

"I remember being taught, as a child, from one of our huge old books," said Aurora as she opened her eyes, "that there was a time of perfect peace and harmony between the humans and the fairies. Fairies were humankind's – were *our* – guides in all matters. They taught us to plant crops, tame animals and imitate the angels. But we stopped farming and playing music and began to fight, desolate the land and curse. In sorrow the fairies left and started to forget us, even to the point where they no longer realised they were created as our protectors. That was when true fairy ways distorted into the revelling, hedonistic and shameful paths we see them taking now." Aurora perceived she had been speaking very passionately, although not loudly, and had transfixed her listeners with a surprised and confused interest. "Of course," she said with a mock laugh, "that's probably just a story."

Lady Urvasi chuckled good-naturedly. "Oh, these tales!" she said, patting Asher on the arm. "We shoot ourselves in the foot by exiling the Boanerges, we really do! Sweet little stories; just as if *fairies* had a code of honour like Knights!"

Both the humans laughed – Asher more restrainedly – whilst the fairies tried their very best to look as if, instead of being mortifyingly patronised, they were very much enjoying the joke.

Asher saw rather swiftly that the Lady Aurora was not relishing this whooping response to what she evidently took as a serious story. Even he, with all his newly acquired bitterness and broken down soul, found that the tale stirred in him remnants of what he used to feel so strongly. "I wish I could say, Lady Urvasi, that the Knights

166

still had a code of chivalry… but as we have seen today at Niebelheim, they begin to fall sadly short of the mark."

Aurora looked up as she heard the echo of a sentiment she felt herself for her own people. How bizarre that sworn enemies, divided as far as far could be, could mourn for the same loss in two utterly different races! If she did not quite smile, at least something of the emotion showed in her aspect, for she took on a sudden brightness which made Asher look at her and then look down, embarrassed.

"Well," said Lady Urvasi, rubbing her hands, "we are none of us perfect, but I hope you will not hold your exile against us. I was once a Riveron; we are all now one big tribe. That was why the Temple was built. I hope you will both treat me like one of your tribe. I hope that you will join me and my ladies in my apartments."

She looked at the fairies with such a winning smile that they could hardly deny her.

"And what is more," she continued, "I will fetch you something nice to eat. Anything you like. You do not look as if you enjoyed your meal."

"Quite frankly," cried Cynthia, "it is disgusting."

Luckily Lady Urvasi found this very entertaining. She laughed very heartily and buried her head on Sir Asher's shoulder.

"For now we must return," she said once the fit was over. She dried her eyes. "We will be missed. But you will come to me straight after dinner? You will not forget?"

"No," Aurora assured her, "we will not forget."

21

CHAPTER TWENTY-ONE

Meanwhile, King Iubdan was pacing up and down the corridors of his fine white fairy palace. Ferns fluttered above his head with a noise like the brushing together of his own wings. It looked more like a bowery walk than a passage, with all kinds of flowers blooming from each side. In the night sky the fairy King observed the moving, flickering yellow discs of fairy lights, and heard the murmurs of shouts along to fairy music far away. He let out a sound of disgust. Then he swept himself into a majestic and awe-inspiring pose, as if awaiting something.

What he expected suddenly became apparent. The air wavered, like it does in immense heat, before splitting open in a fountain of cascading light. Minuscule fairies danced on this river in the air, winding down and down until they touched the floor. Once grounded they returned to normal size, revealing themselves to be a gaggle of noisy, merry faced revellers, led by the glowing Prince Deucalion.

Through laughter, they looked respectfully at the King. His eyes were grey as stones and unmoving. Perceiving this anger, they turned to Deucalion for reassurance. He was as unmoved and chirpy as ever.

"I congratulate you on the destruction of another human village," said the King, with a voice strangely devoid of congratulation for such a sentence. "I wish now to discuss the matter with the Prince. Be gone and rest, for tomorrow we embark again."

The fairies did not need to be told twice. Running to the crystal pool at the end of the corridor, they dove in and disappeared from sight.

When the water stopped swirling, all fell still. The King glared at his son with a levelling gaze, but the Prince rocked carelessly back and forth on the balls of his feet, humming the remnants of a tune.

"Clearly my age is showing. Tell me, young Prince, since you evidently know more, why we are celebrating?"

"Oh, I know," Deucalion sighed. He commenced in a flat, colourless tone. "How can we ever smile again now Majeseerum has fallen, is it really happiness to take a human village when we are meant to protect them, isn't it ridiculous to keep the soldiers up when they are meant to be fighting tomorrow?"

King Iubdan's chest swelled at this unflattering imitation of himself, but restricted himself to saying: "Precisely. And so...?"

Prince Deucalion rolled his eyes and cracked his fingers. "Father, father! We must keep them on side. See how they love me – the soldiers, the astrals! And who can blame them? I give them gifts, reward for service, parties and outlets from the war. It is extremely condescending of me. They regard me as quite one of their own. And that makes them do my bidding, you know."

"The reward should be in the service! The way of fairies... But I will not cover this with you now. I have received a letter from Aurora Optilete."

The Prince looked interested. "Oh yes? And what does the lovely little fay say?"

The King pulled the parchment out of his robe. "I will let you read it yourself when you are in a more sober frame of mind, my child. It is as we suspected: there is a seer. But for some reason she is not convinced he has been used as an instrument against us. He does not reveal all he is told to the human King, it seems."

Deucalion snatched the letter. He glanced at the writing and raised his eyebrows. "Well, well. A decent human, still. An encouraging thought! But has she found out how they took Majeseerum?"

"Yes," replied Iubdan, sounding choked. He pointed to the paragraph containing the information and coughed. "The rings."

"Goodness! Of course!" Deucalion burst out laughing and put his forehead in his hands. The King looked in horror at his strange mirth. "But the effect filters out after the fairy owner is dead, am I right?"

Looking troubled, the King nodded. "I thought Cynthia and Aurora would be better off there, unsuspected. Especially Aurora – she is the last female of the noble bloodline. I thought if the humans attacked the Colosseum, as they are bound to do, at least we could save her."

"Save her as the next heir to the throne, should I die without produce." Deucalion stated.

"Why, yes. But you know I intended her for your wife long ago. If *she* dies, you would have to marry… some common fairy." The King turned up his nose at the idea.

Deucalion laughed. "Indeed, who could ever prefer a common fairy to that goddess of a fay? But the point I am making father, which you do not seem to understand, is that if we die, Aurora will be Queen."

The King breathed out exasperated. "Yes, she would be Queen. But what does that signify, in this crazy time? Humans are using our rings against us, Deucalion. Can you not see the enormity of that? We did let the fays – Aurora and Cynthia – take their rings for their protection, but now I am more concerned than ever for their safety."

Prince Deucalion gave an odd little smile. "I think you should be more concerned, father, with how much you trust Aurora Optilete."

At this time, when the outlying villages stood at most risk, the human King and his army felt it most necessary to congregate around the capital of Iblees. Though it had been made barren with a scorching wind, and the sand was so hot only hoofed animals could stand upon it, Iblees remained the Capital, and either through fear or a desperate nostalgia for what it had been, Joel clung to it.

Besides, there were many useful occupations for the Knights in that noble city. For example, his two greatest warriors, Asher and Kish, could approach those strange Boanerges ladies and charm them out of their prized fairy rings.

King Joel was deeply interested to discover the effects of these rings upon the wearer. Therefore he instructed Sir Asher and Sir Kish to find out what dim secrets that moonstone jewellery had whispered to the ladies, and why exactly the rings had not yet vanished or broken, like the one used to pillage Majeseerum.

"After which, I trust you will find a way to use them to our advantage," said Joel from his now rather dilapidated throne. "That is what I employ you for, after all."

Sir Kish, clearly spotting it was he the King addressed, presented a smug face to Asher. "Of course. And if these ladies are so good as to aid the great progress of the reign of King Joel, I wonder if he might not let them remain in the kingdom? It would be a great favour to me, as they are, after all, my kinswomen. But if I speak out of line and presume upon the King's grace, I am sure he, who is as just as he is merciful, will stop and pardon me here."

Joel rewarded Kish with a very curious expression and then burst out laughing. "What, let them stay and put one of my greatest Knights in jeopardy? Oh, Kish, Kish! A lady in waiting? You cannot marry her. She does not even know how to make a fire. What *do* they teach these women in your tribe, eh?"

Kish laughed good-humouredly at himself in response. Asher could not help feeling like he had missed something.

It jarred against him suddenly to see proof of Kish's closeness to Joel. Asher was more a friend of young Prince Elihu now than of his father. Years ago, Joel would have told him the moment he suspected something like Kish's liking for the Lady Cynthia. They would have discussed and joked over it together. Asher felt this change all the more strongly because now he was actually in need of someone to tell him all these things. For some strange reason, any symptoms of affection between Sir Kish and Lady Cynthia had completely passed him by. The sudden realisation that there could be an attachment, or even marriage between this coupled filled him with an inexplicable terror.

King Joel stopped laughing and looked thoughtful. "And yet, she does not know that. She does not know you cannot marry her."

Something almost like pain passed through Kish's eyes, but it did not come across in his voice as he said with comprehension: "The Lady Cynthia, at least, would be more willing to give up secrets to her betrothed lover."

Asher experienced a curious sickness.

King Joel traced the toe of his shoe across the dusty floor. "Well, I cannot promise them anything yet. Why not let them have their fun here while they can, poor things? Let us have a dance or a festivity of some sort."

Asher found himself speaking before he could prevent himself. "A dance," he repeated blandly. "You are actually going to have a dance in the middle of tense, stale-mate warfare? Why not invite the fairies too, while you're at it? I'm sure they would provide some fireworks for us."

There was a silence. "Come, come," replied the King in a threatening voice, "do you really believe the fairies can defeat the chosen King, and without Majeseerum? Moreover, how exactly do you dream they would know my Knights are not prowling the perimeters of my kingdom, ready to strike their next major city? Do you really think that I, Joel, your King, would allow these things to happen?"

There was only one answer, and Asher gave it most unwillingly.

"Good. In which case, you *shall* go to the dance. Now you may both leave my presence."

Not only the frivolity, but the heartless honey-trap nature of the proceeding rankled Asher at his core. Unfortunately, Kish seemed to interpret the foul look upon his face as an unwillingness to dance.

"Come, Asher," he said, thumping him on the back. "For the good of the kingdom."

Night fell harsh and cold upon the sands. No one was particularly inclined to be outside in the heavy dark on the freezing dunes with the dust whirling all around, even though the rough beaten trees were strewn with lanterns.

Very little dancing went on. The people had forgotten how to dance. They could only remember how to fight, which could be a type of dancing in itself, and it satisfied them. Instead they congregated in small groups to chatter and listen to the wind-blown notes of the lutes.

Asher found the two ladies of the Boanerges were the sole pair impervious to the chilly temperature. Cynthia was mumbling the words of a song under her breath whenever the flutes or lyres started up. She trailed off when he approached, as if she were afraid to be heard.

"Hello there," she said with an awkward curtsey. Her eyes grew large and she tried very tactlessly to shield Aurora, who stood behind her, bent over something

"Good evening," he replied, and just as unsubtly craned his neck over her to see what Aurora was doing.

At the sound of his deeper voice, Aurora rose with a swift and graceful movement. She turned towards him in a flash of sparkling robes, her long hair sprinkled with jewels. A brief half smile was all he received by way of a greeting. She was then apparently content to ignore him, but all the same stepped back from what had previously engrossed her.

As she did so, part of her white robe moved like a curtain and revealed a fresh little face grinning in the lamp light.

"Elihu!" Asher pulled the boy from his cross-legged position on the floor. The child gave a laughing screech and swung from his arm. "I didn't even think you were allowed to be here. Stand up! What *is* that gunk around your eyes?"

Asher shook Elihu by his shoulders and held him. There were odd smears under the rims of his huge boyish eyes. Asher brushed them away with his thumbs.

"I was tired," Elihu defended himself, "and the ladies said it would make me wake up."

It may have just been the wind and the strange glints of lantern light, but there seemed something deeply sinister about this substance to Asher.

The ladies were looking knowingly at one another. Their unearthly beauty and the rays of the crystal jewellery dangling from them suddenly made Asher shiver.

"Clover, thyme and mushroom compound," Aurora

listed, rolling her pale eyes.

"Anyone would think we'd hurt the child," complained Cynthia. "Look at how refreshed he is."

"I feel *much* better," jumped in little Elihu, physically jumping forwards as he said it. He was about to say something else, but an object seemed to attract his eye. Asher could not see anything. Elihu tilted his head, looked engrossed and wandered off.

He tried to follow the Prince, but soon lost him amongst the squeeze of chain mail and dresses with panniers. Every breath of wind now felt like it was freezing him with a mild flush of panic.

By the time he returned to his two so-called hostages, they were looking very pleased with themselves.

"Do not fear for the safety of the child," Aurora told him calmly before he could say a word.

Seeing it would be pointless to go over with her how important the young Prince was, and the danger he could fall into alone on a dark cold desert, Asher visibly slumped.

A sudden random thought troubled him.

"Where did you get it from?"

"Get what?"

"The compound." He raised his head and gestured to the smooth and unaltered surface of the sand. "There hasn't been thyme or clover here for more years than I care to remember."

Silence. Aurora returned his gaze, steady and expressionless.

Cynthia freckled and looked about to either side. The pressure was too much for her. Without ceremony, she pretended to see something an idled off, ever so slightly in the direction of Sir Kish, who quickly intercepted her.

Now friendless and alone with Sir Kish, Aurora had nowhere to go. Knowing it was rude and probably suspicious to say nothing, she very calmly told him: "We are fond of flowers, my lady-in-waiting and I. Sometimes," she lowered her voice, and for a moment her eyes looked almost dark, "we walk into the forest in search of them. But you probably shouldn't tell your King that."

For a moment Aurora feared she had said too much, though being a regal fairy, she did not show her fear above sticking her lower lip out a little and flashing her eyes, bright as a knife blade.

Sir Asher spoke. "Follow me." He turned on his spurred heel and walked off at such a fast pace that Aurora had no time for thought and was compelled to follow him.

It seemed they walked for a very long time thus; he striding purposefully forward, she following the dark shape always just within sight.

They entered Glass Mountain Castle – a strange, lumpy growth it appeared from the outside in this light. Along shadowy corridors, past ghostly mullioned windows they trod, until they reached a chamber with a faint candle guttering inside.

Asher entered. Aurora waited on the threshold as he picked up the candle. Asher smiled and beckoned to her to come in.

"Look," he whispered, pulling out a loose sandy coloured brick from the wall. He drew out an old beaten book, the leaves of which fell open at a clearly much returned to place. Aurora came towards him, curious to see.

Very slowly, he drew from the book's pages a pressed stem of heather. Almost reverently he handed it to Aurora, twirling it so that the dead dried bells flamed in the spirit of their original purple for a few moments under the candle light. "Here."

Aurora's face took on the eager glint of a child's. She accepted the stem, held it to the light, and stuffed it eagerly into her mouth.

Asher let out a yell which extinguished the candle. "What are you doing? What on Earth do you think you are doing?" he barked into the darkness.

Aurora, terrified, felt all at sea. She tried to pinpoint which of her actions had been so terribly wrong. Then it hit her with a shame that produced a fair few freckles. "Oh. I take it your people don't eat that?"

"Eat it? No, no they don't! What sort of tribe are the Boanerges?!"

Asher fumbled in the dark for something to light the candle with. He could find nothing. "Do you even know what that *was*?"

Somehow, the candle was lit again, and he found himself gazing into her clear eyes, which suddenly appeared shadowed with grief and confusion.

"I – I do not know if we have the same word for the plant," she said hesitantly.

Asher swallowed, and felt immediately weak for making a fuss about a plant. "It – it was the last of the heather. The heather which used to cover the moors when we had plants, grass and crops. It was the last."

"I am so sorry."

There was no keeping anger with this charming creature, even though Asher knew it was right to stay angry. He hung his head. "Well, it is right it should all go. There is no use clinging to the past. I must look forward."

"So you must. There will be more where it came from." Aurora rose to leave, and saw an ill repressed tear slide down Asher's cheek. Her pity welled up in indescribable volumes. She paused, apparently deep in thought, then continued in a rash voice: "Remember, it was not the last." She pointed behind him, turned and fled.

Asher, shaking his head in bafflement, looked to the window sill she had indicated. Upon it were two long stems of heather, smelling and blooming as sweetly as if they had just been cut.

22

CHAPTER TWENTY-TWO

Kish knew his route through the sands now. He knew it as thoroughly as if there had been clear landmarks pointing him to Green Glow forest. His fascination had often led him this way, despite any misgivings.

His ears were tuned to the silent night air; he could hear the whispering of the Deevs from far away, when before he would have heard nothing.

Kish thought it a very beautiful night. The sky was full of twinkling stars and the air was crisp. His senses were fully awake; his mind was infected with the dancing and the time he had spent with the Lady Cynthia.

Kish did not hesitate, as he used to, when he reached the edge of the forest. He marched straight in like he owned the place, fearless and resolute.

The voice that came at his ear, as loud as if someone had been leaning over him, did not surprise him or make him jump.

"You are doing well, Sir Kish. Our strength grows daily. It will soon be in our power to make you King."

Kish stared deeply into the pitch black of the trees. "I need something a little more immediate. Help killing the fairies, for a start."

There was a tittering, and the leaves around him shivered ominously. "This sounds like ingratitude, Kish. Who was it, after all, who gave you the map to

Majeseerum and made you great? It is not our fault you took so long to use it." The voice did not sound as friendly as it used to. It sounded positively threatening.

Kish backed away slightly. He was wondering if he could find his way swiftly to the entrance of the forest in this darkness. "I had to wait. I needed to know I could beat the fairies when I got there. You can't imagine how long it took me to find a fairy ring. And now there are two within my reach – and I just cannot get at them!"

Silence. The voice recommenced, softened. "So you want our help in obtaining these rings? I am not sure there is anything we can do."

Kish sighed. The rings were only part of what he wanted. He realised that deep within him he had come to ask for something quite different, but he could not now he was here. "I want – I want the ones who bear the rings to stay in Iblees. Joel does not seem too keen on the idea. They are Boanerges, you see. I want to keep them. I want my family back."

There was a snicker. Kish's chest flamed in hurt pride; a blaze through the quiet, dark night.

"What you are saying," said the voice, "is that you have chosen a Queen."

Kish contemplated the night air. "I do not know," said Kish meditatively. "Perhaps. What I *do* know is I shall never be King if these fairies carry on destroying our villages, and I will never see my tribe again. To beat the fairies I need the fairy rings. To get the fairy rings, I need your help. There must be something you can do."

A pause. Kish could hear the muffled sound of a thousand whispering voices. At last, the voice replied. "Of course. We are never *quite* helpless. Have you heard, Sir Kish, of a being called a Drake?" Kish did not like to appear ignorant. He hesitated in what he thought was an intelligent way, and replied, "I – I do

180

not completely recollect."

"Let us refresh your memory. There are amongst our kind, ones which we call Drakes. They are wonderful creatures, formed specifically for guarding treasure – be it gold, home or...person."

The voice stopped unexpectedly. "Yes. Yes, I recollect," said Kish, feeling he must say something. He felt vaguely uncomfortable about the voices tonight, but he could not say why. "But how could a Drake help me?"

"They love treasure," explained his invisible interlocutor. "They live to make their masters thrive. They would not let harm come to those fairy rings you hold so dear – or those who bear them."

This was interesting. Kish cocked his head to the side. "Would they let harm come to me in battle?"

"Dear me, no! They would attack your enemies," said the voice, hurt by the implication.

Kish regarded a particular tree. He found it helped to concentrate on a particular object and imagine the voice was coming from it. It stopped him from feeling quite as insane.

"Why have you not mentioned this before? I could have died anytime these past few years!"

A whimper from the forest. The tree branches groaned. "Do not be angry, Sir Kish! How could we speak to you of these things? You seemed so unsure; you did not trust us. If you are truthful, you will admit you did not really believe we were not something to do with the fairies until you found Majeseerum."

Kish felt a little guilty. It was very hard to converse with or reassure something you could not see. He hung his head slightly. "It always pays to be careful. Especially with fairies. You can never be sure."

"Your wisdom does you credit," soothed the voice, rapidly over its upset. "But while you were uncertain – I hope you are not still uncertain – we could not offer you such a thing as a Drake."

Kish pouted. This was bordering upon a harsh reflection on him. "If you really wanted to make me King-"

"Sir Kish, Sir Kish!" The voice was shockingly loud now, and right inside his head. Kish froze, feeling very vulnerable. He was half convinced these voices could read his thoughts. "You must not resent us. A Drake, you see, requires someone to be completely on our side. Once you have a Drake, you cannot go back. A Drake requires a very serious pact."

Kish trembled. He felt on the brink of a great event, but he could not tell if it would be a fortunate or abysmal occurrence. Part of him longed to flee the forest. Yet no matter how far he ran, he was not sure he would be free. These Deevs knew so much. It was much wiser to be for them than against them. And despite his hatred of fairies, some queer fascination was leading him back on a daily basis to Green Glow forest. He was not certain he would be able to stop now.

Other than prudence and fear, ambition joined to root him to the spot. Besides his own resources – extensive as they were – these Deevs were the only ones who could help him beat the fairies forever. Joel would aid him about as much as the Fairy King himself, and Asher seemed rather to want to be conquered. Kish's mind expanded with the noble deed he would be doing to rid the world of fairies; his mind's eye saw him remembered in history. And then there was the prospect of the Crown, Glass Mountain Castle, Queen Cynthia, Iblees at his command... Whilst there was a chance of achieving this, he would be a fool indeed to run now.

"What kind of pact?" Kish asked through a very dry throat.

"One which will require your complete allegiance. It

is better that your Drake himself should explain."

"And where will I find him?" Kish looked around with startled eyes. Every shadow seemed to take on a strange form, and any of a thousand shapes he saw could have been a Drake to his mind.

The voice did not reply, but there was a faint sizzling above his head. Kish looked up and saw the trees lit with hundreds of tiny little flames. One leaf on each tree was glowing the colour of fire, and guiding a path.

Kish knew he was to follow it. Very slowly, he put one foot in front of the other and began on the path. His legs were not completely stable. He did not know what he would do when he reached his destination. He tried to swallow his pride. It would take a lot of reassurance and convincing to get him to make a pact with one of these creatures. Kish felt it would be a debasement for a Boanerge.

But if what they said was true – and he certainly had no reason to doubt them so far – what then? His mind raced and his heart rejoiced at the millions of possibilities. Kish walked faster and with a lighter step. If they could do him good, if they could help him in his life, if they could watch over him – wouldn't that be wonderful?

Thinking back, Asher noted it was shortly after the heather incident that life started getting blurry. Concentration became increasingly difficult, and seeing a sign next to impossible.

He was aware of his brain becoming like a giant smudge, incapable of any thought – except when he was thinking over little incidents of the past again, and again, and again. At times there were moments of complete clarity which hit him like a blast of cold air – but he could not hold on to them. These clear moments ultimately depressed him, as the only purpose they served was to horrendously contrast his old brain with the confused grind he now kept inside his head.

Lady Aurora, on the contrary, grew every hour, so it seemed, a little brighter. She looked strong and happy.

Asher had seen Aurora that morning, with Urvasi and Cynthia, from his window. They were laughing and picking the mushrooms which had somehow grown where the dance had taken place the other night. He envied all three of them their carefree glee, and their vigour.

Some hours may have passed before the three ladies came back inside. Asher did not know – he had no conception of where the time had gone, or how he had spent it. But he saw them enter the Castle. They did not regard him.

Lady Aurora looked ethereal and shining as she walked up the uneven staircase, he noticed, and to his horror, she noticed that he noticed. There was a circlet on her fair hair and a star upon her forehead, the skin of which beamed white as snow. She must have felt his eye upon her. Her lips, red as rowanberry, curved ever so slightly as she turned to look at him.

Suddenly, she grimaced. Her moonstone ring, stolen from a fairy, had snagged on the banister. Asher could see even from his position standing bored before the King's throne, that it was bent. He watched with compassion as Aurora gaped down at her almost ruined jewellery, thunderstruck, and galloped up the stairs.

Then he returned, subdued, to listen to Joel's continued drone.

"... and some new course of action is necessary. And so, Sir Asher – the fine and mighty Sir Asher, as our villagers are calling you – what does it mean?"

Asher only knew what Joel's tone meant. He always became increasingly barbed and sarcastic when he was afraid. Asher could see jealousy, suspicion and fear in the glaring eyes of the King.

Asher felt a heavy longing for Joel to realise that he was his friend. He need not fear the fairies, for Asher would stand by him. He need not fear losing the love of his people, or the love of his son to Asher. But he did, all the same.

"Mushrooms," debated Alfred in a musing voice. "Does it mean the fairies are near? Their fruitful world overlapping into ours as they approach?"

There was a general murmur of worry. Many pale faces turned towards Asher. He tried very hard to look like he had all the answers.

"Of course not," interrupted Sir Kish from the circle of Knights. "They are a sign that we will prosper!"

The point was loudly argued. Joel did not appear to be listening, or doing anything except brooding darkly.

Asher refrained from comment. He was sure the sky had become darker whilst listening to the same facts repeated again and again, and wondered vaguely how long he had been standing there. Though it was awful to admit, he had his mind on other things than the war, and these other things seemed inexplicably more important.

Eventually, both arguing sides fell silent and looked to the throne, each trying their hardest to look convincing.

"And what does Sir Asher say?" drawled King Joel at last. "He is curiously restrained about the subject."

"It is too early to tell, your Majesty." Asher felt it wise to be as respectful as possible when Joel was in this frame of mind.

"You do not *want* to tell me," returned Joel moodily.

There are certain situations that have to be handled very carefully. When a monarch, with the power of beheading you at any chosen moment, thinks you are withholding information from him, you can be sure it is one of those situations. Asher paused to think of the most political response. If Joel was angered any further while he was in this mood, there was no knowing what he might do.

It was very unfortunate that Elihu chose that moment to come swooping into the room and fuss about Asher.

"Zoom! Zoom!" he cried with arms outstretched to the side, running forwards and backwards.

"Will someone have that child removed from the room?!" demanded Joel testily. His angry eyes looked with intense jealousy at Asher. "What *are* you doing?" he asked the Prince without even moving on his throne.

Elihu swooped again, and then screamed. The whole court covered their ears with their hands. Only Asher looked slightly amused.

"What *they* are doing! The giant insects," the Prince giggled.

Whilst the rest of the court murmured and told Elihu to be less imaginative – to behave himself like a proper, uninventive Prince – Asher moved towards the throne in alarm.

"We must go outside. Give me permission to mobilise the archers."

Joel looked derisively at his friend. "Scared of the huge locusts from Elihu's mind are we?"

Asher would not even waste the time in sighing. It was here – a moment of perfect, pure clarity – and he would not let it go unused. Especially over something this important.

"I think he may mean something else. We must go to the houses of the workers."

Everyone turned to look.

Asher's energetic haste had the unwanted effect of making Joel more determined to provoke him by replying particularly slowly. "Oh, must we? Last time I looked, I was King. Whatever would you have me go there for? Leaving Glass Mountain Castle undefended?"

"By all means keep a guard here, but everyone else must be spared to go," cried Asher, increasingly loud and desperate. "Please!"

The other advisors and Knights were alarmed by Asher's tone. A worried chatter spread.

The King looked confused and sceptical, but Asher bore his eyes through the back of Joel's skull; he made Joel look at him.

"Trust me," he said simply, and for a moment, it was almost like they were simple shepherds again.

But the trust did not spring half as readily into Joel's face as it used to. He fought internally with something. His brow hardened. Then, all at once, he said in a phlegmatic tone: "Very well." Joel raised his hand.

The soldiers, having sensed the panic in Asher's voice, leapt into a frenzy of action. Running boots, rapid movement and cries of preparation replaced the atmosphere of bored tension that had filled the hall but moments before.

It was not the worker's huts; Asher had been wrong there. But as soon as the feet of the Knights left the drawbridge, they knew he had not made them leave the Throne Room in vain.

In the endlessly burning blue sky that scorched above the sandy land, there hung a cloud. A huge, black rain cloud, such as they had not seen since the days when the earth was covered in heather and gorse. Nothing could look so oddly out of place as that giant ink blot floating in the same air which had not housed even a white, wispy cloud for so many years.

Many of the Knights drew up short at the very wonder of it, leaving Asher to gallop on ahead alone.

"It's a miracle," whispered one of Sir Nehemiah's men.

"We will have rain again at last!"

The archers reacted with more fear than awe. They shivered as the sun dipped behind the dark cloudy mass. They did not want to follow their leader in that direction. They could not trust this sign to be a good thing.

All of the army, however, raised their heads in expectation of feeling the first drops of blessed water on their faces. Quiet and concentrated, they waited.

It was then they heard the screams.

The cloud was flashing, but not with lightning. Small darts were falling down, but they were not raindrops.

"Come *on!*" screamed Asher, returning to the archers, and they hesitated no more.

They were jumping over bodies long before they were directly underneath the cloud. Dead men clutched parts of transparent wings; mingled stains of deep red and glittering purple congealed the dust. Although there were precious few landmarks in the wasteland, Asher could tell they were heading towards Sir Kish's small castle.

The desert was shaken by gusts of wind like a giantess shaking her petticoats. Scratching sand flew into the eyes of the Knights and archers. Barely able to stand, Asher shielded his face and looked up.

He had never seen a fairy before. At once beautiful and dreadful, a whole swarm of them wheeled through the sky, covered in green mantles with golden tassels and golden helmets. Whether it was the sun reflecting off these helmets, or something else, Asher found he was forced to squint at the great light burning around them.

Stranger still, over all the cries of human pain, and the muffling wind of the sand storm, he could hear a haunting, unbearably sweet melody. The power of enchantment breathed through every man standing there, and held him, mesmerised.

A crack split the air. Asher leapt suddenly sideways and fell to the ground. Beside him the ground was burnt black and steaming.

"Archers into formation!" he cried as loud as he could.

Every arrow the human archers fired merely reflected off magical force-fields, which the fairies created each time they sensed a missile approaching them. Sometimes, indeed, the fairies' judgement was confounded, and they exploded in a shower of purple glitter, until the sky was like a red pool of blood. But this was a rare occurrence.

Asher wondered where Kish could be in this great melee. He knew the ways to repel fairies, or claimed to.

Asher remembered that Kish had once told him that fairies were afraid of owls, but he was at a complete and utter loss as to how to acquire one. He even hated himself for the random, ridiculous thought; he, Asher, the great warrior, the slayer of Dybuk! Where were the signs that had guided him in his hour of need every time before? Had they deserted him in this terrifying, awful place? Or were they still there, and only in his hateful, hateful blindness could he neither grasp nor get at them?

Weary, bruised, sweating and bleeding from a wound he did not even remember receiving, Asher raised his eyes in desperation towards the heavens. He saw, beyond the fairies, coming from the shadows of the forest on the horizon, a floating fiery ball.

It grew and grew, streaks of flame flailing out behind it.

Until now, only Asher had noticed, but the attention of all his comrades, and even the fairies, was caught by the stench of rotten eggs diffusing around them.

The ball burst. Outwards shot dragon-like creatures with sinewy necks, made of flame. They did not touch the humans; they streaked back and forth across the fairy cloud.

Asher, putting aside his wonder, took the opportunity of the fairies' distraction to aim his arrows, and evaporate scores of them.

Yet soon Asher was plunged into outright confusion; the fairies, trying to escape the flaming creatures, were swooping around him. Some of the dragon-like things fell, igniting the remains of Sir Kish's home. How could a mere human cope with these scenes? Asher felt he was locked in a battle of the heavenly bodies, where he had no right to be. His archers looked, he thought, nearly distracted out of their minds.

"Drakes! Drakes!" he heard one of the diving fairies cry to a fellow. "Oh, these humans are worse than I thought! A pact with a Drake!"

Eventually the fairies could not cope with the double onslaught. Fighting off the Drakes and the arrows from the humans was too much for their depleted numbers. They massed tightly together, and streaked across the sky like a shooting star.

Without their presence, the rank smell of the dragon creatures – Drakes, apparently – increased. Asher, nearly retching, exchanged a look with Sir Nehemiah. Did they fire upon these things?

Before they could decide, they were knocked backward by a wave of heat. As he lay motionless on the sand, Asher watched the drakes gather up every shiny or golden thing left about the wreckage of the castle or the bodies of the soldiers, and then fizzle out like fireworks.

Then he could keep his eyes open no longer.

23

CHAPTER TWENTY-THREE

Sir Kish wound round and round the spiralling staircase, barely needing to touch the rope which ran along it, so well did he know the steps. The only semblance of light was the distant wavering of torches illuminating some other corridor, which played upon the near walls in spasmodic fits.

No longer weighed down by the tug of armour, Kish galloped upwards effortlessly, his breeches and shirt allowing him to lengthen his stride, his soft boots making no sound on the cold floor. Nevertheless, his face wore a much heavier, more serious expression that it usually did on the field of battle.

He walked past the bedroom of Lady Aurora, pausing only momentarily with a strained ear. Walking a few steps further, he squatted down by the neighbouring sandy wall and began gently to remove a loose brick.

The glowing eyes of Cynthia were already peering into the space he revealed.

"Oh I am glad to see you!" her soft, floating voice said immediately. "I was so frightened today."

"I wish I could tell you it was without reason. But I fear the time we spoke about is fast approaching. You remember the spot?"

"In the forest, by the grove," Cynthia replied straight away. Tears began to swim in her large, dreamy eyes. "Are you sure you will be safe, travelling through there to meet me?"

"Safer than you, my dear!"

"Kish, I'm scared. Scared that if my people find you, they will kill you. How will we ever be together?"

"I will bring you here, of course, after the war has been won. I will persuade the King, never you worry. And as for the Boanerges – why, I am one of their kind! They are more likely to readopt me than murder me. I would be interested in seeing them sometime – my old family. You must talk to them about me – in the future. Far in the future," he added in a comforting voice.

"Oh, far in the future!" Cynthia squealed, disconsolate. "Does that mean – oh, when will I see you again? I do love you so much, Kish."

Kish's eyes disappeared from the gap, which was filled momentarily with the view of the top of his dark head. When he looked up, he was passing something through the gap to her.

"Here. To remember me by when I am not with you – and I think you can guess what else I am trying to say."

Cynthia took the ring and looked at it in bewilderment. No doubt it had some greater significance she was meant to understand. Tearfully, she looked into his eyes – eyes that she trusted – and was on the very verge of apologising and explaining all about being a fairy, and loving him anyway, when he spoke.

"It was the ring they gave me when I became a Knight. It shows my allegiance to the King; you can comprehend how dear it is to me. I want you to wear it."

"Oh." Eager to please, Cynthia quickly put it onto her finger, feeling very touched. A strange human custom indeed! She saw he approved – the limited view she had of his face was full of joy and tenderness. But then she felt rather useless and embarrassed, for he did not speak, and she began to wonder quite what he expected of her.

"Well? Do I get nothing in return, my sweet?"

"Oh dear!" she began to rummage around her. "I am not sure I have anything to give you! Where *is* my handkerchief?"

Kish laughed merrily. "It is normal to give another ring! Have the Boanerges really fallen so far from refinement?"

Electrified, Cynthia whispered, "I only have the one ring! I - I am not supposed to ever, ever-"

Kish's whole aspect darkened. Although Cynthia could not see his lips, she knew they were pouting. "Oh, I see. I thought - well, it does not matter what I thought. I suppose you think I will not get into trouble myself for giving away my own ring? But if I mean so little - if mere jewellery means more-"

"Oh, no, no!" cooed Cynthia desperately. "I did not mean that - look, take it, take it!"

Her heart misgiving heavily within her, she pulled her precious moonstone ring off of her hand, blinking at it to make it large enough to fit on Kish's wider finger.

Kish raised the ring to the gap, kissed it, and put it on. "Do not forget the place, do not forget the times, dear Cynthia. I know I shall not." He gave her one long, serious look, and replaced the brick.

Sir Kish's eyes could not immediately adjust to the increased darkness. He continued to walk, for he knew the route so perfectly, and had some trepidation of being caught if he lingered; but his walk was that of a blind man, seeing nothing but bottomless darkness before him.

Feeling a small sense of pride in not needing to grope along the walls, Kish stepped once more bravely forward, and had the mortifying experience of hitting his forehead straight against a wall.

He recoiled, rubbing his head, although his pride was

the only part of him which really hurt. Devoutly hoping no one had heard, he was about to progress when the wall made his blood run cold by doing a most unconventional thing: it spoke.

"Creeping about at this hour, Sir Kish? Have you no need to rest after that battle? One might almost say it looks suspicious."

Kish instantly recognised Asher's voice, and all fear seeped out of him.

"Ha!" he laughed, although it was not a real laugh. "It is natural, I suppose, to be able to sleep, when you have lost your home, your grounds, and all your possessions? You cannot know what it is like. Kindly let me pass."

Kish could not see in the shadows to move around Asher; he seemed to be always before him, whichever direction he turned.

"Kish..." Asher's voice was no longer sarcastic, taunting or threatening. It made Kish pause and listen. "What *was* that thing?"

Kish shrugged and then realised Asher could not see his shrug. "You should know."

"If – if it was a kind of fairy – why did it come to help us?"

"Drake! It was a Drake, you fool!" For a moment Kish's conceit at his own knowledge overcame his prudence. There was silence for a beat. "Now let me go."

"A Drake," Asher repeated, clearly trying to place the name. "Kish – you actually went into the forest and made a pact with one of those dark creatures?!"

"And a lot of good it did me. I told you inhuman things are not to be trusted, even the Deevs, who hate the fairies. I loathe them all, as I loathe all the people who let my home be destroyed today!"

"Kish, you went into the forest and made a pact – a pact written in blood unless my knowledge fails me.

Anyone would think you were not fighting for our side."

An intense look fizzled between them, although neither of them could see it. Kish shoved past the stationary Asher, and was gone.

Asher stood breathing for a while in the dark. He could hear Kish retreating quickly down the corridors.

With a distant curiosity, Asher realised his heart was beating very fast in his chest, and that his breaths were shallow and quick. There was far too much going on inside his head. All of his back and shoulders felt tense and his brain ached. He did not know if he should tell Joel about Kish – would he be believed? Did he even owe it to Joel to tell him anything? But perhaps Kish was up to nothing, after all. And then there was…

"Who's there?"

A crack of light suddenly thrown into his eyes made Asher squint in pain.

"Is it normal, here, to be running around at this late hour? I was unaware how rude we were being by breaking custom."

Asher sensed his cheeks turn pale, and then glow very hot, as he heard Lady Aurora's weary, tetchy voice.

"No – not at all. Sorry," he stammered. "I was just – sorry. I will leave now."

"I heard voices and steps," continued the lady. He could make her out against the light now, slightly dishevelled, her hand resting against the door. "Not just you. Were you speaking to Lady Cynthia?"

"I – no, I was not." Asher shook his head a little too vehemently. "Perhaps she talks in her sleep."

Lady Aurora rubbed her eyes. "Perhaps she does. Well, goodnight."

He did not know why, but Asher literally could not stop himself from lightly touching her hand.

"Your ring…" he began, laying a finger upon the bent

silver, but he did not make the effort to finish the sentence.

Asher saw her swallow. "Yes. An accident. It got bent. Broken." She shook herself suddenly and shrugged. "Well, we cannot use it to experiment upon after all, can we? It's a pity. Goodnight, Sir Asher."

She gave him a smile, an almost cheeky smile, he thought, and then the door was closed upon him, leaving the darkness, it seemed now, even darker and colder than it had been before.

24

CHAPTER TWENTY-FOUR

The fairies swarmed nearer Glass Mountain Castle every day. They were unstoppable; they never needed to return for food; they could move faster, and with greater surety, than any Knight. The only Knights who tended to survive were those who could combine skilful horse-riding, which increased their speed, with accurate archery (the only sure way to hurt an air-born fairy).

Crawling for a shelter behind some of his fallen comrades bodies, Asher felt an overwhelming pang of guilt. If he had been able to read the signs clearly, if he could concentrate, these blood soaked Knights might have lived to fight again. Only last week, the fairies had attacked a small, out of the way village, and it was not until Asher arrived with his archers that it occurred to him this must be a diversion, so that the winged warriors could get closer to Glass Mountain Castle.

Dodging lightning bolts, which fell from above and left smouldering black stains upon the ground, Asher held his aching head in his hands. There was a struggle, an awful, never ending struggle inside it; it had not even left him alone to sleep for a longer time than he cared to remember.

It was like he was two Ashers – the old one, who could see strange signs but was lonely, dark, and scared; and the new, vital Asher, thoughtless but full of nothing but sunshine and light, who had been created on the day the Boag nearly claimed his life.

He wanted very badly to always be the happy sunny Asher, but something inside him would not give way, would not allow it. The problem was, that new Asher never had a thought in his head about the war, or the signs, or anything much. Except, of course...

He was firing now on automatic pilot. He could not have told you whether he had shot half dozen fairies, or a score of his own men.

This duality in his life was a terrible, terrible weakness; he loathed himself as he realised how heedlessly he had been firing. He recalled with painful shame the hours he had spent recently on one dear, darling project instead of the war effort and winced.

His wince had been a greater one than the occasion called for. When he had finished wincing, he realised that the pain was actually greater, which was not often the case with these things in his experience. Strangely detached, as one observing the scene, Asher saw a slippery, wet red on his hands and the ground around him. It had not been there an instant ago; nor, moreover, had the arrow in his arm.

He raised the injured limb to inspect the damage, but he could barely do that. The arrow head had travelled all the way through his arm, and stuck out the other side. He winced again, and vomited from the pain.

Thus, sitting in a pool of his own blood and sick, Asher waited. He could fire no more arrows like this; he could only wait for victory to be won, hoping to hide under the bodies and pass for one dead, or await calmly his own slaughter.

He did not wait for long. There was a great ringing like an aftershock in his ears, and a wave of red swept across his vision.

He could feel incredible heat, yet, surprisingly, no pain at all, save what was already in his arm. This went on for an extended period.

At last, Asher opened his eyes, and discovered with pleasure that his eyes still worked. He could still hear nothing but the ringing, yet he could see fairies screaming and swarming away. A great red beam shone over them, and was apparently causing them great agony, both in body and in mind. He looked down, and could see the beam originated from Kish, who was holding something up triumphantly towards the sky and warding them away.

Kish fought the fairies now with renewed fury – not a hot-headed fury but a cold, spiteful anger, all the more frightening to behold in its very calmness

After the pain of the red beam had paralysed the fairies, and several had come crashing to the ground, they seemed to collect themselves enough to retreat, still screaming horribly.

Kish began to laugh, just as horribly, and chased them as far as he could with the red-emitting object. But as the cloud of terrified fairies drifted further away, his laugh became strained, and he started to sway. Suddenly, Kish's body gave a great shudder, and he collapsed.

The left guard room had been converted into an infirmary. It was not ideal to have to lay already mangled Knights in the midst of the implements which performed the mangling – and it was very inconvenient that the ladies in waiting had to move the majority of the aforesaid mangling implements to the adjacent room. But the left guard room remained closer to the ground than the soldiers' dormitory, and ensured the wounded could be easily thrown there with the least inconvenience; leaving neither smears of blood along the stairs, nor waking the Knights who had the decency to stay unmangled in the midnight hours.

Asher could barely feel his arm as he was dumped unceremoniously into a corner. The pain had stopped – that was a bonus – but the bluish white colour his arm had turned could not be positive. To take his mind, not to mention his eyes, off the terrible sight, he watched the multitudes of ladies push through the doors and really come into their own. To nurse – to do something – seemed a great excitement to most of them. They bound wounds and daubed with gauze very industriously.

He was surprised to see, and for a moment checked that he did not hallucinate seeing, the Boanerge ladies join them. Their behaviour was less exemplary.

Having stood at the door in a cowed position for the majority of the time she could have been useful, the Lady Cynthia, her eyes alighting upon the motionless Sir Kish, fell into a fit of something near hysterics, even though he had not a spot of blood upon him.

Lady Aurora, as may be expected, was not half so ineffectual, but the service she did perform was a very strange one indeed. She took it upon herself to administer glasses of water to the wounded, and ignore their other injuries completely. He could not see what good it was supposed to do them at all.

Having said that, when the time for his own glass of water came, Asher did not find himself particularly unwilling to receive it. He watched the lady pour it, and saw her drop, by sleight of hand, into it something which looked like a small yellow stone. Dubiously, he drank the liquid. When he put the cup down, he saw that she had removed the arrow from his arm without him noticing. She regarded him in silence, while he could only thank her with his eyes. Impulsively, she gave him a handful of small slippery stones, shaped like the sole of a shoe.

"I think you will put these to better use than anyone

else here, when I cannot," Aurora said, and went to move on.

Asher made a noise. "What -?" he finally managed to say.

Lady Aurora gave a minute laugh. "I call them *Caibe sith*. But I do not think you should try to say that now. I wish your arm better."

She moved towards Sir Kish, seeing that Cynthia would not.

Asher was interested to see not only what was wrong with his comrade, but what Aurora might do for him.

In propping him up from his face-down-spread-eagle position on the floor, Lady Aurora happened to unloose Sir Kish's tightly gripped fist. When she saw what it held – Asher, from his distance, could not – she gave a gasp and a hideous shudder.

Panting, bright eyes flaring, she took the object hurriedly and stuffed it down her stomacher. She then proceeded towards the door, where she gave the Lady Cynthia *such* a look that Asher seriously thought for a moment that she would strike her. But in the end Aurora merely stalked past, high displeasure in every feature.

The disconsolate Cynthia burst into renewed sobs.

The miraculous healing of Asher's arm came as very little surprise to most. He was a sacred man, a man blessed with the sight; of course injury did not befall him for long. He knew they had more important things to worry about, but really, keeping the use of his limb was a big deal to Asher, and he felt the Knights should care just a little more about it.

But they were so busy he could not tell them his theory: that those who Lady Aurora had given water to had survived; and those who she had not had time to see before storming off had not been so fortunate. Nonetheless, he had continued to drop the little stones into the drinks of the sickly soldiers in his dormitory, usually to very good effect, and this satisfied him, though he had no one to share it with.

But to the matter in hand – which, really, should have concerned Asher more than little yellow stones: he was not altogether sure they could actually leave the Castle any more. He had not been sent out to fight for days.

He decided to make his way to the King's solar, to ask the question. Asher had not made the journey at all recently; he had been extremely busy, he defended himself, and yet could not recall with what he had been so absorbed.

Asher walked down the richer looking passages, hanging with pattern painted ceramics and crimson swags of material. Glass Mountain as a whole did not look as dark as it was wont to, these days – to Asher, at least. Whatever the reason for that might be cannot be covered here, but Asher soon found the cause of the brightness in this part of the fort, at least: little Prince Elihu stood on tip toes by the window, shutters flung wide open.

"Well now," said Asher in a low voice, so as not to startle the lad, "is this entirely a wise idea?" And he pulled Elihu back slightly by the hood of his cape. "Those fairies have quite a range, you know."

But Elihu, his eyes huge, shook his head and drew back to the window as if magnetised. "Look," he whispered, pointing a chubby hand to the field of battle.

There were two strange forms of creature weaving in between the bodies; a large black thing which came closest to resembling a crow, and white ladies, frosted all over as if with snow, with wings and clothes made of swan feathers.

Asher narrowed his eyes and gave a low whistle. "The fairies are getting stronger. I had not realised they were this strong," he commented, and wondered how it had escaped him before. "Yet they are not exactly good fairies... I don't know what this means."

"What *are* they?" inquired the fascinated young boy.

"That one," said Asher, pointing to the crow, "they call Macha. It serves no purpose, you see; just rejoices and carouses over the slain."

"It was drinking their blood. It was gross."

Asher laughed that it was not gross enough to stop Elihu from looking. "That is not a good fairy. It is a bad one. They came when the war began."

"Father says there are no good fairies. But I do not think Father is always right, is he, Uncle Asher?"

Asher bit his tongue and said: "No one is always right, Elihu. Look there – the snowy ladies are called Valkyries; it is said they take the souls of the brave to dwell with the angels. I have never seen one before – only read about them. They are quite beautiful, aren't they?"

"When I grow up, I want to be wise and knowledgeable like you. I am sure *you* are never wrong."

"Oh dear, I assure you I am, quite frequently in fact."

"But you are kind, and you see things that the others cannot. When I rule my kingdom, I must be like that also. Will you teach me?"

"I will try. Only you must tell me first where your Father is."

Elihu pointed out the direction, and Asher left him to gaze, still untiring, at the window.

Asher's walk continued, down to where the walls were made of salt blocks. He began to muse on the future, when Elihu was grown up, and wondered what it would bring. Glass Mountain Castle appeared once more in his imagination as a thriving place, full of the sounds of peace instead of war. Asher could see Elihu seated on the throne; he could see them together dispelling the superstitions about fairies and living in harmony with the creatures. He could see it so vividly he could almost touch it. If only he could be transported through the mists of time to that day and skip all this painful waiting! He longed with an aching heart for the future to come.

He walked with less and less attention to his direction until, rounding a corner, he nearly plunged straight into another person.

Typically, it was Lady Aurora, very dignified with a gold fillet gleaming on her head. Her feet moved her out of his way as lightly as rays of sun on a lake. She barely noticed him; she was looking ahead in absorbed preoccupation.

"I am sorry," Aurora said politely, dismissively. She looked at him a little guiltily, Asher thought, and had nearly walked away before he had time to arrange his thoughts.

But her retreating back paused, and she turned around. "I suppose it would be wise to take this opportunity to bid you farewell. The time when Cynthia and I must leave to rejoin our people is fast approaching. We have had word of them, and it seems they are safer than we are here. I understand that as your prisoners, we should not take the liberty to assume we can just leave; but really, given the circumstances, I think we are the least of your worries."

Asher nodded his head quickly. This action was easier than speech at first. "Of course. I had not given a thought to the matter." If she was going to speak to him with cold apathy, he was going to do the same. "You may do whatever you please." His voice lost the indifference he had so professionally maintained until now as he asked: "You – you will be sorry to leave?"

Perversely, he almost hated her at that moment, for making him feel so sorry at her going; she: a Boanerge! She was entirely objectionable. Well, it would be better so. She would leave, and he would return to normality.

Aurora looked as if it was a funny question, and answered: "Yes. Yes, I will be sad. It is strangely pretty here sometimes – with the waves in the sand, and the deep colours." A look of deep reflection took possession of her features. She looked to be considering greater questions than he was asking.

"But you will have the sand wherever you return to?"

Aurora actually giggled. "Oh! It is a little different where I come from. I cannot explain how. But yes, I shall miss Iblees from time to time," she shook her head and perked up. Her delicate fingers touched lightly upon his healed wound. "I am glad to see I leave you with your arm entirely recovered." She gave a smile which was warmer than she usually allowed herself, and nearly left again.

"Will the Lady Cynthia really go with you?" Asher called after her, unable to stop himself.

Aurora stiffened. "Yes," she said rather tensely. "Although she tells me her and Sir Kish are actually engaged."

Asher swallowed and could not meet her eyes. "The King won't like that," he chuckled.

Asher had observed that Kish was deeply changed since the wastage of his castle.

He was more sullen than usual towards the bulk of the Knights, but became extremely friendly with a select group of the most talented and brawny. He retreated away with this circle of comrades frequently. He did not seem particularly ready for a wife.

Moreover, although Kish's relationship with the King continued very close, Asher thought he observed something in Kish's manner – an increased politeness, and the occasional contemptible look from behind his back – which made him feel Kish's attitude towards Joel was not entirely cordial.

"Well, precisely," agreed Aurora pursing her lips. "She has to go and consult her own people first. I should not worry; I cannot imagine they would allow it."

Maybe because he knew it would be the last moment he could, Asher looked into her face and let the sunlight in. It flooded into his head; it cleared his eyes and illuminated his brain.

Aurora looked confused. Asher was sorry to see he was something like a shield, a filter to her light. In brightening him up, she appeared to pay a price within herself.

"Well... goodbye Sir Asher. May you be granted safe passage in battle."

"Wait – I have a leaving present for you." He arrested her hand. "This ring – you looked very upset when it was broken."

Aurora stared into the moonstone. Her little face fell. "Oh! Yes, yes I was. Silly, really."

With one deft moment he pulled something from a concealed pocket and placed it in the palm of her hand, closing her fingers upon it. "I used to work in the blacksmith's with my father, before I was a shepherd," he said, in an explanation which was no explanation at all to one who never even knew he had once been a shepherd. "I hope you like it. Goodbye."

And he now had sufficient embarrassment to wish to be out of her presence, from which he fled very rapidly.

Aurora opened her hand and saw the ring he had made inside, golden and set with rose quartz. For the briefest instant she looked like she would cry, but instead smiled and walked away with her head held high.

Consequently, Asher was admitted into the King's presence in no very composed state. Trying to pass unnoticed, he slunk to the side wall guiltily. He was not successful; Kish stopped mid fairy-bashing rant and gave a look to the King which clearly said: "Didn't I tell you it was so?"

"We do not appreciate one of our advisors turning up so late on an occasion like this. Unless you were actually entangled with a fairy previous to coming here, you will be punished, Sir Asher." Joel frostily delivered.

"An – an occasion like what, sorry?" Asher attempted to wear the face of concentration which Joel was so admirably sampling, as if in a hint it was the one he should also adopt. He only succeeded in deeply furrowing his brow.

"You see? What did I say? He plays the innocent now." Sir Kish eyed Asher with a very pure and sincere hatred.

Asher could almost smell the metallic twang of fear in the air. The faces of the King's advisors were drawn with suppressed desperation.

"Either he is on their side or this seer is burnt out! He had a gift, I do not deny that, but your Grace – it has clearly gone! How many months have we waited for signs from him? We have relied too much on that, and now this has snuck up on us and caught us unawares. He is useless – and if you say he is not, well, he must have been purposefully concealing the truth to aid the fairies. I would not be prepared to risk it – if I were you I would keep him under guard and key until the victory is won."

"You do not think like a King, Sir Kish; you presume we have the guard and key to spare, and that it would make a blind bit of difference. Where can he go from here?"

Joel stared at Asher. There was still nothing but a vague, dreamy look written all over him. "Go to the far right corner of the room, Sir Asher, and lay down upon the floor. Be sure that one of your ears is pressed against the stone."

Asher considered it one of the strangest punishments he had been made to undertake, but performed it nonetheless, hardly sorry for an excuse to lie down.

The floor was cold and scratchy against his cheek. And there was something else. A patter – but it did not sound like a mouse.

"What do you hear?" commanded the King.

"It sounds like... digging, Jo- Your Grace."

"Pre-cisely. Digging. We are entrapped. Our food supplies are running out. It is strange that you could not stretch yourself to see, or even hear, the fairies mining underneath our Castle. You see their positioning. If they set the props holding their tunnel alight, this part of the Castle will collapse."

"Then begging your pardon your Majesty," said Asher, hastily removing his ear from the floor, "but why are we still using this room to..."

"It is not for a fairy to remove King Joel from his Council Chambers," barked Joel with more pride than sense. He recollected himself and continued: "They are filling the moat with the rubble. We are constructing a counter mine to meet them, but who can say if it will be in time? *You* certainly cannot – not anymore. Unless – do I do you a wrong? Have you any bright idea?" Joel asked in no very encouraging way.

"Yes. Make another tunnel and get the women and children out."

There was silence as they all faced the enormity of the situation.

"That will be done," Joel decided grudgingly. "Now, go about it. You are dismissed."

Joel did not look particularly vexed. He was still counting, no doubt, on the idea that the chosen King could not be beaten. Well, it was no longer in Asher's power to dissuade him from these fancies. He pulled himself to his feet, and began to leave, in order to... to speak with his archers, of course, that was it.

"Asher? You do not think you have escaped a punishment?"

Asher stopped – a delayed stop, for he was not aware he was being spoken to until several other advisors glared at him.

"Oh – I – given the circumstances..." Asher looked at the King's angry, hard eyes and hung his head back down. "No, of course I did not, your Majesty."

"Good. For I cannot spare many soldiers. This tunnel for the women and children – you will dig it. I shall leave it to you to decide where. Well, don't stand there. Get to it."

CHAPTER TWENTY-FIVE

Many of the Knights flew to the towers; they were the only vent of attack open to the humans now. It had even been ordained that several dummies stuffed with straw were to sit constantly upon the battlements, to give the impression of a constant and undaunted Knightly presence.

Some felt it would have made more sense to place Asher, the critically acclaimed best archer of Auchriachan up there, instead of on his own in a tunnel; but as always in war, nobody mentioned these things, because the higher authorities must somehow know better.

Besides, it was a frightening place to be, on top of the towers. None of the Knights were able to mention much, being bombarded with fairy arrows, fairy lightning bolts in a variety of colours, and huge rocks catapulted towards them by a trebuchet. The number of soldiers in the fairy army had grown – quadrupled, the Knights given to exaggeration claimed – since Sir Kish's use of the strange flashing instrument.

But as the days passed, there came a new sight, and no one could decide if it was more beautiful or terrifying. It was simply this: the start of a river.

It glistened at first merely as an unusual blob of blue on a yellow horizon, but it spread, branching out, growing longer, growing stronger, until it met and flowed into the moat of Glass Mountain Castle.

On its own, the river would remain only as a bizarre occurrence. But the river did not stay on its own. Those with keen sight divined something moving up it.

The boat was made from a nautilus, and drawn by two sea crabs of unusually large size. Those within it were clothed and surrounded by a glow of rainbow colours. No arrows could permeate this shield.

One side of the shield was a deep blue, and seated an older (almost thirty!) weather-withered, equally blue personage inside. The Knights aimed more at this side than the other, but the arrows all mysteriously went astray, falling wide, no matter how perfectly aimed.

It was at this point a messenger was sent to Asher, dirty and sweaty in the failing lamp light of his emerging tunnel.

"He is coming, Sir! King Iubdan himself, sir!"

Asher froze. A lump of earth fell upon his head. "Here?" He took the messenger boy roughly by the shoulders and brought his muddy face uncomfortably close. "And this tunnel still not finished! Well, but what does it matter? He is coming here! Really, here?"

The messenger boy felt the solitary occupation of digging must have had an adverse effect upon poor Sir Asher's mind.

"Yes, Sir. The King wishes to consult with you."

Asher's face gleamed bright through all the splatters of dirt. "Of course he does! Sanity is returning, my boy. I will go to him at once. Stay here and finish this tunnel – no, wait, come with me. Tell me all you know and have seen about King Iubdan. Well come on then, don't just stand there!"

They ran incredibly fast, with more exultant joy than was altogether proper for a losing side in a war, and fell into the Presence Chamber ruddy faced and out of breath.

Asher was forced to temper his smile, seeing as everyone else looked incredibly grim, and moreover, the Ladies Cynthia, Urvasi and Aurora were witnesses to his manic grinning.

"My King," said Asher, kneeling down and kissing Joel's ring. "This is a happy day! If the Fairy King himself comes, peace must be in the offing! Go out and speak to him: if my studies prove me right, you will find him more than reasonable."

"Oh, this is charming," announced Sir Kish with a slow clap of the hands. "If Asher were not against us, he could not be so happy. See how joyfully he sends our precious King into danger?"

"Oh no, no; you do not understand," replied Asher very earnestly. "This blue faced creature they bring with them – it is Cailleach Bheur, a very sacred fairy. They do not normally go anywhere near her, for she alone is trusted with the staff that symbolises their command over the destiny of the human race: to avoid any temptation to use it for wrong, she sits in the forest alone. They have brought her to remind us of the bond we share – and, and I almost forgot: she brings the Winter! That is her job, to bring the Winter, and we have not had a Winter for so long! Do you think – perhaps the landscape will return to how it was – oh, go and talk with her Joel!"

Joel could not avoid being caught up in Asher's very genuine excitement.

"Of course we shall go and meet with him. It will take more than a fancy fellow riding in an oversized sea shell to shake King Joel of Iblees!" Though to Asher it looked very much as if it had already shaken him, and he was stalling for time. "But as this decorated insect is not yet with us, we will sit a while longer, and enjoy each other's company, while we can."

"I think," said Lady Aurora, her voice very thin, "we

will leave all the same, Cynthia and I. It is safest."

Lady Urvasi grasped Aurora's hand very tightly. "You will leave me alone, will you? How shall I manage without you?"

Aurora stroked Urvasi's hair. "You have been strong before, and you will be again. I am sure you will come to no harm."

There was much weeping and hugging taking place between the three ladies. Asher did not feel it polite to watch.

Cynthia soon broke off to have a whispered conference with Kish. There was an equal measure of crying again on Cynthia's part – Kish did not seem to be so given to the habit – and more kissing than hugging. The others tried to have a very meaningful conversation and find something better to look at.

When it was quite over, to everyone's relief, Aurora and Cynthia solemnly made their way to the door, curtseying to King Joel as they did.

"You forgot, my hostages, I have not released you." The ladies stood electrified by this, and opened their mouths in silent remonstrance.

Joel laughed. "I shall let you go, never fear. But you must perform a task for me first."

"As you wish," said Aurora, a little too politely. Joel looked very hardly at her.

"Queen Ganieda was a very great musician," he said, the words coming out tightly, "or at least so I thought. Did you ever have the pleasure to hear her?"

The ladies silently shook their heads. Lady Urvasi looked for an instant like she was going to break down in tears.

"Then I pity you. The lute is in the corner, there, as you see. I wish you," signalling Aurora, "to play something upon it. It has been a long while since we have

213

had music in this hall."

There was something in the way Joel looked at Aurora which Asher did not like. Her flowing hair and her pure eyes reminded Joel of Ganieda, Asher was sure.

Aurora looked slightly wary, but said: "Certainly, if it is your Majesty's pleasure – though you will derive no great satisfaction from it, I warn you in advance."

"Quite the contrary, I am sure. Proceed."

Aurora and Cynthia with her moved towards the instrument uncertainly. There was a little whispered conference, a shrug, and then they began.

If asked to describe the event, Asher would have to say that Aurora played, and Cynthia sung, yet neither of those verbs was appropriate in the sense he knew them.

This music – if indeed music it was – resembled nothing they had ever heard before. In fact, it was not just music that was heard: it filled up every sense, with the smell of meadowsweet flowers and the taste of fresh fruit. Cynthia's voice flowed smoothly, more lovely than any nightingale's, Aurora's fingers were producing low, unearthly strains of a tune which was unbearably sweet.

Every member of the small court was struck silent. Not one of them could move. They were pierced, frozen, entrapped.

Seeing this strange effect of their melody, the fairies stopped sheepishly. They had never heard human music, but they gathered what they had played was not it. Aurora lay her instrument down with a discordant twang which made her wince.

Everyone stared. In their eyes Aurora could see strange workings: hostility, shock, betrayal, unhappiness, fear, wonder, and a vague, haunted look. Clearly they knew what fairy music was meant to sound like, even if they had not heard it before.

"You are fairies." It was Kish who said it, stiffly,

accusingly. Aurora was glad that Cynthia did not have time to look at his face. The expression she saw there would have slain her on the spot.

Aurora did not spend any longer observing her briefly beloved human companions. She grabbed Cynthia's arm with a tight vice like grip and pulled her towards the door. "Run!"

They fled as a tangled crocodile. All the swiftness and agility came from Aurora. Cynthia was nothing but a sobbing bundle hampering her progress.

Behind her sounded the crashes of feet scrambling after them. Somewhere in the distance they could hear King Joel roar and Lady Urvasi weep.

They were coming to the end of a corridor. Aurora wheeled them round in a sharp right. Cynthia nearly tottered over. Still they kept running. The Castle was nothing but an intricate maze to their eyes; so many passages, so many lanterns, and none of them familiar.

Aurora took a turn that she thought she recognised. They nearly collided with a worker carrying a large roasted pig on a tray. It flew over their heads and clattered to the floor behind them. Cynthia screamed.

A volley of voices followed the noise.

"Knights! There are Knights trailing us – be quiet!" whispered Aurora.

Cynthia stifled a sob and ran along as best she could. The fairies were at an advantage; they were far too light-footed to be caught in a chase. But should they get lost, or a Knight spring on them from an unexpected corner...

"This is ridiculous!" Aurora cursed and unclasped her human dress. It crumpled on the flagstones like a deflated person. Her astonishing aqueous fairy dress was revealed beneath. Its sparkles seemed to illuminate the corridor, and Aurora felt reborn.

Quickly she unrobed Cynthia in the same way, and

they were both free to run much faster.

"We must be near the Banqueting Hall, because of the poor pig," Aurora assumed quietly. "Help me, Cynthia. Can you remember the way out from there?"

"You told me not to talk," complained her companion.

Aurora sighed. Hopefully they were leaving the Knights far behind. It was impossible to track two ladies who ran without their feet making a sound.

She looked at all the doors before her and her head swam. She picked one at random.

Her head was too full of panic to concoct some magic to free them from this place. The Prince Deucalion had once taught her to transport herself as a stream of light, but she could not remember it perfectly.

Moreover, Cynthia did not have her ring, and Aurora had not tried hers since it was broken. Even if it did work, and not backfire, she did not know if it would be strong enough to use for both of them. She did not want to try it at so vital a juncture.

All of a sudden her feet were nearly taken from underneath her. Cynthia jolted behind her and released her hand. Aurora stumbled and felt the impact of the dirty floor.

Her shock did not last. Straight away she sprang back to her fairy feet and saw Cynthia clutching a bundle in her arms.

"Farvann! We nearly forgot him!"

Glad as Aurora was not to leave the fairy dog to be tortured by the humans, she did not display her emotions. She circled Cynthia's shoulders with her arms and shoved her forward.

They ran for about five minutes before coming to an abrupt halt. They were in the dirty, dank environs of a tunnel. The very the tunnel which Sir Asher had been digging at laboriously minutes before.

"Oh!" Aurora looked at the wall of mud in despair. Farvann felt her pain so intensely that he barked at her.

The clanking of weapons and armour sounded alarmingly close by.

"This way! The tunnel!"

Cynthia grabbed Aurora's ring finger. "Get us through! There must be a way through!"

"I'm thinking, I'm thinking! The spell – I can't remember…"

"Aurora! It must be now!"

Footfalls sounded right outside. Without thinking, Aurora raised her ring and muttered a few rapid words.

The Knights bundled into the tunnel with ferocious cries. Their spears were raised and ready for action. Those at the front stopped short as they nearly collided with the muddy wall.

The other Knights piled into their backs. Someone stepped on Asher's spade and cursed very loudly.

The small tunnel reverberated with arguing voices. More dirt fell from the ceiling, and there might have been a real danger of it caving in had not a firm, authoritative voice raised itself above the rest.

"Where are they?! Show me! Bring them to me!"

Somehow the Knights found room to part down the middle and make way for Sir Kish, bristling in bronze and red. He stalked between them. His face was as fiery as the breath of the Drakes.

His words came out like cannon balls. "Where are the fairies?"

Collectively his men hung their heads. One that had ridden with him to Majeseerum was brave enough to speak.

"They are not here. The tunnel was empty."

"Impossible!" Kish spat. He rounded on the Knight

with a murderous look. "I heard them! Look," he gestured to the lump of slimy ground in front of them. "Could they have gone through this tunnel? It is unfinished. Where exactly could they go?"

The Knight that had spoken looked at the end of the tunnel and looked at Sir Kish. "They are fairies. They could have gone through this tunnel," he affirmed.

Kish's frame convulsed in a shiver. His eyes did not leave the end of the tunnel. He bit his lip extremely hard. "I'll kill her. I swear it; I'll kill her."

The Knights did not reply, but filed uniformly out of the tunnel, leaving Sir Kish alone.

Although he remained stationary and silent as a mute, Sir Kish was undoubtedly active. In the hush of the abandoned tunnel, his rapid and bitter cogitations were almost audible. For what was nearly half an hour he stood there, sour faced and clenching his fists. The air could have crackled with his ill-will; he filled the entire half-tunnel with his spite. At last, he straightened himself and left the tunnel almost gracefully.

Within a minute of his departure, there was a soft pop. Aurora and Cynthia reappeared, squashed up against the wall.

"I told you to get us *through* the tunnel," Cynthia scolded her friend. Her delicate fairy limbs were trembling.

"I could not remember the spell. That was the best I could do. Now we will wait here for a bit longer, and -"

Cynthia interrupted Aurora with a forlorn cry. "I cannot stay in this tunnel another moment!" Her fair face crumpled in desolation.

Aurora put her arm on her shoulders. She could see that the strain of hiding from Kish, with him in the state that he was in, had taken its toll upon her. Had she known the reverse spell, Aurora was sure Cynthia would have revealed them to Kish in an instant and fallen at his feet.

Even now she had some foreboding that Cynthia would run out after him calling his name.

"Alright. We will leave the tunnel. But -"

Cynthia had dashed out of the opening even as Aurora finished her sentence with "slowly".

Aurora dived after her. If she kept running at that speed they would collide with Kish in no time at all.

"Cynthia! Wait!"

Fixing her view on Cynthia's flowing robe, Aurora dashed wildly down the corridor. She looked at nothing else. She was more used to running, and less hampered by distress than Cynthia. It did not take long for her to catch up. As she rounded a corner, she lurched for Cynthia's dress and caught its wispy material.

Neither of the fairies had seen what was approaching from the other direction. One blind with tears, one leaping to catch hold of something, they stumbled round the turn straight into another worker carrying a water pitcher.

This collision was less fortunate than the pig incident. The pitcher travelled vertically rather than horizontally, and returned to earth directly on top of them.

Cynthia shrieked and Aurora shivered in shock as they were baptised with icy water. But they soon realised it was not just the sensation of being unexpectedly drenched which made them feel so odd.

Every fibre of their spines was tingling. They shook uncontrollably. The worker they had bumped into gaped at them with infinite concern as their eyes began to roll backwards. He was going to offer to fetch them some water, but realised it would be as ineffectual as it was inappropriate.

Suddenly, sparks of blue and purple covered the ladies he was observing. There was a faint *whoosh* and wide banners of colour erupted behind them. The vibration of their backs slowed and finally stopped.

"Our wings! Of course! Immersion in water," Aurora muttered with shaking lips. She stretched herself. The pair were an incredible sight in that dark castle, arrayed in their full fairy glory. Aurora smiled.

The worker fainted with a stony clatter. Aurora smiled a little less widely.

"Come," she said, taking Cynthia's hand. "Now we are free of those burdensome human restrains. We will fly home!"

Even Cynthia brightened at this idea and shook out her mahogany hair amongst her wings.

There was a casement window with a seat about two hundred yards down the right hand side of the corridor. Half of it was propped open to let in whatever breeze might flit over the hot dunes. Aurora looked through the black lattices and was overwhelmed with felicity. The hot dry air on her skin reminded her that soon she would be in Laseri, where the air was neither too hot, nor too cold, but just wonderful. They would fly across these sandy deserts, hopefully into the care of a fairy army nearby who could escort them through the forest. The journey had been difficult enough last time, and she did not fancy attempting it again with a mangled ring and no Blanchard. But however they got home, she would take with her the image of the one she was sworn to protect, in her new perfectly formed rose quartz ring. To know the name and the face of the person she was created to guard; that had been a privilege she had always dreamed of.

She pushed open the other side of the window.

Cynthia looked down at the drop. She wriggled her shoulders and stiff wings.

"You first."

Aurora held out her hand. "Together."

Cynthia nodded.

The two fairies climbed upon the window seat, their four dainty feet tottering on the edge. The vast continuous landscape of Auchriachan was beyond them.

"One, two," counted Aurora. She left a pause "Three!"

Simultaneously the fairies took a huge leap and cycled their pretty white legs through the sky. Still their hands were clasped fast. They dropped a short way – then there was a sudden rushing noise, and a parachute of brilliant coloured wings spread out above them. They began to travel upwards upon the warm air.

Laughing with the intoxication of freedom, they soared higher and higher. Their figures streaked across the smouldering sky with perfect beauty and grace, travelling in the direction of Green Glow Forest.

26

CHAPTER TWENTY-SIX

Trumpets flared in triumph for the coming of the Fairy King and his dashing Prince. They were merry, almost peaceful trumpets, causing the blood-stained, dusty, rusty Knights to pause in the middle of battle, faces full of amazement.

The atmosphere fell eerily quiet, and it was as if all the soldiers had just woken up, and began to turn around in horror at what they had done. Bodies were strewn all over the blood-stained sand. Some of the only remaining trees were scorched or hacked apart. Everything was waste and dust, but here – here were magical, amazingly bright and clean people, almost resplendent with the power of goodness.

The winged royal personages alighted from their weird conveyance, without a hand to stop them. King Iubdan smiled.

A scuttling around the portcullis interrupted them. It creaked opened a few inches and Sir Asher rolled under. He was clearly agitated but managed to run down the slope very fast. He called out hoarsely that the army were to hold their fire, for King Joel himself was coming to speak with the visitors.

Yet almost simultaneously, a brigade of Knights rode from the curtain wall, heading in a completely opposite direction, with torches and sharp axes. Everyone was startled at the sudden sound of their loud clatter. They looked to the front of the snake of horses. The troops were led by Sir Kish.

Stupidly, Asher allowed his attention to be focused on this crazy group riding helter-skelter and shouting. He stopped speaking, and turned to look. A second later there was a hard knock on his chest and he hit the ground painfully as Sir Nehemiah brushed him aside. Troops of Knights (more, in fact, than Asher remembered being alive still) filed out behind him, and leapt into immediate battle with young Prince Deucalion.

Kish had been a mere diversion.

Alert as a hawk, the sharp young Prince was not thrown off his balance, and met the attack readily. But King Iudban stumbled forwards in shock, and the frosty blue Cailleach Bheur ran away screeching. The spell was broken over the Knights; they began to attack again, as if they had never been recalled to themselves in the first place.

Asher, and Asher alone, was removed from it all, standing, as he felt, in a vacuum, watching and mouthing the word: "No."

Arrows began to fly from the Mural towers.

What must he do? He must find that Blue Fairy and her cherished staff! Sir Kish must have his eyes upon it; if the trauma of discovering the woman he was practically engaged to was a fairy did not consume his whole mind, he must be thinking of the Blue Staff.

Asher looked avidly for a happy glimmer of blue amongst the melee, but there were too many people. His head was spinning, the fighters were whirling him with them, and every bit of blue in the world had gone. Occasionally he thought he saw something, yet it turned out to be only a streak of colour in a fairy ring.

He would have to search for Sir Kish instead.

King Iubdan was not immobilised for long; he began to use his larger, grander fairy ring. Blue rays flew from it like electricity. One blast from it aimed at the man attacking his son fell wide, and set alight the Inner Ward. All the ladies and remaining workers ran screaming from it, into the throes of the fairy soldiers who awaited them.

Asher stopped at the sound of distress. Instantly Lady Urvasi sprang to his mind, and he ran towards the stream of civilians. As he did so, King Joel came grandly out of his devastated home, ready for battle. He walked right over the spot on the barbican where Asher had stood but moments before.

Cursing himself for not remaining in the place he would be able to stop him, Asher dashed back again, and saw little Prince Elihu running glibly after his father, as if it were all a terrific game.

Asher did not think any longer; his instinct took over. He grabbed Elihu, who responded with a cry of protest, and swung them both into the saddle of the first abandoned horse his eyes fell upon. Asher gathered up the reins, kicked hard, and headed out of the war which his heart could not longer be in, towards a comparative place of safety.

Some of the surviving ladies and workers began to follow Asher, but he was not aware of this. He had seen and felt too many things this morning to notice much else outside the whirring of his own brain. He had a headache like a thunderstorm, and rode as if he were fleeing one.

The horse foamed and sweated and looked fit to drop; the Prince cried and moaned and coughed; yet it seemed to Asher they reached the forest in record time, and without incident.

He saw the dark primeval woodland and began to breathe, sighing for its coolness and stillness – despite the threat of Boags. Sadly, as he approached closer and closer, a sinking sensation in his stomach told Asher he would receive neither.

For the trees looked darker, and twice as high. There was a scent tainting the muggy air, filling his and Elihu's lungs.

They rode close enough to see what their nostrils and hearts had confirmed. The forest was on fire.

Asher had to see it. He had not really believed that Kish would be able to forget the Blue Fairy, whatever other distress had befallen him. Perhaps Cailleach Bheur had run to the cover of the trees and Kish was trying to smoke her out, but looking at Kish, Asher could not honestly believe that was the case.

Kish had clearly not taken the revelation of his beloved's true identity well. He was taking it out upon the trees, for he knew how the fairies loved them.

There was burning and there was felling. Knights were picking up hares and skinning them for spite. Any creature, any nature, anything a fairy might care for was brutally and messily slain. Some of the trees, Asher knew, were but mirages with Deevs living inside them – these ones spurted real blood to the bite of the axe, and fell screaming horribly.

"Uncle Asher," came Elihu's innocent muffled voice. "What's happening? Why is the forest growing?"

Asher noticed it was true. Bizarrely, with each tree that fell to timber, two saplings sprouted in the ground just before them.

"I suppose each tree we kill separates us further from the fairies and their ways," mused Asher, noticing an unexpected and very unmanly lump come to his throat. "But come, these are not scenes for you." He turned the poor exhausted horse about, and rode on to where he knew there was a cave.

The poor bewildered refugees from the Inner Ward

lost sight of Asher. Smoke baffled their vision, and many of them began to be more interested in what was happening in the woods than where the heir to the throne was going.

Lady Urvasi was among them, her pretty gown torn, her hair half-up, half-down and covered in sand. She had been hanging on to Lady Rubezahl – one of Ganieda's old ladies in waiting – but had become disengaged from her along the way. She was so exhausted, hot, thirsty and frightened that she did not actually notice when, or how, and could not even bring herself to care much.

Urvasi held her head in her hands to see the carnage of the forest. "What – why?" she murmured to herself, but could not bring her tired head to understand. She noticed warm blood on one hand – she must have injured her head somewhere along the way. Craving sleep of all things, she collapsed in heap, and for this moment, cared nothing for what became of her.

Urvasi awoke, much more herself, with a great lurch. It would have been confusing enough to wake up from such scenes to find herself not in her own bed but in the middle of a desert. Yet this was not what she found: she found herself in no bed, no desert, but a forest. It had sprouted up so quickly with the relentless malice of Kish and his followers that now all Lady Urvasi could see on looking up were mist enshrouded treetops.

Complete silence reigned. Urvasi arose shakily to her feet. She was held back by liverworts, winding like intestines around her. She brushed them off with a little shudder and moved on.

Dampness and mould filled her nostrils. She passed little mounds teeming with green beetles and felt sick. She was so hungry, and so thirsty. Where had Asher and Elihu gone? What had become of Rubezahl? Urvasi shivered.

She longed most fervently for a noise of some kind. A little scuttle of animals, or the hoot of an owl – even the leaves of the trees brushing against one another. It would take the edge off her suspenseful terror.

The forest looked to be entwining itself around her. Urvasi, seeing a small tree, paused to look at it, and saw the most astonishing thing. It grew before her very eyes, bursting into blossom, dropping its petals, then standing erect with proud green leaves. It had gone through the whole cycle of a year in just an instant.

"I will never find my way out of here," she said to herself, and was somewhat comforted by the sound of her own voice.

No sooner had she said it than she heard another noise to her left. Turning, she saw a hoof of a horse crush a bed of peony flowers. She raised her eyes and saw three men, all of them very fair to look at, sitting on this one horse.

"Well, my goodness!" said the man holding the reins, in a voice like melting honey. "What are *you* doing here?"

"Who – who are you?" Urvasi demanded warily, but she could hardly keep the relief at seeing another human creature from her voice.

"Me? I am Incubi, this is Mart, and behind him Alp," said the same rider, extremely politely.

"But we should be asking who you are," said Alp. "It isn't usual for strangers to be prowling around our home. She might be up to something."

"Oh, leave her be!" cried the one called Mart. "She looks innocent enough to me."

"Oh, you live here," concluded Urvasi. "Then – I wonder if you could tell me the route out?"

"Tell you?" laughed Incubi, in the same alluring voice. "You would never remember! We could *take* you."

"Take her? Are you mad?" complained Alp, still

eyeing her suspiciously. "She could kill us all!"

"You're scaring the poor thing!" Mart pointed out. "She would be far too terrified to come with us. She probably thinks we'll kill *her*."

Lady Urvasi's face was clearly showing she did not know what to do. "If you live in this forest you are – you must be-"

"We are fairies," Incubi said silkily. "No doubt that makes a pretty and intelligent young lady like yourself hate us." He gave her a long, piercing look.

The only images coming to Lady Urvasi's mind were the kindness of Aurora and Cynthia, and the comparative barbarity of the humans.

"I – I trust fairies," she said tentatively, and allowed Incubi to take her hand, and hoist her up behind him.

Joel's horse quivered beneath him. It stepped sideways and jumped as arrows grazed its gleaming shoulder-blade. Joel kicked it on, hewing fairies left and right with his sword, sending up showers of glistening purple into his face.

He could see a very limited space in front of him, obscured as it was through the gunpowder, butterfly wings and flashes of lightning. Sometimes he caught sight of one of his Knights, only to see them fried or otherwise struck down by a bolt. But at last Joel's eyes hit upon what he sought: grand King Iubdan in his furs and majestic robes. Gritting his teeth, Joel spurred his horse on. Coming at a steady gallop from behind, Joel hit the Fairy King firmly on his golden royal head with the hilt of his sword.

Riding past, he turned about prepared to do the same again – or worse – when he felt his horse jolt too far sideways. The next instant he found the world diagonal before his eyes, and himself on the dust.

Struggling free from the wounded animal, Joel leapt

up and located his sword with a rush of relief. It surprised him to see Iubdan already standing and ready to face him.

The sun beat down upon the pair of Kings; one sweaty, enraged and full of sand; the other sophisticated, looking distinctly out of place and weighed down by sadness. They paced around each other in silence, passing hostile, unconsciously fascinated looks.

Joel made a lunge. It was easily parried by Iubdan's thinner, lighter sword. "Joel of Iblees, this is not wise," counselled the Fairy King. "We did not come for this."

Joel set his jaw and attacked again. Once more, he was rebuffed.

"This is madness – all of it, madness," Iubdan swished his sword briefly around the battlefield. Joel vainly tried a third time to break his guard. "We have failed in our duties, that is true: failed for centuries. We keep a poor watch, and from too great a distance. But still, we were predestined protectors of you – our powers should not be employed in wounding you!"

"I need no protection," growled Joel. "My people need no protection except me."

He ran forward, sword held high, and was cut on the arm by King Iubdan.

"We are in charge of your destinies – if you let us..."

"I am the chosen King! I command the destiny of Auchriachan – your time is past, insect!"

In his rage Joel managed to nick Iubdan's cheek.

"Surely you were chosen to do something significant. Do it: bring back the time of harmony between the fairies and humans. We will no longer run away in sadness at your practices. We will work with you, and build a place-"

"Give over my kingdom to your kind, you mean! I did not work so hard – my wife did not work so hard, to build a city ripe to be run by fairies!"

The Kings lunged at the same time. Joel was cut more

seriously on the other arm, and part of King Iubdan's wing was sliced. Iubdan gasped and nearly dropped his sword.

Joel, seeing his advantage, aimed again at the same place. He was blocked.

"Please, Joel. Consider this, let us speak. If I am informed correctly, two fairies have been living amongst you, not inharmoniously."

Joel's entire face contorted. Before Iubdan even had time to register it, Joel had thrown his heavy blade through the air. It tore a gaping, ragged hole through his brightly decorated wing. Iubdan fell to his knees, mouthing in pain – and was gone.

Barely did Joel sigh in triumph before his injured arm was pulled sharply behind his back with a stab of red-hot pain, and his face was forced into the sand.

"I should kill you now," a voice spat in his ear, "but I am not like my father. I believe in a unanimous decision, and I think maybe we should have a vote on the whole murdering Kings issue."

"What do you want?" Joel spat grains from his mouth as he spoke. "Kill me, now you have me!"

"Oh, but I would rather convince you. I just have a slightly more painful way of going about it. No, no, dear Joel, what I want to show you is worse than death – for you, at any rate. I know you would welcome the chance to be cold in your grave with her."

Joel twisted beneath Deucalion's grip, but was forced to stop and cry out as he did so, for he felt like his arm was being pulled from its socket.

Deucalion made a sound of disgust and threw Joel to the floor. Joel, his wits still vaguely about him, groped about for something to throw at the Prince's wings. But Deucalion, with a bored look, raised his hand, and his wings disappeared.

"I am one of the few fairies who can do that," he

mentioned conversationally. He lowered his ring to point at Joel, who crawled desperately in the swirling dust away from him.

"Great King Joel," laughed Deucalion nastily. "What would the Queen Ganieda say if she saw you so? Would she really want you to be fighting these fairies? If I remember, she was not greatly for pointless murder – but then, I did not know her as well as you do. I'm sorry, did I say *do*? I meant *did*. For it was your child, and the stress you put her through with this war which killed her, was it not? Correct me if I am wrong – I rarely am."

Joel threw himself madly at Deucalion with a cry like wounded animal, but his strength was so drained that it was a pointless, pathetic lurch. "How do you – how would you know these things?"

Deucalion caught Joel in his arms, and forced his grazed face towards the large, ever changing moonstone on his ring.

The moving blue colour of the ring began to glow before Joel's eyes. Unable to move his gaze at all, he watched blue expand into other, intangible colours, and swirl round and round.

For a moment Joel thought he had simply been hit too hard in the head, or lost too much blood. The ring was reflecting rays into his eyes so brightly that he could see the ring in his eyes, and his eyes in the ring, until he wasn't sure which was which. Then he saw moving eyes in the ring – weeping eyes – and the eyes became part of a face. A face he knew well.

Horror-struck, Joel ardently tried to turn his face from the sight, but it was clamped down firmly by Deucalion. He could not move at all, could not even close his eyes, and – oh! – how he longed to close his eyes! Watering and sore, they were forced to look upon the countenance of his Ganieda, more beautiful than even his imagination had remembered her, crying from her very core. Her expression – so disappointed, so reproachful – would have twisted a knife even in a less susceptible heart. Joel gasped, he panted, but still he met resistance at all sides, and still his eyes would not shut.

"Her spirit does not seem best pleased with you, does it?" Deucalion detachedly observed.

"Make it go away! What sorcery is this?" howled the struggling Joel.

"Do you believe now? Have you finally realised the power of the fairies, and the tie we have with you?"

"But how – how?"

"For one, I have no interest in your worthless kingdom. Keep it, do as you wish – I do not think your people particularly worth saving, but-"

"That is as well, for you will never have it! Not even this – this witchery you practise on me – will make me forsake it!" Joel said through a clenched jaw, though it sounded as if his resolution wavered.

"That is unfortunate. When they said you were chosen to do a significant thing, I did not realise that thing would be to demolish any remnants of peace between fairies and humans."

Joel squirmed and deflated as if fainting, but Deucalion held him up by the roots of his hair. Deucalion longed at that moment to kill him. Only the strictest remembrance of his duties as a fairy stayed his hand, although he did not love these duties with particular ardour, and could hardly be bothered to carry them through.

"Oh, what, " cried Joel at last, nearly completely shattered, "what will it take to remove this from my sight?"

Deucalion looked suitably smug. "Here's a little concept I've been working on. You disband your Knights, you get every worthless one of them clear of Laseri, and you stay in Iblees. All of you, only in Iblees. And we, in return, will leave you alone. Completely alone. You come nowhere near us, we come nowhere near you – does that sound fair?"

"To confine my whole kingdom to the capital?! No, it does not sound – it – oh! – oh!" Joel felt his arm twisted again, and his face pressed even nearer the painfully bright ring.

"Alright, alright, I agree!" Joel nearly choked on the words; he choked even more at the thought he had been wrong about the fairies all along, and the terrible realisations that brought upon him.

"Good! For remember, her spirit dwells with our ancestors – they have charge of it, and they love us. A little something to think on if you ever plan on violating the agreement."

The sudden release from Deucalion's grasp gave Joel the sensation of falling much further than he actually did. His body sunk low into the sand, and he felt all the substance of his spirit crumbled to grains just as fine.

He heard a snap, as if someone had clicked their fingers beside him. He did not even have the will to raise his head to see what it was. By the time he finally did – he could not say if it was seconds or hours later – every fairy had vanished. His Knights looked around in sheer bafflement for the fairies they had been duelling. There was only silence, and the wind. They all looked to their King.

He returned his face to the sand.

27

CHAPTER TWENTY-SEVEN

They came speeding towards the airy mountain of the Colosseum, beaming light from every direction. Victory was theirs, and it gave a new speed and opalescent beauty to their wings. Despite their shattered fairy cities, despite the damage to the trees, despite the fact they were now divided further than ever from the humans, the fairy army were overflowing with lightness, joy and ecstasy.

In fairness to fairy sensibility, this particular unit had had some days to come to terms with the less pleasant aspects of the victory, such as the death of their well beloved King.

So how could they be sorry now that their new and popular King had already ascended to the Colosseum, awaiting only the things they brought him now in their arms to proceed with his coronation?

So joyful were the populous at the air units' return that they were dancing in rings and waving glowing lamps at them. Coloured streamers shot up in the air and the sky was filled with the richest tinctures of colour.

Apollo beamed with self satisfaction to see the displays below. The thrill of winning this long war was almost too much to absorb. He looked down into his arms, where he held the unconscious Aurora. She looked very beautiful and peaceful with her spangled dress and waving luminous hair, which was blowing around her body like living strands of gold.

To his right, his fellow warrior Erebus carried Cynthia. Apollo did not consider this to be such a valuable responsibility. He, and he alone was carrying the future Queen of Laseri.

Amidst cries of celebration they landed on the juicy green grass of the mountain. Almost immediately fairies of all sizes began to swarm around, pushing for a view.

Apollo could barely breathe, he was so crushed, but that did not matter so long as his charge was safely cradled in his arms.

"Stop it! Stand back!" demanded an imperious voice.

Apollo made out tall banners bobbing their way through the masses, and heard the orderly tread of feet.

The on-lookers pressing in around him whispered and gasped. They began to fall back respectfully.

Apollo now had room enough to see the Guards of the Gate marching towards him, conveying between them the safe passage of the new, if not official, King Deucalion.

The fresh King's young face was still scarred from fighting, and the rims of his star-bright eyes were red and purple. He looked very serious, but his tone was light as he flicked back his hair and said: "Well, what do you have for me? Is that her? Give her some room, fairies, give her some room! What are you thinking?"

The fairies shuffled or hovered out of the way. It was a messy, disorganised business but soon they formed a wide circle a good distance away from the newly alighted soldiers.

Deucalion walked up to Apollo and inspected the fair bundle in his arms. "It is you who has my treasure, is it? Lay her down, then, if you would." Together they gently placed Aurora and Cynthia on the fresh green ground. They looked very serene, with their bluish-white eyelids shut as in a profound sleep, and their rosy lips slightly parted.

The prince bit his fingernail as he looked down upon them. "They are not injured?" he asked Apollo.

Apollo shook his black head. "No, not to our knowledge. We only had time to check them quickly. It was exhaustion that made them pass out, I think."

"And where did you find them?"

"Very near the fairy camp. They must have been trying to get there."

Deucalion nodded. They must have had a reason to bring back their wings. "And you carried her all the way?" Apollo pulled himself up as tall as he could. It still fell short of the height of an average fairy. "Yes, your Majesty. I did."

"Good fellow! I will have you made a Guard of the Gate for this!" Deucalion slapped the glowing soldier on the back. Apollo nearly choked with pride. "Now, get her inside and put her to bed. She has much to become acquainted with."

Apollo's smile drooped. He hung his head. "I suppose she does not know about –" he raised his face slightly to ask the question "– about her parents?"

The King shook his head. "No. How could she? But I will give her a royal family in replacement, never worry." Deucalion was starting to walk back when Erebus stepped forward, calling his name.

"Your Majesty, we saw a terrible thing as we flew." He came closer to the King and began to whisper confidentially. "Some Deevs had taken hold of a human lady. I will not describe what we saw. But I think she will be injured, and maybe with child, and there will be no way to get herself home. Is there anything we can do? May I have your permission to go and seek her?"

Deucalion thought about this. It was rather a complex moral issue for so early in the morning. He sighed. "I am not sure what we would do with her once you did find her – if you did. I have no want of a human! It is regrettable, but…"

"I will build her a little place in the woods," Erebus invented, "like you are doing for the Blue Fairy. I will look after her; you need do nothing."

"Well," said Deucalion warily, "it probably isn't a good idea to be so close to a human at the moment…Especially a multiplying human. We do not even know what kind of creature will sprout from her ill fated womb."

Erebus would not be appeased. "Please, your Majesty! I feel this very strongly."

Deucalion looked into his flaming eyes and saw that he really did. He did not have the energy to fight against someone with strong feelings today. Besides, it wouldn't hurt his reign to be seen to be granting a few favours at the beginning.

"Very well. You may take whoever is mad enough to go with you. Only – don't bring her to Laseri! And when she is well enough, her and the "baby" – if there is a one – are sent packing to Iblees. Is that clear?"

"Very clear," beamed Erebus, and ran off to find the Lady Urvasi.

Aurora awoke feeling very luxurious. The pillows beneath her were soft and billowy, the covers around her so beautifully snug and warm! She was reluctant to open her aching eyes. This comfort must be a dream, and she did not want it to fade. She stretched her limbs. It felt divine.

"The beauty wakes," commented a low, companionable voice.

Aurora started. Her eyes flicked open in an instant.

She blinked and rubbed her eyes as she looked

around her. It was amazingly bright – not only the light, but the colours.

A thousand rainbows shimmered around her. She was in a cave of dazzling white crystals. The floor was paved with burnished gold, and the room was lighted by the glimmer of diamonds. To her right, the Price Deucalion sat astride a rocky stool.

Aurora thought she dreamed. She gave a start and cried, amongst other incoherent words: "The war!"

"Ended weeks ago," Deucalion finished for her. "I am sorry you missed it. It turned out well." He smiled at her.

Aurora put her pounding head in her hands, and lay back on the squashy pillow. Was it really over? Final and complete at last? And the fairies were the victors! It was too great a triumph to take on board so soon after regaining consciousness.

Ere these happy sensations had finished, a thousand concerns claimed her attention and pushed them away. What would happen now? What had become of her human friends; of Asher, of Urvasi? If the fairies had won, there was a strong chance that the human King was now dead.

Aurora shuddered, and realised for the first time that Cynthia was not with her. This thought galvanised her more strongly than the rest. She flung her pretty white legs over the side of the bed and stumbled to her feet.

Deucalion aped her motion. He was there ready to catch her as she swayed.

"Cynthia! Where is Cynthia?" she challenged him, searching his face ardently.

Deucalion laughed and tightened his grip on her shoulders. "There, now! You are worrying yourself over nothing! She is quite well. I have returned her to her parents. She awoke from her stupor a little before you. I think it is the only thing she will ever have to gloat over you with."

Deucalion had the pleasure of seeing the face before him erupt with the most gleeful smiles. A cloud cleared from Aurora's forehead and her lips curled upwards. "My parents!" she beamed at him. "Oh, take me to them Deucalion! How glad this victory will make them!"

Hard as he tried, Deucalion knew his efforts to control his expression failed appallingly. He felt his joyful mouth closing. He could almost see the sparkling light pass out of his own eyes. Aurora observed it too. She mirrored his face in her own. But she would not be the first to speak. She looked at him mournfully, yet she would not ask.

"You know – I cannot," Deucalion stuttered at last. Aurora nodded, and her shoulders slumped. That was all.

Deucalion felt it incumbent upon him to explain further. The less she said, the more her wan face, her world-weary eyes screamed out. "Many terrible things have happened," he continued. "I do not know where to begin telling you about them. Many of our fays were taken prisoner and raped – or maybe they were not, I do not know. But they are bearing *creatures* in a matter of weeks – vile, sickly *green* things. Most of their mothers are afraid of them; they throw them out into the forest. I have not allowed any of them back into Laseri with their – offspring – the astrals say we cannot know what such unnatural creatures will do. This suits the mothers; they are either in terror of their produce, or loathe it as a reminder of the ordeal they suffered."

Aurora shivered. Deucalion looked as deathly pale as if he was one of the mothers himself. "That is ghastly. What have you done with the mothers?"

Deucalion looked doubtful. "Well, they are back home. But they are not like proper fairies anymore. I do not know how to explain it. And the other fairies are angry at them. They say they have disgraced our name. They demanded punishment." His jaw set suddenly.

Aurora looked thunderstruck. She seemed to be thinking alternatively of her dead parents and these injured fairies, and reaching no merry conclusions either way. "Punishment for being captured? That is the strangest thing I have ever heard! What have you done to them?"

"I have tied back their wings for a start. If the astrals are right, I cannot risk them flying all over the place to aid their Knight lovers."

Aurora considered, and tried to be reasonable in spite of her initial horror at this information. "I daresay that is right at such a crucial time. But it does seem awfully-"

"And then I have cut their hair short, so they can be easily identified," Deucalion spoke over her. "You cannot be too suspicious at such times as these." He looked so defensive of his action, that Aurora suspected he was ashamed of himself.

"Oh, really!" she cried. "To maim a fay of her beauty, as if she asked to be taken captive! That is not like a fairy, Deucalion. That is – " It was too horrible, and Aurora turned her face away. She was still fighting back the tears for her parents. That news was seeping in very, very slowly, filling her heart with a heavy weight every instant.

Deucalion let go of her suddenly. Aurora felt herself wobble as he walked away and turned his back on her. "So they can be easily identified," he repeated. "I have been on my own here. It is unkind of you to judge me. I have been all alone, and I have done what the astrals asked of me." He raised his head, and looked at her hopefully out of the corner of his violet eye. "But now *you* are awake, and it may go better with me." He returned to her with his hand outstretched and took hold of her fingertips. "Our marriage and coronation can be celebrated straight away.

As the official King, I will be in full control of the astrals. You can help me to decide what -"

Aurora snapped her fingers away violently. Her whole frame trembled. "Marriage?" she repeated incredulously. "I could not think of it! So soon after my parent's death – I – I -" The vision of her mother's enthusiasm whenever they discussed the subject of her intended marriage to Deucalion floated before Aurora's eyes and filled them with bitter tears. She did not feel ready to become Queen of Laseri; she felt fit only to curl up into a ball and sob.

"You are not the only one to have lost parents," Deucalion reminded her acidly, and it struck her for the first time that Iubdan must be dead for Deucalion to be making such a request of her.

She had been counting on King Iubdan to help her in her new determination. Now that she had met the human she was sworn to protect, she meant to dedicate herself to bringing the fairies back to the golden age. She did not feel like making the same requests of Deucalion. She doubted he would understand.

"I am sorry for your loss," Aurora murmured. The tumult of her feelings and scarcely awakened mind was too great. Invalid as she was, she groped her way to the door and began to walk shakily away.

Deucalion was fast on her heels. She could hear his footsteps coming towards her as if from underwater. "Where are you going? Were you not listening? Laseri is in peril! We must marry and receive our crowns immediately!"

Somewhere deep inside Aurora knew it to be a wise course of action; a path she would take one day. But the various shocks she had received were playing upon her heart and mind. Every instinct revolted at the thought of what Deucalion proposed right now. Aurora was deeply confused and distressed. She wanted only to flee.

"No! I am in no fit state to be a Queen. Delay no longer; be crowned yourself and leave me be!" she pleaded and tried to run.

Deucalion had no trouble keeping up with her. "Impossible! Everyone expects our wedding," he insisted. His frustration and disappointment were written all over his face. "If it does not take place people will ask why. They are suspicious enough of you and Cynthia, being so long amongst the humans. Do not give them, or me, reason to question where your allegiances lie."

There was a threat, an accusation almost in the last sentence.

Aurora felt herself stiffen. How impossible it was to convey that her allegiance *was* with the humans – and as a fairy, his should be too! Now she had reasons for refusing him: she was angry, she was insulted, and she held him in great contempt.

Aurora ran out of the cool white cave and found herself in the bustle of the market place outside the Colosseum. The fast moving fairies and clamour of haggling voices did nothing to alleviate her light head.

Hardly cognisant of her direction, Aurora continued to walk. She was surprised she did not bump into any person or object. She had taken many steps before she realised that fairies were standing out of her way on purpose. The babble of voices was rising – not because she was entering the heart of the market place, but because everyone had seen *her*.

There was a stamp of feet, and Aurora became aware that the Guard of the Gate were closing in around her. She flinched, but then understood they were protecting her from the advances of over-eager fairies.

"There she is!"

"Our Queen, look, it's the Queen!"

"Stay back my fee, she's been amongst the humans."

"Is she any different? She looks curious."

"What do you think they did to her?"

The circle around Aurora began to spin. She tried to stand tall and stare back at the onlookers.

In unison the chatter crowd hushed their noise. The King – or, almost King – was heading towards them with another barrage of soldiers.

"May I congratulate you, Prince Deucalion, on the safe return of your bride," one of the Guards of the Gate spoke up. "May we hope to see you crowned at last?"

"My bride?" asked Deucalion. He shrugged one shoulder. "I have no bride, though it was my father's wish. What do you think? She affirms that she will not have me!"

Outraged cries rang out through the market place. Only Apollo, somewhere to the back of the circle of Guards, manifested small signs of pleasure.

The soldiers Deucalion had gathered on-route exclaimed, confounded.

"Will not have you, Deucalion!" erupted one called Leto. "What else is she aiming for? I thought it was settled?"

Deucalion put up his hands in a hushing motion. "I was gullible enough to expect a thing settled between our parents was settled between us. But promises seem to have died when they died. My father always trusted her, but I knew she was good at misleading. That was why I recommended her to go to Iblees. She *wanted* to help the war effort. I thought she might have some gratitude towards me." Deucalion pulled a tragic expression. "But what can you do? We shall have to abandon our idea of a Queen, dear Leto."

Some of the young pretty fays perked up at this new opening. They fluttered long eyelashes and bright wings in the Prince's direction.

"But this is despicable!" exclaimed another soldier, Tethys. "What are we going to do with her in the mean time? Has she given a valid reason for her refusal? It is her duty to Laseri!"

Aurora used every last morsel of energy in her to return, "My duty! Oh, you still do not see! When I am well I will explain it. My duty and your duty to Laseri have nothing to do with noble families and fine palaces – it – it – " she swooned forwards, but Apollo was there to catch her.

"I do not trust her!" cried someone from the gathering. "It is these humans; they have infiltrated her, they have warped her!"

"It *is* incredible that with all her magic, attacks on Laseri kept coming from the human kingdom. Why didn't she stop them?"

"Maybe she helped them!"

Hungry, wary eyes darted at Aurora from all directions, assessing her from blonde head to dainty toe for some sign of corruption.

Deucalion found the more incensed the crowd became against her, the angrier he became himself. He was hourly more affronted. He did not want to show himself as a King easily swayed by emotion – indeed, on the seldom occasions he felt strong emotion, it rarely swayed him – but he felt he must do *something*. After all, he had searched so hard for her, he had delayed his own glory, he had relied upon her – and how had she repaid him? He was stung. He could not deny it and he became desirous of stinging her likewise.

"It would indeed be wonderful if she turned down a position of such honour for the sake of those who murdered her parents and her King," Deucalion said coolly. "A terrible shame! We could have used her to help reconcile them with us eventually. But never mind; she does not want that! What would you have me do with her, my people?"

"Kill her!" cried someone wildly, probably one of the pretty ambitious fays.

"Banish her!"

"No, no – if she likes the company of humans, make her go and live in the hut with that one Erebus has!"

Deucalion turned to that soldier with interest. Erebus averted his face at the gaze.

"Ah yes, Erebus, I forgot your charitable act." Deucalion appealed to his intended Queen once more. "You see, Aurora, we are still trying to look after some humans, despite all they have done to us. You judge us too harshly. Ask Erebus – ask him about his little – what did you call her?" Deucalion questioned the solider.

Erebus' lip trembled. "She told me her name was Urvasi, sir."

Aurora nearly leapt from Apollo's supporting arms. Colour returned to her pale face, and she reached out eagerly for Erebus. "Urvasi! I know her! Oh, take me to her! Is she safe? You have rescued her! You do me a great service!"

This outburst of attachment to a human did nothing for her in the crowd's eyes.

"Shhh!" hushed Apollo. "You are proving them right; you are confirming their suspicions."

But Aurora did not care. She looked appealingly at Erebus, trying to walk towards him regardless of her weakness, Apollo's restraint and the barrier of people.

Erebus' wings drooped. He lowered his eyes. "I am sorry. I cannot take you. There were two – I almost called them fees. The birth was too much for her weakened frame. She died."

Aurora looked like she was choking. She fell backward and was suddenly glad once more for Apollo's arms. "Fees?! By the Angels, what happened to her?!"

The Last Fairy Tale

"Deevs," Erebus replied quietly.

A great sob shook Aurora. "Poor Urvasi! What have you done with her children?" She thought she would care for them if she could not help Urvasi now. But the other fairies did not see it that way.

"Listen to her!" shrieked one in horror. "She has feelings for those green monsters!"

"Oh merciful Angels, it is true after all! She is tainted!"

"Did you hear how she calls them *children*? That is *their* word!"

Deucalion felt himself turn sick. Suspicions that had not occurred to him before began to taunt his brain. "Quiet! Answer the fay, Erebus."

Erebus looked up, surprised. "Well," he said uncertainly, "I have done what we did to the rest. The Blue Fairy has taken them out to a distant part of the forest."

"Where?" asked Aurora. "She need not care for them; I will."

"Care for them?!" repeated Erebus. "No, it is a part of the forest known only to her. She has left them. They should never have been in the world, any of them. They are a horrible reminder of a horrible war."

Aurora did not cry out or reproach him. But she lost her sudden burst of energy; she sagged, and tried to take listless steps away from the circle. Apollo tried to support her, but she brushed his hands away from her.

Every fairy was crying that she must not escape – she could be dangerous. But not one stood in her way as she advanced towards them; they dove away as if she would infect them by close proximity.

"Do not let her go! Prince Deucalion – do not let her go! Chastise her!"

"This concern for the green creatures cannot be innocent."

Aurora reached Deucalion and placed her hands on his arm. He did not shudder like the rest of the fairies did. She turned her forlorn face up into his stern one. Her violet eyes were all clouded with unspeakable sorrow. "It is as you say, Deucalion: I may be of help to you *eventually*. You must forgive me. I did not mean I would never marry you. Perhaps I will, as I see I cannot do what I wished to alone. But look at me. Too much sorrow has afflicted me. How can I make such decisions now? Go, receive your crown and be a good leader. Maybe I will receive mine one day too. But not yet."

It was impossible to see this pretty sorrowful figure, suffering in such refined martyrdom, and not melt inside. Deucalion began to soften. The fairies fell quiet.

Deucalion took her cold white hand in his. "Little Cranberry Blue wings! What scrapes you get yourself into! I -" he stopped short and turned her hand over. All the gentleness fled his features. "What is *that*?!"

He held her hand aloft. Plainly there, for all to see, was the golden rose-quartz ring Asher had made for her. Complete bedlam ensued. Some fairies screamed and a volley of insults rang out against Aurora, who stood there, very grave, saying nothing.

"Aurora," demanded Deucalion, his wings bristling, "Is this - is this a human ring?!" his voice entreated her to contradict him. His mouth was open, aghast, and from the expression of his eyes, Aurora feared he really did love her.

When the uproar had died down slightly, she replied with a wavering voice, "It is. A very good human made it for me. I believe - "

"Oh Aurora!" groaned Apollo, "How can you wear such a thing! Take it off!"

Aurora stiffened. "I will never take this off!" she said fiercely. "You do not know what it stands for."

"Aurora," cried Deucalion, his voice higher than usual. "You must tell me something. Did a male human make this for you?"

Aurora was deeply insulted by his insinuations. She could not help the freckles appearing on her face. They were the freckles of true modesty, but the fairies of Laseri saw them, and took them to mean something more sinister.

"Yes. But if you will let me explain – "

No one would let her explain. The affirmation a male human had made the ring was enough. She had as good as signed her own death warrant.

"I knew it! A male human!"

"No wonder she showed compassion for the pixies! She will soon bear one!"

"She would not marry our King because she wanted to return to her human lover!"

"No! No!" wailed Aurora, "It is not like that!"

The crowd advanced, truly murderous now. Some civilians grabbed spears from the soldiers and advanced menacingly. They would have used them too, had Deucalion not called the soldiers to stand in their way.

Deucalion gathered her to him. He looked desperately at Aurora. There was sympathy in his face, where before there had been none, but the respect she had always observed in his demeanour toward her had flown away completely. "I can save you," he said, "I do not forget the family of Optilete. But you must take off that ring. I will protect you, I will marry you – but will you take it   off?"

Aurora crumpled before him. He asked too much. She knew her duty as a fairy, and it mattered more to her than the good opinion of her people, the love of a King, or her very life. She shook her head. It was an effort, but she shook her head steadily. "Never," she affirmed.

Aurora felt a cold rush of air as Deucalion released

her from the safety of his arms. She turned her face to the floor so that her long blonde hair hid her tears and prepared herself for pain.

"You heard her. She is a disgraced fairy." Aurora did not need to look up to imagine the scornful, scalded figure Deucalion was as he said this. Great blows of guilt and fear struck her by turns. "Do not kill her. We must honour the memory of King Iubdan. But so long as you keep her alive – do with her what you wish."

He stalked from the crowd with a confident, daring stride, as if nothing had happened to nettle or hurt him. A mask of complete apathy fell over him. He did not look back to see the fairies close in upon her; he did not even look back when the general clamour was pierced by the screams of Aurora.

28

CHAPTER TWENTY-EIGHT

There is only mist now in the wood; heavy, all consuming mist. The sun shoots clear rays through this fog from where it is setting in the west, causing the whole mass to glow bright white. It is possible, therefore, for Apollo to observe the figures before him as he trudges wearily on, over ditches and lumpy ground.

"She is – she is kind of pretty, almost, isn't she?" he suddenly whispers to Demetrius. It would make more sense for him to confide this sort of thing in Aurora, who he has known forever, but for some reason he feels a decided caginess about approaching her with subjects like these.

Demetrius, who is paying strict attention to his surroundings, turns to him with an irritated face, and then looks vaguely at the twin pixies leading the way. He makes a disgruntled sound and continues to break branches along the way, and arrange small rock piles. He is trying to secure their path back, should disaster strike.

Everyone else seems held in tension, expecting this great disaster, but Apollo – perhaps because he is a soldier and used to dangerous situations – finds himself quite at leisure, looking at the pixies.

"You wouldn't think it, if I described her. But she is – almost. In a weird, green, long eared sort of way. Prettier than that Daireann, at any rate."

Aurora, somehow omnipresent, has missed none of his ill concealed words.

"Only you, Apollo," she says dryly in his ear, making him jump. "Only you could look at a pair of identical twins and call one more attractive than the other."

Apollo turns very hot – he thinks it might be the rays of the dying sun suddenly shining upon him – and says no more. When at length he almost thinks of a comeback, the twin pixies have quickly dropped their linked arms and frozen solid.

The fairies and Demetrius follow suit, scared to move an inch. Their eyes question the twins.

"Listen to that," Daireann breathes, rather than says, in the lowest voice possible.

They listen. The trees around them seem to vibrate, they are listening so hard. Then they hear again what Daireann heard the first time: a snort. Demetrius shivers.

A sound of heavy breathing is getting louder and louder. They all shrink visibly inside themselves, looking for a place to hide.

Except Aurora and Daireann. The former raises her chin and cranes her neck with watchful, dangerous eyes; the latter has an arm around her sister, and is shooting out threatening sparks from her face like a bear guarding its cub.

A tread. Apollo and Aurora wheel round, hands poised, but only this blinding mist fills their view. Another step.

Demetrius judges it prudent to stand completely motionless. Something – it sounds like something coming through a bush – moves again.

Then there is a sound of sharp inhalation. It sounds like some creature sniffing, scenting them out.

"This fabled pixie magic would come in real handy right now," Apollo mutters to the still motionless

Demetrius.

He wishes he had never said a word. At the sound of his voice the footfalls start again, fast and determined this time, running. The whole party feel a gust of wind as the thing approaches. The sound of running stops.

Something else is there. They can sense its presence with them, although they can see nothing, barely even each other now the sun has moved even lower in the sky. Caelia looks close to fainting with apprehension.

Aurora tries to find the location of the presence. Her skin tingles. She tries to decide where it is warmest. She turns her head and feels a blast of hot breath on her neck. She gives out a little scream.

Apollo, quick as lightning, shoots a blast from his ring. It cracks against a tree branch, which falls heavily at their feet. As it does, Apollo hears a frightened whinny.

The oddness of the noise makes him squint at Aurora. He can see her now, beaming like a mad thing, and throwing her arms around a large shape beside her.

"Blanchard, Blanchard!" she tells them all, caressing her beautiful dapple grey steed. "He has followed me! Why was no one watching him carefully? It does not put my trust in my husband if he lets my animals career about in the most dangerous place imaginable."

"You do not have much trust in your husband anyway," Apollo points out. He feels an obscure sulkiness whenever they speak of her husband, even though he is Apollo's King and the one he is bound to serve and love. Apollo cannot really remember how, when or why this started.

However, his attention is soon caught by Caelia, who has disentangled herself from her sister and made her way towards the animal.

"Beautiful, beautiful horsey," she murmurs to it, plus some other nonsense baby-talk he cannot distinguish. She strokes its cheeks and looks deep into its eyes. Blanchard seems to calm her, and Apollo thinks how sweet and adorable this pixie is.

Demetrius, who seems to have forgotten this whole episode ever happened, shrugs his shoulders and begins to walk onwards as normal. "It will come in handy to have a horse around. Their instincts, you know, are quicker than ours, and he can carry us when we're tired."

The others stare at him in amazement. But they are obliged to follow, lest they misplace him in the mist. His small green figure is rapidly being swallowed in its shroud.

Apollo is swift to offer Caelia an arm and guide her forwards to her sister.

Aurora brings up the rear with Blanchard. Even he, her dear horse, looks strangely distracted in this eerie forest, she thinks.

The woods continue as dark and mysterious as ever. Dead leaves on the less thriving trees look, from a distance, like berries; a cruel deception to a hungry traveller, who reaches it to find only a mouthful of dry decay.

"I'm hungry," says Apollo, this fate having befallen him several times. "Can I not at least have some of that dry bread, Aurora?"

Blanchard gives a little lurch which prevents Aurora from replying, as she tries to regain control of the horse.

It is Daireann the pixie, who rounds on him to respond, her green face glowing spookily out of the mist. "You know you cannot. It protects against the Deevs; she told you."

"Well I'm sorry, but when fairies bring any kind of bread, it's usually for rations."

Daireann turns contemptuously away; Caelia gives a consoling little smile before following her sister. This, somehow, makes the hunger worthwhile.

Having given the quest for food up momentarily, Apollo walks on. This is not like an army march. It seems nothing will break the stifling stillness of this forest. He begins to whistle.

"Shhhhhh!" A stern hush comes from every member of the group – save Caelia, who looks on in pretty green ignorance.

"What?"

"No whistling, no shouting," explains Aurora, but looks far too tired to explain why. Apollo tells her how tired she looks; it comes out sounding more like an affront than the kind, caring remark he had intended. Yet it does not seem to matter as much as it used to.

"I *am* tired," admits Aurora, and in another second swings herself gracefully onto the back of Blanchard.

There is nothing else to say or do now. Apollo amuses himself with watching Caelia, although it is not possible to do this all of the time without detection. He watches the tree tops in the interims. He manages to find something beautiful in the leaves and the mist-cloaked branches. It seems at times, just for a second, as if the sun is about to burst through – and then it does not.

It is as he lowers his gaze that he sees it. It is past mistake now; those twigs are weighed down by shining, bright red drops. Apollo starts towards the berries eagerly.

One moment he is running, the next, he feels a sea of feathery moss against his face. Hurting along both sides, Apollo realises the world is wonky, and he is laid upon the ground. He can hear the muffled sound of repressed laughter. Dizzily he raises his head, and looks to where the tree was. It is gone. He looks in the other direction. It is there. It is moving.

"What – what?" he begins helplessly, pointing at it.

"The trees move," Demetrius informs him helpfully.

"Clearly. Does no one else find this strange?"

The pixies blink. Aurora merely yawns. "They have always moved," sighs Daireann irritably.

Apollo stumbles to his feet and runs after the retreating party. He is at a loss how everyone except him knows these things – and he an experienced soldier of King Deucalion!

"But then every land mark will move! How will we find our way back?"

"That is why I am dropping twigs, leaves and crumbs," Demetrius tells him, in the manner of one teaching a small child.

"Oh. Right. Yes, you – continue doing that, then."

As they continue, blobs of light float through the trees. They are there for only a second, their form and shape as elusive as a dream. They become more frequent, and are soon accompanied by a gentle lapping sound.

"Water," Demetrius decrees, a grin suggested on his lips. "Now, we must be very careful about-"

The sickening scream of an animal interrupts him and throws them all off balance.

It is the cry of Aurora's horse. They turn to see what is happening.

The white blur of Blanchard brushes past them, mane flying wildly. Aurora speaks soothingly to him, tries to sit back and calm his frenzied whinnies. Even her calm composure cannot stop his pawing and constant side stepping. He dances round and round the group.

"Hey now, little fellow!" says Demetrius as calmly as he can.

They are all now speaking softly to him, placating him with raised hands. Apollo is chilled to see a flash of red in the horse's eye – it must have caught a ray of sunlight, from somewhere.

"Be a good boy," whispers Caelia.

Blanchard finally breaks Aurora's masterly grip on the reins and plunges at a gallop through the trees.

Thoughtlessly, they charge after her as one. Demetrius barely remembers to drop crumbs as he goes, they are forced to sprint so fast after the four retreating hooves. Divets of mud fly into their faces.

Finally some of the heavy growth thins out – they see an immense lake, looking enchanted through its thin cover of mist.

"Perhaps he is only thirsty," chirps Caelia, oblivious of how stupid she sounds. "We do not need to chase him any further."

Surprisingly, her friends will not stop as she stops. They run all the way to the edge of the lake, just in time to watch Blanchard leap wildly into the frothing water, still giving that horrible neigh.

The pixies scream. Just visible through the splashes is Blanchard's untamed mane, growing to an unprecedented length and taking on the form of seaweed.

Apollo runs unthinkingly into the churning water. The cold smack as it hits his body freezes him for an instant. Immobile, he sees a wild green tress sweeping towards him. Closing his eyes, Apollo feels the cool, slimy lick of it against his skin. It smells of salt and dead leaves.

The slithering seaweed-mane withdraws – and comes back a second later with force redoubled. Apollo winces from the impact of the weed and the water it pushes with it. He can see himself being propelled backwards, lifting into the air with an almighty splash. Just before hitting the ground he thinks to use his wings, and rises up, determined and dripping like a miniature rain cloud.

Aurora's useless wings are weighing her under the water. She comes up occasionally, hair plastered to her forehead and gasping for air, but Blanchard's mane, like tentacles, is wrapping round her body, drawing her under.

Apollo fires a blast from his ring. It snaps a coil of the horse's green hair, giving Aurora a moment's longer breath.

Blanchard grunts in pain and turns to face his opponent. Apollo is shocked to see the noble steed has turned into an entirely different creature with sharp, pointed teeth. Apollo fires again.

"Oh, oh, don't hurt the horse!" pleads Caelia. No one remarks on her stupidity. The other pixies are trying vainly to get into the water and prise Aurora from the tangle she is in.

Demetrius is trying to mutter a pixie spell, but every time he nears completion, an arm of seaweed-mane dunks him, splashes him, or knocks him from his feet.

Apollo has nearly managed to unloose Aurora enough for her to struggle back to shore. Yet each snare he breaks seems to grow again from elsewhere, bringing her irresistibly nearer to the ready teeth of her past horse.

Seeing this, Apollo increases the rapidity of his fire. He swoops and battles with such fury that Blanchard is entirely distracted by him for a short while.

It is enough for Demetrius. He has a sudden idea. Taking off, with one deft snatch at his neck, a piece of red thread hanging about it, he swims like any stream-lined dolphin across the lake, and pounces on the very head of the beast.

It shrieks a painful, ear splitting shriek. Aurora is dropped completely and sinks in a burst of bubbles under the surface. The mane of what was once Blanchard thrashes about insanely, whipping branches from trees and throwing up fish from the lake. Yet still Demetrius sits firm upon its forehead.

He is making a contraption around the horse's head. He is bitten, he is bleeding, he is nearly thrown off several times but holds on with purpose, hands and thighs straining.

He makes a small improvised bridle, with a cross on the face – straight down the forehead and intersected high up the nose. As he ties the last knot, the water quells. The tentacles stop, fall off, shrink and retreat back to the roots of the mane.

Soon all that is in the water is a horse, out of its depth and swimming to the bank, a triumphant green rider upon its back.

The animal comes ashore, leaving no one with anything much to say. They make no attempt whatsoever to crowd round Blanchard. On the contrary, Daireann backs away from the now, to all appearances, placid horse, expecting him at any moment to launch into another frenzy.

There is a loud splash. Caelia gasps, probably thinking for a split second Blanchard really is about to turn back. But no, it is only Aurora, coughing and spluttering as she drags herself along the bank on her stomach, hair plastered over her face and her dress slicked to her body. To her own, and indeed, Apollo's surprise, he does not run over to help her.

Although Aurora's beautiful face has waned in colour through the lack of oxygen, the expression upon it is as dark as night.

"Do not worry, Fairy Queen." Demetrius is the only one who ventures to talk – the others are still coming to terms with the shock of the event, and the all too sudden return to normality. "You could not be expected to know that your horse was an Aughisky. Only pixies really know-"

"I know what an Aughisky is, thank you very much!" Aurora cries, in something very like a strop, and pulls herself to her feet.

"Well I do not," says Caelia with a blink. "We were

so worried – please explain what happened to the horsy?"

Demetrius pats the animal's neck and vaults off his back. "He is perfectly safe now. Really Caelia, what type of pixie are you that you do not know this? It is a Deev horse – they can be very fine horses too, only if they return to water they take up those highly unpleasant habits again – eating flesh and the like. This is the only way to bridle them." He waves a self-satisfied arm towards his handiwork.

Aurora is brushing the dust from her gown and wringing her sopping wet hair in a coil. "I have ridden him near water before. Do you think there is no water in Laseri?"

"That cannot be!" Demetrius' green forehead creases. "How else would you suggest..."

But he stops when he sees the way Aurora and Apollo are looking at each other.

"Pixies," says Apollo, and not very pleasantly. "I told you about pixies."

"Perhaps I should have listened. With a Deev for a father – I – I thought the mother might bring about balance..." Aurora looks pointedly at Daireann.

A sudden tumult breaks loose. Demetrius, in high indignation cries: "Wait, you think *we* – didn't I just save your life?" at the same time Daireann repeats in shellshock: "A Deev? My father a Deev? It isn't true! Stop lying, stop lying!" Caelia does not seem as shocked or surprised. She looks, in fact, as vacant as if she understands none of the words, which she probably doesn't.

They begin to argue, they all talk at once in increasing volume, until Daireann, who has really had enough, blasts a jet into the ground with incredible force. They all fall quiet to observe the smoking black crater. This proof of violent magic does not cause the fairies to view her with less suspicion.

"Look," she pants, her voice shaking with anger, "we did nothing to your horse. I have never even seen one of those – *things* until today. But now we are extremely lost, and I suggest the best course of action is to find our way back again."

Apollo is all for killing Daireann on the spot, convinced she is only trying to further lead them out of their way in order to attack. Aurora cannot be sure Daireann does not have this purpose in mind, but acknowledges the truth of her statement.

"When we find our way back to the path," she hisses to Apollo under her breath, "perhaps we will find a way to leave them behind. I planned to find Calleach Bhuer and see if she could grant us a safe passage through. But until then, it is better to keep the pixies with us and on our side."

And really, looking at Caelia, Apollo has to agree it would be better to keep the pixies with them for a while longer.

29

CHAPTER TWENTY-NINE

As it transpires, they have to keep the pixies with them anyway. They find it is next to impossible to get rid of the pixies, even if the pixies would go of their own accord. There is, in fact, no way out for either pixie or fairy.

Demetrius has neglected his crumb dropping duty, so after scanning the earth for a hint in vain, they decide to try walking through every inviting gap in the trees. But whichever path they take, no matter how many cunning little twists and turns they take, they end up back by the lake.

At first this is amusing, and it is some relief to laugh at their own stupidity after the frightening scenes of earlier. But an hour of this practise is more than enough. It rapidly becomes downright frustrating, and whoever is walking in front takes a serious scolding for choosing the wrong path – again.

The trees, standing in a gnarled mossy watch over the travellers, seem to mock their efforts as they twist about them. The foliage has concocted a plan to carry no distinguishing marks, or differ from the plant next to it in any way at all. It is as if the plants are *trying* to get them lost.

Before long, the sun joins in the game of making the voyagers uncomfortable. It sets, so that the air has a nip, and all light is gone.

Apollo thinks he can see the same fear in the glowing eyes of Caelia as that which is taking root in his stomach. But he could be wrong, for he can barely see at all.

Or can he? Is that light? Pale white lines moving to and fro? No, it is the moon upon the lake. The lake again. He lets out a groan, which sounds very similar to a whimper.

"Shhh," murmurs Aurora, not in the harsh tone of earlier. There is a catch, a panic in her hushing noise. It is not without reason.

Apollo turns towards the rippling water, and begins to fear himself that they may be overheard by the strange phenomenon upon it.

Skimming over the mirror-like surface is the same unearthly mist, but another glance reveals it to be more than mere vapour. There are figures made from it, dancing; ghostly figures of women with flowing hair and haunted faces.

They are both mesmerising and terrifying to watch. Blanchard gives a disapproving snort.

Caelia giggles girlishly at her companions' frightened expressions. "They look as if they mean no harm," she decides, and makes a tentative movement towards the misty creatures. Daireann holds her back firmly.

"It is not safe Caelia."

"Let me go!" pouts Caelia, in a voice too loud for Aurora and Demetrius' liking.

"Shhh!"

"It is not fair! I am not asking *you* to go near them. They may be able to help us."

"They may be able to kill us," returns Daireann. "You cannot even protect yourself with magic."

Caelia nearly sparks with umbrage in the dark. "Oh! How *could* you use that against me? How *could* you be so unfeeling?" She pulls a pinch of Daireann's green skin, twists hard, and escapes her sister's grasping fingers.

The travellers can only look on in horror as Caelia tiptoes near the lake. Apollo has half a mind to cast a spell and bring her back, but the glowing of his ring would surely get them notice.

Aurora swears the lake ladies catch sight of the pixie at least once. Yet they appear to accept her presence as nothing unusual.

Caelia smiles at the mist dancers. They ignore her. For some reason Caelia is encouraged by this, and beckons the others to join her. They do not.

Her companions cannot move at all for fear, although Apollo is perhaps more strongly tempted to follow her call than the others. But he knows only too well that Deevs can trick an entire regiment to their death with such initially friendly movements.

The group stay standing, aching and trembling from the cold – the still wet Aurora trembles most at the side of her dripping horse – all night. They stay until the sunlight comes, and melts the figures on the lake away. By the time dawn is full blown, it is as if they had never danced over its surface at all.

"I cannot tell you how glad I am that you allowed me to come on this journey with you," snipes Daireann suddenly. The others regard her in amazement. It seems awfully courageous and unnatural for anyone to speak, after the long, still and silent watch.

"Oh," she exclaims, stretching her seized up green limbs, "do not look at me like that! Stop being so cowardly. It is not as if anything I say could possibly bring back-"

She is cut off by a loud droning. It hums through the ground and vibrates every part of them. Daireann gasps, her bravado gone.

Demetrius and Aurora pass wild "What shall we do?" glances back and forth. Only Apollo, for once, appears to have retained his presence of mind.

He looks rather more comforted than scared by the sound. He walks out from the cover of the tree and throws his head up.

"Look," he invites Aurora over, pointing at the sky. Being a fay of substance, Aurora obeys him without much misgiving.

She sees a shape like a giant bug moving steadily through the clouds. Each part of it is well ordered and straight. A closer look reveals that it is made up of tinier parts, and all these tiny parts are moving individually. She recognises what she sees easily enough.

"The fairy army," she tells the pixies, her lips pale and trembling. Yet they are trembling with anger, not fear, and her fair face sets in new determination. She strides away from Apollo.

"Deucalion thinks he will get a head start on me. Well, we'll see about that! Come on! Why are you standing there! We must escape this lake!"

"Erm – he sort of has already got a start on us," Apollo tentatively points out.

"I don't know why you are bothering. Against him – especially against the Deevs – you are going to lose!" Daireann points out, not very helpfully. "What forces can possibly be stronger than the combined greed of two kings and the dark Deevs?"

"If you do not know that," cries Aurora, grabbing hold of Blanchard's bridle under the chin, "I will not waste my energy in speaking to you."

"You show yourself to be very much your father's daughter," she adds in a bitter breath as she starts to walk away.

Ere she has finished speaking, Daireann has launched herself upon Aurora with a furious howl sounding very like "My father was NOT A DEEV!"

They scrap on the ground, shrieking, neither able to use their magic in the tangle of their limbs. Aurora has her hands deeply imbedded in Daireann's ink black hair. The horse scrambles away from them with the whites of his eyes showing and hides behind Apollo.

Apollo does not know what to do with himself. He is somewhere in between disapproving of and taking pleasure from this female scrap.

Daireann is about to go for the wings.

Suddenly the pair scream once, together, even louder. Everything is illuminated, and the fighting duo are surrounded by a flash of purple light.

Demetrius has pulled them apart and is floating them in the air in separate purple bubbles.

"This is really not helping," he says very sternly, although Apollo looks as if he was rather enjoying it.

"We need to cross the lake!" exclaims Aurora, in a muffled, bubbly voice. "It is the only thing left to do."

"Cross the lake?" scoffs Daireann. "What could that possibly achieve? You are wasting precious time -"

"Do not ask me why! But it is right – I just know somehow it is the right thing to do!"

Demetrius releases the girls with a pop. They fall to the ground with groaning noises.

"We are cold already," he shrugs. "We may as well be cold and wet. I will trust you, Fairy Queen. For whatever reason, you make me trust you."

Aurora picks herself up in one graceful movement, as if nothing has happened. "You have acted very wisely," she compliments Demetrius and shakes his hand. "You are a credit to your race, and you shame us in our neglect of you."

"Oh, so it is only Demetrius' opinion that counts, is it?" says the indignant Daireann.

"If two of you say we should do it, we do? How is

that at all fair?" She glares. "It is very like a fairy, I will give you that."

She is not alone in her rebellion. "I do not think crossing the lake is a good idea at all," nods Caelia.

"Oh, do not be afraid," says Apollo, undisguisedly tender. "I will look after you. I am a soldier, you know."

There is nothing Caelia can really say to this. She and her sister still do not think it a good idea, but they are over ruled.

"If you want to stay in this clearing for the rest of your life, you are very welcome," Aurora concedes reasonably. "But as for us, we cross the lake."

She stalks purposefully over to the water's edge with her faithful steed trotting behind her. She hesitates only momentarily as the greenish liquid laps about her pretty little feet. The pressure of the pixies watching her makes her precipitately brave. She arches her slim form and dives straight into the water. Blanchard shows no inclination to become a green frothing monster again as he puts each hoof cautiously into the lake.

Apollo follows next, teeming with needless injunctions for Caelia to stay back.

He leaves his protective armour on the bank before wading waist deep. He looks to Aurora already swimming strongly, looks back to the pixies, and swims after Aurora.

The water is surprisingly calm and non-threatening. Apollo watches it gleam in front of him, a beautiful miniature sea. For a time just the feel of the water gliding past his arms and its gentle hushing sound calms him. It makes him feel they will really find their way after all.

A splash in the distance disturbs him, but a glance over his shoulder reveals it is only the pixies, who do not have enough fortitude to remain on the maddening shore alone.

Now that Apollo knows they are coming too, he feels

comforted to an even greater degree, and swims contentedly on.

But where is Aurora? He scans the waving blue horizon hurriedly. He had turned his head for but a moment, yet she is gone! Where *could* she have gone in so short a time? Drained inside with panic, he swims harder, his strokes becoming short and rapid.

"Aurora!" he calls, when the fear lets breath back into his body. How he expects her to reply without being there is anyone's guess, but predictably, she does not.

He calls again, this time water flooding his open mouth. Apollo realises he is struggling to swim. In his worry he must have forgotten to pay attention to how he was propelling himself. He tries to settle down and focus on his stroke. Strangely, it does not get any easier.

He is falling downwards, downwards. No matter how hard he fights the current, flailing limbs, flapping wings, the water comes up to his nose. He can hear the pixies beginning to weaken and thrash about also. Blanchard gives a terrified, deep throated scream.

Apollo has a sudden impulse to lie completely still and see what happens. He is a soldier, used to making split decisions, so he does it. He gives up swimming.

Apollo drops through the water. He does not simply sink, in the natural token of a body; he can feel himself being *sucked*, fast through the lake. Water rushes loudly in his ears. He begins to want breath. His head turns dizzy, he is nearly fainting…

He hits something with a sickening impact. His sore head is swimming, but it gradually dawns on him that *he* is not. He is lying upon something, and it is dry.

Blinking, Apollo opens his eyes and hazily sees Aurora, with the same dazed expression he must be sporting, on the ground beside him. *Ground*. It *is* ground!

Apollo goes to smile at her. A sudden blow to the

back deprives him of the ability. He chokes for air as a weight presses him deeper into the dirt.

"Pixies!" Aurora calls weakly. "Welcome."

The fair Aurora – somehow *still* fair, white and glowing, though she has been drenched and battered about – climbs shakily up and helps Daireann to her feet.

Apollo rolls unaided from underneath Demetrius and Caelia. He urges them to get out of the way before the impending weight of Blanchard slaps into the ground and misses them by an inch. The horse does not look impressed.

They all look giddily about them, and see the now familiar sight of ground ivy and overgrown furze bushes. They are back in the wood again.

30

CHAPTER THIRTY

All is not well in Auchriachan. The leaders of the kingdom are not well, and this spreads like a poison in the water throughout the whole stream of people.

Joy and happiness are gone on little fairy wings of their own. There are shouts, but they are not prompted by either of these two emotions. There is fear, there is occasionally crying, but that is only when the people cease to be indifferent. Although there is peace in Iblees, the whole city is broken and unwanted like old pottery.

Who can be inspired by a King like Joel? His face carries a permanently introverted expression, his figure frailer and thinning. It is not the figure of one who can win battles. Indeed, he did not win the fairy war, even in greater girth. The people do not trust in him.

Yet no one *needs* to trust in him. He does nothing proactive, holds none of their greater interests, neglects the interests he does hold, and keeps but a funeral court – and that rarely.

Kish currently attracts more devotees, due to the vibrancy about him – the alluring vibrancy sprung from pure anger. In his great rage, the citizens of Iblees feel he will at least get something done.

He has only one fault: Kish remains as constant and flattering to the King as ever. His followers suspect that he would like to open forces against the fairies more often than King Joel allows him.

Kish was made to look a fool by engaging himself – and some people rumour, his heart – to a fairy, the most hated creature he could imagine in all the world.

Nonetheless, there is not a soul in the whole of Auchriachan who would dare call him a fool. They respect and fear him, because of his great anger, and are very pleased with the provision the King has made to leave him as overseer for young Prince Elihu, should the King die whilst the Prince is still a minor. Undoubtedly Kish is also pleased with it, but the feeling does not show itself manifestly through the aforesaid anger.

Asher misses her. That is the sum of it. It was hard to recall life before the fairies came, and he still cannot recall it, in all the time that has passed. He has been somewhat mute since the day the three ladies – Aurora, Cynthia and Urvasi – disappeared. He says nothing, and says nothing with a distinctly vague manner.

Asher cares little for the kingdom now. He has a sense of a kingdom inside himself, greater and brighter than any on Earth, just waiting to be discovered. But that is it – a whisper, a sigh, and no discovery, none at all.

Asher spends his days in memories, infrequently varying to day dreams. They give him headaches and make him impatient with the real world. He thinks he must be in love, and wonders how it happened.

Sometimes he thinks of *her*, breathing out there beyond the forest, and convinces himself she loves him too. He is not sure if he believes it in his heart, but it keeps him going. It is nearly all he has left.

He cannot see the future now. It may as well have been decreed that he could not see at all, so great the loss of this sense impacts upon his life. It is a thing, like Aurora, he had no idea of missing until it was gone. And now he is alone, groping in the dark without either of them.

The King – his friend, Joel – who had long been cooling towards Asher, now regards him with complete disdain. The Sight had been Asher's one constant saving grace, and without it the King has no use, affection, or apparently even remembrance of him and the times they shared together. If it was possible to put Asher down, he would.

But as it is, even the Chosen King Joel cannot pass that law, and Asher hangs uselessly around Glass Mountain Castle, teaching the odd archery lesson. He spends the chief of his time with Prince Elihu, who has grown into a fine, strapping boy. They are very thick, the two of them. Elihu loves Asher as himself, and a great deal more than his father.

His father does not take kindly to this, when he does see or remember it. Which to be honest, is not very often.

Today Asher and Elihu are returning from a hot and sticky ride across the desert. They are quite ready to return their horses to the stables and plunge themselves under the nearest outlet of cold water. But it is not to be.

The sun is high in the endless blue sky, and there is no wind to break the way the air clings. It is near impossible to think of anything except the heat, although Asher, as we have detailed, somehow manages to do this.

King Joel evidently also has his mind far from the heat, for one of his guards suddenly thrusts the camel he is riding into the path of the two horsemen and demands their presence in the Castle.

"Whatever for?" demands Elihu.

Asher silently shakes his head and signals it would be best for them to follow.

They arrive, almost white from sand and dust, sweating and very unsavoury.

"I wish I knew what all this was about," cries Elihu

petulantly as they trail the guard through the castle. I can barely concentrate – I feel dizzy."

"It's probably the smell. You stink, your Grace," Asher helpfully informs him with a cheeky smile.

They are turning into a room and Elihu begins to giggle in a glorious, child-like melody.

"Yes, but why should that make me dizzy now? It's not as if it's any different from usual…"

"I concede that; you do stink consistently, but today is quite an achievement even for you. Yet fear not. I daresay your father will not notice the whiff, or even if you faint from it."

They are laughing and pushing one another as they turn to see that they are in the State room, surrounded by some very important people in very important and smart clothing, looking very important and serious. They are looking very serious, and very silently, at *them* in particular.

"Where have you been?" Joel immediately barks at his son from the heights of his throne. "Is this a fit way for a Prince to present himself?"

"I – I was with Asher." The Prince waves a redundant and awkward hand at Asher beside him for illustration.

"You were with Asher," repeats Joel scathingly. "Is it compliant with your duties, *Sir* Asher," he continues, as if the distance of adding a title is the only thing that can make it bearable to look at or address Asher, "to distract the Prince of Auchriachan from his duties and prevent him from attending the Council Meeting?"

Asher says the wise thing – namely, nothing – and hangs his head in what he hopes is a very meek manner. He is not really certain *what* his duties are now.

"Hey, Asher," calls a member of the King's advisors in a taunting voice, who is clearly having the same thought. "Seen any signs recently?"

Asher is on the point of making a very rude sign in return, but doesn't. This advisor is no better than him; purely a nominal advisor, whose advice carries the power only to be ignored.

"You will not spend your time with Sir Asher any more. Be seated."

The only seats available on the lower level are very far asunder. The pair separate towards them with reluctant looks.

"You may continue, Sir Kish," allows the King, when his beady eyes have ensured they are still and not so much as looking at one another.

Sir Kish pulls his face very grave. "There is the matter of the riot in Nibelheim. It is a long distance from the last, but imagine if they *should* band together. It stinks of rebellion, your Grace."

"Rebellion," scoffs Joel. "What have the people to rebel about?"

"They are restless, your liege. The court is too quiet for them. We lost many a man in the war, my King, and the villagers hunger for revenge."

Joel swallows. "I will not attack the fairies. I have said it before. It is insolence in them or you to question my judgement. We are at peace, we have food enough, we get along."

"But your – "

"I will *not* attack the fairies!" thunders Joel, in a way which suggests he may attack Kish, if not the winged creatures. He knows he has disobeyed his pact with Deucalion by letting his people live in the villages outside of Iblees. He dare not risk any more.

Kish feels it wise to say little else. He does, however, bestow a very mutinous look upon the King he loves so well.

"All that needs to be done," continues Joel, more

composedly, "is to locate the leader of this treason. I will wage war on *him*, fear not."

From the overall bored languor, several ears prick. No one has a care for much else other than attacking; the fairies or a person – either is good.

Elihu alone carries the appearance of one distressed that something violent might actually happen. His chest is expanding and contracting rapidly with the sharp, cold breaths of fear. Still more boy than youth, his eyes glimmer with the seeds of tears. Whether they are born of terror, rage, or misery is a mystery even Asher cannot fathom.

"My King, I do not believe there *is* a leader," Kish sighs heavily. "My job would be a world easier if there *was*. It is the workers – and a few latent Knights, it grieves me to add – resident outside Iblees who are expressing discontent."

Once, it is ironic to remember, Asher and Joel themselves may have been among these workers.

"The land is dry, unforgiving and unyielding, your Grace. They appeal to their King for aid in the only way they know how," Asher speaks out, surprised at himself. But he is ignored, and finds this less surprising.

"Plebeian minds that cannot call for help by using the authorised channels deserve to be treated as the land treats them," Kish comments dismissively. "The King, in his great wisdom, does not give them a war, so they amuse themselves with their own. This ingratitude should be punished most severely, but really it is only encouraging them. And it is such a shame, after all, to launch an attack on your own people." He shakes his head grievously, the picture of a good Knight torn between the love of his King and his people.

"I know you will serve us to the best of your ability in this matter." says Joel. There is a stress on the word *will*. It is no condescension. "There must be a rallying point, an organiser, if not an all out instigator. You shall hunt him out."

Kish bows. A rather disturbing smile plays around his lips.

The meeting passes without further incident. As it winds up, and the saddened advisors file slowly away from the bleak, shadowy room, Asher feels suddenly like the chamber he is leaving: as tall as it is empty and gaping. The shivers of losing a close friend consume him once more. It is worse than if Joel had died.

Asher has seen Joel turn into this figure left on the throne – foreign in being, marred in memory, and leaving him wondering if Joel had ever been what he thought he knew him to be.

Yet these ponderings are soon checked by renewed concern for Elihu. The boy, despite numerous inward attempts, stands visibly wondering how to love a parent like the one he is leaving in this chamber.

Despite every prohibiting word, Asher walks straight to the child, to relieve him from his mixture of awe and frustrated feelings for the man who is to be both father and mother but will not even look at him.

They leave the hall together, and it does not pass unnoticed. The piercing, yet motionless and silent eyes of the man who is supposed to be so much to both of them, follow their path up until the very moment the door is shut. Elihu cannot help entertaining a fancy they follow him further.

31

CHAPTER THIRTY-ONE

"We are lost," Demetrius states. "Hopelessly lost."

The others know it, but are angry at his unfeeling announcement of it all the same. There could be a gentler way to break to them the crushing failure they already know.

"Perhaps we could ask for directions?" Caelia suggests very quietly. "Not all of these Deevs can be evil... can they?"

Even her sister eyes her with decided scorn. Nay, even Apollo rises to the level of viewing her with deep disdain, and finds his attraction only multiplies with it.

Aurora looks to the place of the dying sun, tinting the sky amongst the mountains to the colour of ripening apples. Each peak is illuminated by turn, casting a long, long shadow, highlighting how very tall, very wooded and very, very impassable it is.

"It has been a long time, has it not Apollo, since the humming of your army stopped?" she says abstractedly, whilst the others abuse Caelia's stupidity.

"I should think so! The speed they go! Why, they'll be there already."

Aurora heaves the most dissatisfied breath and seats herself haphazardly on a boulder encrusted with some strange moss-like, unsightly plant.

She has many a distressing premonition of human

faces she once knew twisted in pain. Her imagination will not stop its unhelpful process, and absurdly conjures Sir Asher and King Deucalion fighting bloodily to their deaths.

"Then I am too late," Aurora's voice wobbles. "My friends… I had hoped to protect at least some of them. I could not protect Urvasi last time…"

"Your friends now, are they?" Apollo wheels around, livid. It is curiously possible to be angry at Aurora nowadays. "Who can say if your *friends* even survived the last battle? So much for the great fight to serve the fairies' true calling!"

"I do go on for that!" wails Aurora, tears stubbornly held behind her beautiful eyes.

"If the soldiers flew without getting attacked by the Deevs, I don't see why Apollo might not," Caelia adds defensively.

Apollo hurriedly begins to explain why this course of action is entirely inappropriate.

"I knew it was stupid," says Daireann helpfully. "But we've come this far on a fool's errand, so we might as well go on. I for one don't want to sit here and get eaten by Deevs. Who knows, maybe they'll let us join them if we ask kindly enough."

She is answered only by very dark looks. Demetrius mutters vaguely about her being "up to something". Her unseasonable, reckless optimism is entirely out of place in so bleak a moment.

"I don't know how I possibly thought I could protect fairy kind. I could not even protect Cynthia, right under my nose!" Aurora exclaims irritably and stamps her foot in sheer frustration at herself. "I cannot find the Blue Fairy, if she is even still alive. I cannot find my way to Iblees, though I have made the journey before!"

"Shhh!" Daireann looks intently at the undergrowth.

It is only dark and leafy. There is no movement, though they stare and imagine it until their eyes ache. It is only then they realise they are not meant to be staring, but listening. There is a sweet little melody, methodical, repetitive and hypnotising. Beginning weakly, it grows louder, until the fairy words *"Se do leine, se do leine ga mi negheadh"* become audible.

Demetrius approaches Daireann, his voice an angry low note. "What new spell is this you are weaving?"

Almost the moment the words are out of his mouth, there is an awful cry, like a goose screeching, a lost child sobbing and a wolf howling all at the same time. The group spontaneously clamp their hands to their ears and wince. An instant of pain, and then it is gone.

"Se do leine," starts up again.

Daireann pulls an amused face. "Now really Demetrius, I know I have some tricks up my sleeve, but I could not do *that!*"

"Oh, who would want to?" shudders Caelia.

"Come away," advises Demetrius. "We will go in the other direction."

But Aurora has already stood up and is looking for a passage into the undergrowth.

"We will kill it," improvises Apollo. "It could be the right way to Iblees. Or maybe that is what humans sound like?"

Daireann cocks her head so that her pointy green ear stands erect. Her great eyes sparkle. "Or perhaps it is that Blue Fairy your Queen is so eager to seek."

Aurora, judging she has nothing to lose, plunges herself into a thicket and chases the sound. If she could but make sure that staff and its bearer were protected, she would have achieved something! Though hanging back, the others follow, pausing only to block out the screech once more.

Apollo goes first, Daireann after him, Caelia holding her hand, and finally Demetrius when there is no one left to listen to his remonstrations, although he takes care to put on a very disapproving mien.

As the lichens and grimy green leaves are brushed aside, Aurora sees a vague shape. It is clean white and knelt beside a pond, around which the reeds grow. Aurora tiptoes forward. It is a hooded lady, singing gently to herself as she washes.

It cannot be Calleach Bheur, but it is a pleasant discovery nonetheless. Aurora listens, almost soothed, to the lap of the water on the laundry and the tune of the song. There could be no scene more lovely, more tranquil, until the hooded lady pauses suddenly, grasps her hooded head in her hands and utters the awful moan again.

The pixies waste no time in shutting their eyes and ears, but Aurora, somehow hardened to the noise, strains forward aghast. As the white lady cries, her despairing hands push her hood ever so slightly back, and Aurora catches a glimpse of something that compels her forward.

She freezes once her body has entirely passed through the hedge dividing the pond and their previous path. She can see now that the pond is the rich sticky red of blood.

But Apollo, only poking his head round enough to see what made Aurora gasp, cries out in an astonished voice: "Cynthia?! *Cynthia!*"

For the shrouded figure does indeed bare an uncanny resemblance to that fay. With that he plunges forward, his steps moving faster than his eyes to the sinister appearance of the pond.

His short but rapid legs bring him instantly to the figure. Quick as a flash, she lashes out, one of the sheets she is washing twisted like a whip in her hand. It strikes him on the leg – he cries and falls down.

The girls are horror-struck – Aurora all the more so, for she sees in the twisted features of the enraged woman the friend she held so dear for her journey to Iblees. Already weak from walking and lack of food, the fairy Queen nearly collapses. A thousand thoughts race through her aching brain.

Did Cynthia not die? Is this a ghost? A twin? What is it, and why will it not go away?

Demetrius dashes forward to rescue the howling Apollo. He pulls him back, green arms straining, as the odd Cynthia-like creature shrieks and howls. He clears him from the reach of the lashing sheet, but not without incurring a blow upon his face. Demetrius stumbles, still pulling Apollo for all his life, but his eyes are closed and swollen, blistering to an angry red.

Between them, Aurora and the twins manage to drag their injured companions through the bush once more. The Cynthia-creature has not moved, but remains shrieking, and now Caelia begins shrieking too. Demetrius and Apollo are wailing in pain.

It is wondrous then that Demetrius still hears Aurora mutter: "Oh my friend! What was it? What *was* it?" and that he sees, though his eyes are puffy and dimmed, that she means to go back and confront the thing that resembles her past comrade.

"I presume," he gasps through his agony, "that the creature who mortally maimed me is a friend of yours?"

"I – I thought she was murdered!" is all Aurora can reply.

"And so she was," Demetrius says forcefully, clamping his fumbling hand on one of her limp wings. "I have read of them, but never seen them: cut down in their prime, doomed to wash until the day they naturally would have died."

Speech is entirely suspended from Aurora for some

moments. "It cannot be true. You may study fairy law, my pixie friend, but I *am* one. Such things cannot happen to our spirit."

"These are strange times, Fairy Queen. A war is being launched by fairies against humans; fairies take to mischief and revelling; you yourself, the monarch of your kind, are marching through a forest, disgraced, with pixies. If I had told you that a few years ago, you would have replied to me that *such* things could not happen."

At a time when perhaps she should be despairing to a greater degree than she was even a moment ago, given that they are just as lost and now two of her companions will slow her down by being wounded, Aurora is renewed with strength. She recalls why she is on this quest, and if all that she can do is save Cynthia from this slavery of the soul, then she has accomplished something dear to her heart at least.

The woods no longer look dark and mysterious, but familiar and full of opportunity. Aurora is viewing them with the art of the possible, as a tool to something that must be achieved.

"Ow! For goodness sake, can I not just fly the rest of the way?" moans Apollo as they trek on. He is seated upon the snowy back of the now perfectly behaved Blanchard, but every bump in the path chafes his blistered, peeling red legs. Before his injury the idea of flying over a Deev-ridden forest was petrifying, but now it begins to look rather appealing.

"You can fly *home* if you wish. You will be more use there with legs like that," replies Aurora tartly, not turning back to him.

"I have no wish to go home," he says, rapidly looking between Aurora and Caelia. "What would King Deucalion say, after all? Me helping his wife in her madcap schemes and all. But really, all I can feel is pain. This cannot heal – it is too painful! Something must be done; I am no good to you, no good for this quest in this state."

Demetrius snickers as he thinks he hears Aurora make a comment under her breath.

"We could leave you here," offers Daireann brightly.

"No, I do not think that would help the mission either," is Apollo's firm opinion.

"Vervain." Aurora stops, and pronounces the word again.

Demetrius weighs the silence, before breaking into it with the comprehension only he has. "Do you really think we could find that herb?"

"I have no doubt it would cure you; I have seen it cure worse."

"Of course, of course," Apollo nods wisely. The pixies are not fooled by him.

Caelia looks to the grabbing branches of the trees, and the possibility of something dark lurking in the undergrowth. "We will only get lost. Even more lost!"

This chance is certainly not to be taken lightly. It is not funny to be lost, but to Apollo's selfish mind, to be hurt is even less funny. Humans have bought this war upon themselves, whereas he – a fairy, a mirror of grace and majesty divine – has not deserved his pain in the least. A war, after all, is not as important as his own immediate comfort. Yet strangely he appears to be the only one who realises this.

The least to comprehend this truth is Daireann. Still supporting her sister, she quips: "Yes, let us not forget our main purpose! This is all for nothing if we do not get to Iblees in time. We can worry about healing you afterwards. For now, we must go on."

"Oh, but I am in too much pain to go on!" groans Apollo tragically.

Each is fed up with the other. Apollo is still hungry and cranky, the pixies are resentful, and Aurora – well, aside from being upset about her friend, Aurora is perfection as always.

Interestingly, it is Caelia who comes up with a solution. Twisting a leaf around her green fingers, she says with a raised inflexion: "Queen Aurora knows what this herb looks like. Why does not she go to find it, and the rest of us push forward?"

Aurora scuffs her fairy feet in the dirt. It is not really viable to reveal her doubt that the rest of them could impede the war should she not return to them in time.

"It *is* a good idea," acknowledges Daireann in surprise. "You can shoot a flare from your ring when you have found it, and Apollo can respond in kind. We will stay put and you can come to find us. Then once you are back the whole mission will be sped along. It is the only way, save for leaving them here – which I must own is my personal preference – that we will get there in time."

Aurora sees all the wisdom of the representation. "I suppose," she sighs, running her hands along the tight bark of a tree, "if any of us can survive alone in this wood, it is I."

Apollo remonstrates loudly. He is afraid for her.

"I would go myself, with my sister," shrugs Caelia, all gentleness, "only I do not know how this herb looks, or how to send up a flare. I am altogether useless!"

Apollo remonstrates loudly against this too – perhaps even louder.

"This is wasting time. I will go. But none of you know the way," Aurora remembers with a moan of frustration. Seeing that they truly are watching the drops of the precious little time remaining trickle through their fingers, Demetrius cries: "Yes, go, and go now! We are pixies; we shall find some way. There is not long left. Go!"

Feeling all his urgency, Aurora nods determinedly, and goes. She does not say farewell, and she does not turn back. This is the last we may see of her for some time yet, as her beautiful blue wings disappear into the moist, shady background.

She is gone.

"Well," begins Daireann. She rides out another sickening, useless silence before finding the end of her sentence. "Let's be moving on, then."

The continuation of their journey seems more difficult and altogether purposeless without Aurora. They are just a huddle of tired, hungry creatures, who would not naturally choose each other's company, stranded in a dangerous forest.

Apollo realises with no great elation that he is abandoned on his own to the pixies. Added to his injury, it empties his spirit of all joy. At least he still has Caelia to look at, and without Aurora to test his loyalties. This must be his sole staying force as they drudge continually forward.

The walk becomes tiring and to be honest, completely boring, as quests often are once the initial zest has past. Even the novelty of losing Aurora has its day, and becomes far less consequential.

The trees are thinning to reveal a bruised sky, black and blue all over, yet it does not portend their arrival anywhere near Iblees. They are merely walking through thinner trees. Thinner trees mean more wind and increased shivering. Moreover, they let the rain through. Although there is none falling at present, the grimacing clouds show clearly enough that there has been, and may be again.

Subsequently, the ground is boggy and strewn with puddles. Blanchard finds it increasingly difficult to pick up his hooves, and it is all the twins can do to stop the blinded

Demetrius sliding down muddy banks.

"It smells," complains Caelia, as if she is the one in all this to be pitied for the assault to her nostrils. "I don't think we should go this way."

"Do you want to venture back over all of that?" responds her sister, nodding her head to the slick ground that they have traversed with some difficulty. But even she has to admit in her heart that the scent of rotten eggs is less than appealing.

"Have patience," says Demetrius. "Once I can see again, we can follow back all the twigs I have snapped and tokens I have dropped, if indeed we have gone that far astray. Just let us be moving and feel we are doing *something*."

There is a gurgle, almost like a burp. Caelia giggles and looks at Apollo.

"I didn't do that!" he immediately flares up, both in colour and tone.

Before they can tease, the mud immediately in front of the pixies bubbles. Big, pregnant bubbles full of reeking air.

They jump away and eye it suspiciously – even Demetrius, although he can witness none of it – but it does not happen again. It happens behind them.

Blanchard dances to the left. It is as well he does so, for a millisecond after, up shoots a geyser – a long fountain of dirt, slapping back to the ground with a disgusting squelch.

"What in the world is going on?" demands Demetrius breathlessly. He can only feel the earth moving beneath him, and hear the squeals of his companions.

Apollo is whiter than the white spots of the horse he sits astride, looking very much like he would love to run, but powerless to do so. Glances to the sky suggest he is thinking of using his wings, but is equally afraid of the

Deevs up there.

It is Caelia who, rolling her globular eyes around in anticipation of the next eruption, first sees the shape. It is about two yards to her left, and spherical.

She thinks it may be another bubble, but it is darker, and does not burst. Even stranger, it has what looks like little twigs growing from it.

"How strange!" she cries, and irresistibly walks nearer, ignoring the virtual minefield around her.

"Caelia!" Daireann leaps after her sister, but is unable to track her closely. She is soon surrounded by hot pools of molten mud, and can only watch Caelia walk closer to the round muddy blob.

Demetrius has more success, somehow sensing but not seeing where the wayward pixie and the danger are. He approaches close behind as Caelia reaches the round shape.

As she leans over, Caelia divines that the strange protrusions are not twigs. They are arms – scrawny, spindly arms which flap and grab towards her. And in the dirty ball supporting them, her huge pixie eyes make out a scrunched up, sorry looking face.

"Oh, isn't it cute?" she cries, clapping her green hands together.

"What have you seen?" demands Demetrius. "A Deev?"

"We said we would ask for directions. Excuse me, Mr. Muddy thing, do you know the way to Iblees please?"

A squished, grumpy looking face becomes apparent in the round mound of mud. The creature only grunts and dribbles. Wrinkling her green nose at it in distaste, Caelia is about to repeat her question, when the dirty creature splutters, sending up a shower of mud pellets.

"Eugh!" exclaims Caelia, jumping backwards and hiding her face in disgust on Demetrius' shoulder. The pair are not joined so for long.

Air rushes between their feet and the ground. Something grips tightly, painfully on their shoulders, and the next thing they know, they are laying on a mudless, sulphurless ground.

"What happened?" enquires Demetrius, blackly blind to anything. There is a humming noise in his ear.

It is Apollo, hovering on his wings, somewhat unstably. "We flew. *I* flew. What were you thinking, leading Caelia into that danger?!"

Ignoring the obvious retorts he could use, as Demetrius sees very little will penetrate through Apollo's blanket of obstinate stupidity, he merely says: "There was no danger. If my sense of smell does not fail me, they were Ballybogs. They are only capable of grunting and dribbling, in a manner reminding me of someone. What we *need* to find, if we are going to ask directions – not that I condone this, you understand – are Laminak. Now Laminak always say the opposite of what they mean, but if we could find their grotto and interpret, they really are harmless -"

"Lies." Apollo's voice has a chill to it. It does not permit any reply. "We have had nothing but trouble since we ran into you pixies. I don't blame all three of you – but this one – he is lying to us."

There is a silence. Without vision, Demetrius knows everyone is looking at him with no very charitable looks.

The weight of this accusation is so crippling and painful that no one dares to break it. In the end it is Daireann – who rather likes these frictions, and therefore feels compelled to stop them, lest she should start being happy – who says with great intelligence: "I don't know if that is true, Apollo. The Ballybogs *did* grunt and dribble."

"How is it possible," continues Apollo, refusing to be diverted, "that these things keep happening to us, without

someone being on the side of the Deevs? Blanchard –
someone bewitched that horse. Look, look how he
purposefully gets injured to deflect our suspicions!"

"Oh really!" gasps Demetrius in disbelief.

The leaves rattle in the trees. Demetrius can hear
nothing but the wind, and the burden of blame pressing in
on all sides. He hears nothing for so long, he begins to
think he has been left alone, and his insides freeze.

"All the same, I am not moving," comes Apollo's
voice at last into the darkness, making Demetrius flinch. "I
go nowhere under *his* direction until Aurora returns."

32

CHAPTER THIRTY-TWO

The first hint of trouble is the spear in the ground. It stands brazenly out of the dry, cracking earth, and Asher cannot make his head explain how it got there.

He has been teaching pages and squires all day. They have been tilting, they have been hawking, and they have been practising archery, but none of these, to the best of Asher's knowledge, involved the medium of spears.

Asher rubs his eyes. He has been feeling rather unwell of late.

Last night he read that once a mortal is enamoured of a fairy, they are bound to them, and cannot escape except by replacing them.

The fairy, according to this book, pays for the relationship with a short life; every embrace drawing life and breath from the winged apparition, while the mortal becomes bright and strong. It is his opinion that the book has confused the role of fairy and mortal. Surely it is he that is slipping a little further from reality and radiance each day?

Asher is certain life cannot mean to hold on to him for much longer. There have been so many near accidents in the past few days, suggesting to his befuddled brain, still straining to see a sign in anything, that death means to claim him for its own.

Why, even today an arrow has narrowly avoided him

twice, a horse has nearly run into him, and a hawk has aimed itself intently at the crown of his head. Then again, that could be down to the stupidity of the squires today. With no wars to aim for, they are feckless and inattentive to their lessons.

Asher takes up the long spear and wipes the sand from its sharp point. He looks to the windows of Glass Mountain Castle. It is possible someone has thrown it from there, but who…?

Death, death, everywhere! One of the pages, Ezekiel, with whom he had been wont to share his wine, had died of a fever but last week. Running a hand over his tense forehead, Asher wonders if he has the same thing, and cannot make up his mind whether he cares anyway.

He disassembles his targets and puts the squawking hawks into their yellow stone enclosure. The sun is reaching the highest point of the sky, and Asher knows he must get himself inside before the very heat stifles him.

As he begins to walk with heavy steps, his head bent to the ground in order to shield his eyes from the sun, Asher feels something heavy smack into his side. It rings against his armour.

The clang wakes Asher from his reverie, and he spins bewildered to see Elihu scrambling in the sand.

"Oho, my little Knight! What are you doing out at this time of day? You will burn that fine stately skin, you know." He pulls the disorderly boy to his feet by his elbow.

"*My* skin? It is yours I am trying to save. I – I meet my father in five minutes. You must follow me," gabbles the Prince, nearly falling over his own feet in his frenzy to pull Asher along behind him.

Asher digs his spurs in, quite amused at the gangly boy's efforts to have a man's strength.

"Go then, and send him my regards. *I* have no desire

to see your father."

"*He* intends that you shall never see him more! I tell you the truth, Sir Asher! Please, please come with me. It is important."

Asher, seeing the young Prince really is distressed, shrugs his plated shoulders and follows.

He is obliged to keep a very quick step to match Elihu, who scarpers as if there were no tomorrow.

They do not cease their crazed pace until they have alighted upon an acacia tree with a large, irregularly shaped rock beneath it. Scarcely does Asher have time to catch his breath, before he is shoved behind it.

"What *are* you doing?" pants Asher, sounding very ill used. "I thought we were meeting the King?"

"*I* am meeting my father here. I arranged it to be here. *You* cannot see him here. He is trying to kill you."

Asher cannot respond for a good few seconds. Overcoming the icy, creeping suspicion in his veins is a strong pang of frustration. Elihu, his only loyal friend, has not overcome childish ways yet after all.

"Oh, really," Asher goes to rise from his crouched position. "I appreciate your concern, Elihu, but this is *me*. What reason would Joel have to kill his best friend?"

Elihu shoves Asher back to his knees with freakish strength. "I thought you would say that. But I overhead Kish talking with him. I know what I heard. That is why you are here."

"For goodness sake! I watched sheep with him; I saw him crowned; I killed Dybuk! He may not like me any longer, and he may not be what he was, but he has no cause to want me dead. Why, I doubt he even has passion enough left in him to plan such bloodthirsty plots."

Elihu listens very calmly, his face inexpressive, right to the end of Asher's speech. Then, squaring him in the eye, he asks: "Is it me you are trying to convince, or yourself?"

Asher starts a sentence but gives up on it half way.

"Look," says Elihu, shoving his friend further behind the rock every second by stealthy pushes with the side of his foot, "at worst I am wrong. Then what harm has it done you to follow my bidding? I do not like to remind you at this time that you *are* my subject..." he adds with a twinkle. "If I am raving, you can tease me the rest of your life. But if there is a chance, just the slimmest hint of a chance that I am right, don't you think it is better that you listen?"

Asher does not retaliate, for he sees the long shadow of the King stretching towards them and ducks down.

A deep voice, unmistakably Joel's, reaches Asher's ears. "So there you are. Why here?"

"It was the only place out of the way enough," replies Elihu. "I needed to ask you what I am to do."

"What you are to do? What do you mean?"

The boy's voice trembles, and Asher thinks it very impressive if Elihu has put it on. "I heard you talking. I think I could help you stop the rebellion. I am - I am closest to - "

Joel's voice jumps in, accusing and eager. "You knew it?! You admit it? That he leads them?"

"I know nothing, father; only what I heard from you. And I wish to serve you..."

There is a low laugh. "I believe nothing you say." Joel pauses. With a sudden inspiration of confidence, he confesses: "We will kill Sir Asher in his bed this night. He always thought he was better, with his signs and great sights. The people always chant for him, preferring him to me. Even you... but enough of that. We will forget all you have done in the past. Come now, don't whimper; you're a good boy after all. Make sure he is asleep early. Wear him out. That's what you can do for me. Then I will call you my son, through and through."

Asher thinks he can see Elihu's shadow shudder. "I will. But hasn't he always been a faithful servant, father? Hasn't he always loved you like a brother? I don't understand…"

"I tell you as long as he lives you will not become King, have my kingdom or have my love. Enough of this nonsense. Do you want me to throttle you as well, boy? Who could think such a son could come from *such* a – " It is clear Joel intends to pronounce the word "mother" but cannot. Again his voice becomes gentler. "But there, you are a good boy, and you want to help me. You won't tell Asher?"

"Upon my soul, I will tell him nothing you have just said to me. But I will make him walk very far for tomorrow night."

"Well, that is all I wish." There is an awkward pause. A King cannot say "thank you" and it is an inappropriate moment for a mark of affection, even if they were used to giving them. "Well, goodbye then," says Joel, and returns to his obscurity.

During the dead of night, King Joel's own deadly Knights commit a heinous assault upon Sir Asher's pillows.

Stealing stealthily into the dark, sandy cavern of his room, they noiselessly advance on the bed, their dull shadows of weapons raised.

There is a moment of wicked, delicious hesitation as the enormity of the act is digested, and then they let loose upon the pillows.

Granted, the pillows were not expected, but the Knights discharge their task admirably, despite the surprise, adapting well to the slashing of feathers instead of flesh.

Incomprehensibly, King Joel fails to see the merits of the attack.

Their one-time general proves more liberal. Far away in a rocky, uncomfortable cave, he appreciates all the advantages of their butchering his bedclothes as opposed to his own dear self. He sees out with silent, shivering approbation the night of the attack from his cold desert cavern.

Extremely cold is that night in his rude shelter, chilled still more by the knowledge that he is hated and loathed. Several hours after dawn-break, when his capacity for inward reflection and self condolence is spent, Asher wearily puts a shawl around his head. He is preparing to move on from this place, numb in both body and spirit.

He hears a spray of sand against the rocks. He does not freeze or manifest any signs of panic. The sound of feet scrambling over the stones equally fails to move him.

He is unsurprised by it all, not because he has foreseen the event, but because he has abandoned and resigned himself to a hopeless fate.

The one bonus of no longer possessing the power of prediction is that Asher is more likely to be, and is, pleasantly surprised. Rather than being arrested by an armed guard, his arm alone is arrested by a very affectionate boy.

"Elihu! What do you think you are doing? Don't you know they will follow you?"

Pulling a bewildered face, the boy proffers a parcel. "I thought you would be hungry."

Asher takes the parcel eagerly, unwrapping and devouring it in one swift movement. Nonetheless, he states: "Running off in the dead of night will not make you look less suspicious. You know you will be in trouble already, without this. Run back so that you are not missed. It will be hard enough even then to deflect blame from you."

Elihu fidgets like one dispelling a cramp. "Let me come with you. I do not want to stay here."

"And steal away the only hope left for Iblees?" Asher shakes his head sadly, with indulgence. "I cannot do it."

Elihu sighs and stoops under the great weight of responsibility upon him. "Where will you go? While I am trapped here to be 'hopeful'?"

"I do not know exactly. Before it was a desert, I knew this land well. Now I can only plan to go far enough not to be caught. I have a fancy for the woods."

"The evil fairies – Deevs do you call them – ?"

"Ah, but beyond the Deevs – Laseri. I do not mind dying trying to get *there*."

Elihu looks alarmed at Asher's indifference to his safety, but only shuffles in reaction to it. "Well, you are right in one respect – we will both die if we linger here much longer. I think I know who leads the rebellion against my father. I must hasten to tell him, if he will hear it. Do you think the Boanerges would help me, if I can find them?"

"For myself, I would not involve them. The one time they would have been useful was the Fairy War, and then they were not to be found. They are more likely to rebel *against* you than aid you to crush someone else's riot. But whom do you suspect of leading the rebellion?"

"Do not concern yourself," says Elihu evasively. "I must learn to cope with these things myself."

"And so you must. If I find the fairies – and I do not think I shall – I will send *them* to your aid. But for now, we must part."

They do, and very soberly, with a restrained embrace lest the revolting emotions within should burst forth and break their resolve.

Asher proudly watches the Prince withdraw and

walk towards the light mouth of the cave without looking back.

After a few moments pass, Asher judges that he can watch his little friend run safely home across the dunes without him knowing.

Asher is not sure if it is the weather or because the boy has left, but the cave looks darker. He hopes it is not about to rain, for as welcome as water always is in that dry region, wet clothes or hair would be a sure sign of the Prince's treachery to his father.

Asher collects his belongings and wraps his makeshift headscarf tighter, so that he can be ready to leave after watching Elihu cross the horizon.

As he stands up with his belongings in hand, he hears a deep buzzing. At first he thinks there is an insect in the cave with him. But then he sees the rocks minutely tremble, and dashes to the cave mouth.

He is greeted by a wave of gritty sand in the face. Spluttering, he looks out into the developing storm, now depressingly dark and thundery. Sand is swirling in great whirlwinds, almost knocking him back into the cave.

Vaguely in the distance he can see a dark shape that must be Elihu, struggling to stand.

Asher retreats slightly himself, to save his stinging face, and tries to call Elihu to return. "Come back! Elihu, it is too dangerous!" But Asher's voice is carried away by the wind, and Elihu continues faltering forwards.

It is growing continually darker and louder. Beyond the howl of the wind, that rumbling buzz comes again. Suddenly, a spring of memories rises up in Asher's mind; he is on the battlefield again, and he knows that hum…

He forces himself to look up through the scratching whirls, and sees a sign he does not want to see – the fairy cloud. Only a small one, to be sure, but flying fast and, alarmingly, *descending*.

Elihu is blown sideways by a gust and falls to the ground. Asher can just make out a blanket of sand covering the exhausted Prince, and a more disturbing shadow over *that* – the falling fairy formation.

Dropping everything that he holds, Asher launches himself outside. Instantly he feels how powerless he will be to help; coughing, stumbling and blinking, he is sinking into the sand and unable to move quickly no matter how fast he runs.

The fairies are aiming for the fallen form of the Prince. Asher shouts and pulls forwards with all his might, yet they are moving with such streamlined speed!

By now the hovering fairies are so low that the wind is unbearable. Asher is nearly buried in sand. All he can see, hear or taste is sand and the panic within him. He fights frantically, trying to regain the surface.

At last he can breathe again, but his vision is still heavily impaired. It may be sand in his ears, but to Asher it seems the flapping of wings sounds quieter.

It continues to fade as he sits there, brushing the yellow-brown mist from his eyes and trying in vain to stand. Gradually, the sand clouds begin to diminish too, and Asher can climb to his feet. He can see...nothing.

A vast space of nothingness. Both the fairies and his dear Elihu are gone. Completely gone.

33

CHAPTER THIRTY-THREE

All of them spot the flare. It is not exactly an immense distance away, and they have precious little else to look at. Even Demetrius notices the change in the light patterns against his eyelids.

Apollo is prompt to reply, standing and raising his arm into the air with pride. A silver starry shower shoots upwards, giving all the pixies black blobs before their eyes for minutes afterwards.

Scarcely have these blobs faded than the foliage begins to crash and rustle, and Aurora thunders through, her face markedly lacking its usual serenity.

"Why are you still here?" she barks.

The pixies can see clearly now how terrible she would be in her rage, had she her full fairy apparel. With flowing hair and working wings unleashed they would fear her even more than they do at this moment.

"We – Apollo -" Caelia feels for once all the stupidity of what she is about to say and holds her tongue.

Apollo screws all his soldiery bravery to the sticking place.

"I am not going any further with *that* pixie," he says stubbornly, barely condescending to wave his hand at Demetrius. "He is trying to have us killed. Caelia almost died. Aurora, listen to me, he is trying to sabotage our mission -"

"Could it *be* hampered any further? These are people's lives, and you are here sulking over petty jealousies! The pixies mean us no harm, Apollo! For goodness sake!" Aurora nearly weeps with frustration.

She starts towards him. Apollo flinches, thinking she is going to hit him, but instead the Fairy Queen bends down. With frantic energy she rubs the vervain herb clutched in her hand upon his blistered legs.

Apollo cries out in pain. Demetrius' cure is not administered with much more tenderness.

The effect is almost miraculous. Apollo is striding about again with ease and Demetrius blinks his lids open, but they do not notice. They are all too angry.

Apollo in low, urgent tones tries to press upon Aurora their imminent danger, rooting from Demetrius. The pixies disclaim and bicker amongst themselves. All is chaos.

Suddenly, they are taken by surprise. The trees rattle madly, the grass dances in a manic sway and they are blown off their feet by a blast of wind.

Daireann groans and lifts her head. "What on Earth was that?!" she asks the horizontal figures of her pixie kin.

Aurora is standing up again already. "Fairies. The fairy army. Going the other way! Oh what is happening?"

To the rest of them it is but a game; because they have not seen dangerous Deevs, they doubt their existence; because they have never met a human, they do not care what becomes of them... or *him*.

"Deucalion's father told him he was breeding a work force like this. Selfish, undisciplined – oh!" Aurora cannot voice her emotions. She feels as if she will be torn in half with anger. It has gone far enough. She forms a desperate resolve. "If you do not wish to go on Apollo, then very well. You return. Here we separate. I go on alone."

Apollo is wounded by her words. He gives a visible

shudder and turns mournful.

"I will go – I will follow the troops. I will find what they do," he says, air and voice subdued. He looks at her very softly, suddenly remembering himself and all their past. He feels that now he can even accomplish this dangerous task to help her progress, and not feel hard done by.

Aurora very nearly relents, recalling she is alone in a perilous wood with pixies. Bad as the fairies have become, and as much as she would like to be noble minded and trust the pixies, she must admit she would prefer to have *some* company of her own kind at this time.

The moment is broken by a plaintive voice.

"Take me with you," pleads Caelia. "I am so afraid."

As she speaks, Apollo positively glows and ceases to look upon Aurora so kindly.

"With the greatest pleasure – but you do understand how dangerous it is to fly here…?"

Caelia trembles but grins winsomely. "Oh yes! I do not know if my poor moth wings would carry me that far – your stronger ones might, though! It will be risky. But I will not be afraid… with you."

"Take her, take her," urges Daireann, embracing her sister. "She is brave enough; she often walks alone in the woods, though I urge her not to… Take her to safety!" It is novel to see Daireann suddenly so caring and earnest.

Aurora is writhing her sylph's figure about in impatience. "Fly swift Apollo – may all speed and luck be with you – but be gone! Time is of the essence." Now he has shown himself to be silly again, Aurora remembers how much more important it is to get to Iblees and warn the humans than to keep her friend Apollo with her.

The pixie sisters separate fondly, their large eyes full, beneath a venerable tree. Given the recent dangers and feelings of trapped boredom, Daireann is eager to free her sister of this failed quest, even if she must abandon her to a fairy – something she could scarcely imagine a few days ago.

There is much Apollo would like to say to Aurora, who he followed with such loving motives, but who has, inexplicably, shrunk in stature and importance to him on this journey. He settles for simply saying in a low voice, avoiding her angry freckled face, "I am not comfortable...leaving you with him...with what I suspect. Take care. Think of what you do."

She nods her cropped blonde head irritably and turns to go on, looking at no one and nothing save the things invisible to the naked eye – the scenes running through her distracted mind. He leaves her.

Apollo, now every inch the dashing soldier, places a hand respectfully around Caelia's waist and flies slowly upwards. The pixies watch the pair ascend through the trees. They watch until Caelia's bell no longer rings in their ears.

Then, surprisingly, Daireann, who they all thought a very heartless creature, bursts into tears. They are not going to be moving quickly after all.

"Good grief!" despairs Aurora. "Curse the resemblance to your mother! I should never have brought anyone along!" The usually dignified and majestic Fairy Queen is fit to scream or rip out her short hair.

Little as he liked Apollo, Demetrius regrets being left the only male in this situation.

"Look," he says affably, all complacence now his sight is restored, "I will fetch us some water. She will calm after a drink and then we will be all stocked up to take it with us on our voyage. I doubt your charming *friend* would have followed us this far upstream?"

"Cynthia? Every second you speak I betray Cynthia, I betray *your* mother," to the sobbing Daireann, "and...

and..." But Aurora lets Demetrius take the empty bottle from her nonetheless.

Demetrius crosses behind a gathering of shrubs to where Caelia had discovered, in their boredom when Aurora left them, a broad expanse of flowing water. To Demetrius, so lately returned to the land of the seeing, it appears a wonderful thing; bubbling, diamante and strewn with the brightest red petals he ever beheld.

"I see what Caelia meant," he calls out, musing.

"What?" barks Aurora from the distance.

"A tree has shed its blossom here, and it is quite, quite beautiful."

Aurora makes a moan of frustration and he says no more. He should probably just hurry up and get the job done. They are pressed for time...and yet... He shakes his head. There is something so wistful and alluring in those petals.

Stooping, he runs the bottle gently through the bright blue water. One of the petals sticks to the spout, clinging with all its red, transparent might. He peels it away gently and observes this is going to be a recurring problem.

He knows he is taking too long already, but is irresistibly compelled to gather all the petals bobbing on the surface.

Out reaches his green hand, cupping at them. He captures a few and they slide around, ineffably lovely in his palm.

He goes again to pick out another shard of floating red and, disturbingly, cannot withdraw his hand. There is a strong pull in the water, sucking it downwards. At first it pulls softly and he thinks a little force will break him free. It rapidly develops into a powerful tug, like quicksand. He cries out in horror.

Demetrius is so absorbed in wrenching his hand from the growing whirlpool that he is startled to see Aurora at his side.

"What -?" she begins, rushing to take hold of his shoulder, just as another lurch swallows the rest of his arm. The bafflement in her air is turning to dismay as she grasps the gravity of the situation.

Demetrius knows she is like him, able to see what is unseen and the forces at work here.

"No!" he counsels as she goes to help him. "I know what this is. If you try to rescue me, it will let me go. But it will seize you instead – and much quicker."

The forlorn despair in his wide pixie eyes prevents Aurora from asking how on Earth he was caught by it if he knew what it was. She can only stare helplessly on as Demetrius is yanked to the ground, smacking his chin, his whole shoulder now submerged.

"Just go!" he orders her through the blood filling his mouth. "It is my own fault! I was not alert! Do not be foolish too. Your mission is too important."

They exchange one lingering, agonised glance before Demetrius disappears with a large slurping noise beneath the surface of the water.

All is quiet.

Aurora falls back against the trunk of a tree, quivering. Somewhere in the distance, Daireann is still crying.

34

CHAPTER THIRTY-FOUR

Back in the land of Laseri, the warmest season is, as always, in full bloom. Tender blossoms share their branches with budding leaves; the fields are glowing; everything smells of fresh grass and sun-warmed lagoons.

Deucalion is vastly pleased with both it and himself. He feels he is indirectly responsible for the gorgeous weather, the gorgeous landscape, and his own gorgeous appearance. Standing on the windy rock face of the grand Colosseum, his long fairy hair flying out in wisps on the breeze, he is awaiting with immense satisfaction someone to whom he means to show his immense satisfaction.

Through the clear, cloudless sky come the fairy troops, appearing on the horizon with astonishing speed. Deucalion smiles.

Into the dulcet landscape they bring Elihu, too introverted in his own raging thoughts to notice the glory of the warm air he is borne through. Deucalion wishes he would notice it. It was part of his plan.

The fairy air force wheel round in position and very elegantly deposit the sand-caked, dishevelled Prince at Deucalion's fine booted feet.

"You are welcome, young human," the King hails him at once, without bending to pick him up. "I understand you are a Prince, and if so, you are much more at home in these splendid environs."

Elihu, still feeling air borne, scrambles over the rocks and climbs shakily to his feet. "Who – Sir – I –". The boy's brow furrows in troubled bewilderment. His pretty coral mouth hangs agape as his faculties struggle to take in the wings and the majesty of the figure addressing him.

Deucalion cannot hold in his winged and majestic laughter. "Oh, it is worse than I imagined!" He scrutinizes Elihu's windswept hair, the dirt on his face making his bloodshot, frightened eyes glow, and the slim boyish build. He laughs again. "This passes as a Prince! Tell me, my good soldier Aubrey," beckoning with friendship to one amongst the ranks, "if I ever cut so gangly, skinny a figure in all my childhood? No wonder they cannot command their armies! Oh, it is too good!"

The confounded Elihu barely realises that the group of tall, lightly clothed men surrounding him are making him an object of mockery.

"Sir," he says, crimsoning, "I can see you are a very important person. I do not know why I am here, but I must beg you to return me to my land. I have matters of great importance to resolve…"

There is renewed tittering and guffawing amongst the ranks.

"Bless it!"

"It talks as if it were a leader!"

Deucalion laughs along for a while before silencing them, albeit with a twinkling eye, by raising his elegant, tapered-fingered hand.

"I believe it, little one," addressing the Prince with great condescension, "but so, indeed, do we. We have no leisure to return you. Besides, look at this fine land. Can you really tell me with a clear conscience that you wish to leave it?"

Dreading to be thought an ungrateful idiot by saying "Yes" immediately, Elihu looks about him briefly in order to satisfy his captor with a little well placed admiration before repeating his request to go home.

However, as his unprepared sight meets the verdant hills, exploding blooms and magnificent colours, all these plans drift from his thoughts as gently as the fluffy clouds are drifting overhead.

To someone who has never seen a blade of grass, who was born to a land of waste, ignorant that such a miracle as flowers existed, the view of the Noble Village is a dream-like revelation.

Returning to Deucalion in dumb wonder, Elihu begins to piece together the flying, the whole new world and the strange apparatus on the men's backs.

"You – you're *fairies*!" he declares incredulously.

Deucalion claps his hands slowly. "Who said humans were less intelligent? Which one of it was you? Here is proof that you are wrong." He rolls his violet eyes and nods pleasantly to his troops. "Now, get the brat cleaned up, if you please. I will not receive the wretched thing in this state. Go to it, go to it."

The army enclose once more upon Elihu and bear him wide-eyed and mouthing wordlessly away.

After nodding again at his shining kingdom in speechless admiration, Deucalion follows them at a leisurely pace, and breaks off into a grand chamber resplendent in the rainbow glow of the astrals.

"I am extremely pleased with our decision," he tells them. "The boy seems a perfect imbecile. I will keep him with me constantly." He throws himself into his throne at a jaunty angle and curls his legs up beneath him as he twirls a vine around his fingers.

"It has all worked well," says an astral, "as would any kingdom run in this way. Why I believe it was Hestia who had the idea of making the humans launch an attack..."

"And Leto who knew the little human Prince would be the key to that."

"Do not forget it was *I* who started the idea of circumventing the Queen in a way that she could not complain about," chips in another astral.

Deucalion chuckles. "It is a great pleasure to me that you can all take pride in what has and will be achieved. Now all we have to do is wait for their armies to come – and if we have turned the boy to our side in the meantime, it will not be the worse for him."

No circumstance occurs to quell Elihu's amazement. He is escorted through high domed rooms of astonishing colours, pavilions and bowers. Everywhere he smells a floral fragrance and breathes a pure air. It is all amazingly supernatural to his unaccustomed nostrils. He sees exotic creatures he could never have imagined and nearly falls several times into fresh bubbling fountains.

Although he manages to elude this dunking, his escorts eventually throw him fully clothed into an enormous circular bath with tiny neon fish inside it – and do not appear to think this ceremony out of the common way.

Elihu is left alone and dazed amongst the sparkling bubbles and steam. It would be a perfect time to escape if he had his wits about him, but he does not. He is too peaceful watching the plants creeping around the trellises, hearing the birds swooping – sometimes visible to him, sometimes not – and unwinding in the soothing water whilst playing with the fish.

All too soon smart male fairies in crisp white robes appear, strip him without embarrassment (save an ill disguised disgust at his wingless back) and bundle him into soft, loose clothing of a pastel shade. His skin is glowing and fresh, though he does not recall scrubbing;

even his face is clean, but it has not touched the water. They brush his light hair until it curls and shines.

Dazzled, Elihu is led onwards again, this time through great halls, still drenched in that heady scent and those rich hues. Everything is so vivid; it looks to Elihu like someone has spilt a pallet of paint all around.

Ending his journey in a large, cool chamber with arches looking out onto the mountain top, he is seated at the largest of many marble tables covered in giant banana leaves.

"The King requests the pleasure of your company at dinner," he is informed as his chair is pushed in.

Surveying the room, Elihu cannot decide by which he is more awed: the kaleidoscope glow of the astrals, who glide in from behind and, to his embarrassment, seat themselves beside him; or the lack of procession and pomp – he feels exposed without its sober restraints.

In comes the King, laughing with a fairy carrying apples. Elihu was not aware kings were allowed to laugh.

Upon sighting Elihu, he sits down and notes with pleasant surprise: "You have cleaned up remarkably well, young human."

Deucalion has to admit, on closer inspection, there is something almost charming in the child's aspect. His bright clean face, still bearing smooth cheeks which have never needed shaving, looks at Deucalion with such shining eyes, such an expectancy, as the King has rarely beheld.

Elihu's smallness, helplessness and winglessness stir a protective, paternal feeling quite unexpected and wholly unpleasant.

"Do you still wish to go home?"

It takes Elihu a very pensive few minutes to respond: "Oh. Home," in the manner of one to whom that place is long forgotten and foreign. "Yes," he says with deliberation, "I must go back to Iblees. But...I would not mind having something to eat first."

Deucalion bangs a palm on the table and laughs uproariously. It shocks Elihu that the astrals around him are not obliged to laugh uproariously too, but merely smile indulgently.

"Yes, yes, you shall have something to eat, fear not!" Deucalion summons the banquet in a loud voice. "Give this boy food – it is all Laseri can offer him!"

Mountains of berries and platters of nuts fill the tables by themselves. Elihu cannot catch sight of one hot or meaty substance, but is ravenous enough to eat what he can reach without complaining, and swill down the strange coloured liquid he is given to drink.

"We certainly do not have this in Iblees!" he comments gaily, raising the blue glass cup again.

"Oh, Iblees!" titters Deucalion dismissively. He swallows the mouthful he is chewing. "You will soon forget Iblees and all that nonsense. You are the first human in Heaven knows how many centuries to be brought into Laseri, and I have to admit that I expected you to be a bit more grateful, little – what *is* your name?"

The Prince draws himself straighter. "My name is Prince Elihu of Glass Mountain Castle, son of -"

"Yes, yes I know very well, don't bother with all that, Elihu," Deucalion ruminates, trying to resist wrinkling his face. "Elihu. Well, don't let that get you down, old chap," he says bracingly, wrapping an arm around the boy's shoulder. "You'll fit in here despite that. You'll like it. And we hope very soon to bring some little friends to stay with you."

Abashed, Elihu squirms free of his grip and replies: "I appreciate your hospitality – but why *am* I here? You are fairies, yet you do not seem inclined to hurt me. To be sure, Sir Asher always *claimed*..."

"Hurt you?! Bless you, no! We are meant to *protect* you and... and all that."

"And this is done by waging war on and kidnapping us?" cogitates Elihu innocently, thinking out loud.

Deucalion looks sheepish. "Well, I had to kidnap you to *prevent* me waging a war," he explains defensively. "My wife would not let me. But now your father will come after us, and everything will be peachy. You'll see." He throws another nut in his mouth and looks away with mock easiness.

Elihu swishes the nectar thoughtfully in his glass. "I do not understand," he admits.

"Oh? Well, I daresay you do not – you are a human. But the gist of it is, that your father does not know what is good for you at all." Elihu finds it hard to disagree with that.

"He broke the peace treaty and killed one of our fairies not so long ago. Merely because of this, some of my people have been sick – it is in our make up to be ill when we do not get along with you. Some of the traditionalists even hung themselves over the first war, you know. So we will bring you humans here, where you are meant to be, so we can look after you, as *we* are meant to.

My Queen is en route to talk with your leaders regarding this; it is not a good idea, because it was her own one. So now your father will try to come and get you and we will make him yield. Those who will not accept fairy protection... well, we want to bring all the best ones into Laseri. And who can blame us?"

Elihu begins to chuckle joyfully as blossom sprinkles down upon his head from above. He is dimly aware that some part of Deucalion's speech contained a hint he meant to kill some humans, but oddly enough, finds himself past caring. He is content, sated and indolent, as he would be if he had sat outside on a summer's day or eaten a large meal. He can not give a thought to consequences or the welfare of anyone else.

But Deucalion has himself discovered several flaws just by heeding his own plan. With an actual human before him – and such a fine boy – it seems suddenly pointless, and even cruel.

What *is* protection? What if Aurora was right, and there is a spirit out there that Deucalion is specifically formed to watch over? What if that spirit were killed in the coming battle? What if this very boy before him *is* that spirit?

It seems, inexplicably, that his wife has been right about something.

It did not occur to Asher to return to Iblees and alert the King to his son's kidnap. He knew that this would be the wisest course of action, but he also knew there would be sharp, pointy things awaiting him there to bring about an untimely death, possibly before he could have time to inform them why he came back.

The upshot of this is that Kish is left to fabricate his own version of events, which, if not strictly true, have at least nigh on the same effect as Asher's returning with the full story would have done.

"Your Majesty," he cries, bursting with a huge creak and slam of the large wooden door into the King's solar. "I do not know how the constable or guards let this happen: Sir Asher has gone, slipped through our fingers due to their incompetence -"

"I know we have not disposed of him as planned," growls Joel, who is still being dressed, though sitting as if he has no conception of what is going on around him.

"Yes, that is true. But we have also disposed of something which … which we did not mean to."

"What on Earth do you mean?" demands Joel

impatiently.

Kish draws in his breath. "Prince Elihu. The Prince is nowhere to be found."

Joel is so stunned that he cannot even move to look at Kish. Only a muscle working in the base of his neck denotes he is still alive. A thousand theories of kidnaps, murders and sand storms jump around in his head. It is only now that Joel begins to have anything like paternal feelings, now that the child is not before him, and these are heightened by the hopeless speculations of what his mother would think.

Kish sees his sudden tenderness, and humanely puts an end to it. "It is clear to me what has happened. Asher has swayed his vulnerable young mind and they are run off together – run off to join the fairies!" he surmises. "We knew that rogue Asher was leading a rebellion but we did not realise how far it stretched – to the very Castle! It is all for that wretched fairy he loved. She has bewitched him to destroy Auchriachan from within!"

Blanched and horror-struck, Joel says nothing.

Taking full advantage of this favourable turn, Kish presses: "Give me leave, my King, to lead your armies out! There is a fairy I know of in Green Glow forest. Her capture would bring the fairies to their knees. Would you be invaded by *their* kind?!"

"No!" cries Joel, before Kish has finished speaking. The noise reverberates around the beige room. "We launch no war against the fairies. Is it not bad enough I have lost my son and heir? With him I will cut off all inheritance, of course... but I... I will not break a peace treaty."

Kish is flabbergasted. "But your liege – "

"No buts, Sir Kish. Remember your place." Kish does remember it and takes a step back, but he is retaining rebellious eye contact. "I will be obeyed in this." Joel challenges him with a burning look.

Kish bows meekly. "As you wish. It is not my role to question." And in this subservience, he continues to bow himself out of the room.

Cautiously the servants move to recommence the dressing process. They are hastily brushed off. Disliking the ferocity and belligerence of Joel's aspect, they likewise disappear through the stony passages.

Once alone, Joel can weep out his agony. They are the frustrated tears of one who is aware he cannot win either way.

He is *not* aware, however, of Kish's actions. Little does Joel suspect that Kish has left him to walk at full speed, spurs clinking, towards the stables, all the while muttering "I gave him the chance - I did give him a chance."

Each Knight Kish passes at his rapid gait looks to his determined face in expectation.

To some of them he says "It is true. He means to do nothing and watch us be destroyed." Occasionally he adds, "Is it possible - that he was in league with them all the while?"

To others he announces excitedly, at a greater volume, "I have the King's orders. We are to charge on them - through the forest - the route I went to Majeseerum, you know."

Both comments serve to actuate the Knights addressed into running for horses and arms. A select few Kish urges to stay behind. They either respond with knowing looks or groan out sorrowfully: "Yes, I will stay by the King in his time of distress," at which patriotic words he pats them with wordless admiration on the shoulder.

This done, Kish saddles his horse ready for combat, mounts him with one jubilant spring and rides out through the frenzy of preparation going on in the stables around him. Straight as an arrow he heads into the desert, regardless of heat or sand.

He travels, camel like, for a long time at a steady pace, until the edge of a large dune appears rising like a grainy sun over the horizon. Its peak is covered in a scrubby black line, like an imperfect charcoal drawing. On closer inspection, the line undulates, and is revealed as being in fact a mass of people – a veritable platoon, crudely armed, wearing scruffy, handmade clothes. They are awaiting his arrival.

The motley row wavers in excitement at his approach. A low mumble and a cheer well up across the warm desert air. By the time he is before the dune, they are ecstatic.

So avid is Kish in his cause of self advancement, he finds no difficulty in hollering after his lengthy ride: "Boanerges!"

His voice is triumphant, nearly loving. The exiled tribe raise their weapons, cheering, until they resemble a noisy forest.

"The time we have awaited is here! No longer will King Joel keep us out of Iblees – the city we helped found! No longer will you need to fear that the fairies can attack you through his incompetence! There will be a new kingdom – a kingdom of Auchriachan and Laseri combined – with the Boanerges at the font!"

Renewed, maniac cheering from the Boanerges. Any past treachery on Kish's part towards their tribe is forgiven in his swift rhetoric.

Leaving them suitably roused, having embraced his estranged brothers for effect, he heads to Glass Mountain Castle.

The crumbling courtyard is by this time a sea of orderly, patiently waiting Knights, fully mounted and clad in armour. Profound silence engulfs them – the King has not even noticed the quiet party assemble.

To this group, Kish troubles himself to say only two words – handily accurate for both factions of soldiers – "For Iblees!"

The yellow, rocky walls ring with resounding enthusiasm. Horses toss their heads and pull their bits at the noise. Kish raises his sword to the sky and launches his steed forward from its haunches. Like a river bursting through a dam, the Knights follow his path, rippling light from their armour and babbling a victory cry.

It is only then that King Joel is drawn to his grimy window. It is only then that his red, sore eyes can comprehend the full extent of his loss.

Charging irrepressibly onwards, the Knights gain sight of the forest. It is here, subtly, they are tailed by the Boanerges, who creep out from the woodwork.

Few of the Knights riding at the rear notice the jolly addition; even fewer realise who the turncoats are. Those that do are not inclined to raise screaming objections.

Kish and his horse, both still superhumanly energetic, effortlessly trace the route back to wasted Majeseerum. A long and treacherous ride awaits them, but no valiant Knight heeds this. They hurtle onwards to fight for whatever version of the story Kish has told them. Some ride to protect their King, others to their freedom, and the Boanerges to their birthright. Only Kish knows he has already been successful in safeguarding what he set out to protect: his own self interest.

35

CHAPTER THIRTY-FIVE

Apollo's white wings are not spread for many miles before his fair charge begins to grow restless.

"Is it really safe flying, Apollo? I am sure we are pushing our luck – the Deevs must spot us soon!"

Apollo thinks they are unlikely to see Caelia. Her green skin blends so well against the heaving forest canopy that only her bright eyes stand out – and they could belong to any animal.

"Do not be afraid," he comforts her. "I am a solider of Laseri! I know what I am doing. Besides, it is quicker this way. I promised Aurora I would do what I could with the King."

He swerves to avoid a rogue branch.

"Oh yes, and she is your Queen. Of course you serve her." There is something bordering on resentment in Caelia's tone. It cuts Apollo to the quick.

His cheeks and heart burn. He cannot conjure a sentence of response that will not accidentally offend her again.

They fly on in silence through the grabbing twigs and birds nests. Squirrels poke their heads inquisitively out of the curtains of foliage as they pass. It is a comfort to see them again; Apollo was beginning to think nothing could survive in this wood – but up here he sees hope.

The air begins to grow warm and misty. The smell of

bark and leaves is now so close it begins to become a little suffocating.

"The sound of your wings, and us shouting to talk above them alone might attract the Deevs," whines Caelia as she begins to feel the heat.

"It might," Apollo admits, and takes this as a signal to stay quiet.

Caelia, however, so afraid of detection that she will shout at the top of her lungs to avoid it, recommences: "We should at least fly a little then walk a little. If we combine the two it will be safer. Oh! It is very hot and bright up here! I am not used to it – it burns!" and she gives out a little whimper.

Apollo has to concede that without the full shade of the trees, the sunlight is much stronger. It finds its way very easily through the thin layer of top leaves that still cover them. He is relishing the return of the sun on his face, and a light level somewhat nearer to that of Laseri than he has seen for a long time, but he readily comprehends how painful it must be to a pixie accustomed to the dark – especially combined with this increasingly subtropical heat.

Truly tired himself, Apollo begins to relent. His wings move more slowly, and they float a bit lower.

"Perhaps – perhaps we could find something to eat?" he debates hopefully. "You must know what is edible. You glean your own food from the forest, don't you?"

Caelia's green face beams up at him. "Oh yes, some food and some water would be lovely, wouldn't it? It's so HOT!"

This sways it. Apollo's own crying body begins to picture filling itself with nourishment. These urges conquer everything else. Besides, he would not be taking very good care of Caelia if he let her starve, would he?

They dip, skimming the air with small bumps and

land painfully in a bed of pine cones.

"Sorry," Apollo apologises. "I'm not used to travelling with passengers."

They stand with crunching steps and look at their surroundings. A heat haze hangs in the air, blurring the edges of objects. It smells, feels, and even sounds warm. Apollo can hear it humming in his ears.

"We must be near," he sighs in relief. "I can hear birds again. They don't sound like Laseri birds, but..."

In fact nothing looks quite right. The bushes are dark, pointy, long-leaved and completely incongruous with the trees, which are gnarly and twisted.

Some have fallen and are propping themselves up diagonally against others. The floor is a carpet of dead leaves, acorns and sycamore helicopters. Nevertheless, Apollo strides onwards with purposeful, soldierly steps.

He takes Caelia's clammy, green hand gingerly and pulls her along with an air of defence.

"Do stay under the shade of the trees! It is so hot," she emphasizes again and again.

They walk close to the side of the beaten track. Apollo does not enjoy being in such close proximity to the knotted, warped trunks. They almost look like they have faces.

His hand tightens on Caelia's, in case she has the same creeping fears as him. She must do, as despite the sweltering heat that she is so frequently lamenting, she is edging further away from the shadows she was but a moment ago eager to seek.

They are approaching a particularly large sycamore tree with a great branch span, spreading wide cool pools of shade. Just looking at it makes Apollo thirst. He picks up his pace, keen to gain the relief for his sweating skin all the sooner.

Caelia, caught up in his renewed activity, gives burst

to a spout of glee and capers off to the side, picking flowers as she goes. Apollo laughs.

In skipping off she avoids entering the coveted shade of the large tree. Apollo is not sorry to have more room to bask in its soothing touch himself.

Moreover, he loves to watch her, this strange, extraordinary creature. She is making something like a daisy chain, picking her flowers with care.

Almost the moment Apollo's feet touch the shade of the tree that he has been seeking, a weariness comes over him. Perhaps his sudden exposure to refreshing shade makes him more aware of how he has missed it in its absence. He is very unwilling to move at all. He leans with his arms folded against the tree in a kind of contented lethargy, observing Caelia through a bleary smile.

The lulling heat causes his eyelids to droop. Before he is aware of it, he has dozed slightly, and wakes up in a minor panic.

Caelia is still there – it takes him a frenzied minute to spy her, cross-legged on the floor.

"I thought you were in a hurry," she reminds him with a saucy green look. "Are we moving on?"

She stands and brushes the crunchy leaves from her drab clothing in a business-like fashion.

Sheepishly, Apollo goes to follow. He cannot.

His lithe fairy limbs feel lead weighted. With supreme effort he staggers forward on rubbery legs. It is as if his entire outfit has been saturated with water.

Caelia's dish-like eyes gleam. "Are you quite well? What is wrong? Oh don't be ill! You cannot be ill and leave me all alone!"

At any time when he was in less pain, this concern would have been most gratifying.

"No – don't worry... I just – I – my body is so stiff. Perhaps it was falling asleep against that tree." Apollo inspects the source of his pain, and recoils at the sight of his rather swollen body parts.

"Look at my arms," he draws Caelia's attention, trying to conceal his overwrought voice. "Maybe I've had a reaction to that herb Aurora rubbed on me."

"Oh!" wails Caelia, wringing her hands. "It is not that. It *must* not be that. What would I do? I am sure you are only weak from not eating for so long!"

It does seem reasonable, particularly to his growling stomach, that this is the case. Lack of nourishment or drink for so long is likely to produce unfavourable physical symptoms.

"Let's find some food straight away! You'll be better then, I just know you will!"

Caelia's appealing face and Apollo's long and now remembered hunger make this option extremely enticing.

"Of course. You may – just – have to help me along." He freckles over with consciousness of how he will enjoy that despite his pain.

"Oh no, *that* cannot be! You became ill after you stepped under that tree. We cannot risk the same befalling me. That would do us no good at all!" Caelia represents with a righteous shake of the head. Apollo feels his skin burn even hotter at this rebuff.

Tortured by pain, he manages to creep forward. He is ready to weep with shame as Caelia watches his laboured movements. In trying to underplay the agony in his swollen limbs, he finds he is actually increasing it.

Slowly, very slowly, he is clear of the farthest reach of the tree's branches. Caelia, who has been watching him intently, proves her friendship by now coming forward and taking his arm.

"You should probably not touch me – it may be catching," he demurs feebly, really very glad of the support.

"Like we said, it is probably weariness. You just concentrate on keeping in step – I will find us something to eat."

Moving on with Herculean effort, Apollo observes the landscape altering. It hits him as a sequence of strange, bleak images, so fevered is his brain by the pain.

The trees become barer. They are still gnarled and twisted in shape, but there are odd chunks out of their sides and wood shavings on the floor. Soon the green leaves are so sparse that nearly the whole sky is visible, and he wonders fleetingly how Caelia can bear it.

But there is no ray of sun now; the atmosphere is filled with that overcharged stillness that comes before a storm. Clouds coat the sky in a grey blanket, threatening to rain, but shed no drops. And it is still so, so, hot...

"There!" Caelia points, her face glowing with pride. "Acorns. Fairies eat nuts and seeds, don't they?"

Apollo looks and nearly falls back in horror. His heart still pounding horribly, he turns his flustered eyes back to the boughs – and there is nothing there.

He could swear he saw ladies in the tree; ladies with skin the colour of the bark, clad in oak leaves. They had wings like him, but they were pointy and black. They did not look very cordial creatures.

He rubs his eyes. Still nothing there. Most likely his brain is hallucinating because of the pain.

Before he can tell Caelia what he thought he saw, she is in the very tree itself, climbing with perfect ease through the branches.

"Be careful!" he cries weakly, sick with the terror that he will see her snatched by a Deev at any moment.

This whole place makes him shudder. He wishes more than anything that they had never landed. He wishes Caelia had tried to fly on her own, at her own height beneath the cooling leaves, so that this stop-over had never been necessary.

There is too much tension in the air here. It makes his head feel like it will burst. With every passing moment the chunks out of the trees look more and more like bite marks to him. Having been brought up in Laseri to consider all plants precious, it is a hideous, hideous thought to Apollo.

Lost in these thoughts, it makes him jump when Caelia springs out of the oak tree and lands in front of him with a mound of acorns. She has filled the front of her top like a bowl with the cupped seeds. "Here! Take some!"

Apollo thanks her and eagerly begins to devour what is presented to him. It is only once he begins to eat that he realises how starving he was. Soon he has eaten nearly all that Caelia gleaned from the tree.

"I'm sorry," he says, suddenly recollecting himself and putting an acorn back. "The rest are for you. You must be just as hungry."

Caelia shrugs and sighs. "I am. But pixies cannot eat acorns. They are indigestible to us. I will look around for something else."

Finishing the harvest off, Apollo feels a little revived. He is able, and even happy, to follow Caelia on her quest for something edible. But the places they walk to do not cease to give him the creeps.

"As soon as we get you something, we should fly again," he tells her, "even if you fly on your own wings, in the shade. We can stop again when you get tired. It is not safe here."

The wood is thinning. The trees look like they have been coppiced. Everything becomes increasingly brown, until they turn a corner and are faced with a sea of wasted trees. Logs and splinters are heaped upon the ground. Nearly an acre of forest has been felled, and very untidily too. There is not an erect plant as far as Apollo can see. It is impossible to follow the path and climb over this mournful assault course.

"How horrible!" ejaculates Apollo, surveying the butchered trees with dismay. "Let's turn back."

"We cannot do that. Back there was were you got ill," Caelia reminds him equably. "It will be far safer for us to hover over this."

Little as Apollo wishes to do so, he concedes it is the most sensible plan. They flap their wings just enough to lift their feet off the ground. Caelia leads the way, for Apollo is still a bit weak. Her bell jangles with every change in altitude.

Apollo has the sensation of flying over a graveyard. Each dead tree carries the sense of tragedy, the sense of something not quite at rest. Apollo is uneasy. He feels an icy fear in the pit of his stomach. It winds round and round his insides like a tentacle as he flies. Suddenly he realises it is no longer fear, but pain – a sharp, sudden cramp that sends him off balance.

His great white wings no longer work. He drops out of the air, clutching his stomach.

"Caelia! Caelia!" he groans, then sees that she is floating over him. The sight would give him comfort, but for the sinister grin warping her pretty green face.

"The acorn lady punishes those who eat her produce," she titters gleefully.

Apollo writhes on the floor, feeling wood cut into his back. "But if you – why -"

"Fairy, stupid fairy! Did you really think you could beat the Deevs? They are more powerful than you'll ever be – and I shall reign with them!"

Betrayal crushes into Apollo with awful, incomprehensible clarity. "You – you cannot even do magic!"

"So my kinsmen think. They hate Daireann and I – why should I care to share it with them?"

All his old concern for Aurora returns with choking dread. "Daireann too?"

Caelia's green face creases. "She knows nothing of it yet. But she will. She will be brought round. Did you actually believe we wanted to live in Laseri with you hideous creatures? You abandoned us, you outcast us from the moment of our birth – you will be repaid!"

Apollo groans and rolls over.

"Your King knows Deevs attack humans, and therefore thinks they will be on his side. It is partly true – they will obliterate any human who crosses their path! But they will do the same to *you*. We will watch you destroy each other, and Deevs shall inherit the land!"

"Aurora. Aurora," moans Apollo, and finds there are tears rolling down his face.

"Her mission will fail," Caelia tells him brightly. "We will finish her, do not worry. As soon as I find my sister again, it is all over for her. You will be with your precious Queen again soon." She sneers and spits in his face.

With that kind farewell, she flies off, now as strong on her wings as any fairy and, Apollo vaguely notes with useless depression, perfectly capable of flying long distances alone.

She is gone, and the tree cemetery is motionless. Apollo is pinned down by pain, as heavy and redundant as the logs around him. He squirms in an effort to relieve himself, even for a moment, but finds no rest.

His body convulses suddenly, and he too is completely still.

36

CHAPTER THIRTY-SIX

How it has happened, where it started, Deucalion does not know. He wishes he did, for he could have nipped it at the bud.

Somehow, unstoppably and irresistibly, the human boy has begun to fascinate him. Rarely in his gleeful life – and it has been one filled with much revelling and carousing – has he known a greater joy than observing Elihu's delight with Laseri.

To see the child happy somehow makes Deucalion happy himself. He smiles uncontrollably to see him clad in bright, flowing fairy clothes; Elihu's chubby arms look so plump and boyish where they emerge at the sleeves.

Talking to, listening to, and trying to teach Elihu about his own kingdom, his own people and their ways gives Deucalion a feeling of importance and purpose even greater than that of ruling the fairies, for the effect he has on shaping this young mind is almost palpable.

As he leans out of an archway on the upper story of the Colosseum, watching Elihu slide down waterfalls and swim with catching exuberance in the lagoon below, Deucalion is forced to admit a painful fact to himself. He has tried to repress, deny and reason himself out of it, but it will not do.

Elihu is the spirit that he is meant to nurture and shield. He is Elihu's guardian, and this charming realisation puts a most inconvenient halt to all of his plans.

His new found desire to shield, to defend at any cost, could not come at a worse time. A gorgeous young fay, wrapped in a dress sprinkled with rosebuds and wearing a tiara of woven leaves – exactly the picture, in short, to inspire credibility – came tripping in on light ballet shoes only yesterday and had a vision.

This in itself was not unusual. A week or so ago, a prophecy that Auchriachan had launched its armies would have been a welcome piece of intelligence. Today, confirmation that he has started a war does not make Deucalion's heart sing with joy.

It is a strange, disquieting turn of events. He is not even sure that he wants a war after all; he wonders what possessed him to desire it in the first place.

Tearing himself away from the vision of youthful ebullience, he walks through the glowing white corridors, through archway after archway framed by glistening golden pillars, rubbing his smooth forehead all the while.

In this meditative walk, he almost falls over the eager fees sharpening spears and charging about in a mad, hyper fashion. Deucalion does not altogether approve of the wild, thirsty look on their faces.

His fine Romanesque courtyards are full of precipitant soldiers, already wearing elaborate silver headgear, like a silver web over their brows. Each is trying to assemble the best multi-layered armour; preferably to match the exact shades of their individual wings. They are optimistic, cheerful, patriotic and completely ill suited to the task. To Deucalion, they look like they could wage war with no compunction, walk right into Iblees and win.

He clears his throat and catches their eager, smiling attention. "Stop this preparation," he orders them. "You are all far too ready."

The soldiers look ashamed and try to be more

slovenly. "That's better," Deucalion encourages. "You're not going anywhere for a while yet."

All his life Deucalion has been cocooned in popularity. He has bent, he has adapted, and he has shown fairies a good time. There has not been a fairy since his infancy with whom he has not got along; if they did not love him on the virtue of being a Prince, they loved him for his ability to morph his opinions and pursuits to fit theirs. He has always managed to get his own way through this tactic.

Never before has he been in danger of expressing an opinion which he knows will be unpopular; when he opens his kingly mouth, he is used to the assurance of his statement being universally applauded.

But with this war – this war of his building, which he must now stop – there is something that savours strongly of hypocrisy.

He broods around the leafy stable yard. How to convince fairies out of the actions that they now so desire to take – because he has convinced them to do so – is a problem that fills his insides with clay and his heart with bubbles. Deucalion loathes this semblance of cowardice.

To doubt his own abilities – what has become of him? All for this boy? He wishes Aurora were here. She would say something controversial, which he could deflect with a witty put down and feel much better about himself. Or, more helpfully, he could use her to speak his own opinion without incurring the displeasure of his court.

If only Aurora had married him sooner – if only he had been able to overcome his own jealousy regarding the rose quartz ring sooner – he might have learnt to be humble and listen to her. Having her love, he might have cared less for the love of other fairies and planned his policies better. One thing is clear: all this is mainly Aurora's fault.

"Aurora! Of course!" he slaps a hand against the side of a horse-box, and sends the unicorn inside dancing across it in protest.

Deucalion still has the hope that Aurora will reach Iblees in time to prevent the war! He sent Apollo with her, and even untied her wings, but all in all, he wishes that he had done more to assist her. He now sees his failings as a husband.

What are the real chances that she could convince the humans not to fight; especially now they have taken King Joel's son? Looking back, that kidnap was rather a silly thing to do in the first place, and Deucalion wonders what ridiculous fairy put him up to it.

Yes, he will leave it to Aurora – he should trust in his wife, after all – but his conscience and his nerves cannot be satisfied with merely that. He must do something decisive and kingly. He should help her along a bit after all.

With a heart beating alarmingly fast – almost too fast to be healthy – he picks his way carefully down the mountainside, the wind in his long fair hair. He passes some fays picking posies to send the soldiers off with, then walks into the midst of chattering groups of more influential fairies collecting water from the river in wobbling buckets. Deucalion's face clears with recognition.

Casually, he integrates himself into the group, who greet him with smiles.

"What are you doing there, Erebus?" Deucalion asks, trying to lace his voice with unconcern. He plunges his hands into his pockets to complete the picture.

"Water supplies for the armies, your Majesty," replies the strapping fairy as he bends down and slops water all over his feet. "And the Colosseum, of course."

"Of course, of course. So they really plan on marching soon?"

Erebus laughs. He is paying more attention to his

task than the King, walking back and forth with heaving pales. "I would think you would be the person to ask about that! Did we not reach a consensus – forgive me if I am mistaken – that you wanted us to mobilise as soon as possible?"

Deucalion nearly quails there and then. "I have been thinking that perhaps this war is not a good idea after all. Is it really fairy-like? My ambassadors to the pixies have achieved nothing – the blighters will not even talk to them – and as for the humans... I questioned the boy. He does not know of any plan to overthrow us. He even doubts that sword really was Joel's. These things should be considered. I do not like to see my people act rashly."

Erebus is aghast. He stands up straight and puts his hands on his hips to consider the matter, red and breathing deeply. Deucalion wishes he had an excuse to reveal that he is breathing just as quickly.

"I am surprised you have not raised this in a meeting. You know how we value your wisdom. But it is ill timed – your speech, the glory of humans in Laseri, the pixies!"

Deucalion can feel himself freckle.

"Yes, but true wisdom is to know when you have made an error. Perhaps I should have listened more to Queen Aurora. In my defence, she wasn't Queen then, which must account for it." Deucalion hangs his head, and announces bravely through a lumpy throat: "I would like to take back some of what I said, at any rate. Perhaps you and your friends at least will be so good as to delay your leaving."

Erebus positively gapes. "But – we cannot go against your speech! We respect your wisdom too much!"

Deucalion frowns. "In that case, you should respect it now. I will order you not to march on Iblees."

The fairy shakes his head in something between fear and incredulity. "Oh no, you could not do that! It is not fairy-like to be ordered."

Squirming inside with embarrassment, Deucalion realises he must be a tad more humble. "Then I will request it."

"You could do that. But we could not act contrary to what King Deucalion told us to do."

Deucalion chokes back an uneasy stammer. "But I just – then I *tell* you not to march!"

"Everything with fairies should be done democratically. We should not do anything because one fairy tells us to do it. King Deucalion told us that."

"But I *am* King Deucalion."

"I know, your Majesty. I respect your wisdom very much."

Deucalion resists the urge to weep. Anyone who had heard his comments on the verdant hillside, or who he approaches with increasingly timid applications, responds in the same way. They refuse to listen to him, out of respect for the advice of King Deucalion.

With a vague sensation that he is going mad, he slinks back to his Colosseum. He eyes everyone with extreme suspicion; perhaps they are the insane ones, and they could hurt him.

He cannot blame them for lack of obedience to their King – on the contrary – but failure to recognise their King, and shift with his whims, is to Deucalion's mind most reprehensible. He wishes with all his heart that he had listened to his father; if he had given his followers less power, and less sway, he could merely tell them what to do. But now it seems that these fairies are running themselves. He also damns his own eloquence and handsomeness for persuading them so thoroughly into war to start with.

Perhaps it will not be so bad. Perhaps he is only being ignored by his subjects because he *is* insane. This sudden change of mind, these rushes of love towards the human Prince certainly aren't natural, after all. Deucalion has to admit to himself that he has been acting very uncharacteristically. It is a good thing really, if the fairies are not swallowed in his private madness. They know what they are doing. All he has to do is calm himself, and become resigned to the fact that the boy may suffer. Steeling himself, he bends his steps towards the pool.

As if intent on wounding his own feelings, Deucalion pauses under a cypress tree to watch the Prince and the fees he is playing with diving off rocks, splashing one another and basking in youthful jubilance. He sighs.

Edging toward the tinkling lagoon, he is spotted by the fees. They are less defiant than their elders; they smile at their King and nod in deference. Smiling in return, he squats down by the side of the water, breathing in its delicious scent. Elihu's head bursts through the surface beside him.

"Oh! Hello," Elihu says, pushing the sopping hair out of his eyes.

Deucalion swallows, which takes longer than he has ever remembered it doing before in his life. "You look very happy here," Deucalion observes with pleasure. "You are not homesick at all?"

As always when the human world is mentioned, a strange flicker passes over Elihu's countenance, like he is trying to process a complex sum internally. "No, how could I be? You are all so very kind." He passes a wistful look at his fee friends still frolicking under the waterfall.

Deucalion feels himself glow within. "I am glad you have made friends. I made a promise once, to bring some people from Iblees to keep you company. Do you remember?" As Deucalion pronounces the words, he is suddenly painfully aware of how impossible his task is. No inward steeling of himself, no resolutions to stand firm and disregard the child are working. Nothing he can do will sever the golden threads woven between them, and nothing, no matter how he may lie to and reason with himself, can alter his purpose in life. The madness he had been lamenting such a short time ago was returning, and as usual it did not feel like madness, but rather the most powerful rationality.

"No, you actually said you were going to start a war," Elihu highlights with all the acuteness of children in general.

"I did? You must forgive me; I am old – nearly twenty three – and I forget these things."

"That *is* old. Have you not learnt better than to start wars yet? "

Deucalion laughs in spite of himself. "It seems that I must go to war. I will be leaving you soon."

It is gratifying to see that the pain inside Deucalion is reflected for a moment in the features of Elihu. Had he been in any doubt of the sacred trust, this mirroring must have allayed it.

"You may get hurt!" he warns the Fairy King, as if this may not have occurred to him. "Do not go. Or if you do, let me come with you."

"And fight against your own people? You do not understand what war is about," Deucalion counsels him fondly.

With a troubled brow, the young Prince runs a hand through the sparkling water and watches it. "No, I would not hurt them! But can't I talk to them? Show them that I was not really kidnapped, and that you fairies are very nice after all? And – and if they do not believe that," he continues, hanging his small head, "I will return with them."

Deucalion resists the impulse to embrace the child. "That is very noble, dear boy. But I fear this has gone beyond you now."

"Why can't you do something to stop it? My father would just say the word, and no one would stir. Aren't you a King?"

He leans back and sits on the grass. "I am a Fairy King. I have built a kingdom so fair that I cannot stop what is wrong. It is a great achievement of mine."

"Oh."

Deucalion pauses to look at the sky. It is incongruously bright, still. "Tell me one thing, Elihu, and it must be very seriously. Would you, once this war is over, work with me if I restored you to your kingdom? And I mean *your* kingdom, if you were in charge of it instead of your father. Would you let Laseri visit Auchriachan and Auchriachan visit Laseri? Would you let us protect you?"

Elihu laughs. "You are silly! Of course I would. We will always be friends – won't we?" He looks troubled with a moment of doubt.

Deucalion rolls on to his stomach and peers into the lagoon. Raising his eyes to Elihu's face, very close, arresting his gaze in his purple eyes, he vows: "I will not let any harm come to you, my boy. It shall be as you say."

Elihu rewards him with a smile full of all the richness of summer. Deucalion can say or bear no more; he stands and strides off abruptly to his fate. The sun continues to shine upon him in hideous mockery.

37

CHAPTER THIRTY-SEVEN

Aurora and Daireann alike suspect, deep in their nagging hearts, that it is all for nothing. The forest is sombre. The whole world around them feels in thrall – a singular time capsule. It is like wading through stagnant water.

Aurora is lucky enough to have a passion, a purpose within her to march forth and defend. But her misgivings grow the longer she traipses through this insensate wood.

The shock of Demetrius' death, the fear of going the same way, and Daireann's grief at parting from Caelia all overpower her by turns. Every so often she heaves an enormous sigh.

"If we could control what is going on outside, we would get there quicker," she announces. She runs a hand through her short blonde hair. "Why did I not realise it before? We saw Deucalion has sent soldiers to Iblees – that will only make the forest grow! Who knows what is taking place outside this hateful cocoon? The forest could be expanding at every moment!"

Daireann thinks she hears a waver of tears in the Fairy Queen's voice, but when she turns to look, Aurora is maintaining perfect composure.

"I always thought it was a pretty stupid idea, but you have tried. That's what helps you sleep at night, after all." But this will not do. Daireann's chest swells with pity. She rakes about objectively for something to comfort. "We must be getting *nearer*. Those dandelion seeds floating in the air have gone and I am half convinced the earth is almost sandy. Do run your foot over it – we must be *approaching* a desert at the very least."

Aurora does so obediently, her gaze fixed and glazed. She is not paying the least attention. What does it matter? It all feels dust and sand to her – everything.

Daireann shivers to see her pretty face contorted with lackadaisical disregard. She may as well be a zombie as a regal fairy. Daireann senses there is more bothering her than a quest for human kind – even more perhaps than the death of her dear fairy friend who had caused them so much trouble – but she cannot ask.

Reflecting for the next few meters, Daireann searches within herself to find a way to animate, to revive to life her companion. The answer is close to her own heart.

"How," she begins with a light, unstable voice, "how did you know her? Tell me about my mother."

Aurora wheels around at her in surprise. Her purple eyes are softer. Even the very remembrance of the past tenderises every feature. "Certainly, if you wish it."

Her expression becomes wistful, and her gaze far reaching – as if she is stripping the trees, shrubs and undergrowth away to resurrect the whole past world before them with just the power of her mind. "Her name was Urvasi. Lady Urvasi – as they are all ladies in Iblees. But she had a greater claim to the title than most. I believe she was cousin to the famous Queen Ganieda, and very like her."

Daireann gapes. "Royalty? I was born of royalty?" To one hated and despised her whole life – by her own kind no less than her parents – it is an exhilarating revelation.

Aurora, used to greatness all her life, smiles at the pixie's youthful simplicity. She cannot recall a time when she found it wonderful, or something to covet. All she remembers is that her noble parents had been slain when she returned from Iblees, and that they had been slain by the humans for being related to royalty.

"Yes of royalty, and of a good woman. She was always very kind to me at a time when I was a complete stranger. She fed me, and she supplied me with fresh clothes when I had but one set. Her gentle looks were a great comfort to me. I met nothing but glares and suspicion elsewhere."

Forcibly imprinted in Aurora's memory are the kind looks of one such other – she sees them suddenly, and says no more.

Daireann's green face has never looked less sullen. "So – so -" she stumbles in her great eagerness to form her tumultuous thoughts into words, her huge eyes expanding and contracting. "My mother is not my shame, as I have so long been told?"

"On the contrary; she is your pride. Your father was nothing but a sneaking Deev – it is *that* which makes you unique among pixies. They must have kidnapped her in the last battle. All of Iblees was in uproar. She ran out; I saw her heading towards the forest." Overcome, Aurora says no more.

"It could have been a fairy, all the same," reasons Daireann, her pride a little hurt at being associated with a Deev.

"I am sorry to pain you, but it really must be so. I am a fairy. Do you not think we can sense our own kind?"

Daireann remembers her skin *is* a little darker green than the other pixies, and her magic had always been of a kind to alarm others. "Then I am glad to have followed you," she admits, a very becoming humility overtaking her for the briefest spell. "The fairies of Laseri have done me no harm. As for my mother... I should fight for her."

She is amazed at her own revelation. Up until now she could not dream of considering her mother with anything other than scorn and resentment.

Aurora smiles at her with the zeal of a friend. Each feels, as their eyes meet, a sudden and unexpected comradeship. But the sound worming its way towards them dispels the charm as quickly as it was woven.

Their faces lose the elasticity, the warmth of attachment and expression. All colour is drained away and replaced with two vacant, dreading countenances as they hear the weeping.

It is a female, or a very young boy, sobbing in a way to break hearts. The forlorn cries come as fast as the person has breath.

Daireann starts forward. Her arm is checked by Aurora, who shakes her head noiselessly. "Caelia," Daireann pleads in a whisper.

"It is not her. How could it be her?"

Daireann shivers, afraid to let herself be comforted. "It sounds so like her."

Aurora gives her a knowing look. "It is designed to. We must lay face down on the path until it goes away. Trust me."

Reluctantly Daireann nods. She is still sporting a rebellious pout. "I have been caring for her since we were very small. I know what her cry sounds like."

Aurora gives an understanding look, but nevertheless gathers her flowing dress and lies down on her stomach. There is no time to lose. Her arms are folded, and she rests her fair forehead upon them. She gazes up and commands Daireann wordlessly to do the same.

The pixie flicks her eyes once more at the source of the pitiful sound, then imitates Aurora's position.

They lay still for a long time. Aurora can hear only the beating of her own heart, and the quick pant of her breathing. Every contraction of her rib cage feels over emphasised; it is a great effort just to take in air. Her senses seem heightened. Her skin tingles and her eyes pick out every vein on every leaf and every blade of grass on the earth to which her face is pressed.

Aurora catches her breath and pauses. The weeping continues. Air bursts from her mouth in a rush of disappointment, and she closes her eyes.

She continues this process at regular intervals. Once or twice she fancies the sound is quieter. Her head swims with relief, yet still she stays, glued to the land. Not until she is sure, absolutely sure that nothing but silence meets her strained ears, will she venture to even look up.

When two or three stints of listening prove the creature, whatever it was, has gone, she warily lifts her beautiful head. The trees before her are just the same. All is peaceful and still. Aurora's breathing begins to resume its regular pace.

"All is safe, Daireann," she whispers. "You can get up now."

She turns her head to look over her shoulder, eager to see a friendly face.

"Daireann?" It is more a gasp than a cry; she genuinely expects to be answered.

Nothing but leaves and sandy grass lay beside her. Daireann has gone.

It is the vagary of this wood, this unnatural divide betwixt Auchriachan and Laseri, to warp logistics and appearances. You would not believe Asher to be travelling in the same place as his beloved Aurora, so swift is his passage.

At first he follows the air-bound fairies, moving as the crow flies, but soon this becomes impractical. They are too fast to keep in view, and sometimes try to lead him on a route cutting straight through the thick bark of an ancient tree. Nonetheless, he has gone a good way under their directions, and his own memories of where he first found the two fairies in peril help him to ascertain which way they must have come from originally.

Now the trees are clearing, which can only be helpful. The air is thicker and warmer, resembling the atmosphere of Auchriachan. It slows but does not hamper Asher, so used to it is he.

Onwards he goes, crunching acorns beneath his feet. He cannot think of stopping even to rest. His chest burns with exhaustion, and with grief. Somehow the loss of Elihu has become intrinsically linked in his mind with Aurora; it feels implicit that saving him will be saving her – though from what she needs to be rescued, or if she would even care to remember him at all, is still unformed in Asher's thoughts.

A burst of light tells Asher there will be an open glade, or a parting of the trees very soon. He rushes into it before he expects to, and comes to a tripping halt. Before him is that self same tree-hunting ground that Apollo and his pixie found.

One look tells him how difficult it will be to pass, but he has committed himself thus far, and must see it through. His mind is so focused, or so deranged with the long journey of silent, torturous rumination, that he begins to clamber and leap over logs without a sigh. He falls down frequently; he rights himself, and continues, bleeding. No groan of pain passes his lips.

In fact, Asher does not remark anything outside the well of his own writhing thoughts until he sees the body.

The hum of flies first attract his attention, whizzing around his head until he has to look at where they are coming from. Foremost to catch his eye is a pure white wing.

He vomits with the surety it is *she*. It slams into him with the force of a brick to the rib-cage.

Coughing and shaking, he is finally able to raise his eyes to the sorry sight. He does not want to see it, but something tells him he must and compels him against his will. His diluted gaze sees short, black hair.

He rubs the bridge of his nose and shakes his head. That same hair – it is not a blob before his vision – and the figure too – much shorter and stockier than Aurora's – confirm that it is not her.

Whether elation or shame is uppermost in Asher's sensations he cannot decide. A fairy is dead: that has not changed. His senses are heightened again. His hand moves deftly to his quiver.

He creeps forward. His steps are now careful, and noiseless where possible. The smell is not too strong; the fairy cannot be very long dead.

Asher inches along in such stealthy suspense that crossing the remaining half of the tree charnel-house feels eight times as long. Nothing attacks him, however; he almost wishes it would. Anything – death itself – would be painless compared to the dreadful anticipation he now suffers.

As he nears the grove on the other side – painfully slowly – a whisper licks his ear. He flinches. He looks to either side.

Dead trees. Nothing else is near him, but still it comes – the eager, hungry whispering. He thinks it is coming from the trees.

Asher is careful not to venture too near the trees. He knows they have magical properties here; he knows so much as stepping on the red earth under a Sasbonsum's tree would cause immediate death. But it is not necessary to come to close for him to make out the words. His hearing is heightened by the fear and adrenaline screaming through him.

"You have proved yourself one of us. Incubi always boasted of you as his own – but today we are sure of it."

"We do not disown you like they would, if you were one of theirs. Did we not always, from your infancy, speak to you, care for you and warn you not to use your magic?"

"Yes, yes, you did. I am yours. We shall reign victorious over them all. As soon as the humans break through and grant us a passage into Laseri, it will be over for both of them."

"Even if they do not, we can kill the fairies who try to cross themselves. You have just shown it is more than possible. But your sister – why does your sister not join us?"

"I have never spoken to her about what we are. You have seen her – you know what she is like. But now the crisis is here – now she will understand."

"Then find her. Find her and between you kill the one who travels with her. If a reconciliation is brought about – that will not do for any of us."

"It was always my plan. This is but a detour. Ha! To kill Aurora! Imagine how the fairies will writhe at the death of their Royalty!"

This time the link between Aurora and death does not make Asher sick. It makes him angry.

Almost as if sensing the irate fumes he is emitting, the voices in the tree hush one another.

There is a pause of complete and utter silence; not a breeze, not a twig crack, not a breath. Then, from nowhere, a fireball.

A split instant before the ground beneath him ignites, Asher leaps aside and rolls under a bush. He feels the heat char his whiskers.

He pants, looking through a tangle of branches. The magic missile is sizzling in a bright blaze behind their cover, making a crackling noise.

A green head sprouts cautiously through the foliage. In his initial horror, Asher's mind commands him to draw an arrow. But his body will not obey. There is a glimmer of recognition in that face.

Though green and frightening, wearing a murderous look, it is familiar. Suddenly Asher is reminded of his friend Lady Urvasi. He knows very well in both heart and mind it is not her – but the mere resemblance causes him considerable pain.

It is lucky he does not make a movement, for the green apparition lets loose another fireball, very close. Asher's face is toasted with warmth.

The creature has moved, ever so minutely forward, to launch the second shot. It is all Asher needs to get a perfect view. In one deft movement, he rolls from his shelter and gives flight to an arrow.

His aim is straight and true, coming to rest in the centre of the green forehead. Caelia drops lifeless from the tree.

Asher's heartbeat begins to slow to the normal rate. He is about to start whispering calming, soothing thoughts to himself when all at once there is a truly terrible cry, and a black mist swarms out of the tree.

Asher's memory whisks him backward. He is on the hilltop with Joel, watching an identical haze swallow foliage and lay waste to the land. The same grief, the same devastation grips his insides with an aching hand. But this time he is determined.

Out he leaps from the bushes, firing arrow after arrow in rapid succession. Each straight-aimed point floats clear through the dark smog, and falls to the floor. He shows no surprise or disappointment, but goes on firing.

Chilling laughter encompasses all his senses as the black vapour coils around him. The mist fills his ears, his eyes, his mouth, like water fills one who is drowning. The voices of the Deevs mock him. Yet still he is firing. He will die trying, and go out like a Knight of Auchriachan – what *was* Auchriachan – if he can help it.

Asher is shooting with all his heart, his soul and his mind. Every morsel of useless, suppressed rage he has accrued since he stopped being a shepherd finds a swift vent. He shoots an arrow for Iblees, for the moors, for Ganeida, for Joel, for Elihu, for Urvasi, for his fairy…

The last, impassioned arrow drains all the energy from him. As if in slow motion he closes his eyes, and raises his sweating face towards the sky. Exhausted, Asher slumps backwards and lies on the earth. Dust rises up in a powdery cloud around him. The air does not stay brown for long; the darkness is enfolding it.

Asher remembers it is in the pocket next to his heart. Still there, still shining as new. His tired, bruised fingers grope for the only thing she ever gave him.

He clenches his fist around the small, yellow stone. He wishes to hold it to his breast, but his hand is shaking. The precious, tiny rock drops on to his clothing, and sits on his stomach.

Almost the instant it is exposed to the light there starts a horrid shrieking. Asher flinches in spite of himself; his body, prepared for the worst, thinks they are stooping to attack.

But they are doing no such thing. They are burning – burning without fire.

Asher's amazement enables him to sit up and gaze in exhilarated wonder.

The sun peeps out from behind the cloud as the Deevs are dispelled in a smoky vapour. Its rays shine through the blackness, and he can see how transparent it is. What was a moment ago forming itself into human shapes is now floating in harmless wreathes up to the sky –

there thinning, and disappearing completely.

Asher picks up the yellow stone with a keen thrill. After considering it with affectionate awe, he raises it determinedly in his hand. The shrieks are renewed, twice as loud. The black is nearly gone. Asher grins wildly.

The Deevs are clustering together above like a thunder cloud. They tremble, suspended in the air. Asher can hear crackles of friction and feel vibrations. The cloud swells, shrieks once more, and implodes. With a faint "poof" they are gone.

Asher brings the stone eagerly to his mouth and kisses it with frantic lips. He is astonished to see it is now completely white. He must have drained some kind of power from it – but it does not matter now. Such wild glee is pulsing through his body that he verily believes nothing will ever stop him again. To be alive, when he had resigned himself for death – to still stand a chance of saving all, when all seemed lost – it is a glorious, glorious thing. He feels like a man with the opportunity to turn back time after a great tragedy, in order to prevent its occurrence.

He springs to his feet, no longer weary, and runs with the pace of a gazelle.

Speeding through the trees, leaping over ditches, knocking aside branches, he knows in his heart he will see Laseri. And the surety of that fills him with an ecstasy beyond words.

38

CHAPTER THIRTY-EIGHT

Asher's elation at the prospect of Laseri is in proportion to Deucalion's dismay at leaving it.

You would not think to look at him now, hurtling along desert dunes in an open cart, flanked by chariots in front, behind, to the left and to the right, that he is struggling against despair. Behind the focused, resolute violet eyes he is looking back to his beautiful land and the dear boy; almost hopeless of seeing either again.

Although the memory of that wonderful place and of that wonderful person steels him with a desire to fight for them, he doubts himself. He wonders what Laseri really is, really stands for, and what is best for it. As for Elihu – it grieves Deucalion to think that any human who might die means as much to some fairy somewhere as Elihu means to him.

The shining silver car rattles on. The elegant white fairy horses pull the chariots with unearthly speed. Fairies riding unicorns alongside the ground troops are just landing on the Auchriachan side of the forest. The air force carries on over head, flying with unabated stamina.

Deucalion fears they are depleted. Before the thought can fully process in his brain, one of them is hovering by his ear, making the sound of a humming bird.

"Human Knights, your majesty – in the forest. We have killed a great many." Deucalion feels sick. "Yet I fear some will get through. Will our defences at home hold against them?"

These humans! Deucalion cannot decide what makes him feel worse: killing them or having them in his kingdom.

"We must hope they shall!" he shouts above the noise of the wheels. "We must not let thoughts of what is happening there distract us!" The fairy nods and visibly strains for fortitude. Having achieved it, he soars upwards again, leaving Deucalion laughing at his own effective hypocrisy.

There is a great crack from the forest border. Deucalion looks back to see dozens of Kish's vagabond troops spill out, hauberks hanging off their bodies, destriers – such fine warhorses! – bleeding. They run, crazed and scattered like frightened chickens.

Some try to attack the fairies and fail. One or two fairies fall, to be sure, but the humans are too hysterical to be effective. A Knight in a blue surcoat wheels his foaming bay steed very near the wheel of the chariot on Deucalion's left. Their eyes meet for what can be only a fraction of a second – but Deucalion feels he will never forget the man's look. The very expression behind his eyes makes Deucalion sure he has seen a Deev.

The bay horse stumbles forward, being directed every which way by his deranged rider. The man goes to drive his spurs home – he pauses with legs in the air as he is struck hard in the back from nowhere. He slumps on his horse and falls from the charioteer's spear.

Deucalion turns his face away.

Other Knights, in the disturbance of their minds, beat a hurried retreat to Iblees. They think they are escaping while their comrades attack the fairies; they do not stop to consider at least one of the enemy must be following their movements.

How long must it have taken the fairies to find the way to Iblees, though they had travelled it before in the first war, without the aid of these coward Knights! Every short cut, every path to avoid a hazard that can be taken, is taken by the poor wounded soldiers hurrying home.

Fear, their injuries and concern for their horses prevent the Knights from even noticing they are being chased. They see the great yellow mound of a city with waves of the highest relief. They dash through the gardens full of palm trees, creak over the bridge and bundle through the dilapidated gate house – then, and only then, as their senses return do they comprehend what they have done.

The guard rooms are in uproar. Seeing the advance of horses from a long way off, the depleted army have been preparing for battle for some time, under the directions of Sir Nehemiah.

"We should never have let you in!" he curses the returning army. "And if we did not need the extra men, I assure you I never would have allowed it."

One Knight, who truly believed Kish had led them out under Joel's orders, gapes at the upbraid. Sir Nehemiah hits him over the head with a pike.

"Take your arms, then! You may be traitors but you're all we have!"

Half of the Knights, still dazed from blood loss and terror, continue to be astonished at the glaring looks of the Knights who stayed behind as they grab swords from the wooden racks. It is not a bright day for them; the word "traitor" suggesting if they are not killed by winged creatures, they will be beheaded by the King or pulled apart by their comrades at arms.

Nehemiah gallops up to the southeast tower, where Joel is pacing, hands travelling repeatedly through his unruly hair, to relate the news.

"Some of the renegades have returned my liege. They are wounded and hardly fit to stand, but it gives us a greater chance. Whatever their past intentions, I hope they will fight for Iblees now."

"They will be fighting for their very lives; they will not be able to help it."

Nehemiah grimaces. "It is dire, your Majesty, but there is always some hope…"

"Not for me," Joel shakes his head rapidly, eyes wide, "not for me now." With a sudden burst of energy, he runs to the edge of the tower and peers over. "Oh, and are they really here? The fairies? There is no way to stop it now!" he cries wildly. "They have done it! My Ganieda, my Ganieda!"

Sir Nehemiah judges the only correct response to this is one that does not directly relate to anything the King has just said. "Some of the Knights, indeed, looked amazed that we disapproved of their running off."

Joel slumps against the wall. "Kish! Kish, all this time, not Asher!" he shudders as he says the name of his former friend and draws a ragged, shivering breath. "Oh Asher! What have I done? I need you now, old friend. I can save a lamb, but not a kingdom! Never before have I felt so strongly that I wish to serve and protect Auchriachan, as now, when all desire must be in vain."

Seeing he will get no help here, Sir Nehemiah returns to his Knights, to shift as well as he can. Joel does not notice his removal. He sits, hugging his knees, his lips silently forming the names of Ganieda, Asher and Elihu over and over again in a reproachful mantra.

"Kill the fairy carrying the banner if you can," Nehemiah instructs his soldiers. "I seem to remember Sir Kish – or it may have been Sir Asher – telling me once of its magical properties." But he does not think it too likely they will be able to.

The archers speed to the battlements. Losing no time they begin to fire, rather too frantically. They have no Asher to guide their shots, and they feel it most acutely. But they hold the advantage that their castle is now concentric – they can fire upon the fairies from three levels. Considering the fairies have not yet come to a standstill, and were not expecting Iblees' forces to be mustered so soon, this many tiered onslaught is no small benefit.

The burning blue sky is streaked full of arrows, flying in every direction. Sundry fairies drop from the air, twirling round and round like sycamore seeds to the ground.

Deucalion and his chariots are now within perfect range. His troops begin to conjure the apparatus for attack. Ladders, ramps, forks and mangonel catapults are materialising from a hundred moonstone rings. Deucalion dismounts from his car in an elegant swoop.

"Wait! Leto, Tethys, wait!" the two fairies he addresses lose their concentration and drop half finished ropes to the sand. Deucalion's body buzzes at the silence he is suddenly expected to fill. He cannot help noticing every second he searches for the right words, more fairies are dying.

"Peaceful means first. As fairies, we should *try* to avoid a battle…" he sees their incredulous eyes flick to the castle, and the waves of arrows, before returning to his face.

"Yes, I know, they have started a battle. But remember the Queen may be within. I will send an ambassador, therefore, to see what may be done. I must do this first, for the safety of Queen Aurora."

Grumbling under their breath – neither have they forgotten that only a few months ago, this fairy was held in disgrace, nor have their suspicions of her wholly died – they acknowledge it must be so.

"Good!" cries Deucalion, rejoicing from his heart as his conscience begins to approve of him once more. "Erebus – you have always had a high respect for my wisdom. Go, then, and carry it to them; I know no one more qualified. Be quick!"

Whatever his former opinions may have been, all visible reaction from Erebus denotes he no longer values the great wisdom of Deucalion as highly as he ought to.

Wrapping the fairy banner around himself for a shield, he runs like a cheetah towards Glass Mountain Castle. He will have to climb through the sewerage system to gain admittance. It is a circumstance that makes Deucalion smile a little more widely than is appropriate for a war.

Meanwhile, the fairies must do something industrious. They begin to dig, shovelling huge handfuls of sand into the air. Others fly swiftly over the moat and stand in preparation.

"Was ever a captain so spectacularly unlucky?" exclaims the frustrated Nehemiah. "How can I guess the enemy's tactics when they are such brainless animals? They are digging. *Digging.*"

"The trebuchet is ready, Sir," one of his Knights consoles him.

"Good. Begin using it immediately. And lower a mattress over the door. They look like they would begin battering. But they are so *still*! Apart from the digging. What are they doing? Do they not see their soldiers falling from the sky?"

There is a sudden clamour from the garderobe.

"A fairy! A fairy!" Nehemiah hears.

He grieves for the intelligence of his army.

Any moment now, thinks Deucalion, he will be

reunited with his Queen, and hailed as a wise King. Every second Erebus is away strengthens his conviction. What could take so long, if not peace negotiations?

Deucalion raises his face to the bright sky in a blaze of exaltation and gratitude. He sees the heavens full of the silhouettes of his air force, and is proud. Until… They are halting, swerving; something is not right.

With jerky movements they are parting down the middle like the red sea.

There is another shape in the air. Deucalion watches it fly like a well fired canon ball towards him, his faculties frazzled. He should move, he knows it – yet has no desire to. He wants to see what the thing is. He squints against the sun as the object becomes larger and larger.

It is falling through the air now with a rushing noise. His charioteers Tethys and Leto run from him; the diggers Himeros and Iapetus scatter from their trench with loud lamentations.

Deucalion remains perfectly still until the moment Erebus' head lands at his feet.

There is an instant where Deucalion hears nothing, save the blood rushing past his ears. It is like he is under water gazing into the glazed, bloodshot eyes of Erebus.

Then, with a pop, he is aware of how painfully loud and full of sorrow the desert around him is.

"Evil, evil, unnatural creatures!" shrieks Himeros – a tall, noble faced fairy.

Deucalion notes with a dull surprise that every fairy, even those who had no acquaintance with or reason to like Erebus, has tears streaming down their faces.

He knows, rather than feels, that this is one of the greatest outrages on a fairy. He is too numbed by shock to process the emotion. True, many fairies had died in the first war – but that was a battle. Cynthia had been killed, undoubtedly by premeditation – but he had not seen it.

Here, in cold blood, an ambassador is slain. It is an irrecoverable truth, sounding in his heavy heart like a leaden knell, that he cannot save the humans. For some reason this is the last straw - the rebellion to break the fairies' hearts.

Tethys' mouth looks like it will rip with screams. "A peace mission! He went to propose peace! Oh what in the world have they done to our Queen?!"

This unlucky conjecture gives birth to new agony. Never have the fairies loved Aurora more than now, when they may have no chance to love her again.

The air force wheel about in the sky with cries like hawks. Several of them - and some fairies on unicorns too - turn tail immediately and flee in the direction of Laseri with the news.

Deucalion had read once, as a boy, that every time a human upsets fairies, the fairy decreases in size. He had dismissed it as nonsense at the time, but now he fears everything is true. Every horrible possibility he hid himself from is coming vividly to life. His army no longer looks like it will outnumber that of Auchriachan; it looks small. He feels small and frightened inside.

But Aurora - Elihu - to mope will not do. Though he feels powerless to act, Deucalion knows he must do something. He knows, moreover, that he must do the last thing he wants to do, for all fairies.

"Get a hold on yourselves!" he reprimands the fairies in an authoritative bark. "Are we going to let them do this? Are we going to let Erebus die in vain?"

The soldiers are calmer.

"But - your Majesty, they have our banner."

"And we have our magic. Finish that mangonel!" Deucalion begins to stride powerfully forward, addressing grieving groups by turn. "I want to cover the Castle from all sides. We could do with a tower. Someone tell those near the drawbridge to start the battering. And whatever you do, keep digging!"

His violet eyes are burning so brightly it hurts to look at them. The fairies are only too glad to be told what to do in this situation. They are comforted, though shaken, and apply themselves with a sense of mission once more. But every so often they stop, their impish faces suddenly bewildered, and look to him.

Deucalion has but an instant, when their eyes are not upon him, and his face is averted, to let out, one bitter, silently howling sob. And then he is ready to give the next directions.

39

CHAPTER THIRTY-NINE

Another minute more, and Daireann will completely lose her senses. Every slight noise assails her with the dual artillery of hope and fear. Her heart rejoices as it hopes the sound is a signal of life – perhaps she has retraced Aurora, or better, Caelia. Yet at the same time her body flinches, suspecting a Deev, an animal, or a monster of her own vivid imagination.

There are more sounds the further she walks. The wood in which she now wanders is more verdant, rich in leaves and flowers. It seems there are birds, for occasionally she hears a flutter of wings – there is definitely *something* living in the trees. She was sure for a moment that she actually saw a rabbit, but now she thinks she may have deluded herself.

"What am I doing here?" she thinks suddenly. Leaving the pixie fort, meeting fairies, the death of Demetrius and her sending Caelia away to Laseri do not feel like things she has really done; it is all a nightmarish chain of events, and she cannot recall how or why they started. And why on Earth did she leave the protection of the Fairy Queen to wander alone in this suspenseful, dangerous forest?

Daireann trembles, barely able to endure it. Her huge eyes turn to the thin strip of sky visible between the leaves. She cannot see the Deevs she suspects to find there.

Caelia. The name leaps into her mind as she gazes upwards. That is why she is here: Caelia. It is her desire and her duty to protect Caelia. She was foolish to let her go with Apollo; she should have known it would be too great a separation.

As Darieann remembers the horrible cries which convinced her to leave Aurora, she shivers. If they were Caelia's – and if the same thing which befell her was about to happen to Daireann – what then? Daireann begins to shake, but something steadies her from within.

She thinks of her mother. Daireann's fancy paints a beautiful, noble lady, wronged past endurance – and yet she *did* endure it, long enough to give birth to her sister and herself. Daireann sees this imaginary Lady Urvasi and has a burning urge to please her, to emulate her. The pretty blonde lady smiles at her with perfect teeth and brave eyes. She beckons. Daireann begins to walk more evenly.

Daireann recalls the look of Aurora's face as she talked of Urvasi. It had spoken unutterable tenderness. They had been great friends, the fairy and her mother. Perhaps her mother had wanted to be like the fairies. Daireann feels like a fairy herself now, trying to protect her own precious one: Caelia.

As she journeys onwards, Daireann sees little of the trees and hears nothing of the torturous noises. She feels cocooned and safe with the image of her mother. She must find Caelia for her mother's sake. How could she forgive her if she let her dear daughter die?

The chimera of Urvasi encourages Daireann onwards with glowing eyes. She looks as divine as an angel. And what was an angel? Self-sacrifice, tenderness, never-ending devotion and courage. Daireann throws all concern for herself to the wind. She knows what she must do to find Caelia: she calls out.

"Caelia! Caelia, where are you? It is me, your sister!"

The hollows and the glens ring with her voice. It is strong, level and unafraid.

"Caelia, can you hear me? Come to me, dear!"

Daireann walks firmly on, calling and calling. She feels invincible.

"Caelia?"

The leaves on her left shiver. There is a sound of crunching from far away.

Daireann is not quite proofed against this. She looks at the foliage in big-eyed suspicion, and backs away from it. "Caelia?" she asks again.

There is a creak like a falling tree. The bushes and branches are swaying in a frenzied dance. Something is coming. Something larger than Caelia, she fears.

Her voice is quieter, but just as stable. She grips onto the bud of a flower behind her. "I am here, dearest."

At the sound of her voice there is a ghastly roar. The green leaves convulse in one last paroxysm and fall still. There is no noise now.

Daireann wrinkles her green forehead in green confusion. Should she take a step towards…

Suddenly a small green figure ejects from the trees, coming at such an uncontrollable speed it might have been fired from a gun.

It hurtles unstoppably towards Daireann; she does not even have the time to sidestep before the green figure is thrust upon her and grips her round the arms.

She involuntarily closes her eyes and utters a small scream.

"There you are! And without *her*!"

Daireann hardly hears the voice at first; her momentary fear has muffled all sound. Her body remains frozen in shock, but her brain is beginning to process the words, the voice…

Inhaling a long, fortifying breath, she lifts her green

eyelids. No sooner have her large pupils focused on the object before her than she flinches back in revulsion.

It is like looking into a mirror of horrific predictions. A dark green face like her own stares back at her, contorted by anger and pain. Its cheeks are stained with streaks of blood, in varying shades of dried brown, flowing red and deep purple. Protruding out of the centre of its forehead is a broken wooden stick, like the snapped off shaft of an arrow.

Once the initial dismay has washed over her and ebbed out again, Daireann rushes forward with arms outstretched.

"Oh Caelia, my darling Caelia! What have they done to you? Who did this?! I'll – I'll-"

Caelia's slim green fingers, like strips of asparagus, stop her mouth. "Hush! Do not tell me of your rage; show it. A filthy human shot this through my head – a human who fights for the Fairy Queen. She must have been plotting this the whole time. Our people were right all along: the fairies are evil and the humans are no better. We must fight back against them. There are some who can help us..."

Daireann steps back and shakes her head violently. She cannot believe it. Aurora's graciousness and nobility is too inspiring to be an act. To lose the conviction of Aurora's virtue and truth would force Daireann to forsake the new found image of her good, glowing mother. She cannot do that. Although the picture has so recently been conceived, it has taken root in her heart; she cannot pull one up without the other.

But this cruel arrow in her darling's head! There must be some explanation; the poor injured dear cannot be thinking straight.

"Are you listening to me, Daireann? Stop looking at the arrow; I will survive yet. It has not gone too deep. I plan to pull it out and jam it through the one who put it there."

Something has changed in Daireann's sister; she is suddenly unrecognisable. When Daireann would expect her sobbing at her feet, she is shooting off sparks of anger and revenge. But in fairness, she does have an arrow lodged through her head. Something must be dislodged in the cranium.

Daireann scoops her twin into her arms with deep pity, heedless of her struggles.

"Of course I am listening. But sit yourself down! You must rest! How did you get this far in that condition?" She pushes Caelia down on a rock and fingers the arrow tenderly. How painful it looks, how easily fatal! It pierces her heart as deeply as Caelia's forehead. She cannot comprehend how her sister has survived this far; her heart bleeds with the doubt she will survive it much longer. What spell could she perform for this? Alas she knows none that can do good!

Caelia's hand arrests hers. She pulls Daireann down to her knees with surprising strength until they have total eye contact.

"I have survived because I have been aided. I told you there were still some who would help us; there is a medicine they can make. I healed myself the best I could, and they will do the rest."

Daireann is disconcerted. Caelia's eyes are nearly entirely pupils. "Healed yourself? You cannot do magic, dear. I will try my best to help – if I could think of a healing spell!" She runs distracted fingers quickly through her dark hair. "I fear it is only the fairies who know those!"

"Sister," Caelia's voice drops an octave, and is gravely serious. "You do not know what I can and can't do. My friends – our allies – have taught me many things. I should have told you before. But you were always so passionate. They urged me to wait until the time was right. Now you cannot raise any objections; now you must see how right they are."

Daireann, who is almost certain these friends are no more than a hallucination caused by pain and blood-loss, makes no reply.

She smoothes away Caelia's blood-caked black fringe and manages to cleanse some of the splatters off of her forehead with her magic.

Caelia allows her to do so without complaint. When she is finished, Caelia merely says: "Think, Daireann – think what they could do with power like yours."

It is now beginning to make Daireann feel eerie. Her poor, poor sister! This is like being trapped with a mad person. To think that these might be their last moments together, and Caelia is gone in spirit already! She tries to reason with her.

"It takes all my power to bear seeing you like this with composure! Sweet, sweet Caelia, what are you talking about? You are being ridiculous. Do sit and think calmly. Who are you even speaking of?" Caelia gazes at her with complete serenity. "The Deevs, Daireann. The Deevs. They have tutored me from childhood in preparation for this day. They accept us as their own. They want you to join us." She puts her hand upon Daireann's, who flinches minutely at the touch. "*I* want you to join us. We will be safe, my sister, and free from shame at last!" Something in the way these words are delivered prevents Daireann from dismissing them as nonsense. There is cataclysmic, undeniable truth in every look.

Daireann's head and heart begin to spin round in an incomprehensible division of loyalties and morals. She does not move.

"You have not backed away," crows the gleeful

Caelia. "I knew you would understand. Between us we will crush both fairies and humans alike. We will be Queens among pixies. Why, there will not *be* any other pixies – all those who have so long taunted us will die!" She smiles broadly.

Little as Daireann liked the other pixies, she feels suddenly a great surge of comradeship towards them. They were awful to her, undoubtedly, but they were her own kind; they were all she and Caelia had had by way of family. She thinks of how Queen Aurora was shamed by her fairies, and how she is now fighting to protect them. It made no sense to act in such a selfless way, and yet it felt so right.

"The – the Deevs killed Demetrius," is the sum of all Daireann can say.

To her horror, Caelia beams. "He had it coming, the know-it-all! You do not know what it cost me to hear him harp on about Deevs and their ways, when *I* should be teaching *him*! How well they avenged us! Do you remember how he used to push us out of his way?"

Daireann ruminates, and does remember. A small prickle of bitterness taints her thoughts. Her heart drops. Yes, perhaps she is glad. Perhaps he did have it coming.

Her prejudices begin to wane. Her hatred towards Deevs is softened, ready to see their pros and their cons. Could her idolized Caelia, so sweet and lovely, have wrong thoughts? No, surely she, Daireann, is mistaken in her thinking. And yet...

"Are you sure, Caelia, that you are not taken in? Deevs do not seem to like pixies, if they will murder Demetrius and all the rest."

Caelia laughs. It is not the pleasant childish laugh Daireann used to love. It is altogether more spooky and mirthless. "Like us? We were never like the other pixies, Daireann. We were fathered by Deevs. We are above the others; that is why they tried to crush us. We were born of a nobler breed." Caelia stands up. "Come, there is no time. I will take you to them, and you will see how they are ready to exalt you."

Curiosity alone nearly makes Darieann rise. She looks at her eager, pretty sister beckoning to her. Is this her chance to be raised to nobility at last? With Deevs? The two words feel incongruous. Her ambition prods her on, and yet she does not rise.

She needs a moment. She cannot change allegiance so quickly; she cannot give herself fully to this course whilst her heart is upbraiding her at every moment.

Caelia has no patience with her dilemma. Hesitation is close in her mind to cowardliness. She knows if she lets Daireann think too long she will become afraid and stubborn. "Come, Daireann, come!" she demands petulantly. Then, looking as appealing as she possibly can, fluttering her long eyelashes, she coos: "You have two choices, dear. You and I have the simultaneous misfortune and fortune to be half dirty human, half supreme Deev. Your paths are set before you. Will you be brave and strong like your father, a Prince of the Deevs, or will you take the way of disgrace and uselessness, like our weak mother? Will you go amongst the humans, who would never own you, who would tread on you like scum, when their offspring our mother was but a plaything of the great Deevs?"

Had she drafted it for a year, Caelia could not have written a speech less likely to achieve her end. She brought Daireann's wronged mother immediately before her. On the one side she sees the bright angel who guided her through this wood, urging her to be humble and brave in order to achieve true nobility; on the other, a shadowy, deceiving Deev luring her down to a pit darker than hell.

Everything within Daireann clings to the image that

is good – she knows she must follow it at all costs. But to keep it she must accept that Caelia is corrupted – perhaps mistakenly corrupted, but nonetheless, she must sever the tie between them.

Daireann wants very much to be bold and courageous, but she is crushed beyond words. Her sister! How hard she tried all her life to protect her – and never once tried to save her from herself! Daireann starts up, and in tears, makes one last desperate attempt to clear her sweetheart from all blame.

"Oh how ill you are!" she cries. "My love, you have seen things in the wood! Where is Apollo? How did he let this happen to you? Perhaps he knows a spell that might cure you!"

From Caelia's look, Daireann already knows all is lost, and sobs bitterly.

"You are the last person I expected to be so weak and silly! Apollo is dead. I killed him with my own tricks; it is my greatest glory. They are all so proud of me. I thought your appearing without Aurora meant she was dead too. I hoped so. But we must finish her if she is not. Come!"

This is the final blow. Daireann literally feels the twin-link snap; she is filled with an intense sense of emptiness and isolation. She looks upon her sister as upon a complete stranger. Never in her life has she felt afraid of her before.

"You *killed* Apollo? He was our friend! He doted on you!" she says it calmly, for all she is shocked and grieving inside.

Caelia turns fully on her. There is far less benevolence in her aspect – and there was precious little in it to start with. "No fairy is a friend of ours, Daireann. Don't be foolish. I promised them you wouldn't be. I cannot disappoint them."

Daireann crosses her arms in a mute show of her

immovability.

"Come!" Caelia stretches out a green hand and gestures impatiently. "Your last chance, Daireann! Come!"

Daireann looks upon the hand as if it were a snake winding towards her. "I will not join the Deevs. You are wrong."

The hand drops. Caelia's impatience rapidly gives way to a smouldering fury. Every sinew of her green shape shoots out vibes of rage and darkness. "Think, you fool! I am loyal to our kind. I will not let you live to disgrace me; you will not live to fight against us."

"I," growls Daireann, annunciating every syllable, "will *never* join the Deevs!"

As she shouts the last word, a gale of paralysis sweeps over her. She feels her limbs tightly pinioned to her sides and falls sprawling off of her seat.

Once she hits the ground, she recovers enough feeling to be aware she is being pulled roughly to her feet and hit around the face. This physical pain, so closely coupled with her emotional trauma, is not to be borne. A weight of injustice presses down upon her, and Daireann roars.

With a sudden jump she fights back, hissing and clawing, great sparks flying from the end of her defensive fingernails.

"It is useless!" Caelia taunts. "Your magic can never match one taught by the Deevs!" She soars up on her moth wings, out of Daireann's reach and laughs horribly. Daireann shoots her to the floor with a well-aimed jet of fire.

Caelia drops like a stone, looking shocked. She rolls to her feet just in time to miss the blow dealt by Daireann's fist.

"I will not let you kill the Fairy Queen!" yells Daireann as she stumbles. Caelia is concocting an evil-looking red beam, but Daireann shields herself with a misty force-field that repels it at once.

Seeing that long, powerful blasts are not working, Caelia begins to fire short, sharp bullet-like flames from her fingers. They fly in all different directions, and Daireann is hard pushed to block them.

She darts about rallying each one. They continue like this for a long time: Daireann sending back each shot, Caelia defending against each missile her sister manages to aim. They are almost evenly matched.

"I never thought, in all the years we were children," muses Caelia, "you would grow to be so idiotic. All the cares and times we shared – and you were a corrupt fairy-lover all along! You were nothing but the scurf of our human ancestry; a pitiful, snivelling wretch like the dog we are forced to call mother! To think *I* let *you* pretend to look after me!"

For the briefest time, Daireann loses her concentration in a fit of anger. She launches herself forward with an offensive attack, and is caught out. A blast hits her and knocks her tottering backwards, smacking against the hard trunk of a neighbouring tree.

Whilst she tries to recover from the dizziness, Caelia swoops in upon her. Each of her hands is clamped firmly in one of Caelia's; she holds her firmly against the tree so that she cannot move.

Through the stars in her eyes, Daireann can see they have entered a deeper region of the forest once more. There are splintered trees around them that look as if they have been recently struck by lightning. Or perhaps their very battle has done this to the trees around them. She cannot remember.

She struggles futilely against her twin's grip. In the vicious, bloody figure before her, she feels as if she were fighting a darker, unwanted shadow side of herself. She presses all the harder against her foe, straining to get free. But Caelia will not let her go.

"It is too late now, Daireann," she whispers with terrifying relish, a strange fire glowing in her eyes and expanding. "I will show you my greatest spell yet."

At that moment Daireann knows her sister is beginning to weave the magic to take her life from her. She has one last chance. In a final, Herculean effort, she stops trying to pull her hands free, and instead pushes.

She pushes with all her might and strength, bruising her back painfully as she uses it as a spring against the tree trunk.

Caelia does not expect this. Her concentration wavers, and the flame disappears from her pupils. Still Daireann pushes, like a thing possessed, pushing furiously against the surprised figure of her sister. She does not care where they go, but they will keep going backwards. She locks her eyes on Caelia's face and sees the deep hatred there.

Caelia struggles to push back, but to no avail. Daireann watches her sister's expression become fraught with effort, shadowed by loathing and irate with frustration.

Deeper and deeper grow the creases on her face – and suddenly, Caelia's eyebrows shoot upwards. She looks surprised, and gradually the lines are smoothing, disappearing from her forehead. Daireann does not trust this; she pushes harder, only to find Caelia will not budge.

What strange magic is this, that she is matching Daireann's force without the least sign of effort? Daireann casts about for a clue in Caelia's eyes, her forehead, her mouth – and is startled to see her whole head slump forwards, and drop upon her chest.

With a start Daireann releases her hands and jumps back. Caelia's limbs fall equally limp at her side, but she remains standing. A trickle of blood runs from her mouth.

It is only then Daireann sees she has impaled her twin on a hunk of shattered tree. Its splintered bark has run through her neck and severed the vital links between head and body. There is no mistaking this time. Caelia is dead.

Daireann regards the sight for a beat, then falls to the floor in choking sobs.

The time becomes a blank. Daireann has wandered, but she does not know where or for how long. She was not aware of leaving Caelia's body, but she is now in a different landscape and suddenly wide awake, like coming round from a deep trance. Everything is foreign and strange. All she can think of is finding Aurora, helping Aurora, serving her cause. It petrifies her to think of anything else. She cannot think of what she has just done.

The trees are closing in upon her, but she is not too afraid of that. They are bright and alive. Daireann feels almost like she is being wrapped in a comforting embrace by them.

She sees she is approaching a great tunnel formed as the trees grow over from two parallel rows and meet in the middle. This is certainly not the way she came. Nor does it look like a desert. Aurora is unlikely to be here.

Daireann hesitates. There is something so inviting about the tunnel – too inviting, perhaps, to be trusted. She really must help Aurora. But what is the best way to do that – through the tunnel, or away from the tunnel?

Tentatively, she ventures her head around a tree trunk and peers shyly into the green tunnel.

She gasps. Her head immediately abuses her for the stupidity of gasping, but she cannot help it. Half way down the tunnel is a tall, comely man, clad from head to foot in glowing armour. This sight would have surprised her enough alone, but it would not have caused her to make a sound.

The Knight – for such a creature she presumes it must be – is smiting, with extreme vigour, another, stranger figure. A lady, with porcelain blue skin and hair whiter than snow, is lying crumpled in a pool of purple, glittering liquid. She is clearly on the point of death, yet clings with the tenacity of a young, fit person onto something like a pole in her left hand.

This pole – or perhaps it is a staff – appears to be the Knight's object of desire. He is pulling on it as hard as he is hitting with the hilt of the sword in his other hand.

Daireann's gasp makes them pause. They look at her – pleading bloodshot blue eyes and ferocious dark brown ones.

The Knight is momentarily motionless. Daireann's feet begin to run, and before she knows it, the Knight has stopped his assault to run after her.

Leaving his previous prey, who he knows cannot move, the Knight swoops down upon her with astonishing speed. Daireann, whose strength has been sapped by her tussle with Caelia and the long walk in the woods, does not have the power to fight him off. He seizes her by her bell chain and holds her up in the air, neck burning and gasping for breath.

"Who are you?!" He demands.

"Please – sir – I am just a pixie. I – I – mean you no – harm. J- Just let me – go on my way."

Something even darker spreads over him. He bites his lip. "Go on your way?! Don't you know there is a war going on?"

Daireann cannot reply for some minutes. She chokes and dribbles. "But – but I am – half human – half – fairy. How – can – can I poss – possibly be on – either side?"

She does not know why her words make his face turn

the deepest shade of red, or why the Knight is suddenly drawing his breath in pants. He looks at her with utter hatred, and draws his sword into the air.

Perhaps it is better this way. She had never envisaged being able to live without her twin anyhow.

Casting her frantic eyes left and right, Daireann retains only enough consciousness to be aware that this is the last she will ever see of the world. She sees the blue lady, with one great last motion, fling her precious staff deep into the bushes. And then the blue lady is still – gone, Daireann thinks, to wherever she herself will be travelling in a moment.

She closes her eyes and braces herself.

It is strange what fear and apprehension do. So powerful is the adrenaline surging through her that Daireann cannot feel any wound, though she hears the rush of air and a loud thunk. The hold on her neck feels less severe, like it is slackening gradually, and she assumes this is happening as she is passing from her body into the next world, where nothing ties her down.

She experiences a brief sensation of weightlessness, and then the shock of impact. She certainly feels pain now, bouncing all over her tangled body. Dimly she can hear a metallic clang. She senses everything as if – as if she was alive.

Daireann opens her eyes.

It is the same world she closed them upon. She is lying at the foot of a tree. The Knight is a few feet away, bleeding from the back of his skull. He is pacing round and round a leaner, dirtier looking man in light chain-mail with a bow on his back and a dagger in his hand, who paces round and round him likewise. From the red stain on the hand that holds the dagger, she apprehends this stranger is her saviour.

"So you do fight for them, after all!" Darieann's

assailer accuses the newcomer. "I knew it."

He lunges at the other man, who dodges with a hair's-breadth to spare.

"I do not fight against my own people – my own King. But when the war is between the fairies and you – oh yes, Kish, I fight for them."

The Knight called Kish launches himself furiously towards his opponent. His blows are only just repelled by the swift movements of the dagger. But the dagger is too small a weapon to hold out against a full blown sword for long. The archer moves a fraction of a second too slow, and is sliced across the shoulder blade.

Daireann is too weak to stand, or help. But she remembers she can do something. Groaning with great exertion, she raises her hand out and concentrates.

She continues to moan and pant as if in agony. But tiny stars are sparkling in her hand and the air before it. They are forming into a shape, gleaming along its edges. Brighter and brighter they shine, until they are a great glowing ray of light.

The beam fades slowly, and leaves behind a perfect sword.

The flash has already caught Asher's attention. He sees Daireann's intention before she throws the newly made weapon into the air, and is ready to catch it.

Kish's face flashes angrily. It is only the technicality that Asher stands between them which stops him running Daireann through there and then.

"So beloved by them all – even their bastards," Kish spits at Asher.

"You were beloved by one – once," Asher reminds him.

It is like a red rag to a bull. Kish's skin mantles red again in pure shame, and shame transforms quickly to blind rage. He leaps at Asher, with a movement more like a beast than a man. "You will not hold that against me! She is dead! I made sure of it with my own hands; she is dead!"

They fall to furious sword play.

Daireann scuttles as far as she can out of the way. But wherever she moves, it seems they are all around her. Every direction she looks she finds moving feet, and blinding light ricocheting off the swords.

Her ears are full metallic sounds and stamping noises. She hears a quick breath, and the occasional groan. She looks up through her tangled black hair.

Asher is fighting with skill and grace, but he is no equal to the swordsmanship of Kish. His talents lie in the bow – and even if they did not, the blood flowing freely from his wound would still prove a severe impediment.

They fight in a wild waltz; Asher is just able to avoid Kish's stabs, for they are made with more passion than calculation.

Daireann feels a deep surge of pity and affection for her rescuer. She is sure she would feel it, even if her life did not depend on his staying alive. She watches him tire as he weaves in and out, ducking the great swings that cut through the air with a soul-shaking swoop. If only there was something she could do…

Kish is grinning maniacally. He can see victory before him in Asher's pale, sweaty looks. The realisation of many long cherished, painfully repressed desires is looming. He can almost see the coronation – King of Auchriachan, no more Laseri, the darling of the Boanerges… He has been waiting a long time.

Asher can see how sure Kish is growing of himself. He is dropping his guard, letting his sanguine feelings carry him from the fight. He seems to be slicing at Asher now for pure fun. He nicks him in the calf and Asher draws back, but is not disheartened.

Daireann hears the cut of material and flesh. She sits

bolt upright, and cries out. Fear gives her the energy to do so.

It is just that second – just the split second in which Kish's eyes flick irresistibly as they register a movement in the corner. No arrow Asher shot ever travelled so straight as the sword, clean through Kish's stomach and out the other side.

He gasps – an awful, squelching gasp – and clutches at the point of entry. Kish's sharp, shrewd eyes do not meet those of his slayer, but lock with the great black orbs of the wounded pixie. Darieann doubts she will ever wipe that face from her memory. She even has sympathy when she sees his expression, though he would have killed her without the least compunction.

Shock and fear predominate in Kish's countenance at first. Then, as he falls to his knees and is level with her, Daireann sees the abhorrence she witnessed when he was trying to strangle her. Inexplicably, his abhorrence gives way to a flicker of tenderness – or at least, something that would have developed into tenderness – but she will never know. He falls heavily to his face, and the breath of life leaves him.

All is still. The Knight and pixie gaze dumbfounded at the corpse. Then they look at each other. Asher looks back to the slain Kish, removes his sword, and walks on.

Feeling suddenly abandoned and cold, Daireann is startled to her feet.

"Wait! Wait!" she calls, with more desperation in her voice than she intended to betray.

Asher slackens his pace, but does not look back.

Straining all that is within her to run, Daireann limps to his side.

"Go back home, little pixie," Asher advises her. He is still facing resolutely forward.

"Who are you? Who was that? You saved my life!"

Daireann pours forth in a mixture of curiosity and gratitude.

A little amused, Asher finally favours her with a look. "You are welcome," he says graciously, a small benignant smile playing around his lips. "My name is Asher. Now you may go home, and be safe."

"You humans *are* slow," Daireann realises. "I am a pixie. We have no home; you must know that."

"We are alike then; I no longer recognise my home. I have lost it," says Asher grimly, but without bitterness.

"That is careless."

"No. For I am going to save it." He smiles briefly and gives her an earnest look. "So whatever kind of resting place you do have, pixie, go to it. It is better than following me on the task I must complete."

Daireann pouts at his condescension. "I may be a pixie, but I have a name. It is Daireann." She pauses. He is still very serious. "Where is it you are going to perform this task?"

"Well then, Daireann, I am going to Laseri – or certain death," Asher adds as an afterthought. "There is a boy there who can heal the future of our lands. That is worth me risking the latter for."

Daireann's face becomes a brighter green. "Then it is true – what that wretch said? You fight for the fairies?"

Asher looks wary. He remembers where his sword came from. His hand unconsciously grasps the hilt. "Would you like me to be fighting for them?"

Daireann laughs. She is so happy she could dance. "Then I must come with you! We are – I mean, I am – helping Queen Aurora – the fairy Queen, you know."

Daireann is surprised to see her companion's face blanch whiter than Kish's cold body.

"*Queen* Aurora?" he repeats at last, in a somewhat strangled voice.

"Yes," she confirms carefully. "I thought you must owe allegiance to her. Have you never met her?"

He looks to the floor, the trees and straight ahead – anywhere but at her. "I – I – er… somewhat. I am going to find the boy."

Daireann is willing to give him the benefit of the doubt. He may not have heard of her yet. "I believe she is rather a new Queen, but recently wed to the King."

"Oh." There is something profound in that noise, almost like a moan, that Daireann cannot put her finger on.

Before she has time to question this further, they both chance to look up. Unconsciously they have wandered the whole length of the green leafy passage.

Daireann makes an involuntarily exclamation herself. She knows now that it was the passage to Laseri.

CHAPTER FOURTY

"I cannot fight any longer!" the Knight slumps against the battlement.

"You must! The fork, the fork!" Sir Nehemiah pushes his inferior aside and attacks the scaling ladder with a large fork. Several fairies climbing upwards are toppled in a flash of fluttering wings.

"For goodness sake," Nehemiah pants, "load the catapults if you cannot fight. But don't wait there for an arrow to go through you!"

"I haven't the energy – I -" the tired Knight blinks. A strange look sweeps his features blank. Nehemiah can see he has lost consciousness. He runs forward, but it is too late; the Knight has fainted, and plummeted over the wall.

Nehemiah watches the shape of his solider become smaller, until it lands on the ground, making a shower of sand. Then, he runs.

Nehemiah finds the King in his Throne Room, pouring over a map. He is considerably more animated, and gigantically more revengeful than when we saw him last. There is a stubborn concentration in his look. Joel will not turn his head and see the fairies at the window; he will not notice the urgency of their situation.

"Your Majesty, we are completely surrounded," Nehemiah reports, slumping against a stone chair. "Our food supplies have run out. This is all strangely familiar."

There is no reply. "What are we to do?" he demands. "The Knights cannot battle without nourishment or water."

Joel grunts. Although he is looking intently at the map, his eyes are not moving over it. "They must," he says at last. "They can eat the flesh of the dead fairies for all I care."

Nehemiah grits his teeth but cannot show his ire. "Not many of those. We are losing."

"Losing?!" Joel slams his palm upon the table. It echoes through the empty halls ominously. "What are you talking about? We have the fairy banner!"

Nehemiah nods wearily. "Yes, yes, we have the fairy banner and it is meant to give victory three times. But it doesn't. It will not work against them. Maybe it is only for when humans fight each other."

Joel is incensed. There must be a way, some way, to make them pay for what they have surely done to his wife. He shakes for a moment, suspended between tears of rage and sorrow. Then he turns back to the map.

"Carry on, then. There cannot be any food, if we do not have any." Nehemiah goes to speak, but Joel stops him mid-breath. "And we will not surrender, so do not even ask. You do not know, like I do, what they will do to us."

Nehemiah can see his King's hand is shaking. It does not instil him with the confidence he needs. "So what *do* we do?"

"Keep fighting," is the murmur from the table.

"How?!"

"That, Sir Nehemiah, is why you are head of the army. Now if the case is so dire, why are you not doing your job? Go!"

Nehemiah goes, very quickly. The door slams behind him. Joel's hands grasp the table. His knuckles are white.

A deadly calm has come over Nehemiah. He sees the necessity of what he must do, but it does not make it easier.

He has not noticed that the fairy army is twice decreased in size. He has not seen any fairy getting shorter, or some vanish out of thin air. He would not, since his own soldiers are dying at an equal rate. He is afraid, he is angry and he feels betrayed.

These vibes appear to magnetise his Knights. As he walks rapidly through the Castle, some leech on to him. It is as if they sense what he is about to do. His face says enough of his despair.

As the set near the King's gardens, they break into a run. Nehemiah throws himself down at the door and peers cautiously outside. Nothing but the warm blaze of sun and the hum of bees meet his inquiries.

He takes his momentary chance, and runs. They all run, stealthily through the tropical plants, under the cover of exotic trees. One or two of the less fortunate are picked off by well aimed fairy arrows before they can reach the gate, and finally desert Iblees.

A strong breath of wind sends a shower of sand up to the sky and drops it again; a brief mirage of a sandy tidal wave. The grains clatter against the window as it falls. At last Joel lets his eyes slip from the map.

He would have done better to keep them down. Much happier for him if his eyes had seen nothing but that chart until the moment they closed forever. He sees now the backs of his last faithful warriors, retreating through the only garden left in Auchriachan. Joel runs to the window, desperate to contradict his eyes. He is stubbornly certain that if he only looks closer, it will all make sense.

The view awaiting him does make sense. Sadly, it is the kind of sense Joel does not wish to see; the dreadful sense he would give his life's blood to be able to deny. It is the sort of sense that says he has lost the fight, the siege, the war, his kingdom. And sense tells him he is now utterly done for.

A huge fairy camp spreads around the city, perfectly enclosing it. More weapons – some recognisable, some strange – are contained in one half of the circle than Joel has ever had within his Castle. Surely their magic has evolved since the last war. These walls of leafy tents and artillery are now the only perimeter of Iblees; the stone walls are cracked like miniature earthquakes, or shattered completely in parts.

Joel can see his Temple on the breast of the hill. His great Amber Temple designed supposedly, to honour peace and placate the fairy-lovers. It has always shimmered to his sight, but now it is glittering threefold.

Warm rays of the desert sun gleam upon bowls of gold, bronze statues and precious gems, all being transported away in the eager arms of fairies. From the amount of gleaming going on, it would appear the place has been looted completely.

The temple itself is glowing with a stronger flame than is caused by light behind the honey coloured amber; it is roaring in the glory of real live blaze.

Amongst all these shimmers, the greatest is the glaze of tears over Joel's eyes, lacing the whole with diamonds and streaks. He can only look, his soul a blank, and curse the sun that shines on everything but him.

There is hardly a division of time between the moment Sir Nehemiah leaves the Castle and the fairies enter it, erupting through the ground like rainbow lava. A tunnel. Of course. Joel had been so used to see the fairies in the air, that he had forgotten they would go underground.

Every fairy looks less serene to Joel's eyes now than they did in the last war. At that time, there had been a calm air of detached superiority about them. Not so now. Those whose countenances he catches a glimpse of are livid, half crazed. They make very short work of the Knights left in the courtyard.

Joel drops them from his sight and focuses beyond, where the workers, the ladies and the children are being led over the dunes in bronze chains. His spirit has a terrible longing to follow them.

He is startled from his contemplation by an almighty crash behind him. He does not look around. He has learnt his lesson.

A sharp yank on his hair pulls his head around. Joel's neck twists, and his crown clatters loudly to the stone floor. A whole spectrum of wings fills the room. Every moment brings a new fairy, shoving a human before it. Joel recognises the grey, bearded men as his advisors; the younger, mutinous looking ones as members of his court.

He thinks he sees, lurking in the shadowy doorway, the great Prince who cost him the last war; the face that haunts his dreams with threats against the spirit of his wife. But perhaps that is only a hallucination; a manifestation of his fear.

Leto, dusty and bleeding, grips Joel's hair with savage force. "You have wronged fairy kind for the last time, Joel of Iblees!" he snarls. "Today we have lost a Queen who was a light to our kingdom; and I have lost a most beloved friend. Now you must take your loss in turn."

Notwithstanding his words, Joel feels surprisingly calm looking upon this fairy. What essence it is in Leto that feels familiar, soothing – bizarrely akin to him – Joel cannot say. But he is glad to be looking at his face, instead of the Prince's.

There is a splattering sound. Joel winces. There are screams. Joel shakes, but looks fixedly forward. The more his neck is turned to look at the horrific sight before him, the more he pulls back to look at Leto. But soon a spray of blood falls in red sprinkles on Leto's face, and Joel's body automatically recoils in horror.

He turns, just in time to see the venerable, wrinkled throat of Alfred crossed with a fairy blade. Joel gasps for breath noiselessly, like a person who has just been hit in the chest.

"By this time our air troops will have reached Laseri," the voice of Tethys hisses in Joel's ear, "and your son will be dead."

Again Joel thinks he sees the Prince at the door. He sees his face turn pale. Then the colour in every other object fades with it; Joel looks down to see a blanched liquid draining from him, as the vision of everything else drains from his eyes, and he drops to the floor, sapped of life.

41

CHAPTER FOURTY-ONE

Asher has never seen blue like that before. He has looked upon countless desert skies without a cloud, seen the sapphire streaks in Aurora's eyes; he has bathed in an oasis with water so turquoise he could almost taste it. But the blue of the expanse above his head in Laseri; this is something different. This is Heaven itself.

He feels warmth in his left hand. It is Daireann. Unconsciously her hand has crept into his. She turns back from gazing – her eyes at least half the size of her face – at the shockingly vivid hills before her. They look so bright it is almost painful to see them. When she notices what her traitorous hand is doing, she snatches it hurriedly away.

Asher laughs. It is impossible not to laugh or smile, or sing. Just look at the sight before them!

The undulating hills are dotted with little snowy white caves and succulent diamond lagoons. White cascades of water spray out from every direction. It is all so fertile and rich, it does not seem possible.

They walk onward. Butterflies dance around their faces. Asher's mind empties for a moment. The reason they came feels like a dream. He has almost forgotten it completely. How can war exist, when there is such a place? Asher cannot reconcile this incredible beauty with the terrible ugliness in his mind.

Even if it were feasible to feel a sense of urgency here,

neither Asher nor Daireann would dare to run. It would feel disrespectful in this enchanting, peaceful place.

Asher's eyes trace the open, wheaty fields, the birds in the sky and the animals grazing all around in perfect freedom. Yes, he is struck by an overwhelming sense of peace. Peace is the word, even though everything he sees is alive and musical.

"We should head for the mountain," Asher whispers to Daireann. When she does not answer him, he looks at her, and sees she is nearly falling over.

"This is – unimaginable – I cannot focus on it – it cannot be real!" she cries. The sudden brightness is clearly playing havoc with her large eyes, accustomed to the darkness as they are. But she does not look to be in pain.

Asher picks her up and carries her in his arms. She gives a yelp of injured pride, but submits.

Nothing has ever felt as surreal to Asher as this climb up the fragrant slopes of Laseri, a pixie in his arms. In all their fearful talk, the Boanerges had forgotten to recall the wonder of fairyland. He can believe now that it is dangerous, for already he is spellbound, walking on in a blissfully dazed trance. The red and yellow flowers in the ditches are breathing sweet scent at him as he passes.

"How," gasps Daireann, "did the atmosphere grow twice as big?" She can hear a faint ringing around her; she holds her bell still, yet the noise continues. A bright smile of recognition makes her face look, for a moment, a natural part of this amazing landscape. Then it yields to the same restful, happy surrender that appeared in Asher's look the moment he cleared the green corridor.

They pass through some deep green lanes, with hedges closing in all around. As they round the last twist, they find they are under a canopy, painted like the night sky.

"What is this?" asks Daireann. Pretty little stalls,

bedecked with flowers are lined in neat rows. They look as grand as little pavilions, with their small spires and decorations sparkling with all the lustre of stars.

"Some kind of market, I think," Asher replies. It is strangely quiet for a market. The stalls are deserted, although the produce – crystals, plump fruit, glowing vials – lays gleaming on display. "Perhaps you do not need to fear thieves in Laseri."

"Shhh!" Daireann throws herself out of his arms, and awkwardly to her feet. The cover of the canopy has helped her sight somewhat. "Can you hear?"

The sound of ringing has been replaced by a dull hissing. They look at each other in bewilderment. So deeply have they been laced with the serenity of this fairy world, they have almost forgotten how to prepare for danger. But prepare they must, for something is coming; the sound has turned into a definite sizzling.

Suddenly the abandoned market feels very eerie.

"I think we came the wrong way," Daireann whispers slowly. "Is there another entry to the mountain path – one that doesn't -" She interposes her sentence with a great shriek, as lightning falls from the sky above.

Daireann jumps backwards and falls to the floor. Something glowing and warm narrowly avoids her head. The next thing she knows, she is being pulled up by Asher.

"What was that?" she gasps. But she can see for herself in a moment. There is a frazzled hole in the canopy, charred around the edges. She can see the material is beginning to fray all along. A lump of something hot and fiery – it looks like wood – is burning on the ground inches from where her face lay.

The sizzling begins again.

"Run!" Asher orders, and pulls her through the market. On and on through endless, grave-like stalls they run. Daireann looks over her shoulder. More lumps of wood and ash are falling through behind them. She runs into a stall, and sends watermelons rolling everywhere.

Asher yanks her arm, forcing her to hurdle over displays and carts, to dodge around obstacles, until she is finally towed, panting, back into the fresh daylight. She is forced to cover her eyes again, but she can feel from the slant of the land that they are going uphill.

She can hear echoes ringing high above. They are not pleasant sounds. Sometimes she thinks a battle cry reaches her ears on the wind; as she travels further, she is startled by an agonised moan, which reflects back off the rocky mountainside and sounds twice as pained on the return.

Asher is running now. His awe and reverence for Laseri has been replaced by a dreadful suspicion that something disastrous is happing to it – and by extension the fay more radiant than the whole kingdom put together.

At last Daireann opens her eyes, and gropes her way along as best as she can. The cries of suffering sounded more mournful in the darkness – she is glad to have her eyes open again. It feels very wrong, to hear those sounds in so beautiful a place. She looks up at the majestic mountain, ascending with pride over the amazing panorama beneath and shakes her head.

They lose the path and scramble with their hands up the last peak of rocks. Grazed and snatching for breath, Asher heaves his chest on to the cliff edge. His legs kick behind him and propel him forwards. He lies on the ground, panting.

But the warier Daireann pokes just her head over the precipice. From this view point, she can see what Asher does not.

"What – oh what are they doing?" she moans.

In the very same pristine courtyard Aurora rode out of many years ago, stand gaggles upon gaggles of fairies. Their wings vibrate in an unpleasant hum. Flashes of bright colour sting Daireann's eyes and make her dizzy. A faint breeze from their manic flapping lifts her black hair from her forehead.

She can now feel the heat of the fire wafting towards her. It is dancing in a rabid glee, throwing sinister shadows over the writhing fairies.

They are in distress, or something close. Their clothing, so bright and beautiful it could have been woven from the stars, is ripped and torn; the garlands of leaves or flowers on their heads lay askew or broken completely.

"Our Queen, our Queen," a fay in the softest rose pink, a flower each side of her head, sobs whilst ringing her hands.

She is comforted by one who looks like she has been clothed entirely by a primrose. But she herself is trembling. "The King knows. He sent the messengers to us. And has he been told she is avenged?"

"Of course!" the defensive reply comes from a solider, his face so tired he seems to be years older than thirty.

"And what are we to do now?"

"I do not know! There has been no trace of him since!"

A pretty little fairy, in a jagged dress of red and purple is gazing upwards with such penitent, despairing eyes that Daireann automatically follows her forlorn look.

In the very epicentre of the fire stands a proud marble pole, wound with vines and lotus blossoms. It is black and unsightly where the flames have licked it. A charred mass is suspended half way down. Daireann presumes it to be a fruit, or a larger plant-like offering.

But a closer inspection plants the seeds of suspicion in her mind. Her rib cage drops beneath her as she realises it looks like... Barely has the unwanted thought passed through her mind, when she hears Asher cry out aloud.

Then she knows it is the boy.

It is all over. Aurora should have known days ago. Everything that had made her life joyful or given it purpose has gone. Her one great ideal is no more. How can anything in the world be bearable?

After spending a few hours searching aimlessly for Daireann, she gives her up for dead.

She can almost hear the forest laughing at her. Or perhaps it is the Deevs. But Aurora no longer has the energy to be worried by Deevs. She feels nothing but a great, blank void. But for a void, it hurts an awful lot.

She strokes the soft white face of Blanchard. He is the same as ever; warm, bright eyed and affectionate, though everything has changed. Aurora takes her hands from his bridle.

"Go."

The horse looks askance at her.

"Go, I told you!" yells Aurora. She grabs a large stick from the floor and brandishes it at him.

Blanchard snorts and flashes the whites of his eyes. He backs up.

"Go!"

The horse turns tail and flees.

Aurora listens until his hooves have beaten into the distance, and breaks down in tears.

She doubts there has been a person in all of the world as miserable as her.

Aurora walks robotically forwards in no particular direction, dragging her feet. Dark faces seem to peer out of the trees at her as she passes. If they are Deevs, she wonders they do not kill her now.

There is certainly a thrill running through the forest. "Well," thinks Aurora, "they must be pleased. Apollo cannot have been successful. Many humans are certainly dead."

She wonders if Apollo, or even her husband, is still alive.

"Fairies are not well equipped to look after humans on this Earth. They cannot even save themselves from danger!"

She had resigned herself to Asher's death almost the moment they saw fairy troops cross the sky. That had cost her enough pain. But she had not doubted she would have Deucalion and Apollo to give some comfort to her.

And then when she had found the children of Ganieda, she had hoped she might do them some good. But to be forced to cave and admit that all these things are no more is to create a world that cannot hold. Her very essence recoils from it. Everything is black and cold, no matter how hard she reaches.

"There must be some way," Aurora keeps telling herself. "There must be some way that fairies can watch over humans as they were made to. But oh! Are there even any humans alive to look after?!"

These thoughts are snatched from her brain as her leg catches. Feeling her foot smack against something hard, she nearly falls over.

Aurora's heart pounds within her. She is being stupid; what is there left to be afraid of? She takes a breath. Her chest lands from its leap, and she is able to look down, her disturbance transformed into curiosity.

At her feet lies a long object of translucent, cornflower blue. As Aurora looks at it, she feels her eyes and diaphragm radiate a warm glow from within. It is winking at her in the dimming daylight; she could almost say it is smiling at her.

Slowly Aurora bends down. She takes the object into her hands with great reverence. She is almost afraid of it. It is too beautiful to be quite right.

Aurora realises it is a staff, or a sceptre. It is cold to the touch, like a great blue icicle. She raises it in her hands. Mounted on the end is a brilliant blue stone, at the heart of a cluster of snowy diamonds.

A switch flicks in Aurora's brain. She realises why her hands are trembling, and they begin to shake the more violently with her consciousness. She drops, practically throws the staff away from her and stumbles to her feet. Backing away from the staff, watching it all the while, she positions herself half behind a tree.

"*Cailleach Bheur!*" she mutters to herself in disbelief. "Oh, and have we lost that?! She is dead, surely she is dead."

She peeps out from behind the tree. The staff is obstinately still there. Unmistakeable, inescapable. The staff of Cailleach Bheur. It is too great a responsibility!

Aurora cannot think what to do. She cannot think at all. It is some wonder to her that her brain still regulates her breath and her heartbeat. Her whole world is destroyed. Her head wheels wildly.

The fairies have lost the sacred trust. Without that, what is their purpose? What is she to do? To go on living, selfishly, as if it had never been? Aurora could never, never forget. She can never more be alone, now she has met those she was born to protect, but she cannot dispel this nightmare world where she is forced to live apart from them.

Aurora paces around her side of the tree. She does not cry and she does not scream. She runs a hand distractedly through her now slightly longer hair. She pulls at her wings. She does anything to stop the truth from hitting her brain with the weight of an avalanche. Were it to fall, she is convinced it would destroy her. Even if her little yellow stones worked on fairies, they would be quite insufficient to cure *that*.

No matter what the odds, an inveterate spark at the root of her insists on striving for the sublime. *There must be something*, it says, *to make all this misery glorious. There must be a passage to air, and light. Nothing is lost; all may be found.*

Aurora creeps lightly from behind the tree. Her elfin features are tense with anticipation. With great caution, she edges towards the staff.

She gets within a metre of her object unmolested. Here she stops and looks. She turns round, and comes back again. She has not quite decided on her course of action when she reaches it once more. At last she puts forward a dainty foot.

The screams begin before she has replaced it on the ground. Agonised, terrible cries rush on her and roar like the waves of the sea.

They echo from the Colosseum of Laseri, frolicking about her head. They bring with them the smell of smoke and the stench of burnt flesh.

The crushing weight of acceptance dangling over Aurora's head drops at last.

She gasps and falls to her knees, as if she were pushed. The world transforms before her eyes to an ugly, shapeless mass. She looks to the sky, and although it is bright, she sees no light. All the birds have deserted it. The hills and the trees shake in her vision. Dread overwhelms the very core of her.

She kneels there, motionless, for at least half an hour.

But then – as suddenly as the wretchedness oppressed her – it is blanketed by a profound calm. Aurora is not steady. Her hands grope at the grass and her knees turn to jelly beneath her. But her mind – her mind is regaining all the clarity it possessed before, and more.

The screams still ring around her ears, but they do not rip the heart of her. Aurora doubts she will ever feel emotional pain again. Once more she turns her violet eyes up at the world, full of courage, seeing only possibility. Now that the worst has come, what can possibly harm her?

Hampered somewhat by her quaking limbs, she rises up and takes the staff into her hands with the greatest assurance.

"It is very beautiful," she observes, with a hint of wistfulness in her voice. She cannot understand that she ever feared it.

She looks at her hands as they hold it. The ghostly glow of her moonstone ring is appropriately mournful. All the fairies out there, suffering, wilfully destroying themselves with similar rings on their fingers, flood her memory.

On her other hand, stubbornly fixed since the day it was placed upon it, is Asher's ring. It is a warmer looking ring. She stares at its gold fire, and is comforted. She travels back to her days in Iblees. Strangely, her fancy paints them as the happiest of her life. The people, the voices, are before her and around her once more – the smell of the sand, the muffled howl of the wind.

The only thing more painful than a bad memory is a happy one, never to return. Aurora realises there are tears in her eyes and snatches off Asher's ring, dashing it to the ground.

Turning her back upon it, she stands in thought, her delicate forehead resting against the cool blue staff. She ruminates without moving.

Then, from her pocket, Aurora pulls forth her marriage ring. Her delicate fingers trace lightly over the hole. She turns it at every angle, admiring its smoothness. Sometimes the hint of a smile pulls at her cheeks, sometimes her brow furrows as if trying to recall something.

"Aurora Optilete; the disgraced outcast. Queen of the Fairies. Bride of Deucalion. Who would have thought?"

Poor Deucalion. She wonders if he lives still.

She places the stone beside the ring. The stone is put down more delicately and thoughtfully than the ring had been.

Aurora looks down at the two great influences on her life. She observes the symbols of the two honours conferred upon her, from a distance. They catch every ray of sun dropping through the leaves, and look inestimably more beautiful than at close range.

Aurora's left hand bears the ethereal moonstone ring; her right, the icy staff of Cailleach Bheur. They assume a new shape to her as she looks at her hands.

Shock waves of power radiate from them, vibrating right through her heart. Her wet violet eyes swoop from one to the other; the swirling coloured fog of the stone, the translucent sky blue of the staff. Her eyes glow a brighter purple as they reflect the two precious powers in her pupils. A relieved, enlightened smile starts on her rosebud mouth and travels all the way into them.

Aurora's breath is coming dangerously fast. Her chest rises and falls quicker than she blinks. She raises her head.

Desperate cries mourn in her ears once more. Though they are far away, they are pained enough to slice a soul.

But up through the canopy of trees, a pure light is raining down. Aurora finds herself bathed in warm sun, and the forest looking no longer frightening, but like a glorious part of her. It is as if a breath of splendour is rippling through the leaves and painting the scene with enchantment. Filtering through the barrier of foliage, the sun is coming to ordain her, and the spot on which she stands. Everything is so green, so right, so destined.

Squaring her shoulders and tilting up her pointed chin, she holds the staff aloft. Aurora takes an almighty breath, closes her eyes for the shortest of seconds – and points the blue crystal of the staff at her collection of treasures on the floor.

A blue beam shoots forth with a great zinging noise. It is brighter than the very sun shining on Aurora. The staff shakes violently. Aurora's slim arm tenses around it with surprising strength, and holds the ray steady.

The two objects on the floor begin to levitate. Asher's ring glows pink; the marriage stone is encased in a cloud of white. The auras begin to merge. Slowly, they start to rotate round and round one another.

Aurora concentrates. Her whole beautiful face is absorbed with one thought. She is so pale that even her freckles begin to fade. The ring and the stone gather speed.

Aurora raises her ring hand and makes a fist. As she does so, she feels the warm kiss of a sunbeam upon her forehead. It strengthens her to know the Universe is smiling in delight, although it is so black.

Aurora lines her ring up with the swirling ring and stone. It is gleaming in a strange way she has never seen it do before. A force is pulling it, almost lifting it off her finger.

Her eyelids drop and extinguish her glorious eyes.

"If you live, I will protect you."

She shoots.

CHAPTER FOURTY-TWO

The rumbling starts in the pit of Asher's ear and grows louder. He is aware of it stealing upon him, to the pit of his stomach, to his feet, and then he can barely stand. The ground is tilting and jumping beneath him.

The wailing fairies stop dead in panic. They are only silent for an instant; soon they are shrieking as the land slides and they fall skidding into one another. The brighter amongst them take to their wings and hover around the quivering mountain.

As his own sight jogs up and down, Asher tries to make out Daireann. She is trying unsuccessfully to keep her pixie feet. Her hands are outspread, reaching for a hold. Another quake jolts the earth, and she falls.

Asher leaps to help her. Movement is not easy. He takes a few steps, his legs straddled and buckling beneath him. If he can only keep her in his sight…

But now he cannot see anything. His eyes sting. He bats at them wildly. With great effort he blinks them open. His hands and his clothes covered in a white powder. He has a dreaded guess what this may mean. He looks up.

Like balls rolling down a slope, rocks are falling from the mountain top. The whole world around is disintegrating before his eyes. He sees a shelf of cliff collapse, and fall in pieces off the edge of the mountain.

"Daireann!" Asher leaps with a sudden burst of

balance, and scoops the fallen pixie in his arms. Little rocks fall like hail stones around them. Ducking and holding the pixie's head against his chest, Asher weaves his way through the screaming fairies.

A huge boulder shatters the earth beside him. He turns at the noise, and his eyes alight on a little cave. Asher makes for it with all his might. Yes, it may collapse upon them, but it is the best hope they have.

Asher does not know how he manages to walk there. But he does it, and just in time to see another crumbling rock, falling as swiftly as a mudslide, cascade down the mountain and smash the walls of the Colosseum.

"What is it?" Daireann asks.

She peeks out of the opening of the cave. All is panic before her eyes – and beyond that, the forest, her home. She thinks it looks a strange colour. She is about to comment to Asher, when it happens.

A huge wide shaft of pale blue light shoots vertically from the middle of the forest. It is about the width of twenty trees, and reaches to the highest heaven. Even the fairies battling for their lives stop to stare. The ground grumbles, but gradually quiets itself. They are so absorbed in the beam, they do not notice when it stops shaking. But soon there is only silence, and the blue.

And then – a bang. It is nothing but a faint pop from where they are, but everyone jumps. From the middle of the shaft an almost atomic wave is emitted. It gallops through the trees, heading in a broad circle, in every direction. Heading towards them.

Asher grips Daireann tightly as the entire world shakes around them. He looks out on this wobbly vision as the last he will see of it. He could not save his land after all. His eyes cast a wistful glance over the forest to where he imagines Iblees is. But his glance is called back to the forest by the most astonishing thing.

Little puffs of black smoke are erupting everywhere the wave from the explosion passes. Small bright fires flicker for an instant, without burning the trees, and are extinguished.

A thick hot whisper tickles his ear. "The Deevs," gasps Daireann with elation. "The explosion is roasting the Deevs alive!"

It is true! Asher can see it is true. Here they are, disappearing like the mists a nightmare. He and Daireann fall into another's arms laughing.

The fairies have noticed too. The smaller ones are skipping and singing for joy. The others merely stare, transfixed, terrified the wonderful image will fail to be true if they turn from it. In all of their minds, if only for this brief time, all of the wars, the shameful past and the harrowing discord have been blotted out, just as if they had never happened at all.

A rush of freedom and promise sweeps through Asher's spirit. The day may be won, still – he is not sure how, but he is sure it may. He climbs to his feet, determined to rush to the mountain top and observe the death of the Deevs in all its glory.

Daireann cries out after him. He will not be stopped. He stumbles and grazes himself, but moves onwards, eyes dancing in pure delight at the flames in the forest.

"Sir! Asher!" He lurches as Daireann grabs his foot.

"Go back to the cave, if you wish! I want to see it." He turns tear-filled eyes back to the woods, giving profound thanks. It is over. All that he could not stop Joel from doing has come to an end at last. "It is the most beautiful sight I ever beheld."

"Asher. That wave. It is coming towards us. It is coming here."

The Knight pauses in the middle of his breath and holds it. Daireann can see the pious expression in his eyes mutating wordlessly into hurtling fear.

He turns them to her. In his wide pupils she sees the reflection of the sweeping tide, coming closer and closer through the trees. The sheer force of it is making a wind that ruffles his hair more violently the closer it comes, and the side of his dirty face is illuminated with its fiery glow.

The very heat of the explosion tickles Daireann's cheek. It is nearly upon them. She reaches out for Asher's proffered hand, and closes her eyes.

There is a violent blast of wind in her ears, popping her ear drums. Then it comes. It feels like she has been hit by a meteor. Even with her eyes shut the world is bright white. The sensation of being pricked with needles in every body part scratches her. She can barely cling on to Asher, or the rock. Some determined force is pulling her irresistibly away, and upwards, she thinks – but she cannot confirm which direction *is* up anymore.

Her green fingers are giving way. Every sinew in her body is screaming in pain. Somewhere over the din of the wind and her own heartbeat she can hear Asher commanding her to hold on. But she is being pulled higher and higher – she is gripping on to him, clawing him now with only her very finger tips. Her hand is about to let go, it shakes so violently. She wails aloud to Asher and then – she falls.

Falls not up, but to the floor. Under no other circumstances would she be so happy to have her face slammed into jagged rocks. It is not glowing white any longer – only the stars of pain dancing through the pitch black of her closed eyelids are white. There is no wind, there is no force. She smiles in grateful relief. It does not matter that she feels blood trickle down her chin as she does so. She cannot hug the safe, still ground hard enough.

The sun darts out from behind a cloud and kisses her bruised skin. She nestles against its warmth. Very slowly, and very painfully, she raises her banging head to look for Asher.

The Knight is just where he was when she caught his foot by the mountain edge. His hand is bloody and his appearance is windswept, but he is otherwise unharmed. She smiles again to assure him she is alright.

He does not return her grin, and she notices, with a vague misgiving, it is not her he is looking at. She is almost afraid for him, almost afraid of what is behind her.

Although he looks pleased, every feature is so transformed she is convinced it must be some sort of enchantment holding him there. His face is filled with the most heartfelt triumph and delight she has ever seen. His mouth smiles in a way she has only witnessed when a pixie arrived home at the fort after a long, troublesome journey.

But then she hears it. It is a lullaby to bring peace to the darkest soul. She cannot understand the words, but they reach so deep inside her, she is sure she has sung the song long ago. The sensation she is floating fills her blood again, but this time there is not the slightest breeze. She looks where the contented Asher is looking.

It was not the sun that warmed her skin so adoringly. It was fairies. A heavenly choir of fairies, singing with an unspeakable purity and majesty. Up and up they float on golden wings, twirling in ecstasy. They wiggle their golden feet; they beam with joy into their companions' golden faces. They are all gold, and translucent – and they are ascending, to where their ancestors live. What better way, indeed, to watch over their chosen ones, than from a birds-eye view, unblocked by the thick forest?

Over the trees, out where Iblees is, the same golden flare is climbing the sky. And for some reason, mid way in the forest, Asher can see the brightest glow of all, gliding like a jewelled ship through the blue sky.

Higher and higher the fairies travel in their golden mist, dropping sprinkles of silver glitter. Daireann twirls round and round in the showers of fairy dust, her arms out reached. She would grab on to them, she would have them take her with them.

But the music is fading; the light is passing. A greater thing calls their melody and their goodness away. Their brightness rivals the radiant sunshine before blending with its rays. The harmony of their voices drifts on to the breeze, and is swept up in the air.

They are gone.

Daireann has just time to let that truth touch the edge of her consciousness before an enormous creaking startles her from her magnificent reverie. She wheels her head around just in time to see every tree in the great dividing forest collapse.

The fort! Her people! Caeliea! All these bonds of early affection leap into her pounding heart. She has no reason to love any of them; but she cannot see their destruction without emotion. Gasping back a sob, she steadies her shaking limbs on Asher, and raises her traumatised face to his, desperate to convey her mute agony. She is surprised, and a little touched, to find he is weeping too. With joy.

"The hills of Iblees, Daireann. Look at them. They're green."

And so it was that the fairy world passed out of ours. You may hear tales of the occasional visit – you may even speak to a person who has seen a small one in their garden – but they do not belong on the Earth that wounded them so grievously any more. Their place is among the clouds, where they can care properly for the ones they love, without scaring them. It is sad to say that some people, in the manner of the Boanarges, still blame the fairies for their misfortunes, or scoff at the idea of them, or run from them.

But you may rest assured they are, on the whole, rather stupid people who nobody cares for – except their fairy, who will love them till the end no matter what.

I can take you now amongst those green hills in Auchriachan, where the foundations of a new Glass Mountain Castle are springing up alongside the tender buds of flowers.

The congregation is depleted and sombre. They are lucky to be alive. On his first arrival back in Iblees, Asher had seen nothing but dead bodies. Only careful rescue work and determined rooting through the piles – with a little aid by virtue of a yellow stone – saved the lives of as few of them as are there.

The Knights were unable to tell him much of what happened – only that Joel was dead, and that the fairy King had never been seen – even when all the fairies ascended – since the moment it was announced little Elihu had been sacrificed.

But these two facts alone were enough to throw Asher into intense sorrow. He had said he would give anything to see the signs again. But he did not realise he would give his soldiers, his oldest friend and his son – or *her*... now he would give anything to take it all back again.

He does not look much happier as we see him now, but calmer and resolute. He walks regally through the people to the platform decked in leaves and ribbons and heather; he does not hesitate or look back for a moment. The sullen pixies look at him with mistrust, but they have sworn to keep this peace covenant.

They relax a little as Daireann mounts the platform, arrayed in the finest white and jewels. Her popularity with her pixie kind has miraculously increased since her importance amongst the humans has grown.

She too, looks different from on the mountain top – much prettier, for a start – but more like her stubborn, confident self. More, it could be said, like Lady Urvasi.

Asher's absorbed, gravely meditative countenance relaxes in spite of itself as he sees her, and takes her green hand in marriage.

For it was agreed between the humans and the pixies that not only should their half-children be accepted, but they should be intermingled. Only this – the crossing of blood and interests – could ensure lasting peace.

Over the years the green has been bred out, but some of the magic has not. There are still those around, with the powers clearly derived from a pixie ancestor – and maybe from Daireann herself.

The joining of the hands complete, they are seated on their as yet rudimentary thrones.

Asher is intent upon the sky. The many years that have passed since his shepherd days are playing out across it; Joel, Elihu, Roddag. Throughout them all, he had never imagined this day would dawn.

Again his handsome mouth will twitch into the beginning of a grin. He is afraid, but he has his purpose now. And he can feel – in the wind, or in the trees – somewhere always present, but never fully tangible – a presence. A presence like the signs, but stronger. A presence like a hand being laid upon his head.

The heather bursts full into his nostrils as he raises his noble forehead to receive the shining crown of Iblees and Laseri.

The crowd applauds thunderously as he looks at them with that nervous seed of a smile. But someone, not far above his head, smiles the much wider grin that he would like to give, beaming like the sun. And her clap, though far away, resounds through the clouds, and through the trees, to reach her Asher's delighted ears.

THE END